Insufficient Evidence

The Grace McDonald Series
Book 3

SUSAN KRAUS

Flint Hills Publishing

Cover Design by Ashley Honey
www.ashleyhoney.com

Cover Photo by Kelsey Kimberlin
kelseykimberlin.com

Flint Hills Publishing
Topeka, Kansas
www.flinthillspublishing.com

Printed in the U.S.A.

ISBN-13: 978-0-9997547-6-4
ISBN-10: 0-9997547-6-9

DISCLAIMER:

INSUFFICIENT EVIDENCE is the third novel in *The Grace McDonald Series.* This series tackles polarizing social and political issues.

Chapter 1 is an account of a therapy session. A young woman is describing her experience of being raped during her first few weeks on a university campus. It could be triggering for readers who have experienced rape or sexual assault. If you have any concerns, simply start the book with Chapter 2 (page 8).

Readers have described the book as a whole as cathartic and even therapeutic for women who have been assaulted, giving voice to collective frustrations, emotional pain, and needs for validation, retribution, and justice.

Susan Kraus

September 2017

Chapter 1
(September 4th)

"And then what happened?" Grace McDonald asked.

Across from her, on a worn leather couch, sat a nineteen–year-old girl. Her brown hair was quite short, almost punky, and she wore an oversized shirt and jeans. Her blue-green eyes darted, frantically, to a corner of the room as if the answer could be found crouching behind the oak desk piled with files. Late afternoon sunlight filtered through the large wooden-framed windows of the office and played across Hannah's face as her neck tightened and her lips pressed together.

"Hannah," Grace said softly. "This is a safe place. We can go slow. Just take a few breaths."

"I was dozing off on the bed in his room. He'd said I could lie down until my head cleared. I didn't realize he'd come back until I felt him lying down on the bed next to me, like up against my back. I felt his hand on my back, stroking, rubbing my shoulder, and it was warm, sort of nice. But then his hand was up under my shirt, and he unsnapped my bra. I didn't know what he was doing. It was so blurry. I tried to move away, but it was just a twin bed and I was almost up against the wall. He had me pressed down, like his leg was over my legs and braced up against the wall. But then his hand, his right hand it must have been, moved around under my shirt and onto my breast. And his fingers were all over my breast and rubbing my nipple. And then he reached further and grabbed the other breast. The bra was still there, sort of, but unhooked so it could be pushed away. And he was saying stuff like, 'You have great tits, baby, really great tits.' "

Hannah stopped, her breath now more shallow, fast small breaths between the words.

"And then what happened?" Grace persisted.

"I had on a skirt, and then his other hand was tugging it up. I was trying to move but I was pinned down. I tried to talk, to say, 'Stop' and 'No' but my face was in a pillow that was against the wall. I did say, 'Stop, please, please stop. Don't. No. No. No. Please, please, please.' He had to have heard me, even with the pillow. I was squirming to try and get some leverage. The music—the music was so loud from the party downstairs. I could feel the floorboards vibrating with the bass, the bam-bam-bam of the bass, like it was right under the bed. It was just bizarre.

There was this huge party going on. Who did this in their own bedroom with people all around?"

Hannah paused, as if she had a small sliver of hope that her question would be answered.

"I don't know, Hannah. For now, at least, I don't know." Grace paused before speaking again. "And then what happened?"

"When he started to pull up my skirt, I felt my stomach knot up, like, 'What the shit is happening? I'm at a *party*.' And I tried to yell. But then he grabbed my hair in back and pushed my face down into the pillow. I got more scared because I couldn't breathe. I felt my head getting dizzy, and that woozy feeling before you faint. And I thought—I thought, *I could die here.* So I pulled out every ounce of strength I had and jerked my head to one side. And I could breathe again. I stopped trying to yell. I needed air more than I needed to yell, and no one could hear me anyway."

"And?"

"He reached up under the skirt, it was mostly up around my waist at that point, and pulled off my panties. I heard them rip as he did it, the sound that silk makes when it tears. I'd put on a brand-new bra and panties to feel pretty for the party, like I was a cool girl. They were from Victoria's Secret. They were a birthday gift from a friend. I usually go to Target."

Hannah looked at Grace, as if it were important for Grace to understand that she did not buy underwear from Victoria's Secret, that she could not afford underwear from Victoria's Secret, that these were *special*.

Grace sat silently, listening intently. There was no rush. If Hannah needed to talk about underwear, if she needed a few more minutes, that was fine. Whenever someone came in for a first appointment, and Grace knew they had a tough issue: an assault, a death, a loss, a betrayal—a rape—she scheduled them last so they could take as much time as they needed.

Hannah was looking across the room again, then down at the floor. Anywhere but into Grace's eyes. This was too hard for eyes.

"His legs were still pinning me, but he kind of flipped me from my side to my back, and then he was on top, like on top over every part of me. I'm, like, 5'3" and he's really tall, like 6'4". I think his left hand had both my wrists in a grip over my head. Then he used his knees to push my legs apart, and his right hand pulled my right calf up to my thigh. Then he said, "That's good, baby, that's about right." And then he tried to push in, but I was totally dry. And he said, 'Damn, you 're a tight little pussy.' And he reached over my head with his other hand to the bedside table and grabbed at something. I felt drops of something drizzle on me. Then he rubbed himself a few times. Then he pushed into me. One hand still had a grip on my hands and hair and the other was pushing down on one knee, keeping my legs spread. But then it was over. Like in 10 seconds. He came really quick."

Grace said nothing, bearing witness to what Hannah had experienced. Then she directly looked at Hannah, making eye contact. *You're almost done,* the look said.

"He got up," Hannah continued, "and started to get dressed, like nothing had happened. Then he said, 'You did good, girl. You can come to our parties any time you want. And bring your friends, too. Hey, what dorm are you in?' "

"Did you tell him?" Grace asked.

"No, I gave him the name of a different dorm. I even made up a room number."

"And then?"

"He told me to get dressed and come on down, that he'd make me a special party drink that was just for the big girls."

"And you?"

"I got dressed as fast as I could. I tried to brush my hair because it was all ratty, but gave up. I put the torn panties back on. When I opened the bedroom door it was like stepping through a magic curtain—from nightmare into bizarre dream. I just had to get out of there. I somehow got down the stairs. It's a very long staircase, and I pushed past people to get out the front door. I remember hearing one guy saying, 'Hey, make way, let her through, looks like the girlie is about to heave.' "

"What then?"

"I walked as fast as I could back to my dorm. My roommate was gone, but there was a light under the door across the hall. Stacy's room, the Resident Assistant She's a senior. I banged on it and just burst in. Stacy was on her bed, reading, and I saw her eyes get big, like she knew, knew *something* had happened. And I said, 'I think I've been raped. A guy at the frat party raped me. What do I do? What do I do?' "

"Did she know what to do?"

"Yeah. She had the list of emergency numbers we got at orientation. There's a 24-hour line for a rape crisis center. They told us to go to the ER. To bring a change of clothes. Not to change my clothes or to wash up."

Hannah paused.

"That was so hard," she continued. "I just wanted to get it off of me. It was like his smell was all over me, and my belly felt sticky. Staci called a friend for a ride to the ER. Then everything is a blur. There were different people talking to me. The Rape Crisis Center counselor was explaining what was going to happen. I undressed and put on this gown and they took away my clothes. A doctor came in, and he had to take swabs and do an exam. He was trying to be gentle, and kept explaining, like, 'Now I am going to do this' and 'Now I am going to insert a speculum.' But it was awful because I had to put my legs up in stirrups, and it was just like. . ." Hannah's voice faded.

"And I had to stand naked on a sheet while they brushed my body and took pictures of me," she resumed. "The flash kept going off and off, and I just stood there shivering and shaking."

Hannah was crying now, but still talking, oblivious to the tears coming down her face.

"And then they were done, all the medical part was done, and they told me I could get dressed. Stacy had grabbed some of her clothes for me. The pants were too big, and a big sweatshirt, but that was okay because I felt all covered up, like her clothes were safer than my clothes. Then the counselor said, 'We need to go to the police station now, just for a while, to give an initial statement.' And I broke down. I just wanted to go to my room and shower it all off and go to sleep and wake up and find out this was all a really, really bad dream."

"So did you go?"

"Yes, I went. They put me in a little room, but it had real chairs and a round wood table, not like on TV. Stacy stayed outside. The volunteer came in, but she just sat over in a corner. The police asked me questions, so many questions. Like, 'Did you go up to his room voluntarily?' 'Had you been drinking?' 'How much had you been drinking?' 'You are underage, correct?' 'Did you take any drugs?' 'Had you been to this frat house before?' 'Did you know any of the members?' 'Were you alone at this party or did you go with friends?' 'Where were your friends when this happened?' 'Did you protest?' '*How* did you protest?' 'Did you yell?' 'Did you try to fight back?' '*How* did you try to fight back?' 'Did you leave any marks on him?' "

Hannah's tone and voice inflection changed as she listed the questions. Grace could hear how they had felt to her like indictments.

"How long were you questioned?" Grace asked.

"I don't know but it felt like forever."

"And then what happened?"

"They said they had enough and then I signed some papers and they said I could go home. The Crisis Center volunteer drove Stacy and me back to the dorm. As soon as I got to my room, I took off her clothes and got into the shower. I made it as hot as I could stand and scrubbed and scrubbed. I washed my hair and then washed it again. I remember feeling relieved that my roommate had gone home for the weekend because I did not want to face anyone."

"Did you call your parents? Call anyone else?"

"No. I started to but it was 5 a.m. and I didn't know what to say. 'Hey Mom and Dad, I was raped tonight.' How can I *ever* say those words to them? They've always been so protective. And it's tearing me up because I feel like not telling is lying. But I know they'll start asking questions. Like *why* did I go to a fraternity party and *what* did I *expect* and *where* were my friends and *why* was I drinking and *how* could I go up to his room? They'll drive up here and try to make me come home. And that might make it worse."

"So what did you do?"

"I took two of the pills the doctor had given me at the hospital. And I got in my bed and pulled the covers up over my head, completely, like a blanket cave. The pills knocked me out. When I woke up it was about noon and Stacy was sitting across from me on the other bed, reading."

"And then?"

"Stacy put mugs of coffee in the microwave to warm up. And muffins. So I sat up in bed and drank the coffee and ate. Then I told Stacy I just needed some time alone, so she left. She said she was just across the hall and would check in on me. After I went to the bathroom, I felt so weird. Like I had to do something. *Something.* I sat down in front of my desk and propped up a mirror that's usually against the wall. I took the big shear scissors from my roommate's art drawer and started to cut off all my hair. I've had long hair, down past my shoulders, down my back, my whole life. It took about twenty minutes to get most of it off. I needed for it to not be long enough for anyone to grab or hold."

Hannah looked right at Grace, making eye contact, holding it.

"Stacy got a girl in the dorm to fix it the next day so it would look less butchered, but I don't think I can ever have long hair again."

Chapter 2
(September 4th)

"Hey, Katrina, are you up for a salad and a glass of wine tonight? I could use the company."

Grace put her phone down on the desk and hoped Kat would see the message. It had been a difficult day. A few hours with her friend might turn that around.

Grace sat thinking about Hannah. They'd taken a break after the *hair*, but then continued talking. The young woman was still in some shock, but starting to understand everything that had been stolen from her, which was *everything* she'd dreamed about as far as a *college experience*. She'd never really relax, never leave her room without feeling vigilant. She'd never be completely comfortable at a party, or in a crowd. She'd never trust that her friends would be there for her when she needed them. She'd be a girl with a secret because she didn't want to be known as the girl who got raped.

Or maybe not.

They'd scheduled a time to meet again next week. Today had been the first time that Hannah had said *everything* that had happened to her in her own words, her own sequence. No interruptions. Grace knew that there was more that would surface later.

Hannah was a referral from the Rape Crisis Center. Grace had volunteered to work with young women, either pro bono or sliding scale, who had no insurance, no resources. Some had insurance but did not want therapy sessions showing up on their parents' insurance statements, did not want to have to answer the predictable questions: *What's going on? Are you okay? Are you depressed? Why do you need to talk to a therapist?*

It had only been four months and already Grace was finding these sessions both challenging and emotionally draining. She'd been a therapist for over 30 years, with a wide variety of cases. People who struggled with depression, anxiety, or phobias. Or marital issues, from lousy communication to affairs and divorce. She'd dealt with intense grief and loss, the betrayal of trust.

But rape, the kind of rape that seemed to be prevalent in a university town like Kaw Valley—was prevalent in any university town in the country—brought different issues to the table. Grace had been raised with *stranger danger*. But this was insidious. Or was it ubiquitous?

The phone ring interrupted her rumination.

"Hey Gracie," Katrina said, "I'm in. Salad and wine sounds good. Anything wrong?"

"No," Grace replied. "Just a hard case that reminds me of how life can suck."

"How about I meet you at the Eldridge in an hour? Can you go early and snag a back table?"

Katrina Baptiste was Grace's best friend. She had, for many years, been her only friend. They'd met when their kids were young, each juggling childcare, work, laundry, and marriages. Katrina was Creole, from New Orleans, and had been raised speaking French as well as English which gave her a barely discernable yet exotic accent. Her skin was a shade of toffee that Grace had failed to achieve regardless of how much time she lay in the sun.

Kat was an attorney. For years, her practice had focused on copyright, then business mergers and trusts. But she'd been changing direction, doing more elder law, not just wills and inheritance, but how multigenerational families balanced self-determination with the progression of dementia. It was less money but more satisfying.

They'd weathered tough times together: Katrina's divorce; Grace's husband's death; the trial; a decade of geographical separation when Grace had left Kaw Valley. There had been a point when Grace had almost walked away from the friendship, when she'd felt betrayed. Not acting on that impulse had been one of the best decisions she'd ever made.

Two hours later, having polished off two salads, a plate of bacon-wrapped shrimp, and most of a bottle of Pinot Noir, they sat, satiated.

"So talk," Kat said. "What's got you all tied up?"

"Remember how I told you I was taking some referrals from the Rape Crisis Center? Well, they're like some warped déjà vu: girl meets boy at a bar or a party; they talk and flirt; girl likes boy; girl maybe even wants to make out a little. Many drinks later, girl is too smashed to resist or be coherent, or tries to back out, says 'No,' but it's too late. Sex is happening whether she wants to or not. Girl feels violated, but also guilty. Like what did *she* do for *that* to happen? Meanwhile her friends are talking about their hookups like *no big deal*. But what she experienced is traumatizing."

Grace paused to take a sip of wine.

"Remember dating?" she continued. "Getting to know each other? Making out a little bit more each date? Some balance of physical intimacy and emotional intimacy? Does *anybody* do that anymore?"

"First of all, what you describe is a minority, Grace," Katrina said. "Your sample is not representative."

"Thank you, Ms. Statistician. But it's an ever-growing segment. And within this social culture—parties, heavy drinking, and *we can do whatever we want* attitudes—there is some serious shit going down."

"It happened back when we were in school as well," Kat replied. "Or do you not recall?"

"We had *date rape* but this is different. That was an anomaly. This happens a lot. And no one is paying attention. It's like we're all asleep."

"We are asleep, Gracie. At 2 a.m. on a Saturday night, I am very much asleep."

"Shut up. You know what I mean. This shit is *pervasive* and kids, girls mostly, are getting hurt. And if it's happening every weekend, how come we aren't hearing more about it?"

"If one girl calls what happened to her a *rape* but her peers label what they've experienced as *just a bad hookup*—which they then dismiss and move on—there is a disconnect. The girl who says *rape* is out of sync."

Grace looked up from buttering the final shred of crusty roll. Katrina had stopped talking and was staring out the window.

"What?" Grace said. "Spit it out."

"I was almost raped once, and it could have, would have, been a gang rape."

Grace's jaw slackened. "We've known each other all these years and this is the first time I'm hearing this?"

"It's never come up and it was a long time ago, years before we even met. I was backpacking around Europe. Alone. It was like a pilgrimage, going to the places in books I'd read, like Mann's *Death in Venice* and Hemingway's *The Sun Also Rises*. A journey to discover my inner-writer-self, which, as it turned out, was more angst than talent." Katrina smiled, ruefully, then continued.

"I was on a night train, Barcelona to Pamplona, headed to see the running of the bulls. Anyway, trains back then had compartments, could seat four or six people across from each other, but with sliding doors, you know, like in the old movies? I was alone in a compartment, sleeping. I woke up to these four guys coming in, so I had to scoot down. They were all excited, heading up to Pamplona. They had bottles and were drinking. They tried asking me questions, but I pretended to not understand. Acted like I was going back to sleep but watched from the corner of my eye. Then they started talking about me, how American girls like sex, commenting on my body, you know, how it would feel to screw me. They were using slang, but their tone was scary. Like walking down the street and hearing, 'Hey, girlie, gonna give me pussy?' It's the tone. Demanding. Intimidating. And one guy was egging them on, the ring leader."

"Shit, Kat, what did you do?"

"I acted like I was waking up and got up to look out the compartment door and down the aisle. I was hoping for a porter, but it was pitch black, and the train was so noisy. I could have yelled really loudly and been drowned out. So I sat back down, straight up this time, wide-awake, and looked at each of the guys separately. Then I selected one—the one who had not made any nasty comments, had not joined in the trash talk. He wore glasses, seemed shy, the least cool. And I started to talk directly to him, asking him questions. And they could see I spoke some Spanish, which may have unsettled them a bit. I scooted closer to the window and motioned for him to sit next to me so we could talk. I was counting on the female time-honored survival strategy: if you belong to one man, *one* of *them*, the others don't mess with you. And it worked. I stayed with him, with them all, actually, for two days. Which was helpful because Pamplona was insane. And what was really weird is how the guys morphed from predatory to big brothers. After a day, they were telling me what to watch out for and bringing me hot chocolate and churros."

"How did that happen?"

"I hooked up with the shy guy. Not sex, but we were openly *affectionate*. I guess you could say I pimped myself out in exchange for protection."

"That's harsh."

"You got another word? Anyway, that's how it started but I ended up really liking him. Alejandro. We talked about his life, his town and siblings, and how he wanted to be an engineer and build bridges. He asked lots of questions about my life in the States. That's what makes it hard to keep straight. Would sweet boy Alejandro have gone along with a rape if his friends were doing it? Would he have joined in or watched? Do nice boys have the balls to tell the assholes to stop?"

"That's a question for a higher power than me."

"You know what's really strange, Gracie? I buried it for years. And if I ever did think about it, my self-talk was, 'Well, that's a risk you take if you want to travel alone.' "

"Travel alone and you risk getting raped? Seriously?"

"It's a hard world. Now, it's your turn. What's your story, Gracie?" Katrina asked. "Every woman our age has one. If not her own, then her friend or cousin or sister."

"Not tonight, Kat. The wine just hit me. I'm going home. The stories aren't going anywhere."

Grace was home by 9 p.m. and in her PJs in ten minutes. Home was a *casita* that sat behind the bungalow where her daughter and grandson, Molly and Max, lived. It didn't look anything like the cement-floor, three-car-garage it had originally been. Grace had worked side-by-side with the remodel guy, Eldon, to make it happen.

"Stuff any idiot could do," was how Eldon had described her contribution.

She'd mudded drywall, painted walls, helped lay flooring, watched Eldon as he tiled the backsplash and shower. It was mostly open concept—one big room with ocean-gray walls and a vaulted ceiling. The furniture and décor was Vintage Meets IKEA: oak kitchen cabinets reclaimed from an abandoned farmhouse juxtaposed with black granite countertop. Shiny backsplash and stainless appliances. No dishwasher. Grace liked the quiet ritual of washing up her few dishes at the end of the evening.

Her desk, against a wall, was 6 feet of varnished wood resting on IKEA cubes. In another corner, a teal sofa and a few easy chairs were grouped on a worn, patterned rug. The bedroom was painted a soft sage with crisp white trim. In the sky-blue bathroom, a deep, compact Japanese soaking tub sat next to a glass-walled shower.

Out back, through French doors, was a small, private deck, hidden from the bungalow.

This was her home and it had everything she needed.

Grace had never intended to return to Kaw Valley after she'd *run-away-from-home* some twelve years earlier. But her daughter, Molly, had gotten pregnant while still in college. Molly was raising her son, Max, alone. Max had been diagnosed with Asperger's, the diagnosis almost a relief as it gave a name to his mood swings and obsessions, rigidity and meltdowns. But, even with a label, being a single mom to Max was overwhelming, especially if Molly wanted to finish college and have some life of her own. So Grace had moved back, and they'd teamed up. Max was now nine, and Grace and Molly had been working out the kinks of this new relationship for about two years. Molly was definitely *the Mom*, but Grace was available to help out, taking care of Max a few evenings a week so Molly could go to classes. And she had her daughter's back.

Grace turned on the television. She channel surfed, looking for something distracting and frivolous. Nothing. So she went to Netflix and settled on one more episode of *House of Cards*.

Nothing like corruption, perversion, misogyny, and toxic ambition to provide a little perspective.

Chapter 3
(September 5th)

The buzzer sounded twice before the extra-tall wooden door was opened by a gawky looking kid dressed in what seemed to be his pajamas. But then, it was only 6:30 a.m. on a Tuesday.

"Can I help you?" the kid asked.

A man and a woman stood at the front door of the Alpha Phi Beta fraternity house. The man was almost bald with a creased, weathered face. Standing about 5'10," he wore khaki pants and a short-sleeved button-down shirt. The woman was about the same height, in dark slacks and a blazer. She had brownish skin, with glossy black hair pulled tight against her skull and into a knot at the base of her neck.

"Is Logan Whiteman here?" the man asked.

"I don't know. I can go look. Can I tell him what this is about?"

The kid looks 16, but he has to be older, the woman thought.

"Just that we need to speak with him." The woman discreetly held out her hand with a badge cupped in it. The boy's eyes widened.

"Uhhh. Would you like to come in?"

"Thank you," they said in unison, stepping into the front entry hallway. Ahead of them was a tall staircase, to the right an enormous living room with four sofas and numerous chairs. To the left were glass doors that opened into a dining hall, with over a dozen tables and chairs, with more chairs lining the walls. They watched as the boy went up the stairs two at a time and heard a rat-tat-tat knocking. There were muffled voices. Then the boy appeared at the top of the stairs and came back down, this time taking only one stair at a time.

"He'll be down as soon as he gets dressed," the boy said. "Would you like some coffee while you wait?"

"Thanks," the bald man said. "That would be great. Black. My partner takes it with cream and sugar. I'll come help."

Patsy Tsosie gave Sam Hillard a sideways look, but did not interrupt as Sam followed Pajama Kid down the hall and into what Patsy assumed would be a kitchen, probably as super-sized as the other rooms in the house. Sam was checking out the house, so she might as well do likewise. She ambled into the living room and started looking around. Magazines—*Sports Illustrated, Maxim, GQ, Wired,* and something called *Game Informer*—were laid out on the coffee tables. Somebody had left their open backpack, textbooks and notepads visible, on a couch. It was all very innocuous.

Not like they're going to leave roaches in ashtrays or a porn collection lying around, Patsy thought.

"Do you want to talk to me?" a voice said from the doorway.

Patsy turned. He was a good-looking kid, tall, with an open face. Hair not long but not too short either. He wore jeans and a short-sleeved button-down shirt.

"Are you Logan Whiteman?" Patsy asked.

"Yes," he said. "Sorry I kept you waiting. Is something the matter? Has something happened to my family?" He sounded anxious.

"No," Patsy reassured him. "Nothing to do with your family."

"Then what? Why are you here?"

His tone was neither deferential or defensive. More curious.

"I'm Officer Tsosie with the Kaw Valley Police Department. My partner, Officer Hillard, and I need to talk with you about an incident that is alleged to have happened during a party last Friday. We'd like you to come down to the station with us. It shouldn't take long."

"What incident? What are you talking about?"

A door opened down the hall, and Logan looked over as Sam returned to the room, holding two cardboard cups of coffee. "Got it to go, Tsosie," he said before glancing up.

"Are you Logan?" Sam asked.

"Yes," he replied. "But I don't understand what you want."

"There's been an allegation, and we need to discuss it with you, get your side of the story," Sam said. His tone was guy-to-guy, like, *Hey, no big deal, just have to clear this up.* But his eyes never left Logan's face.

Logan looked confused. "What kind of allegation? Against me? Or who? Somebody in the house?"

"Yes," Patsy said. "Against you."

"What are you talking about?" Logan asked.

"We just need you to come with us down to the station. We can bring you back. It won't take long. It's just procedure."

Logan hesitated, as if trying to find a reason he couldn't go.

"Okay," he said. "But I have a class at 11."

"I don't see a problem with that," said Tsosie.

They drove down to the station in under five minutes. Patsy drove and Sam made small talk over the seat with Logan about the lousy football team and how he was waiting for basketball season. Sam asked Logan some questions—if he'd ever played sports, which ones, what position. The universal small talk of men.

When they got to the station, they went into an interview room, with a table and four chairs. There was a mirror on one wall and a video camera was bolted to a far wall. They settled down, Logan on one side of the table and Sam across. Patsy moved a chair to be at an angle so that Logan would have to turn his head to see her and could not look at both Sam and Patsy at the same time. Easier to signal Sam without Logan noticing.

Patsy opened by explaining that there was a protocol to follow and that she had to read him his rights. "Just like TV," she said. "If you watch enough shows you probably have it memorized."

Logan looked confused, so Patsy continued. "It's just part of the script. Got to do it whether we want to or not." Then she lunched into a sing-song recitation.

"Can you tell us your full name?" Sam asked, segueing quickly, allowing no time for Logan to process what Patsy had said.

"Logan Alexander Whiteman," he answered. "Now, will you please tell me what this is about?"

"And your address?"

"On campus or my home address, where my parents live?"

"Both, please."

Logan told him.

"Were you at a party at the fraternity house address last Friday night?"

"Last Friday? Yeah, of course I was."

"And did you meet a young woman by the name of Hannah?"

"I'm not sure. I talked to a lot of girls that night," Logan said.

"Hannah is 5'3", 124 pounds, brown hair, blue eyes."

"That describes a lot of girls," Logan said.

Patsy was getting a little irritated. She interrupted. "Did you have sex with a girl who fits that description? Do you remember *that*?"

"Ok, yeah, the cute freshman." Logan looked relieved that he could provide an answer. "Now I remember. Hannah. Yeah, we had sex," Logan continued. "But it was just a quick hookup at the party. She didn't hang around after. I looked for her, was bringing her a drink, but she was gone. And she told me her dorm but they didn't have a Hannah on the roster. I called the next day—or maybe it was Sunday."

"So, you're saying that you did have sex with Hannah but that it was consensual?"

"Yeah. But, hey, wait a minute. Hold up. Is she saying it wasn't? Like it wasn't just a hookup?"

"Yes, Logan, she is saying that it was *not* consensual sex."

"What does that mean? That she didn't want to?"

Patsy and Sam looked at each other.

"Yes, she states that she did *not* want to have sex with you," Sam answered. "That you had sexual intercourse with her against her will. That she was forced."

"But that's like. . .that's like. . .rape?"

"Exactly," Patsy said. "That would be the allegation."

Logan looked authentically stunned.

There was a moment of silence before Logan spoke.

"This is fucking nuts," he said. "And I want to call my Dad."

Patsy and Sam finished getting the statement from Logan, not much more than what he said at the start: "We had sex, yeah, sure, but it was a hookup."

Logan called his father, Lou, who told him to shut up and that he would call a lawyer. "What the hell have you gotten yourself into now?" was what Lou had actually said. But Patsy and Sam told Logan he was not under arrest so he could leave at any time, go back to the fraternity house and get to that 11 a.m. class. No need for a lawyer quite yet. They'd offered to drive him back, but he'd said no, that he'd call a friend or walk. Turns out the frat house and police station were just seven blocks from each other.

Their final words to him were that he was not to try to contact, or have anyone else contact, Hannah. Not in person, by phone or email, or post on social media. Sam was careful to keep eye contact with Logan when he spoke, to make it very, very clear that *any* attempt to contact the young woman would not be in his best interests.

They watched Logan walk out the door.

"Is it too early for lunch?" Sam asked. "Because I do not recall having breakfast."

"It's never too early for tacos," Patsy replied "Fuzzy's is open. We can be there in two minutes."

Sam grunted, stood up, and they walked over to Fuzzy's. They had their pick of tables.

"Two shrimp tacos, extra sauce, double cilantro rice, no beans, and a queso," Patsy ordered without looking at a menu.

"Two pork, cilantro rice, borracho beans, and I'll just share her queso," added Sam.

"You share, you pay," Patsy said.

"Add two Diet Cokes to my tab," Sam said. "So, we're equal. Satisfied?"

"Yeah, that works. I may even come out ahead."

"Tsosie, you always come out ahead."

Sam Hillard and Patsy Tsosie had been on the Kaw Valley police force for too many years to keep straight. Sam had been Patsy's first mentor, walking her through every step of her first homicide case, respecting her intuition instead of knocking her down, having her back over the years as she moved up from patrol to detective. Now they were peers, and it was clear to Sam that Patsy would continue to rise. He had never aspired to being a captain or chief, but Patsy, he was sure, had what it took.

They made small talk until the food came and then ate, dipping warm salty chips into the white queso, taking bites of their tacos. Then, table cleared, they talked.

"We got nothing," Patsy said. "Again."

These cases were more than frustrating. It felt like every week another girl went to the ER, had a rape exam, made a police report, knew who the guy was and where to find him—and nothing happened. Because the guys didn't deny they'd had sex. So, what difference did a rape kit make? Why even bother to confirm that it was his sperm or his pubic hairs? Why use tax dollars to pay for DNA tests when the guy conceded at the first damn interview that, "Yeah, sure, we had sex. So what?" And most didn't even call it *sex*. It was a *hookup*. Which meant that even if the two individuals had just met, had no prior relationship, sex was a possible outcome. So, if there was sex on a first encounter—and most of these weren't even dates, just parties—you couldn't convince a jury it was rape, not get to *beyond a reasonable doubt*. And DAs like better stats than a 2-14 win-loss record.

"We need a data base," Patsy said to Sam. "We need to keep the DNA on *every* suspect, *every* report. Then we run comparisons with each new DNA. Because we will, over time, come up with multiple hits. And then we have a case."

"So we collect the DNA of men who are never charged with a crime, and just hang onto it for future reference?" Sam snorted. "Without telling them? Because we have a hunch that the guy will do it again? How many civil rights would that violate?"

"Okay, a bunch," replied Patsy. "You got a problem with that?"

Chapter 4
(September 6th)

Hunter Payne turned on his Bose, inserting a CD of flute music. Only then did he go to his bedroom, to the legal file box stashed on the top shelf of his closet.

Hunter liked taking pictures. He liked the feeling of freezing a moment in time, how looking at a photo brought back the experience.

There were eleven envelopes in the box. Hunter opened the top envelope. It was dated May 23rd. There were 25 pictures, all 5 by 7, of a young woman. She had shoulder-length dark brown hair, almost black. Her skin was brown also. She'd been from India, a foreign student, pre-med. She had three earrings in each ear and a very tiny gemstone perched on her left nostril. He remembered touching each earring, twisting them ever so gently, surprised by how easily they turned.

She appeared to be deeply asleep, her face absent emotion. In each picture, she was posed somewhat differently, arms spread loosely across the bed, arms above her head, hands over her face, hands over her breasts with legs together, hands covering her crotch with legs spread apart. . .

He looked at each photo, admiring the angles, thinking in his mind how this pose, or that, was like a Modigliani. He liked the stillness of the pictures. He liked that the woman wasn't talking. Even if she'd been chattering away earlier there was a point when she simply stopped talking. It was only in the quiet that he felt the control. Once he was sure that they were asleep, he would shake them, gently, and call their names. Then he would carry them into the bedroom, After that, he would undress them, ever so slowly and carefully, folding their clothes in a neat pile. When they were naked, he would start the poses. He would retrieve his camera from the bedroom closet, always with a new card inserted.

Each girl was different, her body different, and so there were variations in the poses with each. A few poses were essential: a long shot of the body, hands over head, wrists loosely tied with a red silk scarf, legs spread.

He never did anything that could hurt them. He would masturbate next to them or over them, but he always washed them afterwards.

Hunter knew which girl would be next. She'd been in one of his classes last spring, and they'd worked together on a project. They'd had coffee, talking about school mostly, but no real date.

Hunter didn't date anyone in his current classes. It was better if they didn't share a class, and best if the girls had different majors in buildings across campus.

But he didn't have any classes with the girl this semester and had not seen her at the Business School. They'd run into each other on campus just before classes started, and he'd gotten her cell number.

Hunter had asked her out on a date for last weekend. It had gone quite well. And he could tell that she wanted him. He'd called her last night to ask her out again. He could hear it in her voice.

The second date was this Friday night. In two days. After a few hours out, he would invite her back to his place to listen to some music or watch a movie. He always asked questions on the first date about what the girl liked, her favorite music groups or actors, so he could make the invitation to go back to his apartment more personal and *inviting*.

This next girl had very white skin, and she was curvy, with reddish hair and freckles. Hunter wondered how the freckles would show up in the pictures.

Chapter 5
(September 6th)

Molly was frazzled. She was working 25 hours a week while Max was in school, and taking university classes in the evening two nights a week. Her classes were on Monday and Wednesday this semester. Her mother stayed with Max those evenings.

Grace picked Max up from school, brought him home, tried to get him to do his homework, cooked supper. Then they watched a favorite TV show and, if the stars aligned, Grace got Max to shower or take a bath (his mood dictating which was the least offensive option). Then into pajamas, read a story, and, ideally, got him to sleep. The real challenge was getting through the list without some sort of meltdown, but that was a crap shoot.

Max was, Molly was sure, starting to develop better coping skills, probably as a result of the constant interventions: occupational therapy, physical therapy (the kid could not catch a ball to save his life), coaching in "identifying feelings," and "what to do instead when you feel like screaming." She'd observed him in just the last month catch himself as he was starting to lose it. He'd sit down on the floor and shake both his hands—skimming they called it—in front of his body, and rock a little, repeating, "I do not have to scream, I do not have to scream." And he had not screamed.

Today Molly had raced home from work to gather up her books and a paper that was due. She needed to be out of the house before her mom and Max arrived or there would be a meltdown because Mommy was leaving. It was a lot smoother if Max did not see Molly on the evenings when she had to be in class, so she just stayed away between work and class, at the library, or reviewing notes in a coffee shop. It was her only real down time, and she felt freer even if doing school work. She could, if she chose, meet a friend for an early supper. She could run an errand. These few hours belonged to her and she did not have to explain or answer to anyone. If, after class, the other students were going out to grab a beer, she could go. In fact, as Grace had assured her, it was better if she stayed out a bit later because then it was more likely that Max would be asleep when she got home and not get all hyped up because, "Mommy home, Mommy home, Mommy home."

Molly was aware that her life now was so much better with her mother around to help with Max. The intense stress and anxiety had abated. She was almost able to forget how abandoned and alone she'd felt for those years when Grace had left Kaw Valley.

Almost.

Oddly, Molly had not felt the same emotional pain when Max's father, Jeff, had walked out. Jeff had abandoned his son and Molly for an internet soul mate. But, deep down, Molly had never believed that Jeff would always be there for her, while she'd trusted, to the bottom of her soul, that her mother would.

When Molly returned late that evening, Max was, indeed, asleep in bed. His homework was finished. He'd eaten sausage-and-cheese pasta and salad, on plates with dividers, like a school cafeteria tray, so the foods never touched each other. With apple juice. And a brownie with walnuts. Then they'd watched a *Simpson's* rerun, Grace reported, and he'd taken a shower like a big boy.

All in all, a highly successful evening.

Grace sat on the couch with both feet on the ottoman, holding a glass of what Molly assumed was brandy. Grace was now the one who looked frazzled.

"How was class?" Grace asked. "Is it turning out like you hoped?"

Molly had announced a few months before that she wanted to change her major to psychology, which would require another semester of school, but was more in line with her evolving interest in what made people tick. Her mood had been more upbeat since she'd made the subsequent transition.

"Good," Molly replied. "We're looking at motivation, like what motivates people to do what they do. It's pretty interesting, especially when we start looking at different cultures and social expectations. How motivations can dramatically shift with the cultural tide. How one generation is motivated by security and stability, then there can be a generation motivated by money and accomplishment. And now, especially, the role of the media in defining and reinforcing motivation."

"I could use some motivation about now," Grace replied.

"Yeah, you've seemed a little less, 'Gee, I really enjoy my work' the last few weeks," Molly commented. "What's up with that?"

"Nothing that I want to dive into tonight. More importantly," Grace said, suddenly remembering, "there's a convoluted message on the answering machine from the school counselor about Max. She wants you to call her. Something about Max writing a story where he comes to school with a knife and cuts other children up. So she asked Max about it, if it's what he really thinks or just a fantasy, and he said 'Real.' "

"Damn," Molly said. "Not again. He's learning to express his frustrations in writing but doesn't get how to tone it down. I felt that something was bothering him, but no clue exactly what." Molly sighed. "I'll call her or go in tomorrow. I do think schools are getting more and more anxious when kids express anything that is not *appropriate*. Have they not read the *Grimm Fairy Tales*? They're gruesome."

Molly met with the teacher and counselor the next day before work. The counselor did most of the talking. She explained, a little nervously, that some of the other boys had been picking on Max, making fun of him, calling him names, pushing him around a little. Which might explain the need to express some anger. They had not observed this behavior until yesterday or they would have intervened. It was a small group, about five boys, not all the kids. But Max's story still disturbed them: a story about how a boy comes to school, takes out a knife, a b-i-g knife, cuts up the mean kids, and then gets a reward, a b-i-g hamburger and fries.

"So, Max is being bullied, does not know how to protect himself, and nobody has noticed enough to be able to protect him," Molly responded, trying to sound calm and reasonable. "He uses his words, expresses himself, does nothing physical, and *he* is the problem here? Isn't that what you tell them to do? Use their words?"

Yes, the teacher countered, but the other kids were just doing ordinary kid stuff and Max's description was, "an overreaction."

"Bullying is *ordinary kid stuff* but writing a fantasy revenge is disturbing?" she asked.

"If we could trust that Max can differentiate between fantasy and reality, if we were certain that he's just using words to vent, then we would not be as concerned," the counselor said. "But we can't be sure that Max does differentiate."

Molly didn't know for sure either. Max's world existed in his head far more than other kids. His autism made him see the world differently. His reactions were rarely modulated. He did overreact. But flinging himself down on the ground and screaming was more his style. Taking the time to write down what was churning around in his head was, from Molly's perspective, quite an improvement. He'd had a really good para-professional for one-on-one support the year before, even if just four hours a day, and Molly had seen Max grow. But the para had resigned, as most did, because even being a grocery store clerk paid more. Then, with state budget cuts, service hours had been cut. Now Max had two hours a day, and with different people.

"We just wanted you to be aware," the teacher said. "We want to work together. We do not want anything to happen that would risk Max's being able to attend regular school."

It was meant to be reassuring, but Molly felt their words as a threat. Being Max's mother was scary at times. She could not predict how he would react, could not be sure she could control him. And after the Newtown massacre, by a shooter who was identified as "on the spectrum," everyone was more cautious, especially teachers and schools. People were on edge. A kid without the label could exhibit the same kind of behavior and it was normalized. They were "just being a kid," or having a rough patch.

"Ok, I'll talk with him, encourage him to tell a teacher or counselor when he is being picked on. But, if he does, there has to be some kind of consequence for the kids who are taunting and bullying him."

"I'm not sure I'd describe it quite that way. They're just kids. . ."

"It isn't semantics," Molly interrupted. "Max is being targeted by boys who want to pick on someone who cannot fight back, and they have been able to get away with it."

Molly left the meeting hoping that something could change, and that she was not now labeled as a *problem mom*. But she did not feel confident that she had the power to truly understand or control Max.

Chapter 6
(September 8th)

Logan Alexander Whiteman was having a very bad week.

First, cops showed up at the fraternity house on Tuesday looking for *him*. He'd had to go to the police station. Then they told him that a girl had made an allegation against him. For *rape*. Which was, as he told them, fucking nuts. He'd called his dad who told him to shut up, which he already had planned to do. He'd watched enough *Law and Order* to know to shut up once cops tell you you're being investigated for fucking rape. He was about to insist on his right to an attorney but then they told him he could leave. Just not to contact the girl. Which he wasn't about to do, could not do actually, as she had told him the wrong dorm and so he didn't even know where she lived. He wasn't sure about her last name, just Hannah. At least he thought it was Hannah. He'd tried to call her on Sunday evening, but the dorm said there was no Hannah there.

The sophomore who'd answered the front door had managed to tell half the house that two cops had come looking for Logan and he'd left with them. By the time he got back, his phone was swamped with texts and messages: *What happened? Are you ok? What did they want? It's some mistake, right? Like you're a witness or something? Hey, Logan, spill it—so you're a narc, right? What the fuck?*

And then, the final word: *Shit, Logan, what the hell did you do now?*

This latter was from his father, Lou. Lou was quick to assume that if *anything* went wrong, Logan must have screwed up. Which, Logan had come to realize, after many years of trying to defend himself, was more a projection of Lou's life, in which he did have a hand in a lot of things that could and did go wrong.

Projection had been the subject of just a few pages in a psychology textbook, but Logan had found it very helpful. His dad assumed that everyone operated by the same internal rules and motivations as he did, which meant that everyone was self-serving, scheming, and untrustworthy. Lou thought altruism was a crock. He loved his kids, sure, but he loved them more when they looked good. He wanted successful kids he could boast about who made *him* look good.

The chapter on personality disorders had also been therapeutic for Logan. He'd finally had a label for what he'd lived with for years. The professor had used Donald Trump as an example, which really pissed off some of the students. But the more he'd explained, using specific examples and quotes, the more Logan had seen the parallels.

And Lou loved Donald Trump.

Logan had been so frazzled by the whole thing with the cops that he'd blown off his 11 o'clock class that day—and then blown off his afternoon classes. By then his dad had called back and told him to get down to some attorney's office at 4 p.m.

The attorney, Brad Dorfman, had been in the same fraternity and did a lot of legal work for the fraternity and individual frat members. This was mostly DUI and offenses like pissing in public because they were so shit-faced. But he'd handled assault cases before as well.

Dorfman was reassuring at first, "Nothing we can't handle. Accusations like this are made all the time. Every damn weekend some girl is saying she was raped. They drink too much, have sex, can't remember shit. Then they wake up and think, because they would have made a different choice sober, that they were attacked. Which is bullshit."

But then he stopped being reassuring and started asking questions: How did Logan meet the girl? Had he met her before? Were there people who saw them together? How many people? How long did they talk and drink and flirt before going up to his room? How long were they in his room? Did she stay at the party after leaving his room? Did he take girls up to his room at most of the frat parties? How did he know she was into a hookup?

The questions just kept on coming.

The lawyer said they might go down to the police station to voluntarily give a statement rather than wait for Logan to be picked up or asked to return for a second interview. But, he explained, that would be only after he'd reviewed all his notes, prepped Logan, rehearsed his narrative, and secured statements from other fraternity members as to the *circumstances* preceding the alleged sexual assault. But they had to move quickly.

"What's a narrative?" Logan asked.

"It's what happened, but from your perspective, focusing on the parts that explain or justify your reasoning. Why you made the choices you did. We'll need to review it, eliminate inconsistencies, focus on the important features."

"I didn't rape anyone," Logan said. "It was a hookup. I know what a hookup is."

"Whatever," the lawyer said. "I need to talk to some of the guys who were at the party. And if they have girlfriends, loyal girlfriends, who would be willing to briefly describe what they saw, like how the girl was flirting with you, that you didn't drag her off, that would help also."

Logan belonged to the same fraternity that his father and grandfather had, although they'd attended different schools. That was what was great about a fraternity—it was a loyalty distinct from any individual school. Brothers could be found in every state, in every corporation, in every line of work. And brothers helped brothers.

He'd heard from a young age about how fraternity friendships forged bonds. How these would be the best years of his life.

"Get tied down when you're in college and you'll regret it when you're forty for sure," his father's friends had told him.

But it wasn't until Logan was an adolescent that he'd been allowed to hang around, staying quietly in the background, when his father and some friends would reminisce about "the best years, the fucking best, so keep that in mind" in more detail. He'd heard their stories, stories the men did not tell in front of their wives, memories they kept "in the vault."

And some were not memories, but current. . . "I did this girl down in Atlanta last week, tits like melons. No way they were fake."

"A man can't expect his wife to do things that you get from a whore or with some woman you pick up at a bar," one of his father's friends had told him in the same serious tone he used to recommend stocks and futures. "Even if they don't say it, they're glad not to be asked. They *want* to look the other way."

Logan did not take everything they said seriously, but he did recognize that the men looked backward with more longing than they looked forward.

By the time he was a senior in high school, Logan could make small talk with any age group. He practiced flirting with his mother's friends, telling them how they could pass for college girls, noticing their jewelry or a new hairstyle. He was appropriately deferential with the men, asking about their work and listening attentively as they rambled on. He called them "ma'am" and "sir," which seemed to please the husbands more than their wives.

"Oh, just call me Janet," the wife would say. "That *ma'am* word makes me feel old." He'd agree, smiling, and then ask if he could fetch her another gin & tonic.

Logan fit in. He was tall and trim, with sandy brown hair and sky-blue eyes. He'd graduated in the top 10% of his high school class and was holding steady in the top 20% in college. He'd learned that showing interest and asking questions was a useful tool. As long as he was asking the questions, he felt more in control.

Logan played basketball in high school but dropped out when he realized he would not make varsity. He took up golf. His father said that basketball was for kids, but golf was essential for business.

"No 'foursomes' in basketball," Lou would say. "But chatting someone up over a cold beer at the end of 18 holes? That's where you make the deals."

Logan was a runner-up for Homecoming King his senior year of high school. Second best. Which was how he often felt—almost good enough. He put in hours of "dumb volunteer work," his father's description, to build his college applications.

"Beef it up. Nobody really checks that shit," his father had said. "They buy what you put down. Bottom line, you need personality. Make people feel special. That's how you sell yourself."

The volunteer stuff had paid off. He'd received scholarships from the local Rotary Club, the Masons, the Better Business Bureau. No big deal, but it felt good to win at something.

But, no matter what he did, it was never enough for his father to stop asking, "What score did the top dog get, huh? You gotta' try harder, no more excuses."

Those were the moments Logan wanted to turn it around on his father, to point out to him how *Lou used excuses every fucking day of his life*. That when anything went wrong it was *always somebody else's fault*.

But his father paid his tuition, fraternity fees, room and board. Lou didn't expect him to work during the school year, just caddy in the summer. Plus, his father could hold a grudge like nobody's business. It was never a smart move to piss him off any more than he was generally pissed off.

So Logan kept his mouth shut.

And Logan learned to put his own best interests first, and, if they coincided with the best interests of others, that was an unintended by-product. Logan had managed to extricate himself, with his father's assistance, from the consequences of any adolescent pranks. Like when he and his friends trashed the car of a kid they were, if truth be told, methodically tormenting. Or when he sold his mother Vivian's anti-anxiety pills, or took his little brother's Ritalin, denying, of course, that he had any idea what had happened to the bottles, saying only, "Your memory issues are getting a little scary, Mom. Is there anything I can do to help?"

Logan remembered one night when his father had come to campus for a football game and they went bar-hopping afterwards. Lou loved to party with the frat boys. "Makes me feel like a kid again," he'd tell Logan. That night, Lou was feeling flush, enough so that he was buying rounds for Logan and six of his *brothers*. After he'd had four or five Whiskey Sours, Lou started pontificating on his version of *the facts of life*.

"These are the best years, boys, to enjoy life, when you can have whatever you want, whenever you want." Not that they couldn't enjoy a little "life" on the side later, but then they'd have to be discreet, only do it when they were away on business trips. "Don't hold back on nailing pussy—those are the memories you're gonna' jerk off to when you're fifty."

The next day, one of the frat brothers had said to Logan, "Your dad is so cool. Mine is such a tightwad, he'd never spring for drinks. He's always on me about how I need to develop 'character.' I don't think he's ever said 'pussy' out loud. But your Dad? He's a dude."

Logan just nodded, knowing it was too complicated to try to explain. How his father said when he'd dropped them off, "Great brothers you got there, Logan. Don't let them down. Don't let me down."

In his head, Logan often ignored a lot of what his father said. Unlike Lou, he was not dismissive of women. Not like he'd ever be a *feminist*, a word he'd never understood because, as far as he could tell, girls had it easy. But Lou *never* talked to Vivian's friends just to get to know them. He might flirt a little but with a motive. Like if he wanted to spite Vivian or feed the wives something he wanted their husbands to know.

Logan felt that he was different. He liked being able to make girls smile and laugh, liked how they would lean into his body when he put his arm around them. He liked how they looked up to him, although that was in part because he was 6'4" and most girls were about a foot shorter.

In the past, Logan had pretty much been the one to call it quits with anyone he dated, like if they started to get clingy or had too many expectations or demands. But lately, there were girls who did not return his texts. They would initially flirt with him, seem interested, but then they distanced. And, while he felt the urge to prove he could win their affection, prove that he could *have* them, it was a lot of work. Actually sustaining a relationship, having to consider what *they* wanted to do, being nagged for not calling or being late, having some girl tell him what *she* wanted from sex, or, far worse, be critical of his sexual performance? That was more than he was willing to do, not when he could get what made him feel good without all the work.

"Look, Logan, this isn't working for me," his most recent girlfriend, Lynn, had told him. "You need to slow down, pay attention to what I like. I care about you, and I'm willing to work on this, but you have to want *me*, not just get your rocks off. And if you're with me, you can't mess around with other girls. That's a bottom-line for me."

Lynn was definitely smart, and pretty—a senior headed for a marketing internship at a top-drawer firm. But Logan was not ready to be tied down. Lynn had told him that they needed to, "Take a break," and, *if* he changed his mind. . . "If you wake up and realize what the hell you are losing here, give me a call. But only if you're ready to make some serious changes."

Logan had not called. And, while he did miss having someone to share his day-to-day life with, it was a relief to not feel pressured to live up to her expectations.

Logan was trying hard to not obsess about how he was being set-up.

It had just been days, but Logan couldn't sleep more than a few hours at a time, couldn't study, and felt like absolute shit. He was scared, and he hated feeling scared.

And he hadn't done *anything*. It was just a *hookup*.

Chapter 7
(September 11th)

Hannah needed to go to her classes. She hadn't missed this much since elementary school when she'd had pneumonia. She was more the *tough it out* kind of kid, who would go to school no matter how bad she felt.

It had been ten days since the frat party.

It wasn't that she hadn't tried. She'd gotten dressed, loaded her textbooks and notebooks in her backpack. She boarded the on-campus bus from the dorm to where her first class was on the far side of main campus. But then, looking out the bus window, she thought she saw him, from the back. In a microsecond, her heart started racing. Her right hand began to shake, just slightly, and she could not make it stop. It was like the hand was not connected to her brain. She'd had to stick it under her leg so nobody would notice. Then they'd passed the boy and it had not been him. Just some guy about the same height, same hair, who maybe walked the same. But it wasn't him.

Hannah had tried to make her body relax, to stop shaking inside. She'd done deep breathing, told herself, *I am safe. I'm in the middle of the campus in broad daylight. No one can hurt me.* But the racing heart had not slowed. It was if her entire body was telling her to run—run, run, run.

When the bus came to the stop for her classroom building, Hannah did not move. She stayed as still as she could make herself, forehead pressed to the window glass, as the bus followed its predictable route. It wasn't until the bus returned to the dorm that she pushed herself up and out, making herself walk, look normal, get in the elevator, punch the number for the 7th floor, walk down the long hall to her room, take the key from her pocket, and open her door. Then she'd let it swing shut behind her as she dropped to the floor and sat, hugging her knees to her chest, and, dry-eyed, rocked: forward-back, forward-back, forward-back.

Other than that one try, Hannah had not left the dorm except to go to the cafeteria in the adjacent building. And then she went late, when most of the students had already left for classes. She brought a big textbook to read, to hide behind, and sat in a back corner booth facing away from the entrance.

Except for therapy. She'd made herself go to therapy. The therapist's office was right on Main Street, over a shoe store. She'd taken an Uber.

When her roommate, Nicole, had returned on Sunday afternoon, she'd told her an abbreviated account of what had happened, asking her to keep it in confidence. But it was too big a secret to keep and Nicole apparently told a few of her friends, in confidence of course.

Within twenty-four hours, Hannah was being treated as if she had cancer. Girls on her dorm floor knocked, tentatively, asking if she was going down to supper or if she wanted to give them her meal ticket so they could bring her back some food. She handed over her meal ticket. When they asked what she wanted, she replied, "You pick. Whatever."

Nicole was solicitous, but in a way that made Hannah cringe: "Do you mind if I put on some music?" "Is there anything you need?" "Do you mind if I go down the hall for a few hours?" "Do you need to talk?" And Nicole's friends, who had previously been dropping by daily, never knocking, gossiping as they did each other's nails in the same quirky color, had stopped coming altogether. Hannah, who was less of a social butterfly than Nicole, had not yet established the bonds that all the movies and books and media said would become *friends that last a lifetime.*

So, the room was mostly empty and silent.

Hannah binge-watched Netflix, fixating on a show she'd never seen before: *Lie to Me.* It was about a wacky psychologist and his office cohorts. They were experts in detecting when people were lying. They could see the small and almost invisible non-verbal cues that everyone else missed—and interpret them. Hannah watched it obsessively—every squint, every shoulder shrug, every twitch of the jaw and tightening of the lips, every widening of the pupils. She studied this TV show more closely than she had ever studied anything before.

As if her very life depended on it.

Chapter 8
(September 12th)

Grace was working at her office desk when she heard the door to her waiting room open and softly shut. She glanced at her wall clock. The next client, a new one, was not due for fifteen minutes. She sighed. It was a crapshoot whether new clients would be early or late.

Being early required no explanation and was generally seen as responsible and respectful. But since Grace was often running behind schedule, had five more minutes of paperwork to wrap up, one last email to send, she almost preferred the late ones with excuses. Having spent decades making up excuses herself, she appreciated the creativity they required.

Grace gathered together the necessary intake papers—HIPPA forms, insurance forms, emergency contacts, address, phone numbers and email—and made a neat pile for the new client to fill out.

That would buy her at least ten more minutes.

In the waiting room, a young woman perched on the edge of a chair. The Rape Crisis Center had called with a referral, first name Shelby. Sometimes the women who were referred changed their minds and did not call. In any case, the center just provided first names until releases were signed.

"Are you Shelby?" Grace inquired, smiling as she extended her hand.

"Yes," the girl replied.

"I have some paperwork for you to complete before we get started. It should just take a few minutes."

"Ok," the girl said, accepting the papers that Grace handed her.

"Would you like something to drink? Water, tea, soda?" Grace gestured at a mini frig in the corner of the room, with a tray of glasses and napkins on the top. "Help yourself."

Grace returned to her desk and sent off the remaining emails, mostly confirming appointments, then walked back to the waiting room.

"I can't complete these," Shelby said. "If you need them all, then I can't do this."

"That's fine, Shelby. Don't worry. Come on in and we can discuss what you're comfortable signing and what not. Usually it's workable."

Once they were seated, Shelby on the couch and Grace in an adjacent chair, Grace inquired, "So, can you tell me what you don't want to sign and why?"

It was a familiar refrain: she did not want her parents to know, had not gone to the police or hospital because she didn't even know what *may* have happened. Grace said she needed a HIPAA form and some contact info but could waive the rest.

Shelby filled out the few remaining spaces and handed the papers back to Grace, who perused them briefly and then slid them into a manila folder.

Grace sat back in her chair, a clipboard for her notes in her lap. She took a deep breath and looked at Shelby.

Shelby Stewart was twenty years old but looked younger. Perhaps it was the soft roundness of her face, her curly red hair, or the freckles that dotted her nose and upper cheeks.

"Where do you want to start?" Grace asked.

"I don't know where to start. It's so weird."

"Then how about I ask you some boring background questions and we'll figure that out together?"

Two hours later, Grace watched from her office window as Shelby walked down Main Street. Shelby was from a small Nebraska town. She had two younger brothers. Her dad was a dentist and her mom taught second grade. Her grandparents lived three blocks away. She was a junior, and a business major.

And her life had just gotten seriously messed with.

It was different version of the same story: Girl meets boy. Girl likes boy. Girl wants to date boy. In this case, girl did get one decent date—where they talked and laughed and started to connect—and then a second date where she woke up naked in his bed with no memory of what had happened.

Date number 2 started out fine: a movie, a foreign film, and then out for some appetizers and a beer. They'd walked downtown, sat on a bench outside the Replay Lounge and listened to a band playing in the outside garden. Then the boy had suggested they walk a few blocks over to his apartment. He had the new CD of a band she'd said she really liked. They could listen to it, have a drink, and then he'd drive her home. His car was at his place.

Shelby did not say his name, just "he."

They had walked to his apartment, holding hands. He lived alone, and the apartment had been tidy, not a stinky mess like a lot of guys' places. She sat on the couch while he went into the kitchen to make them each a drink. When he came back, the drinks were in little copper mugs.

"He told me they were Moscow Mules; vodka, ginger beer, and lime. And he told me some story of an over-supply of post-World War II Russian vodka and somebody with a bunch of copper mugs—the start of a drink and tradition. I tasted the ginger beer and lime, not so much alcohol. He put on the music and it was really good. We were just sitting on the couch. I felt so relaxed, comfortable with him. I don't remember falling asleep, just closing my eyes and listening to the music."

"And then?" Grace had asked.

"Then I woke up. I was very groggy, didn't know where I was. But it was morning. I was naked, in his bed. *Naked.* And he was lying next to me. There was a sheet over him but then I realized he was naked. I just freaked out. I jumped up and grabbed the sheet around me. I kept asking, 'What happened? What happened?' "

"What did he say?"

"He started talking fast, and said that I'd gotten drunk, that I was coming on to him, that I went to the bathroom and came out naked. But then I passed out on his bed and *nothing* had happened."

"Nothing?"

"Yeah, *nothing.*"

"And you do not buy that because. . . ?"

"That isn't *me*. I do *not* get drunk, I do *not* come on to guys, and I have never, ever, *ever* gone into a bathroom and walked out naked. It makes no sense."

"So what did you do?"

"I told him that what he was saying was a crock. And my clothes were all folded in a neat pile. Drunk people do not fold clothes into neat piles. I asked if he'd raped me. I was getting louder but not yelling. But then he started yelling at me, that he had done *nothing*, that *nothing* had happened, and I needed to get out of his apartment if I was going to act so crazy."

"And did you? Get out of his apartment?"

"Yeah, I put on my clothes and brushed my hair and left. Just started walking." Shelby had been looking at the floor but she had raised her head to look directly at Grace. "I walked over two miles to get home and I don't remember anything."

"Now I feel like maybe I am crazy," she'd said. "Everything is fuzzy in my head, and I usually remember things word-for-word. I'm not even sure exactly what I said, just that I was angry and freaked-out. But I need to know what happened. I can deal with it if I know."

Grace and Shelby had talked about some possible options for finding out what had happened. Grace was not optimistic. From what she could tell, there was only one person who had that answer and he was on the defense. But Shelby wanted to try. She had nothing to lose by trying.

"Nothing to lose," she'd repeated.

They set an appointment for the following week.

Chapter 9
(September 13th)

Hannah was online trying to file a formal complaint with the university. This was a completely separate process from the police, but was, Stacy assured her, necessary.

Stacy said that the campus investigation moved faster. Court cases could drag on for a year or more, with motions and continuances. This was a way to at least get the guy gone, out of the university, until the legal process was resolved. Then she could stop flinching every time she walked around a corner.

But it was confusing. She'd been on the university website and looked but could not figure it out. Stacy told her to go to Institutional Opportunity and Access (IOA). They handled discrimination complaints, harassment, and a long list of other *violations* of regulations, which included Title IX. Hannah had heard about Title IX, but thought it was about gender equity with sports. But, as she navigated the site, it was clearly more than that. It looked like her complaint would fit under "sexual violence."

"Sexual violence" means any physical act which is sexual in nature that is committed by force or without the full and informed consent of all persons involved. Sexual violence may include but is not limited to rape, sexual assault, sexual battery, and sexual exploitation. Sexual violence can occur between strangers or acquaintances, including people involved in an intimate or sexual relationship. Sexual violence can be committed by men or by women, and it can occur between people of the same or different sex.

Yeah, thought Hannah, *that covers it.*

The first step seemed to be filling out a *Personal Discrimination Form.* It was under the *Discrimination Complaint Resolution Process* which appeared to be a very, very broad umbrella. She started to complete it online: her name, when the *violation* took place, the nature of the violation. But then they asked for a detailed description of the conduct that was the basis for the complaint, copies of documents that supported the complaint, names and contact information of witnesses to the violation.

Shit, thought Hannah, *rapes don't have witnesses. No supporting documents either.* This couldn't be right.

She looked at the contact number for the office. A woman answered on the second ring with, "IOA. Can I help you?"

"Yes," Hannah replied, "I do need help."

When she clicked off, Hannah felt better. The woman had said it might be easier to come in. They could help explain the paperwork. She'd said, yes, this could be a confusing process. She'd explained that the university would have sixty days from the time Hannah filed to conduct an investigation and determine findings. During that time, as soon as they knew who the *respondent* was, he would be informed of the nature of the complaint but prohibited from contacting or harassing her. And they would work with her to arrange any needed *interim measures*: changes in class schedule, some additional time for getting caught up, counseling, a variety of supports. She also repeated that all of the *interim measures* and supports were available to her whether or not she chose to file a complaint.

It was a lot of information to digest, but the woman's tone was kind and reassuring. Hannah said she would come over after lunch. It was close to her dorm, just a short walk. She wouldn't need to take the bus or go through the main part of campus.

By 4 p.m., Hannah's complaint was officially filed. She would be contacted by an investigator who was, the nice woman assured her, an experienced attorney *fact finder*. The woman explained how there were different standards with the university process than the court process, how it was more a *preponderance of evidence* than *beyond a reasonable doubt*. Hannah wrote it down so she could google it and understand the differences.

Hannah had been hesitant to ask about whether she'd be in any trouble for drinking underage, which violated university policies as well as the law. But when she'd hinted at it, the woman told her that there was a drug and alcohol amnesty policy for anyone filing an IOA complaint. "Not to worry."

A letter would be sent to Logan Whiteman that a complaint had been filed against him, along with a brief outline of the complaint. He would have the right to respond and would also be interviewed by the investigator. Both parties could present any supporting documentation or witness statements. The investigator would interview witnesses. At the end of the process, the investigator would provide a detailed summary and findings. Then it was up to—here Hannah was not sure who, but some panel, maybe—to determine appropriate consequences.

There was also an appeal process, but Hannah didn't pay any attention to that. As far as she was concerned it was a slam-dunk.

Chapter 10
(September 15th)

When Logan received the letter from the IOA with the complaint, he was initially confused. What the hell was Institutional Opportunity and Access? He read the letter twice before he understood.

The girl had gone to the university and filed a complaint against him. He had to respond. If he did not respond, the investigation would move forward without him. Consequences could be imposed with or without his participation. These consequences covered a broad range. But the only consequence that jumped out at him, that registered, was "expulsion from the university." He had a certain time frame to respond and to meet with the investigator. He was not to have any contact with the person making the complaint, not harass her, or even try to speak with her.

Logan felt his chest tighten. How could this be happening? Why him? He hadn't done anything different than any other guy in the house. Hell, from what some guys said they did, he was in the minor leagues.

These people wanted a rebuttal, a response? They wanted witness statements? *Screw all of you,* he thought. He'd give them that and more. This was starting to get personal.

When the police had shown up and asked him to go to the station, everyone in the house had found out. Not like he could have kept a lid on that. Most of the guys had been supportive, like, "Hey, bro, nothing to worry about. We all saw how she was hanging all over you." "This sucks, really sucks, but we got your back."

But there had also been a degree of wariness. *If* Logan were to be indicted, not like that could ever happen, but *if,* it would not be good for the house. No fraternity wanted to be known as the frat house with the rapist. So, *if* the accusation did not go away, the frat might need to distance itself.

This had never occurred to Logan until another kid, a sophomore, asked, "So, hey, if this really goes down, where are you gonna' live?"

Logan had not answered the question, just said, "Nothing happened, man. It was a hookup. That's all." But he'd been shaken by the question.

Kyle, a junior, had pressed Logan, as if assessing the cost/benefit factors for himself. "So, hey, was she totally passed out? I had a girl like that last semester. We got to my room, and she was hanging onto me and talking, not making much sense, but talking. So I went to take a piss and when I got back she was, like, passed out."

"What did you do?" Logan asked.

"I started to make out with her, figured a little action would wake her up. I knew she'd wanted it. Then I took off her shirt. She didn't have a bra, it was like one of those tops where the bra is built-in." Kyle had used his hands to try and demonstrate the intricacies of female attire. "So I played with her breasts, and she started moaning a little, so I figured she must be liking it. Sucked on her nipples. Then I started to rub her pussy. Still had on her panties under a short skirt. Pulled those down and started to rub up against her. She had really soft thighs." Kyle had stopped to grin at the memory. "That was enough to get me off."

"When did she wake up? Was she pissed?" Logan asked, feeling curious himself.

"I put her panties back on her but couldn't get the shirt on right. So, I put the blanket up over her and let her sleep. A few hours later, when the party was dying out, I went and woke her up. I was like, 'Hey, how are you feeling? We started to make out, but then you just passed out on me. It's a little insulting to a man to pass out on him in the middle of kissing, you know? Just how much did you have to drink?' "

"Then what?"

"She was like, 'Hey, sorry.' But then, 'What do you guys put in that damn punch, huh? This has never happened before. Where are my shoes? So, maybe we can get coffee this week?' "

"Well, that's about what happened to me, only she isn't wanting to get coffee and she didn't pass out. It would be a hell of a lot less complicated if she had."

Logan felt an edge, a tension, between himself and his brothers. They were concerned about him, he knew that. But they also had a self-interest. The frat did not need any bad PR. That could hurt their party status. They wanted it all to just go away.

Logan left voice mails for the fraternity president and then his lawyer. He started to call his father but decided to leave him out of it for now. Lou would just get all worked up, and that did not help Logan to think clearly.

The police had believed him. He was sure of that. This would be the same. Why didn't the girl see this? Why was she making such a big deal about a hookup?

Logan wanted to scream at her. She was making his life hell. It was no big deal. Just get up, pull up your big-girl panties, and move on. *Don't drag me into it*, he thought. *You don't go to frat parties, flirt like crazy, put out all sorts of signals, and then act all offended when something happens.*

Just fucking grow up.

Chapter 11
(September 16th)

Grace startled awake at 7 a.m., then curled back into fetal position, willing herself return to sleep. *It's Saturday*, she thought. *I deserve to sleep in*. Ten minutes later, she accepted that even if it were Saturday, she still had work to do—and she'd never get back to sleep once that thought had registered.

After a shower, blasting hot, which felt quite good and washed away any lingering grogginess, Grace sat down at her desk to write a to-do list for the day. She had parenting plans to draft for her mediation cases, and references to track down for an adoption home study. But they were flexible, so, in some ways, she was *open*.

Coffee in her favorite mug, Grace tackled a custody plan and property settlement for a couple, Mary and Phil, who had been married for twenty-four years and had three kids. There was a fourth child on the way, but that was with Phil's twenty-eight-year-old dental hygienist, hence the divorce. Poor Phil did not seem enthusiastic about being a new father at 46, just when his kids were getting ready to launch, when he and Mary could finally have traveled and enjoyed an empty nest.

Phil had recognized that he'd royally messed up, begged for forgiveness, said all he wanted was to make it up to Mary for the rest of their lives. Mary had seen the repentance bit before, every four or five years of the marriage, and she'd always ended up forgiving Phil, truly, in her heart, because he was her best friend in so many ways and such a good dad. She'd gone as far as to attribute his serial infidelity to his shitty childhood, with a lack of affection and validation from his mother, and a philandering father as a role model. Mary had made excuses for Phil, and he'd sincerely appreciated her understanding, had always straightened up and been an attentive husband and a good dad—until the next time.

But the pregnancy, a baby, was a game changer.

Paying child support to this other woman for eighteen-plus years?

Feeling torn between asking Phil to have no contact with his own child or seeing his love-child—Mary had referred to the baby as his "lust child"—in their home every other weekend? Celebrating holidays with *all* of Phil's kids?

No, Mary had realized, there was no way out of this pickle.

When Mary was being bottom-line honest, however, the baby made the decision easier. Her children would not judge her for the divorce. She could walk away without guilt.

So Grace was drafting a plan for them. It was quite short-term as the twins were sixteen and their older sister was in college. The kids would call their own shots, time with Dad scheduled around their adolescent activities.

Mary had sobbed when they discussed the holidays. She'd offered, for the sake of their kids, to share Thanksgiving and Christmas, and that Phil could come over to open presents, like they'd always done, and for dinner. Of course, that invitation did not include the baby.

The baby that would be her children's *sibling*.

Then she'd cried some more.

The finances were easy. All retirement was split. Home equity was divided, bank accounts separated. They'd made lists of what each would take from the home. Mary had surprised Phil by saying she would stay in the house until the boys graduated high school but then wanted to move to something smaller, with less yard and upkeep. So, if Phil wanted the house in two years, so perfect for his growing family, he could have it. They could delay splitting the equity until he took possession, and then he could buy out her half. It was paid off so there was no big rush. And it had that fabulous wooden playset in the back yard that he'd built ten years earlier.

It took Grace just two hours to write it up, both custody and property, and email drafts to Mary and Phil. She asked them to make edits and then return the draft.

Grace stood up to stretch, rubbing at her neck. *Time for a break,* she thought. *And a reality check.* She punched in Patsy Tsosie's number on her cell.

"What's up?" Patsy asked, answering on the second ring.

"I want to pick your brain on something," Grace replied. "And I'm willing to pay."

"I'm on duty today, so no alcohol. Gonna' cost you a grande mocha latte, extra whipped cream," Patsy said.

"Done," Grace said. "The sun is shining, so how about a bench by the gazebo in thirty minutes?"

They sat on the bench in a companionable silence sipping their lattes. The sun dappled through the trees, making intricate patterns of light and shade.

Patsy Tsosie was a detective, the only Native American female cop on the Kaw Valley force. Her intuition, and willingness to follow it instead of protocol, had made a huge difference in Grace's life over twelve years earlier. After Grace returned to Kaw Valley, they'd reconnected. Grace found Patsy to be a resource on police procedure and what was really going on—the *underbelly*—in Kaw Valley. On the flip side, Patsy valued Grace's clinical experience and perspective. More than that, they just liked each other.

"So, what's on your mind?" Patsy asked.

"I want to get a handle on rape cases in Kaw Valley," Grace replied.

"What? Did some birdie tell you about my caseload?"

"Huh? No, it's nothing to do with you. I've started taking some referrals from the Rape Crisis Center. And so far they're all campus related. And the girls know the guys. No psychos dragging them into an alley or lurking in the shadows. . ."

Patsy cut Grace off before she could continue.

"That's the made-for-TV-movie stereotype. Stranger danger. But it's not reality."

"So do *most* victims know their assailants?"

"Yes, dear. Most—like 90% from my rough guesstimate—of campus rapes are by fellow students. And most girls are conditioned to be nice to people, be polite, not make waves. I swear they don't trust the intuition that God gave them. They may feel the stirrings of a fight or flight reflex, like, 'Oh gee, something here is just a little *off*,' but they smother it under 'That would be *rude*. I don't want to do *that*.' "

"Are these cases not being prosecuted? Because I'm not reading about trials in my morning paper."

"They don't get to trial. Rape is one of the hardest cases to prove *beyond a reasonable doubt* unless there are piles of evidence. The problem is that what constitutes evidence has totally changed. Now we have to *prove* that sex was *not* consensual."

Patsy paused to sip her latte.

"It really helps if the perp is sleazy," she continued, "with a history of other violent acts, publicly denigrating of women or with an axe to grind. Best of all is if the rape happens in conjunction with another crime like a carjacking or burglary or robbery. Because with rape there is always the question—*was the victim giving it away?* Did she start to give it away and then change her mind, so he maybe *misunderstood* and thought he had a right to take it because he thought she still might be *giving* it away? With any other crime, those questions are ludicrous."

Another sip.

"Connecting rape to another crime makes it easier for a jury," Patsy continued. "Like, *no*, she did not say he could have her jewelry, cash, credit cards and, oh yeah, her vagina. Victims of theft or even assault don't have to prove they did not ask to be victimized, but a rape victim has to prove that she was not complicit or culpable."

"But most rape cases, especially on a campus, never meet that threshold," Grace interjected. "And if the guy is clean-cut, Dockers, articulate. . ."

"Juries do not convict clean-cut, well-mannered, white-boys for rape when there are no witnesses, no broken bones, no blood, no abduction, no *serious* signs of resistance or struggle. The guys never deny they had sex, they just say it was consensual. And how do you prove that it wasn't? I mean, *beyond-a-reasonable-doubt* proof? Would you send a kid to prison for years without a sense of certainty?"

"My campus cases also involve alcohol. Does that complicate. . ."

"Yeah," Tsosie cut in, "that's what makes these campus rapes a nightmare to prosecute. Everything can be attributed to 'We were drinking.' But, somehow, while drinking undermines the victim's account, like can she be *sure* she said no, it flip-flops for the perpetrator and gets used as an excuse for a lapse of judgment—like he never would have missed her *signals* if he hadn't been drinking."

"So, credibility gets shot. . ."

"I'm not finished," Patsy said. "Since the assault is often party-related, or on a date, the defense latches on to other victim-blaming shit, like, 'What was she wearing?' Like clothing implies consent. But she was wearing the exact same stuff as her friends who did *not* get raped. In fact, they probably all borrowed each other's clothes before they went out. But, once you're raped, you're scrutinized. The victim is on trial."

"No, c'mon, that's not still being said—not in our justice system?" Grace said this with a sarcastic edge.

"It was once the cops, so there has been progress. But jurors are just people. No training in unconscious bias. Look," Tsosie continued, "I can get you some local stats as far as reported rapes, arrests, trials and convictions, but the real baseline is unknown. Most rapes are never reported. And of the ones that are, only a quarter or so of perpetrators are arrested or charged. Of those charged, very few go to trial and even fewer are convicted. Rape stats are far worse than homicide stats or robbery stats."

Patsy dug around in her pocket for a piece of paper and wrote something down.

"Start with this. Pull up *The Hunting Grounds* on Netflix. It's a documentary on campus rape. Their stats are compilations of almost every national study. A few seem skewed, but most are based on multiple studies. It will save you hours of research. Then we can talk more local."

Patsy stood up, giving Grace a final look.

"Grace, you do realize that I can't discuss any specific case with you, right? Because it has just registered in my brain that we will, if we aren't already, be involved with the same cases. Am I being perfectly, perfectly clear?"

Grace made a face at her but nodded.

"Perfectly," she replied.

Chapter 12
(September 19th)

Hannah was in her dorm room, sitting on her bed, her back against the wall. Stacy and her friend, Nathan, sat on the vacant bed across the room. Hannah had covered the mattress with a red comforter after Nicole had moved out.

Nicole had told Hannah two nights before that she'd put in for a room change. During the first week following the rape, Nicole had started camping out in a friend's room on another floor. Then she'd put in for the change.

"I just think you need your own space, Hannah. This is a very bad time for you and it might help to not have to share," Nicole had said, looking past Hannah and out the window.

Hannah had tried to not take it personally. She and Nicole had just been assigned to share the space. They were not prior friends. And Nicole had been a little freaked out at having her new roomie get raped.

Hannah agreed it was, no question, a downer.

The room change had apparently been expedited. Housing did not want a student forced to share a room with someone who'd been raped. That was not what the *Freshman Experience* was all about. It had been determined, without anyone ever actually talking to Hannah, that she could keep the double room as a single at no extra charge for the semester. Maybe even for the year.

When Hannah had returned from class—she'd finally made it to two of her classes, which was a start—the next afternoon, Nicole was gone. All of her stuff totally cleaned out. Hannah had stared at the uncovered mattress on the bed across from her own. She'd wondered if she would see Nicole again. She'd wondered if she cared.

Guess she's not one of my 'friends-that-last-a-lifetime,' Hannah thought.

But the stark, uncovered mattress had been too hard to look at, almost a recrimination. *Even your roommate bailed,* it said.

Thus, the red comforter.

Today, however, Stacy had asked Nathan for help. The IOA appointment was looming. Nathan was in law school. He was also an intern with a firm that did criminal defense work. Nathan had helped to prep witnesses for court.

This was not court, just an interview with an investigator. But Hannah had never stepped foot in a courtroom, and certainly had never been interviewed by an investigator. Stacy said that Nathan could help.

"This is not open-and-shut. It matters how you present yourself," Nathan was saying. "Don't come across angry or mad, not even upset. Calm and factual. Don't react to the questions as if he—if it is a *he*—is questioning your judgment. It's just his job. He has to ask, and you have to answer. Now, show me what you're going to wear."

"What I'm going to *wear*?" Hannah retorted. "It's not enough that the cops asked what I was wearing that night, how much I drank—like that matters. Now I have to dress fake just to answer more questions?"

"Yeah, Hannah," Nathan said. "*You do*. Not dress *fake*, but dress in a way that communicates that you are a serious person, a truthful person, who is not misrepresenting the facts."

"But I'm not a liar," Hannah protested, her face dissolving in tears of frustration.

"I know that. So, what will you wear?"

They looked in her closet, deciding after some back-and-forth on black slacks, a mauve blouse—not low-cut, no hint of breasts—sandals, and a scarf to soften it up.

"Let's go over what happened and how you can best communicate it," Nathan said, settling back down on the bed with a clipboard to take notes. "Start with when you first arrived at the frat house."

Hannah began with arriving at the party with some other girls from the dorm. Checking it out. How it was so crowded, so much noise.

With each sentence, Nathan questioned her.

"So, what did you feel when this guy came over and started talking to you, asking you questions?"

"Flattered," Hannah responded. "I was just a freshman and he was obviously not. When he told me he was a senior, I was, like, *wow*. I felt special."

"That's good. Make it clear that he initiated the conversation, he focused on you, he didn't leave you to go off and socialize with his friends when he found out you were a freshman. He zoned in on you, kept talking, kept bringing you drinks."

"But he did," Hannah replied. "So why does it sound different when you say it?"

"Because I'm looking at it as the strategic behavior of someone who has targeted you to exploit, not a nice guy who thinks this naive freshman girl is so wonderful he can't take his eyes off her."

Hannah blushed, hot with shame. Because that was what she'd felt, had wanted to believe, that this cool, older guy had seen something in her, something that no other boy had really ever seen. For that hour or so, she'd felt—discovered? Was that it? And now she felt ashamed for being so naive.

Stupid, stupid girl, she thought.

"I'm sorry," Nathan said. "I didn't mean it like that. But it has to be clear that this is a pattern of behavior."

"I'm okay," Hannah replied. But she was definitely *not* okay.

"Now, why did you go up to his room?"

"Because I started to feel woozy. I don't drink much and wasn't used to it. And he said I'd feel better if I lay down for a little bit, took a break. He even said that if I didn't feel better after a while, he'd walk me or drive me back to my dorm."

Hannah hesitated. That last part—how he'd said he'd take her home if she didn't feel better—was not something she remembered telling the police. But he had said it, and it had made her feel safe, like he was watching out for her.

"What's the matter?" Nathan asked.

"What I just said, about what he said? I don't think I told that to the police. I keep remembering little pieces of that night, and I didn't have so many pieces when I talked to the police."

"That's okay," Nathan said. "If it comes up, just explain that you were still in shock when you talked to the police. It was 5 a.m. and you'd been up all night. "

"But will it look like I'm making it up, adding things later?"

"It could. But if that is what happened and it helps to explain why you felt safe going to his room, you should include it. That there was no discussion of a hookup, no reason other than you were woozy, to go upstairs."

"But it is why I went to his room," Hannah said indignantly. "I've never had sex with a guy I just met. Ask anyone who knows me." Hannah's voice rose with each word. "I've only had sex a few times and it was with. . . "

"You can say that as well if you want," Nathan said. "But more in a factual tone. Like—*this* is who I *am,* and I did not totally change in a few hours that night. I did not initiate or agree to sex with a man I'd just met. Now, let's review the sequence."

The entire time, Stacy sat, saying nothing, listening, leaving only to get them Cokes and small bags of Fritos from the vending machines.

Two days later, on Thursday, Hannah was in the IOA office, in a private room, talking with the investigator. She was wearing the black slacks, but she'd gone rogue with a teal blouse instead of the mauve.

"Can you tell me in your own words about the basis for your complaint?" the investigator asked.

Hannah started to answer, trying to do what Nathan had coached her to do but without appearing to have been coached.

Hannah felt prepared in ways that she had not been able to prepare, to anticipate, when the police had interviewed her. Then she'd been raw with disbelief and pain. She'd answered "I don't know" to many of their questions because, at that point, she had not known. She still did not fully understand why she'd trusted Logan Alexander Whiteman. She hadn't even known his full name when she'd first taken his extended hand and followed him up the stairs. She'd learned his last name at the police station when they'd shown her the fraternity yearbook with photos of the members.

But, this go-around, she'd have answers.

Hannah also had a typed witness statement from Stacy. Not to the rape, of course, but all that followed. The investigator would speak personally with Stacy in the next few days. It was all clearly defined in their protocol.

Stacy had offered to go with Hannah but Nathan had said it would be better for Hannah to ask someone else if she needed support. It was important that the witness statement not be seen as tainted. Stacy needed to remain a neutral party; the RA, just doing her job. He'd even volunteered to go with Hannah.

Hannah had thought it over but no one felt right. So, she was here alone. She'd only been on campus a few weeks when it happened. She didn't have a network of friends.

It was over two hours before Hannah walked out of the IOA offices. She was emotionally drained, but she felt pretty good about the interview. She'd taken time after each question to repeat it in her head, to reflect, not rush to answer.

"Let me take a minute to think about that," she'd even said a few times. She had not gotten defensive even when she'd wanted to scream. She'd refrained from asking if IOA stood for *It's Often Assholes*.

And the investigator had been a woman, not a man. Hannah was not sure, but she thought a part of her had relaxed just a little. The woman looked to be in her forties, with shoulder length blonde hair. There was a moment when Hannah had wanted to say, "You might want to cut that hair, lady. It can be used against you." But she'd bit her tongue.

The IOA investigator met with Logan, his attorney, and his fraternity president on the following Monday, September 25th. His attorney said they could delay responding, but Logan wanted to get it over with.

Logan had been coached by his attorney. He was respectful, but not obsequious. *Answer questions, but don't offer more. No tangents.*

Logan produced a file of typed witness statements from his Lands' End briefcase. Each described the behavior of the girl making this complaint: her intoxication, sexual flirtatiousness, hanging onto Logan, holding his hand and walking willingly up to his room, departing the party of her own accord without saying a word to any of the 100-plus attendees. It was a duplicate set of the witness statements they'd provided the District Attorney. They were not just from frat brothers, but from girls who had been present. That the girls were dating a frat brother, or maybe wanted to date a frat brother, was not mentioned. The attorney had provided directives for witnesses: keep it short, neutral, stick to observations, no insinuations, no conjecture. He had reviewed the statements for consistency before submission.

They'd also discussed wardrobe. The attorney wore a suit, but Logan and the fraternity president wore Dockers, button-down shirts, and ties.

The investigator spoke with Logan for over an hour. When asked if Hannah had communicated her unwillingness to engage in sexual contact, Logan answered "No, ma'am, not that I understood. I thought it was really clear that this was a hookup. We'd been talking for a few hours already. I liked the girl. It makes no sense to force someone when there are lots of girls who want sex as much as the guys do."

Chapter 13
(September 20th)

Hunter was unsettled.

The second date with the red-haired girl had been a week ago Friday. They'd met at Liberty Hall downtown to see a foreign film, then gone next door to the Brewery for some appetizers and a beer. When he'd asked if she wanted to come back to his place to listen to the new release of a band she liked, she said yes.

He'd cleaned his apartment and left two table lamps on for ambiance. He'd put on the CD and told her to just relax on the couch. In his kitchen, he made two Moscow Mules. He mixed the crushed pill particles with the vodka and put the vodka in the Little Ninja for just a second with some ice. Then he mixed in the ginger beer and lots of fresh lime juice.

She had, within fifteen minutes, passed out, drifting off as her eyes closed. Her head was resting on his shoulder. He'd left it there, and waited, listening, feeling the rise and fall of her breathing, until the CD finished.

Then he'd gently lifted her up and carried her into the bedroom. After laying her down on the bed, he'd removed her clothes, first the sandals and slacks, then underwear, blouse, bra, folding them in a neat pile.

He'd taken his time, posing her, snapping from different angles, admiring the soft roundness of her thighs and breasts. Her pubic hair was dense and red. He much preferred natural to waxed. He didn't know why girls did that.

Then he'd taken off his clothes. He'd sat on the bed next to her and gently stroked her arms and legs. Then he'd straddled her, rubbing some oil on his penis, stroking himself until he came.

At that point, he usually got a warm washcloth and wiped down the girl's body, and then, very carefully, put her clothes back on. He could never get it just right, but the messiness could be attributed, in the morning, to having slept in her clothes. Sometimes he just gave up and left their pants on the floor of the bathroom, inside out, as if they'd dropped them there.

"You were tossing and turning a lot," he'd usually say. "I tried to get you walking, to take you home, but it seemed smarter to just let you sleep it off here."

He'd offer to make them breakfast, and they'd say, "No." Then he'd drive them back to their dorms or apartments. On the way, more often than not, the girl would apologize for drinking too much, or passing out, or being a bother. He'd say he'd call them, but he never did.

And they never called him.

Hunter picked girls who seemed shy, less experienced. Nice girls. Foreign students were good because they had no one to turn to. They did not want to get in any trouble or call attention to themselves. They would never tell their families. They just wanted to pretend it never happened, whatever it was they imagined might have happened.

But last week he'd been drawn to her, the softness of her. He'd carefully washed her, but, then, instead of putting her clothes back on, he'd slipped down next to her and spooned. *Just for a few minutes*, he'd told himself.

But he'd fallen asleep. He woke up to her yelling at him. She was saying, "What happened? What the hell happened?" And he'd fumbled for something to put on, grabbing anything from his drawers.

"Nothing happened," he'd said, his tongue thick with sleep. "We were too drunk for anything to happen. You wanted it but we. . ."

"What do you mean? I wanted *what*?"

"You went into the bathroom and came out naked," he'd improvised. "I thought you wanted to hookup. But then I went to the bathroom and when I came back you were passed out on the bed. So I lay down and fell asleep too."

"I've never done anything like that in my life. I've never gotten naked, and sure as hell would not have been acting like I wanted to hookup. I don't do that."

Her chest had been heaving and she'd started to cry.

"You have to tell me what really happened," she repeated.

"I already told you."

It had not gone well. She'd grabbed a sheet to cover herself up and pushed past him into the bathroom and then come right back out.

"Where are my clothes?" she'd asked. "You said I went into the bathroom and came out naked. So where are my clothes?"

He'd pointed to the pile on the chair.

"So you were really drunk but you managed to neatly fold my clothes?" She looked around the room until she saw his clothes. "And your clothes?" she asked, pointing. "You were drunk but you folded your clothes too?"

Then she asked him directly, "Did you rape me?"

And he'd found himself yelling at her. "No! I would *never* do that. How could you say that? Just get your shit and leave. I'll drive you home if you want but you need to go now."

And she'd backed down.

"This makes no sense to me," she'd said. "I've never done anything like this. I'm just really upset."

"Well, I'm pretty upset too. Nothing happened, okay? It's no big deal. We drank too much. Period."

She'd refused to let him drive her home, but had gotten dressed, slamming the door and walking down the street. He had watched her back until she turned the corner.

Rape. She'd asked if he had *raped* her.

Hunter would never penetrate a passed-out girl. Never.

That would be rape.

Her voicemail, just when he'd thought she was gone, had thrown him.

"It's not making any sense to me. I did not drink that much and I've never passed out. Call me."

He had not returned the call.

But she'd called again. "If you do not talk to me I am going to come to your door and bang on it until you do. So call me."

It had not been a productive conversation.

"Look," he'd said. "I told you what I remember. You went into the bathroom and came out naked. I went into the bathroom to piss and brush my teeth and when I came out you were asleep on the bed. I tried to start something, but you did not wake up. So, I lay down and fell asleep too."

"What do you mean 'start something?' " she'd asked.

"Hardly anything," he blustered. "Just tried to start kissing you, and, like, rubbed your shoulders a little."

"Yeah, right. I'm naked and passed out. My breasts are right there and you tell me you just touched my shoulders? Why do I not believe that one?"

"Look, I'm no perv, okay?" Hunter said, his voice loud with frustration. "You got naked first. What did you think would happen?"

That had been effective. She did not believe what Hunter was saying but she had nothing to refute him with either.

But then, yesterday, she left yet another voicemail.

"I can't let it go," she said. "I'm going to find out."

Hunter felt cornered. She was so overreacting. He had the sick feeling that she would keep at him and keep at him.

He went to his computer and brought up the file with her pictures. They were quite lovely shots, and the whiteness of her skin showed well against the navy blue sheets. He used white sheets or cream when the girl had darker skin. But the navy was the perfect backdrop for her.

He got into Photoshop, and, one picture at a time, started playing around with some filters. If she wanted to know what had happened, he'd show her. Maybe that would make her shut up. When he was done with the pictures, he downloaded them all onto an empty flash drive.

"Thought you might like to see these. Do you want me to share them with your friends? I'd be happy to do that." He put the message in size 24-type and printed it. Then he paused. He had an idea for delivery. It was a little risky but sent a more explicit message: that he could get to her where she least expected and that he wasn't going to back down either. He wrote, "Please deliver to Shelby Stewart" with her name, email, and phone number in big block print on a large manila envelope. He put the message and flash-drive in and sealed the envelope. He taped it over, ensuring it wouldn't open.

There was a big box for departmental mail in the Business School office. It was not usually for students, but the staff would contact a student if something arrived for them. The office could get really busy at noon. He was sure he could drop something in and not be noticed.

Chapter 14
(September 21st)

Shelby was having her second session with Grace.

"I called him and left a voicemail," Shelby said. "I said we needed to talk. But he didn't call me back."

"So what did you do then?" Grace asked.

"I called him again the next day. I was mad. I left a stronger message—like if he didn't call me back I was going to go over to his place and bang on his door."

"And?"

"He called back."

"And?"

"The story changed. This time he said we'd *both* had a second drink and that he got drunk, too. He repeated that I went into the bathroom and came out naked. But this time I fell asleep and he tried to wake me, rubbed my shoulders and kissed me a little, but I didn't wake up. Then he fell asleep. He still insisted that nothing more happened."

"But you don't buy it?"

"How did my clothes get neatly folded if we'd both been drunk? I told him his story kept changing. That's when he really got pissed. How I was the one who got naked first and what did I expect would happen? Why couldn't I just let it go?"

"And your response to that?"

"I told him it was a crock and I hung up."

"So where does that leave you?" Grace asked.

"I'm not sure. I'll need to wait and see."

Shelby did not tell Grace that she'd called the guy back a third time and left a voice mail, saying, "I can't let it go. I will not let it go."

For ninety minutes, Grace and Shelby talked.

Mostly, Grace focused on how there was *nothing* Shelby could have done to prevent this. It was an ordinary date. He'd appeared in every way to be a decent guy, had done nothing to make her suspicious, nothing to cause her to not trust him. There'd been no red flags. That it sounded as if she'd been drugged, but there was no way to verify unless he confessed, which was not likely to happen. They'd discussed how, if she had been raped, she would probably have had some vaginal sensation, if not pain, the next morning.

Grace encouraged her to talk to her parents. Shelby was adamant that she did not want to do that, that they were very protective, and she could not hurt them that way.

Shelby said she wanted a few weeks to process things. There was nothing they could do at this point, and she'd call Grace to schedule another session.

Chapter 15
(September 24th)

*"**No** means **yes**. . .**yes** means **anal**!* No means yes. . . yes means anal!"

Grace sat in her living room, staring at her television screen. She was watching a group of young men outside a dormitory of women, chanting, their surging, young masculine voices sounding like a company of military guys jogging. But this was at *Yale*?

No way, Grace thought. *Has to be a mistake.* This would never be tolerated. It was disgusting and creepy.

But it was no mistake. Could the chanting guys think it was funny? A joke? A fraternity *welcome* to the freshman women? Or a warning? Like, "This is what you can expect, so don't come party with us and then whine about what happens."

It wasn't until that morning that Grace had pulled up the documentary on Netflix that Patsy Tsosie had recommended. She'd initially put it on while she was cooking, only half-watching, letting the words and pictures flow past her as she chopped onions and peppers, sautéed garlic and sausage. Then the statistics had only half-registered in her consciousness.

But they registered enough to make her return to the beginning, sitting down to focus with a notebook and pen in hand.

Katrina was coming for supper. Grace had left a voicemail with the invite: "Hey, I'm making a dynamite marinara. Want to come over for pasta tonight? I'll do that Caesar you like, with fresh-shaved parmesan and anchovy paste. You know you want to." But the sauce was done and she still had three hours.

Ninety minutes later, the actual time extended because she'd pressed pause several times to take notes, Grace stood up. She felt like she needed a shower. And she would never hear Lady Gaga singing *Till It Happens to You* in the same way.

Grace went to her desk and typed in her scribbled notes, added what she needed to follow up on, and pressed print.

Can these stats be accurate?

1) 88% of women raped on campus (or campus-connected) do not report?

2) 16% of college women will be sexually assaulted in some way while at college?

3) Less than 8% of college men commit more than 90% of campus rapes. (How did they get this?) Do a cluster of predatory men account for most sexual assaults/ rapes on any specific campus? Most commit six or more acts of sexual aggression.

4) Overall, only 26% of rapes reported to police lead to an arrest?

5) Only 20% of those in which a perpetrator is arrested result in prosecution? And the prosecution process often takes 1-2 years?

6) If only 12% of campus rapes are reported, and only 26% of reported sexual assaults lead to an arrest, and only 20% of those get prosecuted—what is that? What are stats for prosecutions that get convictions? DO THE MATH.

7) Could it really be less than a 3% possibility of prison as a consequence? Roulette has better odds.

8) Compare to homicide stats? Burglary? (In Kaw Valley?)

9) Get a complete definition of sexual assault.

10) Talk to Patsy?

When Katrina arrived with a shopping bag containing a warm baguette and two fruit tarts, the sauce was simmering and the salad tossed. Grace handed Katrina the sheet of paper with her notes along with a glass of a Chilean red.

"Go, sit down, put your feet up, and consider," Grace said.

"I thought I was getting dinner, not work," Katrina protested.

"Dream on," Grace retorted.

Within ten minutes they were at the table, first eating the Caesar salad, the croutons toasty with butter and garlic. Then penne drenched in marinara, tossed with sausage, peppers, onions, more garlic, and cheese.

It was comfort food. They used chunks of baguette to mop up the sauce until their plates were almost clean.

"Kat, girlfriend, there is no possible way I can eat dessert now," Grace said, pushing back from the table, standing and making a half-hearted attempt to carry their dishes to the sink.

"No? No dessert—not possible. Not even a fruit tart? And to think I almost picked chocolate ganache," Kat said. "Give me an hour, though. Maybe with a New Orleans chicory expresso? You have that?"

"Yes, I have it in my Katrina drawer. Since you give me a fresh supply every three months, you are in luck."

Two minutes later, Katrina lay on the couch and Grace sprawled on an easy chair, her feet on the ottoman.

"Tell me about Title IX," Grace said abruptly.

"You mean the federal gender equality regs? Came out when—in 1972? I always think about them in terms of sports, but since you don't give a shit about sports, I'll assume there is a connection to the stats you handed me."

"You are so insightful. Anyway, this documentary I watched today, the one that provided the stats, is about some college kids who file a Title IX violation with the Feds. Mind you, they are not attorneys or even in law school. But they educated themselves about Title IX and put a different spin on it. They filed this petition, or whatever it's called, saying that allowing perpetrators of sexual assaults to remain on campus violates the rights of the women who have been assaulted. In an attempt to not discriminate against the rights of the accused, the rights of those who were violated are again violated. I need to see it again to get a better handle, but they assert that *how* universities and colleges handle complaints of sexual assault, the protocol and process, discriminates against victims. And now over 150 colleges and universities are under investigation for how they've managed assault complaints."

"Smart young women. But doesn't the university process mirror that of the courts?"

"Yeah, but with different standards for evidence—more *preponderance* than *beyond a reasonable doubt*. And yet, if the statistics are accurate, it appears that whomever is adjudicating rarely finds for the victims."

"No big surprise there," countered Kat. "Other factors are at work. People can't sue a court for indicting them, but they can go after a university. So, there is the lawsuit threat from the *wrongfully accused* for imposing consequences prior to due process. And sexual assault lawsuits do nothing for recruitment."

"Nor, I might add, would coming clean about campus sexual

assault," continued Grace. "I don't think there is a university in the country that is prepared to deal with the blowback. Parents could get so reactive, like, 'That campus isn't safe.' Meanwhile, that's just the campus that's addressing the issue and the rest are no less safe. Then they risk losing the support of their fraternities, which is huge. Frat grads are the biggest donors. The kids in fraternities and sororities would feel targeted, while this is more widespread."

"I see your point. And what school wants to rain on the *these are the best and most fun years of our lives'*-parade?"

"Do you mind if I vent? I need to process this out loud. And I did just feed you until your pant button popped."

"Gracie, you will whether I say okay or not. So, spit it out."

"Well, the film had stats for different schools, Ivy League mostly. They list the reported sexual assaults at a school, but the time frame is different for each college depending on how and when they started gathering the numbers. Then they list the number of consequences, like expulsions, or even suspensions, for perpetrators. The *worst* consequence possible is expulsion, so compared to legal system or court consequences, university consequences are much less *consequential*."

"Okay, I get it. Proceed."

"Harvard had 135 sexual assaults reported from '09 to '13 but only ten *consequences*. No explanation if a consequence is being expelled or just suspended for a semester or a slap on the wrist or what."

"That a pretty low ratio," Kat commented.

"No, actually, that's the high end. It gets worse. Dartmouth had 155 reported, from '02 to '13, with only three expulsions or suspensions. U.C. Berkeley had 78 reported from '08 to '15, with three as well. Stanford has 259 reports, but over a longer time frame, '01 to '13, with a giant *one* consequence. University of North Carolina had only 136 reports from '01 to '13, which is insanely low, with zero expulsions or suspensions. University of Virginia had 205 reports, over a long time frame, '98 to '13, and, again zero consequences imposed—*zero* expulsions. Now, they had over 183 expulsions for *Honor Infractions*, like cheating on exams or plagiarizing on a paper. But rape? Not a one."

"Those do seem skewed. You need to verify," replied Kat. "But, *if* they are accurate, it explains why girls may feel it's a waste of their time to report. Get assaulted, file a report, maybe talk about this traumatizing experience in front of some panel, follow required protocol, and for what? It's as if the girls are all liars, all making a false report. Because you can't document rape like you can for plagiarism or cheating."

"I was getting to that. College students have a distorted view of the false reporting of rape," Grace said. "They think it's around 50 percent. In reality, it's the same as any other crime, like three to seven percent."

"If you take each individual case, completely separate from any others, I can see that it could be hard to judge," Grace continued. "It is often a she said versus he said. But, if you step back, look at hundreds of cases, *hundreds* of reports? But virtually no consequences? Then you have to look at what's wrong with the process. The girls are the ones who end up dropping out or transferring. Way more victims drop out than perpetrators."

"Wait a minute," Kate interjected. "I just read about a case right here in Kaw Valley where the guy student was expelled and is now suing the university for violating his rights. But it's a stalking case, documented by dozens and dozens of emails from him. And he was also asked to leave two church groups where he was 'inappropriate,' and there were witnesses where he lashed out and was threatening with anyone who tried to get between him and the women he was targeting. He'd already been kicked out of another university for similar behavior. Sounded pretty delusional. And he did it to two young women."

"Oh, gee," Grace said sarcastically. "So email chains documenting stalking, being kicked out of church groups, acting threatening to other people, acting psycho, and doing it to two girls? Is that all it takes?"

"I was just saying that sometimes. . . ."

"Don't go there."

Katrina asked, "Change the system?"

"No. But I want my clients to be able to make informed choices, not encourage them to report and provide them unrealistic expectations. I can't naively support a system that could re-traumatize them."

"That, maybe, you can manage."

Grace and Katrina sat, staring at the wall. It was crazy-making. Had so little changed over the decades? Even with the legal shifts?

"Can you put on that coffee?" Kat asked. "And is caffeine an anti-depressant?"

Chapter 16
(September 26th)

Max was on the playground. It was after-lunch-recess. Today they'd had chili dogs for lunch, which could be okay or not okay depending on which lunch lady was working the serving line.

The lunch lady with the reddish hair understood that he did not like his foods touching, and she would put the hot dog and a roll in one compartment of the serving tray and the chili in a separate compartment. But the yellow-haired lady never paid attention to who she was serving, never looked up. So, even if he gestured at her, his hands flapping sideways, she wouldn't see. Then, when he refused to take the tray, if he just stood there and waited, she would look up and say, "Move it along. No special treatment. Eat it or leave it, I don't care." If it was the yellow-haired lady, he would have to just step back and walk away because, well, because he couldn't eat foods that were touching. Sometimes, when he walked away and sat alone in a corner, he would start rocking back and forth. Then the other kids would stare at him and whisper.

But today it had been the nice red-hair lunch lady. She'd smiled at him and said, "Hello, Max," and put his hot dog and roll in one compartment and just a little chili, not enough to spill over, in another compartment, and had even reached down the line and gotten him an extra-big brownie and a fruit salad in a sealed cup and put them in the other two compartments. "You're all set," she said, "Just get your milk."

Max ate alone. He didn't like to sit too close to the other kids because then they might touch, their legs rub up against him, with so many kids all packed in together at the table. And if there was anything Max hated more than food touching it was people touching.

Now he was in a far corner of the playground, his back against the fence, where he could see anyone coming from any direction. He did not want to be surprised by those boys, the ones who snuck up on him and jabbed a finger or elbow in his side, or pulled his hair or tripped him when they were waiting in line after recess.

Max had tried to use his words to tell the teacher. But his words fell out of his mouth in a rush, and not in order. His words got all mixed up like when his mom put eggs in a bowl and then stirred them very, very fast. Scrambled. Scrambled words.

"Well, Max, this might be where you need to be a little less sensitive," the teacher had said. "Boys will be boys. They don't really mean any harm in it."

That made no sense. Of course boys will be boys. They're boys. And he did not know what "don't really mean any harm" meant. It hurt when they did things to him. And they laughed at him if he cried. He thought they *liked* seeing him cry but he could not explain *why* he thought that. Maybe because of their eyes. Their eyes did not look sad, but almost glittery.

Standing against the fence, Max counted. He could usually count to sixty in one minute, and he thought there were nine minutes left in recess. So that would be 540 numbers. He hoped that would be enough numbers so that recess could be over and they could go back in the classroom.

While he counted, he let the other part of his mind move forward. In only three hours, school would be over. They would walk in a line out to the sidewalk with the overhang in front of the school. His mother would be waiting for him on Tuesdays and Thursdays and Fridays. And his Grammy would be waiting on Mondays and Wednesdays. This was a Thursday. Tonight was macaroni and cheese night, sometimes with chicken and sometimes with hamburger. And his mother would say, "Eat a few carrots. You need a vegetable." And there would be mint-chocolate chip ice cream for dessert in front of the TV, but not until after his bath. He would wear his Star Wars pajamas. And he had one favorite Thursday night show.

He was up to number 312. Only 238 to go.

Chapter 17
(September 28th)

Grace was meeting with Hannah. It was their third session. Hannah had skipped last week, calling to say she had interviews with the IOA and was trying to catch up with her assignments.

Last session, they had spent time just talking about Hannah's childhood, her parents and siblings, what she liked to do, what she wanted to study. Grace felt it was important to expand the lens, not focus exclusively on this one traumatic experience, but to review all the ways in which Hannah was a competent, connected, loved, and valued person, with a range of interests and options. Grace wanted the rape to be placed in the context of a life that extended beyond the university, as Hannah's life had preceded the university and would extend far past her years on campus.

It was an approach that might or might not work depending on the individual young woman.

Today, Grace thought, *it is back to the present.*

"So, tell me, how are your friends reacting toward you? Has the rape altered the relationships?"

"Yeah," Hannah said. "I'm like the freak show—the girl who got raped."

Hannah had had the illusion, for the first few days at least, that she would have some control over who knew what. That she would get to decide who to tell and what to share.

And that *might* have been possible back in the years before social media. But privacy *now*? Not possible.

There had been *sightings*. Anonymous postings on something Hannah called *Yik-Yak*.

Dorm residents buzzed, putting the pieces together: Hannah almost running into the lobby that night looking like someone was after her. Leaving a while later in the middle of the night with her RA and then returning in different clothing. Looking, as one post described, "Like total shit, man, just blotto." Then there were more observations on how she was not in class, not at meals.

A girl from the dorm group that had gone to the party chimed in: "Well, she was at that party with us and then she just kinda disappeared." "Does anyone know what happened?" "I heard that she went to the hospital." "OMG, what happened?"

And some adolescent angst: "I sure hope she's okay."

But then came a parallel, but more opinionated and judgmental, commentary. "How much did she drink?" "Whatever happened must have been quick because there were, like, a million people there." "I saw her talking to this one guy and she seemed to like him, like all flirty. She seemed really into him."

So much for privacy. So much for control. Hannah felt exposed. She was up for public dissection.

One girl from the dorm told her that she needed to "Get your story out there." That she should post her "side" on Facebook, before "it gets bigger and the tide turns." "What are you talking about?" Hannah had asked her. "What tide?"

"What are you going to do?" Grace asked.

"Just leave it alone and try to get my life back," Hannah said.

"Any word from the police?"

"Nothing. I called twice. The officer said, 'We're in the process of examining the evidence.' "

"Any timeline?"

"I don't know."

"What about with campus? Have you made a report there yet?"

"Yes, and I already did the interview with the investigator."

"Good. They can reorganize your schedule or have someone walk with you between classes if you want. They'll put a No Contact Order. It's a separate process, with a lower threshold of evidence. . . "

"Yeah, they explained," Hannah interjected. "But I'm not sure what they can do that will make me feel better other than kicking him out."

"Have you run into him on campus?"

"No, but I feel like I'm looking over my shoulder every minute. I flinch when someone accidentally touches me, even brushing past. A friend came up behind me between classes, when I was walking along the boulevard. I had my headphones on. He touched my shoulder just to get my attention. I jumped out of my skin and almost slugged him."

Hannah paused, taking a sip of water, then continued.

"So, yeah, I guess I'm concerned about running into him. Only it's not just him. It's like I'm afraid of everyone."

"That's pretty normal, Hannah. It won't stay so intense."

"I hear what you are saying. It's logical. But my body and head don't seem to be connected anymore. And I'm not sure which is more messed up."

"So what's your head saying?"

"Remember that first day how I did not want to tell my parents?" Hannah replied. "And that one of the reasons was that they would start to question me, like the police? I've been thinking about that. I think their goal was to help me understand that I had control, or, if not control, then influence over what happened to me. Like, if I could see how my decisions contributed, I could anticipate and maybe avoid it in the future. And it worked. The problem is that I'm doing it to myself now."

"How do you mean?"

"I'm looking at every possible point when there was a choice and how the outcome could have been different if I'd made a different choice."

"So tell me about these points."

"First, going to the frat party in the first place. The girls who were going were *cool* and so, when one asked if I wanted to join them, I said sure without thinking first. Like, I don't drink much, and I'd heard about how crazy frat parties can get. But I didn't consider that. Mostly I wanted to be included. I wanted to be cool too."

"Which is a pretty normal desire for. . . "

Hannah cut Grace off.

"I know it's *normal*, but it's not good decision-making," Hannah said. "If I'd said, 'Let me get back to you,' I could have talked to the RA or someone and gotten a better picture, or even a warning."

"What are some other points?" Grace asked. She could see where this was going but it was better to let Hannah talk it through than cut her off. The endpoint would be that Hannah should *never* have gone to a frat party, *ever*, and *never* had drinks—all of which was unrealistic for any girl who wanted a college social life.

You had to experience in order to choose.

"When the guy started to talk to me, ask me where I was from and what did I want to major in, I was flattered," Hannah continued. "There were all these really hot girls and he picked *me* to talk to. And he was so focused, all this eye contact, like we were the only people in the room. But a little part of me was doubting, like—*This isn't real. Why would a senior single me out? I'm a freshman.* But I didn't pay attention to that. I bought into it instead of listening to that doubt."

"And what else?"

"He brought me drinks. I had one in my hand when we started talking but was more just holding it. Then I was sipping and talking and the cup was empty. And he handed me another big red cup of punch. And we talked more. Then *another* refill. So, that was another point—if I'd said no to the drinks. But I didn't. I didn't want to seem ungrateful or make waves. I wanted to fit in, and it was clear that everyone was drinking."

"Go on," Grace said.

Hannah described how she started to feel dizzy. How he'd been solicitous, offering his room for her to take a break. And how she had trusted that this nice boy meant what he'd said.

"Hannah," Grace said. "I have a few questions. Now, until he came back into the room, and probably locked the door behind him, were there any red flags? Because it sounds to me like he knew exactly what he was doing."

"No red flags. I *wanted* to trust him because I *liked* him. Or I liked how attentive he was. Now, looking back, I just feel stupid. *Stupid, stupid girl.*"

Grace startled at the anger in Hannah's voice. Her contempt for the "stupid, stupid girl."

"You sound so angry at yourself."

"I am," Hannah said.

"You're blaming yourself but not blaming him. And not just for a small percentage of responsibility. It's like you're assuming responsibility for *his* actions."

"No. I'm assuming responsibility for *my choices.*"

"I don't want to argue with you. But the 'choices' you made were based on what you observed and felt *before* the rape, when he was just a nice, good-looking, funny, engaging guy who seemed genuinely interested in you. You trusted him because he did nothing to make you distrust him. Sure, he handed you drinks, but that was just like every other guy and girl at the party. Now, second-guessing, you're saying that a 19-year-old girl at her first frat party should have intuited that this boy, out of *all* the other boys, was a rapist? So girls should be thinking that every guy they meet at a party could be a predator? You can't live like that."

"Well, that's how I'm living now. That's what it's like inside my head. And I don't see that going away any time soon. Maybe never."

Chapter 18
(September 30th)

"Isn't that victim-blaming, Grace?" asked Patsy Tsosie. "Which is exactly what you think too many of us *po-lice* do?"

"No, it is not the same thing at all," Grace retorted.

They were discussing accountability. Not on a park bench for a quick coffee-and-consult, but at *Genovese,* a locally owned Italian restaurant and bar on Main Street. Patsy was off-duty, wearing tight jeans, suede boots, and a soft violet sweater. She'd let her hair down, literally, from the military-tight bun or clip she wore for work. It now fell to her shoulders, shining darkly in the soft light. A plate of bruschetta and a bottle of Pinot Noir sat between them on the table.

"Look, I'm talking about how young women need to assume responsibility for their choices, to appreciate that drinking to excess can put them in a vulnerable position."

"But no one has a right to take advantage of another person who is impaired, certainly not rape them." Patsy said. "Girls are not handing out a pass to be assaulted just because they drink."

"Of course not," Grace said. "But drinking to excess impacts their ability to protect themselves. Since we last talked, I've been to three bars around closing. Kids were weaving they were so wasted. Boys would yell something like, 'C'mon, let's go to my friend's place. Party on!' Girls were just piling into cars."

"Backtrack here, Ms. Grace," Patsy interrupted. "You went to three bars around closing? You stayed awake past 10 p.m?"

"No, I set an alarm for 1:30 a.m. and dozed on the couch."

"I'm still impressed," said Patsy. "And your findings?"

"Oh, hell, Patsy. We can't just teach girls that they can be whatever they choose, do anything they want, and then give them a pass on this area of personal responsibility. Some behaviors are not *safe*. They are disrespecting themselves by getting into those situations when they have the power to make different choices."

"What if they don't see it that way? What if they're just having fun?"

"It isn't just about sex. It's about safety. To get in a car like that, not knowing, really *knowing*, who they're with? They could end up dead in a field. It's bad decision-making."

"And it could happen to a girl walking home at 10 p.m. from a movie. It can happen whether the girl is drunk or cold sober."

Grace knew Patsy was referring to a case she'd had seven years earlier. A guy walking his dog had seen the abduction, but from a distance, too far to see a plate number or even be sure what make of car. But he'd described how a car pulled up alongside the woman, one man jumping out, grabbing her and throwing her into the back seat, then diving in after her as another guy drove the car off. Her body turned up in the next county in some woods three months later. There was no usable evidence. The woman had been raped and strangled. Gossip was that it had been a possessive ex-boyfriend, but the cops couldn't make it stick.

"Okay, absolutely, you are completely right," Grace acknowledged. "Bad things can happen anytime to anyone. But that does not conflict with personal accountability. Or collective responsibility. *Young women need to watch out for each other*. They need to have each other's backs. You know what I mean?"

Patsy nodded. Yeah, sure, she knew. But they were just kids, and it took some balls to do that. To butt in with, *Hey, my friend is getting really drunk and I think we need to get her home.* Especially when it is just as likely that the girl will say, *I'm not drunk. I'm happy!* and proceed to go off with the guy anyway. Meanwhile, the girl who was trying to be decent and responsible is viewed like she's with the vice squad.

"I do know, but that's a lot to expect from kids," she replied.

"Then maybe they do not need to be drinking until they can self-manage better."

"Which could be age 35. Have you seen the behavior of the post-college demographic? They can be crazier than the kids."

Grace stared at her wine glass and then poured more Pinot Noir from the half-empty bottle. She had a split-second thought that this was somehow ironic, but then it disappeared.

"Do you remember during the AIDS epidemic?" she asked Patsy.

"The warnings, *Whenever you sleep with someone, you are sleeping with every person they have ever slept with.*"

"Yeah, I remember," Patsy nodded. "And it still holds."

"So why aren't these young women more worried? Maybe AIDS is less prevalent, but aren't they concerned about STDs?"

"I see it more as the persistent optimism of youth, the denial that the bad stuff will happen to them," Patsy answered. "But there's also a passivity. Like it's inevitable that bad things will happen and then you just have to deal with them. But, you're right, many do not protect themselves. They just go with the flow."

"Which is neither smart nor responsible." Grace's tone was judgmental, without a trace of therapeutic empathy.

"You keep talking about the girls, but is that fair? What about the responsibility of the other boys, the men, to step in?" asked Patsy.

"Yeah, right, like their primary loyalty is not to the man-pack. And male culture promotes excessive drinking and having sex with girls you've just met. It's envied and admired," Grace replied. "You tell me one really derogatory word to describe a man who has sex with lots of women."

Patsy thought. Nothing came up. She made a face at Grace.

"That's what I thought," Grace said, her voice getting louder and more strident. "But for a girl? She's a whore, a slut, a skank, a cunt. It's all about her tits and pussy and ass."

The words floated across the room and people at three tables turned to stare. *Watch your language* seemed to be the non-verbal message. Except for one man, sitting across from a woman who was giving Grace the evil eye. Only his look said, *I want to sit at your table. That sounds like one interesting conversation.*

"It's complicated, Grace," Patsy said quietly. "Girls can be *raped* by our definition of rape, the legal statute, or sexually assaulted, but *they* are in denial that they were raped. *This is not the guy denying, but the girl.* So, it becomes *a bad hookup* or *I drank too much and it got weird.* That way they can maintain the illusion that they can prevent something like that from happening again. At the same time, they're. . . "

Grace interrupted. "Hold on. So not just accepting some portion of responsibility but denying that *anything* happened?"

"Pretty much. So a guy having sex with you when you're too drunk to consent is not sexual assault. It's like, *If sex happened, I must have consented because I did it.*"

"So guys have no accountability?"

"Not in this paradigm. Some girls wake up feeling like, *Why did I do that? What was I thinking?* But they overlook that they *weren't* thinking because they were unconscious. They couldn't have consented. Then, the next weekend, they party-on."

Grace said nothing. It was simply too much. Had all this happened in the last ten years? Or had she been in denial?

"Just when did blowjobs replace a goodnight kiss?" she asked, puckering her lips with the last word. "Tell me that."

October 2017

Chapter 19
(October 1st)

When Grace's cell rang at 11 p.m., she was disoriented. She started to stumble toward the front door before she realized the sound came from her kitchen counter where she'd left the cell phone to charge.

"Hello," she said. When there was no immediate response she said it again. "Hello? Who is this?"

"Is this Dr. McDonald?" a small voice asked.

"Yes, I'm Grace McDonald but I'm not a doctor. Never mind that, what's going on?"

"I'm Lisa? I'm a friend of Shelby Stewart? She's been to see you a few times? She told me that she was going? I have your card here?" With each short sentence, her voice went up, in what Grace used to call a Valley Girl inflection.

Grace was instantly awake, alert, vigilant. Calls like this did not bring good news. "What happened?" she asked. "Just tell me slowly what happened."

"I think Shelby has taken some pills? I'm her roommate? I came in about an hour ago, and she always wakes up when I come in and we talk. But she didn't. At first I just thought she was sound asleep. But then I tried to wake her, like shaking her. This has never happened before. Never. I went through her purse and there is an empty pill bottle. I don't know if it was full, or how many, but I think they were pills to help her sleep? I don't know what to do because she's, like, really private, and would not want anybody to make a fuss, or, like, know what happened last month. Like she only told me and made me swear I'd never tell anyone."

Lisa had been talking in a rush but she finally paused to inhale.

"So, what should I do? You're the doctor, so please tell me what to do?"

"Lisa, you did the right thing to call me. You're a good friend. Now, I need you to check her breathing. Is she breathing okay? Is it jerky or shallow?"

"I don't know. I know she's breathing but it's hard to tell how because her chest isn't moving much."

"Where are you? Do you live in a dorm? An apartment? I'm sorry, but I don't remember what Shelby told me."

"It's an apartment."

"Tell me the address."

Grace scribbled it down and repeated it back.

"Lisa, I'm going to call an ambulance. We can't take a risk just because Shelby wouldn't want a fuss. And this is on me, so if she is angry, she can be mad at me and not you. You did the right thing by calling me. Now get her ID, and the pill bottle, and whatever other medication she takes, and her wallet in case her insurance card is in there. Okay? Give it all to the ambulance people. Put your outside light on and open the front door. Can you do that?"

Grace felt as if she were talking to a 14 year old, but that was probably just because this girl had a high-pitched voice. She really did wish the kid had just called 911, but too late for that. She wasn't going to leave it up to Lisa to make the call, just in case she decided to wait and see if Shelby woke up.

Grace hung up and called 911. She gave the address, a brief description, and added, "No sirens, please. We don't really know what's going on. Just have to make sure she is okay." Then she gave them her name and number.

Grace stared blankly at the bedroom wall. Not like she was going back to sleep. But what should she do? Wait for another call? Throw on some clothes and head over to the ER?

She thought about Lisa trailing an ambulance to the hospital, not knowing what to do. And she thought about Shelby.

"Oh, shit," Grace muttered. "No sleep for me." She walked quickly to the closet and grabbed her jeans.

The hospital ER waiting room was relatively empty. A thin girl, shoulder-length blonde hair loosely gathered in a clip, sat in the far corner. She looked as if she was wearing pajama bottoms below a 1950's flowery blazer. She was one of those girls who could make anything fashionable simply by gracing it with her body.

She was looking at her phone intently, the way they all seemed to do, as if the secrets of the universe were being displayed for just five minutes and if you missed out you were screwed for life.

Stop being so judgmental, she berated herself. It wasn't just the kids. There were plenty of adults similarly addicted.

She walked over to the girl and stood to one side.

"Are you Lisa?" she asked.

The girl startled. She'd been so focused she hadn't heard Grace approach.

"Yes. Who are you?"

"I'm Grace McDonald."

"I didn't know you were coming." Lisa looked at Grace more closely. "You're older than I thought from how Shelby described you."

"Well, I didn't say I was coming," Grace replied, not knowing how to respond to the 'older' comment. "Have they said anything yet about Shelby?"

"They haven't said anything. The ambulance guys told me to drive myself over here. I got here later. I'm just waiting."

"Okay," Grace said. "I'll check with the desk and see what's up."

Grace walked to the desk, waiting behind a young couple with a baby whose cough sounded like a phlegmatic goose. It was the deep honk of croup if not something worse.

"I'm here for Shelby Stewart," she told the nurse when the couple finished talking and walked away with a clipboard to complete the forms. "She was brought in by ambulance a little bit ago. Can you tell me her condition?"

"Are you family?" the nurse asked.

"No." Grace hesitated, wondering whether to disclose the relationship, if to do so would violate confidentiality. On her intake forms, however, there was a release that all clients signed that said she could talk to whomever she determined was appropriate or necessary if she suspected suicidal ideation.

"A friend," Grace added.

"Is there any family coming?" the nurse asked.

"I'll see if they can be contacted. But if this is not that serious, if she will be treated and released, I'd like her to be able to make that decision."

"We'd appreciate whatever contact information you can provide," the nurse replied. Her eyes were oblique.

Grace went back to Lisa. "Do you have Shelby's parents' phone numbers?"

"That's what I'm doing," Lisa said. "This is her phone. I'm going through contacts, looking for their numbers. But she has her own nicknames for everyone. Like her mom isn't under *Mom* but *Queenie*. But I think I have them."

Grace felt a quick blush of shame for judging Lisa. She wasn't just playing around. She was trying to help.

"Uh, Lisa, can we talk for a minute?

Lisa nodded.

"Had you noticed anything different with Shelby these past few days? Did she talk about anything that upset her?"

"Like other than her nightmare?" The girl's tone was sarcastic, almost bitter, a stark contrast to the initial impression Grace had formed, an impression that was clearly overly simplistic. But Lisa quickly recanted.

"I'm sorry," she said. "It's just been really hard on her. She started out like it was not that big a deal, that she wanted to put it behind her. And it looked like, for a while, that she might actually do that. But she was having a difficult time. She'd really liked him. So, when it all got weird, she was in a deep funk."

"Can you describe what you mean by *funk*?"

Grace knew she was fishing. But she'd only seen Shelby twice, and from what she could get, Shelby had no memory. Just that they went to a movie, out to eat, had a beer, back to his place to listen to a CD—and she woke up naked. And when she tried to talk to him, he was evasive and defensive.

"I think she started skipping her classes. I'd get back to the apartment and she'd be in her pajamas, binge-watching."

"How did she explain it? Was she ill?"

"I asked if she wanted to talk. But she was, like, 'I needed some down time. Had a headache. Don't go all-mother on me.' "

"So more like avoidance? Was she studying?"

"Not like she used to study. Then she was always studying. But I didn't want to intrude too much. I figured she just needed time."

Grace and Lisa sat, not talking, staring at the same hospital-green wall, not even seeing the pictures of wheat fields and harvests.

Grace must have drifted off, because she woke, abruptly, to the nurse and two men in white standing in front of her. She looked around for Lisa, as if she could not speak to these people without Lisa. Then she saw Lisa, curled up on a couch across the room, blonde hair tumbling loose and covering her face.

"I'm Dr. Washington," one of the white-coats said. "Who are you in relation to Shelby Stewart?"

"I'm Grace McDonald, her therapist. Her roommate called me when she couldn't wake Shelby up."

"Do you have contact information for her next-of-kin?"

Those words, that phrase, made Grace's heart stop.

"No, but her roommate should." As Grace spoke, she gestured across the room to the sleeping form.

"Can you get that for us, please?"

"Yes, of course. But, please, can you first tell me about Shelby." She heard her own voice, the plea underlying the words. *Please do not tell me, please do not say what I think you might be about to say, please do not, not, not, not. . .*

"I'm sorry, Ms. McDonald, but Shelby didn't make it. Her heart stopped while we were working to stabilize her. We tried multiple interventions, but. . ."

His voice continued, but Grace didn't hear any of it.

Chapter 20
(October 2nd)

By the time Grace got home, about 5:30 a.m., she was exhausted. Her eyes were bloodshot, head pounding, muscles aching as if she'd done a 5-hour uphill hike.

She looked at her appointments, which, thank God, did not start until 11 a.m. She emailed the clients for the 11, 12, and 1 p.m. sessions and cancelled. She figured she could make it by 3 p.m. but not sooner.

Lisa had taken the news of her roommate's death hard. Grace had gone over and gently shaken her shoulder. Lisa had had a similar reaction to seeing three white-coated medical professionals standing in front of her, a combination of panic and gut-twisting denial. She'd started half-sobbing, her high voice echoing against the walls: "What do you mean? What are you saying? What do you mean?"

Grace had sat with Lisa, carefully writing down the names and numbers that Lisa had found on Shelby's phone. When the doctor asked, "If you know the parents, would you prefer to inform them?" she'd promptly responded with, "No, I do not know them."

She'd had Lisa call another friend to come down to the ER and take her home. They could come back later to get her car. Lisa had ended up talking to an ER doc and had left with her own prescription. Grace had almost asked for some pills for herself but thought that might be overkill.

Grace had not been able to get any specifics out of the ER staff. Like how much she had taken, of what drug. She imagined they were looking at her, not so much critically but questioning: *If you were her therapist, how come you didn't pick up on this? How come you didn't do anything to prevent it? How come you didn't see this possibility?*

Which is exactly what Grace was asking herself, over and over. While she helped the staff get the information they needed. While she held Lisa until the other friend arrived. While she sat with the two of them as they cried.

Lisa was also wrapping herself in guilt for not seeing what her friend was going through, for not acting immediately when she got home, for delaying.

Lisa, Grace knew, would feel this for a very long time.

Grace crawled into the shower and then, hair wet, towel loosely draped around her, fell onto her bed. When she woke up, she was disoriented. The clock said 12:14. But was that a.m. or p.m? For a moment she thought that it had all been a bad dream. And then the night flooded back.

She cancelled the rest of her appointments. She'd be useless. She felt like a fraud.

Then she texted Molly: *Sorry about the late notice, but I can't watch Max tonight. If one of your friends can watch him, I'll pay. Will explain later.*

Intellectually, cognitively, she knew that she was not *responsible*. She'd just begun the therapeutic process with Shelby, was just getting to know her. But these feelings were more than professional accountability—questioning if she'd missed something that another professional, someone smarter, more attuned, more focused—might have seen. That would be guilt, traceable to something specific. Guilt could be reasoned with.

What was consuming Grace was shame—pervasive and insidious. It brought back all the shame she'd felt twelve years earlier, when she believed she'd contributed to her husband's death, because *how* he died was because of her. That had been, as much as anything, what she had run away from.

Now the shame was back, waves of it rolling over her, the PTSD triggered again. She lay in bed, cowering. Finally, about 5 p.m. she got up and made a pot of tea. Then she changed her mind and poured a few fingers of whiskey into a glass. After two quick swallows and a grimace, she picked up the phone. When she heard the beep, she left a message.

"Mickey, hey, it's Grace. Long time, yeah, I know. This is very short notice, but, if you're not booked, what's the chance you could come over to my place for a while tonight? I'll order-in, maybe Italian? Let me know. Thanks. Been a hell of a day and I'd appreciate the company."

Mickey Donahue was—a friend? A man who had been there for her when she was at her lowest? Someone who had also survived a lot of shit? Someone she trusted?

He texted back: *One more meeting, then will drive over.*

Two hours later Mickey was at her front door, carrying a very large pizza box.

"I figured since you said you'd order in that you weren't cooking," Mickey said. "And this is Italian."

She looked at him, her eyes filling with tears.

"Oh shit, Gracie," he said, "It's just a pizza." He put down the box and wrapped his arms around her, murmuring words of consolation. "It's gonna' be okay. You'll get through this."

Mickey had no idea what was wrong, but if Grace looked this bad it had to be a bitch.

Mickey put the pizza in the oven to warm and opened a bottle of wine. Grace, usually the gracious hostess, sat on her couch and stared at a wall. He brought over plates, glasses of wine, put the pie in the middle of the coffee table, and sat down next to her.

They ate in silence, Grace suddenly ravenous. She hadn't eaten for 24 hours. The entire pie consumed, she turned to Mickey and asked, "One? You only brought *one*?"

"It was an extra-large, and I did not eat my usual hefty portion. You forgot to eat this last week maybe?"

"No, just today. I did not eat today."

"So, you want to tell me what happened? Not that I don't enjoy your company, but something is really, really bad."

"You are such an insightful guy," Grace retorted.

"No, Grace, you're not getting out of this by kidding around. Lose the front. Spit it out."

So she did.

It was not a coherent account, not linear, but a jumbled mush of feelings and guilt and *why is this still happening* and *how could I not have seen whatever there was to see? Did I try to get her to move on too quickly? And, since she didn't remember anything, did I come across as not-a-damn-thing-you-can-do-about-it?*

"Mickey, I don't even know what happened to her. I assume she was assaulted. I recall thinking, *Oh, gee, it might be a good thing to not remember anything.* Because remembering *really* messes with your life."

Her rant ratcheted down until she was almost whispering.

"She's dead. And I never saw it coming. Not one sliver of *better watch this one close.* Nothing. What good am I if I miss that much pain?"

Mickey tried to reason.

"You know how impulsive kids are, Gracie. She didn't want to kill herself, she just wanted to escape. Maybe for the secret to come out, for her parents to know what happened without her having to tell them. It was probably a bad ten minutes. A bad hour. Not like she'd been planning anything."

But Mickey knew her history, knew what else she'd missed those many years before. He knew his words were—just words.

So, he took Grace by the arm and led her into the bedroom. He sat her down on the side of the bed and took off her clothes as you would an exhausted child. He found a worn cotton nightgown in her dresser and put it over her head. Then he took her by the shoulders, laying her down on her side, ever so gently. Mickey lay down next to her, spooning. He rubbed her shoulders and back through the worn cotton, in soft, even strokes, murmuring whatever useless words came out. And he kept doing it until her breathing settled, until she slept. He got up only to piss and take off his stiff jeans and belt, then returned to his post, one arm protectively draped along her back, synchronizing his breathing with hers until he, too, fell asleep.

Chapter 21
(October 4th)

It wasn't for two days, when Molly got home from class, finding her mother dozing on the living room couch after an intense evening with Max, that Grace told her what had happened—the middle-of-the-night phone call, the ambulance, the ER, Lisa.

Grace did not tell her about calling Mickey or that Mickey had stayed over.

Grace had been searching her mind for any indications of Shelby showing suicidal intent. She reviewed her notes, going over and over them, trying to remember Shelby's inflections, every gesture, the non-verbal clues that can contradict spoken words. Grace dissected everything she could remember and came up with—nothing.

She and Shelby had just begun to sort out what had happened, or what Shelby thought *might* have happened. Grace had been direct in responding to Shelby's self-doubt, the girl's feeling that she had *done* something, *missed* something, or it could not have happened.

Now Grace was in that same position of self-doubt, questioning what she had missed, feeling that she could have, should have, seen *something*, done *something*. Grace longed for absolution, some power that could take away her shame for not being able to predict and intervene.

Earlier in the day, Grace had received a voicemail from Shelby's parents. Lisa had given them her name and number. They said they were driving to Kaw Valley. They sounded desperate for answers, for some explanation. Grace agreed to meet with them at her office the next afternoon.

It was excruciating.

Bill and Diane Stewart were crazed with grief. They were decent, hard-working, ordinary people. Until now. Their only daughter was dead. Their two younger sons had lost their big sister. Their family would never be the same.

Bill did most of the talking, questions and accusations running over one another: Why didn't their daughter tell them *immediately*? How could she have kept this a *secret*? Why didn't Grace *make* their daughter tell them? *Why had Grace not called them*? Screw her precious confidentiality. They had a right to know.

Then Bill went after Grace, calling her irresponsible, saying that he was going to make a complaint to her licensing board. She should have told them that their daughter was suicidal. They would have done *something*. They could have prevented this.

How could Grace not have seen the warning signs?

Grace almost welcomed their anger, welcomed that they were verbalizing what she was saying to herself.

Their precious daughter had taken an overdose of pills and no one— not her roommate, friends, not even her therapist—had seen it coming.

Bill kept verbally punching, spewing. Grace didn't try to rein him in, didn't try to justify. He might have continued all afternoon, but Shelby's mother reached over, placed her hand on his arm, and said, "Bill, stop. Shelby didn't tell us and she didn't say anything to her. The lady isn't God. She couldn't know."

On that, Bill folded into himself, collapsing, head cradled in his arms, sobbing. Diane, her own tears sliding down her face, patted him on the shoulder.

When Bill stopped sobbing, they stood up, saying they would be back, later, when—but they never finished the sentence.

The next morning, Grace met with the Rape Crisis Center staff and some of the volunteers for a de-briefing. They processed what they could have done differently. The conclusion was *not much*. It had been a by-the-book case.

Shelby had asked for *some* services. She'd never gone to the hospital. She did not want to make a report to police. The Center staff had listened, respected her choices, and referred her to Grace. There had been no red flags.

As they were wrapping up, Grace started to say, *I won't be able to take any more referrals*. The words had formed in her head, had almost come out her mouth. And no one there would have argued, no one would have tried to change her mind. They would have understood. But she swallowed the words.

Grace had made a one-year commitment and she would honor it.

93

Chapter 22
(October 9th)

It was early Monday morning, so early that it was still dark outside, as Grace poured herself a mug of coffee. She was scheduled to testify in a custody hearing, due at the courthouse by 9 a.m., and she was not feeling prepared. She'd felt so strung out that she'd emotionally detached from, if not neglected, her other cases. They seemed, in comparison, to be trivial.

Get it together, people, she wanted to yell. *You're alive. Your kids are okay. Stop being so damn petty.*

But she couldn't yell. Not in sessions, although she often felt the urge, and certainly not on a witness stand.

In this case, she'd been assigned by the court to do a parenting evaluation. She'd hoped that her written report would be adequate, but neither of the parents were completely satisfied with the recommendations and both of their attorneys wanted to grill her.

After a long, hot shower, she took her *court uniform* out of the back of the closet: gray slacks, black shell, Chico's blazer, big silver earrings, black low-heeled pumps. Her notes and reports were carried in a black briefcase. Boring for sure, but it took all the angst out of what to wear. Just putting them on felt like she was putting on armor, preparing for battle.

The courtroom was almost empty. Divorce and custody cases never attracted the courtroom-groupies of the criminal docket. A murder trial in Kaw Valley and the room could get packed.

But this morning was just the parties, their attorneys, and a few family members or friends for support. Grace hoped she would be first on the stand so she could get out by 11 a.m. But this case was with a new judge, recently appointed to the bench. So everything was a crapshoot.

"All rise," intoned the bailiff. The whispering around the courtroom abruptly stopped.

"Be seated," the bailiff said.

"This case is Barrows v. Barrows, Case # DM-17-423," the judge read. "The court ordered a parenting evaluation when resolution could not previously be reached as to a parenting schedule for their minor children. The evaluation has been completed and a written report provided. The parties, however, wish to dispute the recommendations."

The judge seemed to sigh as she said the last line. "Any initial statements, Mr. Williams?" she asked the attorney for the mother.

"Your Honor, my client and I have carefully read the parenting evaluation prepared by Grace McDonald. While there are sections where we concur, there are conclusions that we do not feel are in the best interests of the children. I would like to question Ms. McDonald on what basis she reached her recommendations."

"That's what we're here for, Mr. Williams. Let's get on with it."

"I call Grace McDonald to the stand," Williams said.

It took just a minute for Grace to reach the witness stand, take the oath, and sit down. Williams walked over to his table to get some notes.

"Ms. McDonald, will you explain to the court your qualifications."

Every time on the witness stand was a *Groundhog Day*. It always started with the same questions about her qualifications: education, licenses, experience. It was a memorized script that she could recite in her sleep. Only when she finished would the attorney begin with the real questions.

"Ms. McDonald, can you describe for me the structure with regards to care of the children of the Barrows home prior to the divorce?"

"I'll try. Mr. Barrows is an executive with a major IT firm in Kansas City. He has been with that firm for many years and has worked his way up to a VP position. He generally left the home between 6 and 6:30 a.m. and returned between 6 and 8 p.m. There were, however, nights when he needed to work later. The family tried to have a family dinner each night about 7 p.m. and he made it back for dinner most evenings but not every evening. Mrs. Barrows worked full-time until the birth of their first child, who is now fourteen. She has held varied part-time positions since but has never returned to full-time work. Mrs. Barrows has been responsible for the children's transportation, education, activities and sports, their schedules, coordination of doctor visits, immunizations, and dental care. She knows every teacher, administrator, coach, and school nurse. She has never missed a parent-teacher conference, assists in fundraisers and volunteers for field trips. She supervises homework. She purchases all of their clothing. She does all of the grocery shopping and cooking, except on weekends when Mr. Barrows barbequed or made his grandmother's buttermilk pancakes for Sunday morning brunch."

Grace paused. It had been a very long monologue, but she thought she'd covered the basics.

"Is that adequate, Mr. Williams?" she asked.

"Quite, Ms. McDonald." Williams was surprised at her account. It was accurate, but, more importantly, made his client sound like *mother-of-the-year*. If so, her conclusions made no sense.

"However, Ms. McDonald," he continued, "you are recommending a schedule in which father has alternate weekends, Friday after school to Sunday at 6 p.m., as well as every Wednesday night overnight and alternating Thursday nights. This is for a man who has never taken his children to school, rarely helped with homework, and could not tell you the assorted teachers' names, let alone the administrators or counselors. Ms. Barrows is very clear that the best interests of her children will be served by allowing them to maintain their life-long schedule from their home without a mid-week disruption simply to accommodate Mr. Barrows' newly discovered interest in being a father—which coincides with child support being impacted by the amount of time he has his children with him. In addition. . . "

"Objection, Your Honor." Ms. Rudley, Dad's attorney, was on her feet. "Mr. Williams is. . . "

"Sustained. There is no jury and these are not closing arguments, Mr. Williams." Then the judge turned to Grace. "You may answer the question if you can remember it. If not, I'll have it read back to you."

"I'm not sure there was a question, but I can respond. Yes, I did make that recommendation. Here is why—the Barrows family had a system that was functional for them for many years. It worked well with a two-parent family with clearly defined roles and responsibilities. But divorce changes everything. I disagree that any interest in his children is 'newly discovered' and motivated by a desire to lower support. Mr. Barrows is involved as a dad: he's consistently gone to his children's sports on weekends, participated in family activities and vacations. The kids joked with me that he is addicted to national parks because he takes them to a different one every summer. When the children were in elementary school, he knew their teachers. But once they hit junior high and high school, and they had six or seven teachers each, he did not keep up. But their mother knew all of it, and still does, and she was his conduit to knowing what was happening in their lives. Each parent contributed. They were a team."

Grace paused, taking a drink of water from the glass on the stand, then launched in again.

"Without Mom as a conduit, Dad needs to assume more responsibility. He needs to have weekly contact with their school, be involved at least one-to-two times a week with their homework, take them to activities. And he cannot do any of that if he only sees his children on alternate weekends."

"So," continued Williams, his voice rising in a tone of rehearsed incredulity, "you take time away from the experienced, competent parent who has done all of the work over the years so that the incompetent parent can get on-the-job training? At the expense of the children's consistency? Making them change homes in the middle of the week?"

"I disagree with characterizing a parent as 'incompetent,' but yes, with the schedule the children sleep at their dad's home for one night in the middle of the week. However, they are twelve and fourteen years old, not pre-school." Grace paused, then continued. "The *temporary* schedule provided to the court by mother provided father only four out of every twenty-eight nights. It is hard to maintain a relationship with only four nights. This plan doubles that, to a number that allows for weekly contact, not going two weeks without any contact. But it is far from the 50/50 initially requested by father."

"No, Ms. McDonald, it more than doubles it. He has alternate Thursday overnights as well. That's ten nights out of twenty-eight."

"Yes and no. *Both* parents have a child on those Thursday nights. They provide each parent *one* evening of one-on-one time with each child *once* a month. It's a small win-win. One of the harder things for many kids after a divorce is the loss of any uninterrupted alone time with each parent. In my experience, kids crave some time with each parent without siblings."

"Well, it's a lovely theory, Ms. McDonald, but how can Mr. Barrows manage when he is never home?"

"Mr. Barrows is now a VP who can determine his own schedule.

My understanding is that he has arranged to leave early on Wednesdays to get the kids from school and to not be in the office until 9 a.m. on Thursdays. He will also leave early on alternating Thursdays and Fridays. He'll work overtime when he does not have the children."

"And if this schedule fails? If he is late to pick-up the kids or can't bring them to school?"

"Of course, if after trying this for six months, enough time to get the kinks out, *if* it's not working, then we come back to develop a better alternative."

"So, the children are pawns in this experiment, their lives disrupted so that father can try. . . "

"Objection, your Honor." Rudley was back up again.

"Sustained. Mr. Williams, move along."

"Nothing more, Your Honor."

The next attorney, Ms. Rudley, was more accommodating.

"Can you explain to the court, Ms. McDonald, the underlying reasoning for making recommendations that change the prior system of parental roles in the children's lives to one where mother remains as primary and residential parent but father assumes parental responsibilities other than financial support?"

"Yes," Grace answered, turning to face the judge, who was, after all, the only audience that mattered in this room. "When married, parental roles can be parallel. It's better for the kids if parents can continue to share information and collaborate with decisions on some level, like when a teenager needs to see his parents as a united front. A parent who is marginalized post-divorce will never be as competent or effective as he or she could be."

Grace stopped.

"To be honest, and to reference Mr. Williams's description, there are some elements here of on-the-job training. Ms. Barrows is an outstanding mother. It would be an insult to her to say that anyone could do what she does as competently. But that does not mean that Mr. Barrows cannot learn. He may never be as skilled as she is. But children need to know that *both* of their parents are competent to care for them."

"So you're saying that this schedule is better for the children than ones that maintains the more distinct roles of the traditional marriage?" asked Rudley.

"Yes. And I believe that most parents, when asked a very tough question, agree with me even when it conflicts with what they initially saw as their child's immediate best interests."

"And what question is that, Ms. McDonald?"

"Who will your children live with if you suddenly die? Or are incapacitated? If you are hit by a truck tomorrow? Who will feed them and get them to school on time and help them with homework and go to their games and performances and take them shopping and meet with their teachers and take them to the doctor and cook and—well, the list is endless. Who will be their advocate? *Who will do all of that*? If you're dead or incapacitated, you don't call the shots anymore. Your kids live with their other parent. Period. So, do you want them to be with a parent who has no skills? With minimal experience? Is *that* best for them?"

Grace paused for a few seconds, looked up at the judge, then concluded.

"And that's my bottom-line. Some parents can't manage it. Some parents are too narcissistic, emotionally damaged or addicted to be able to provide what their children need. Sometimes distance makes it impossible. But if a parent is willing to learn, has the humility and maturity to accept guidance, can put the kids' needs first, then I do believe that both parents should try to make it work. *If* parents live in the same community, *if it might work,* then I believe they have a responsibility to try."

The judge called a recess. Grace wanted to take off, but the attorneys had requested that she stay, in case either wanted to call her back to the stand. The attorneys each had quick chats with their clients in the hall and then with each other. When court was called back in session, Mr. Williams stood up and cleared his throat.

"I believe we have reached a compromise on the outstanding issues. Mrs. Barrows agrees to the proposed schedule as long as Mr. Barrows meets the requirements to attend co-parenting classes and meet one-on-one with every teacher, principal and vice-principal, coach, school nurse, school counselor, and physician. It is her understanding that he will take three days off in the next three weeks to ensure compliance."

Then Ms. Rudley stood. "All of that is accurate. Parents have also agreed on other elements of the plan: vacation, holidays, transportation, etc. One minor modification, however, related to the proposed holidays."

Rudley paused to cough.

Grace saw Mrs. Barrows head jerk up. She had fought tooth-and-nail over holidays, and Grace could still see the blood, metaphorically speaking, on her office floor.

Ms. Rudley continued, "Mr. Barrows appreciates that certain holidays hold more meaning for Mrs. Barrows. She has the larger extended family, more religious traditions, and his children have many cousins on their mother's side of the family. So, he would like to offer that their mother have the children for every Christmas and every Easter so that they can continue to celebrate those holidays with extended family. In return he would like set time between Christmas and their return to school, to include New Year's, to develop some of his own traditions with the children."

Grace smiled. It was something that she'd debated with Charles Barrows, a gesture of peace and compromise he could offer, agnostic that he was. *For the sake of the kids,* his wife had begged each year, *could you just stand in the pew and pretend?*

Grace had pointed out to Charles that his kids would miss out on the Christmas holiday they'd known since they were babies, with evening Mass, exchanging presents around Grandma's ten-foot tree with their aunts, uncles, and nine cousins, the feast around the oak table that seated twenty. They would miss *all* of it, every other year, because Dad insisted, *I'm entitled to **my** holiday, damn it.*

Grace could get opinionated when it came to guidelines. What appeared *fair* on paper to divorcing parents was often unfair to their children. If there was a way to make it work better for everyone, to cut the losses and make a difficult situation more win-win, Grace got pushy.

"It's not about *your* rights, Charlie, although you see it that way," she'd debated. "It's about your kids, *their* rights, and, if you can stand back and detach from your feelings, what is best for them." She'd proposed options, like taking the kids on a trip every year after Christmas. Then he could create different traditions and memories with them, but without making them lose what they cherished.

But he'd not come around. He'd insisted on *his* rights. He was legally entitled. So, the plan she'd provided the court had just alternated the holidays. *But now*, Grace thought, *just before the final buzzer—*Charlie had been big on basketball metaphors—*he's scored one for the* *team.*

She gave Charlie a thumbs-up as she walked out of the courtroom.

Grace did not schedule other clients on the days she had to be in court. Not only was court unpredictable, but she often needed a break to clear her head when it was over. So now, she had a whole afternoon with nothing scheduled.

The sun was shining. It was perfect weather for a walk. She quickly changed into her jeans and sneakers, leaving her court uniform tossed on her bed.

Since her return, Grace had developed a renewed appreciation for Kaw Valley and Kansas in general. Kansas was a state that got a bad rap—not for what it was, but for misconceptions that had taken root in the American consciousness. *Damn that Wizard and Dorothy.* And if she had to politely smile through one more comment of, "Toto, we're not in Kansas anymore" by someone who had never set foot in the state, she was going to—well, not be polite.

When she started to describe Kansas, Grace could sound like she was on the tourism board.

"Eastern Kansas is like Connecticut. Or Virginia. Rolling hills, lots of trees, but without the traffic jams." She'd graphically describe how the university was on such a steep hill that streets closed when it was icy. She'd say just enough to see their minds recalculating, the image shifting, from the desolate plains they'd conjured up at the state name.

Grace accepted that there was nothing exceptional that defined Kansas: no Rocky Mountains, no Grand Canyon, no Disney World. Yet there was something about the Flint Hills at sunset that had claimed Grace's heart.

Grace put a credit card and house key in her jean pocket as she went out her front door. She'd walk downtown, check out the shop windows, then pick out a sweet at Wheatfields.

Sweet rewards were the best. Or alcohol. It could be a tough choice. On reflection, however, a Godiva Chocolate Martini could fill both needs.

Chapter 23
(October 10th)

When her phone rang, Hannah was in the middle of trying to study for an Introduction to Philosophy test. Plato, Aristotle, Socrates, Descartes, Kant, Rousseau, Sartre—all were spread across her desk and floor. Hannah had returned to her classes, come out of the black hole, but the actual studying was an uphill battle. She'd read something, think she had it mastered, and then be unable to remember twenty minutes later.

It was the woman police officer, with the Native American name that Hannah had yet to spell correctly. *So-see* was how it was pronounced, but there were consonants in there that Hannah could not get straight.

"Hannah, I have some bad news. The District Attorney has reviewed the case and determined that there is insufficient evidence to charge your assailant."

Hannah's mind went blank. The words, *The only true wisdom is knowing you know nothing,* echoed in her head but she had no idea who had said them.

"What did you say?" Hannah asked, incredulous. "Insufficient evidence? What do you mean? We know who he is, where he lives. We have his DNA. We have pubic hairs and semen. What more do they need?"

"Yes, we have all of that, but your assailant is saying that the sex was consensual, a hookup. He is not denying that he had sexual intercourse with you. So, all the evidence to prove. . . "

"Consensual? Are you kidding me? If I'd agreed to have sex, why would I put myself through this? Why would I call victim services, go to the hospital, get grilled by the police? My life has gone to shit, I'm the *girl-who-got-raped,* and now you tell me they believe that it was *consensual?* Who the. . . "

"It's not that we don't believe you. We do. But there is not sufficient evidence, beyond your words, your description, to expect anything but an acquittal if it went to trial," Patsy said.

"How do they know? How can they predict what a jury will decide?"

"It's not my decision, Hannah. It's the District Attorney who decides what to prosecute, what is. . . " Patsy stopped mid-sentence when she realized the next words out of her mouth would have been *worth prosecuting.*

"Don't I get to talk to the DA?"

"Yes, of course. But we've been down this road a lot. We *want* to charge your assailant, but it is very clear that we do not have enough to get a conviction. We go to trial, and the defense will present an alternative scenario, in which the sex was consensual, or you were intoxicated enough that you really do not recall, and they will grill you on the stand. And that would be much, *much* worse than anything so far. They'll grill you about how much you drank, and were you flirting, and did you go to his room willingly, and they'll have witnesses to all of it. And no matter how persuasive you are, how articulate, how sincere, a jury will never be able to overcome the threshold of reasonable doubt. They will never vote to convict."

"So the truth doesn't matter?" Hannah asked.

"Of course the truth matters," Patsy replied. But even as she said the words, she realized that Hannah was right—truth was irrelevant.

In every jury trial, one side was telling the truth. Or mostly truth. And the jury, of twelve ordinary people, had to decide *whom* to believe. Most acquittals were not that jurors believed the defense, but that there was room for doubt. They could not get *beyond a reasonable doubt.* They could believe the victim, yet still experience that sliver of doubt, just enough that they could not send a college student to prison for years. So jurors turned it back on the prosecution: *The prosecution did not do its job. We needed more evidence.*

"I wish he'd been a fucking stranger," Hannah was saying. "In an alley. Like in the movies. I wish he'd beat me up, and I had bruises and black eyes and blood all over. Just so they could have their *evidence.* And, really, those would heal quicker than what's going on inside me— and being looked at like. . ."

"People who matter, who care about you, believe you."

"Yeah, but I don't get to live with just the ones who care. And now it's going to get so much worse." Hannah's voice cracked. "Oh God, it's going to get worse."

"What do you mean?" Patsy asked.

"The DA says that no charges are being filed. Logan tells a few friends the good news. He doesn't have to say a word. Because they'll post, 'Good news for our bro today' on Facebook. 'Truth wins out.' 'Don't believe what you hear because it turns out it was all a lie.' 'Whores lie.' 'She was a slut and this proves it.' They've already been saying it. And people will think that I've been lying because *if* I was telling the truth then wouldn't they prosecute? It looks like the police and DA believe *him* and not *me*."

"That isn't what the police or DA believe, Hannah."

"But they don't come out and say what they *believe*. They leave me to get judged on YikYak and Facebook and Snapchat and Twitter. That's my jury."

There was nothing Patsy could say. Hannah was right.

"I'll set up a meeting with you and the DA," Patsy continued. "Hannah, I'm really sorry."

"Thank you. I'm sorry I dumped on you. It's not your fault."

"That's okay. You're justified in feeling angry and frustrated." Patsy said. "The system is not working."

Hannah lay down on her bed and willed herself to sleep. She tried to not look at the textbooks piled on her desk, demanding that she focus, memorize, and regurgitate. The philosophers would have to wait.

Later that night, Hannah went across the hall to Stacy's room. Hannah had turned to Stacy several times since *that night*. Stacy listened if Hannah wanted to talk, but she was okay with Hannah just being there and not talking. Her room had become a safe space for Hannah to not be alone but also not have to talk. To just *be*.

Across campus, Logan Whiteman had also received a phone call, but from his attorney. After Logan's initial interview with the police, he'd voluntarily returned with Mr. Dorfman and had provided a detailed written statement. The attorney had prepared a list of potential *witnesses* who would attest that the girl in question had been quite intoxicated, had engaged in animated conversation with Logan, flirtatious behavior, and was observed going quite willingly, albeit weaving a bit, hand-in-hand, to his room. The girl was seen leaving the frat house, of her own accord, with no one preventing her. She had not said anything to anyone about being sexually assaulted even though she passed through a large crowd of other students.

"Just need to let you know that the DA has decided not to press charges," Dorfman told him. "I emailed your father already."

Logan felt a wave of relief wash over him. He'd been stunned at what the police first said. The potential seriousness of his situation had taken a few days to register. It had simply felt too bizarre.

Dorfman had talked to him about the different scenarios that could play out—being indicted, a trial, the remote possibility of a conviction with a prison sentence. But, at the same time, he'd reassured Logan that the odds were in his favor.

The *odds*. He'd used that word. Like they were playing craps.

None of it made sense to Logan.

It was a hookup. She'd been flirting with him, all smiling and cuteness, and seemed happy enough to go up to his room. He lay down and spooned her and she hadn't objected. He remembered unhooking her bra, reaching around and feeling up her breasts. He'd even told her how nice they were. And that she had a tight pussy, which was a compliment. Yeah, he'd gotten a little directive, grabbed her hands and hair, but a lot of girls liked that. They liked when a guy knew what he wanted and went for it.

Logan knew he wasn't comfortable with being mushy and so, maybe, he acknowledged to himself, just *maybe*, he got a little into role-playing in sex. He liked to think of himself as more street-smart than he was, and using certain words made him feel less of a kid and more like a man. And while eye contact was okay when talking with a girl, it felt awkward during sex. It got him distracted. Once, when a girl had insisted that he look into her eyes when fucking her, he'd almost lost his erection. That had been weird.

Logan had been telling himself that it was a set-up, like his father had said.

"She did it and then wished she hadn't," Lou had said. "That happens *all* the time to men. Ask any guy."

And all the guys in the house had been mostly supportive, had rallied around him and told him he was getting screwed over but not to worry. They had his back.

But Logan also felt embarrassed, maybe even more than angry. He didn't want anyone to think he was like *that*. He didn't force girls to have sex. They let him know they wanted it by how they talked with him, how they laughed and flirted, touched his hand or arm or shoulder. Sometimes they wanted to but didn't feel like they should. You could see it in their eyes. And those were the ones who drank more, to make it easier to do it. So they could say, "Oh, gee, I had a little too much last night—but that was fun." He never forced them to drink. He offered, and they accepted.

Okay, maybe she had protested a little. But a lot of girls liked it like that, the guy making the moves. They would say "No," but that was just to show they weren't sluts. They got off on the guy taking charge. When he'd turned her over and oiled himself up, she just lay there, didn't grab for his cock or anything. But he'd been holding her hands up over her head, so maybe—anyway, by then it was too late. He wasn't about to stop just because the girl didn't seem into it. Not when she'd been playing him all evening.

"You dodged a real bullet on this one, Logan," Dorfman said. "Keep it zipped, okay?"

The next day, Hannah met with the DA. Patsy Tsosie was not there but a woman who was introduced as a victim advocate was sitting at the conference table.

The DA was a man. Mark Sorenson. He spoke directly to her, explaining the process of how the district attorney's office went about making a decision whether or not to proceed with a case. How it was not whether or not it was winnable but if they believed there was *any* chance for a conviction. In her case, it had nothing to do with whether they believed Hannah or not. The DA believed her. The police believed her. But the circumstances undermined the potential for a conviction. And they did not want to put her through an exhausting and painful process where she would be scrutinized, her account picked-apart—where *she* would, in effect, be on trial—when the outcome was so predictable.

Across the table, the victim advocate simply nodded in agreement.

When the DA concluded, he asked Hannah if she had any questions. The victim advocate said she would "reach out" in a few days to follow up. They were kind and supportive. There was nothing that Hannah would later wish they had done. They had done what they could do. It was simply not enough.

Hannah stood up, shook hands with the DA and the advocate, thanked them for their work on her behalf, and walked out of the courthouse. She found her car in the long parking lot, got in, and began driving back to the dorm. Halfway there, she abruptly pulled to the side of the road, opened the car door, and retched onto the road, bile and breakfast combining to scorch her throat.

Chapter 24
(October 12th)

Molly and Grace were having supper at Molly's house. Molly had fed Max earlier and he was inside watching *Simpson* reruns. While Grace was caring for Max two evenings a week this semester, she and Molly were finding it more of a challenge to find more than a few minutes in passing for themselves.

Grace missed talking to Molly. Actually, there were many times when Grace forgot that she was talking to her *daughter*. Grace had left Kaw Valley for a decade, during which time Molly's life had profoundly changed—from university student to working single mom.

Grace had returned after Max was born to help out for a few weeks. But Jeff, Max's dad, had still been there and it had been strained. And she'd flown down for a week once a year. But one week was hardly enough to sustain a relationship. Even now, Molly felt somewhat guarded with her mother. And Grace had things in her *emotional vault* that were staying locked up.

When it came to anything outside their own relationship—things like their respective work, Molly's classes or issues with Max—they found it easy to talk.

For Grace, Molly was now a valued resource, just as Kat. Or Patsy. Or Mickey.

Grace needed to be able to process her work, which meant talking things out. Otherwise she ended up like a caged hamster on a wheel, going in frantic circles in her head at 2 a.m. At the same time, she had to respect patient confidentiality.

It was a conundrum.

So, Grace had crafted a release of information for her clients to sign that gave their permission for her to discuss specific issues of their case, *anonymously*, never using names or identifying information, with "relevant professionals and experts, including clinicians, attorneys, accountants, mediators, law enforcement, specialists, etc." The "specialists," "experts," and "etc." covered Molly, who was quite the expert on being a single mom, raising a kid with a disability, returning to school, rebuilding a relationship with a mother who'd disappeared, as well as a wide array of university issues. Molly had a pragmatic common sense that could cut through the crap.

But tonight was just for chowder, salad, warm French bread, and getting caught up.

"How is Max doing?" Grace asked. "Is he still being teased?"

"Seems to have let up some," Molly replied. "But *teased* is not the word I'd use. He doesn't understand teasing, too much nuance. It's more bullying. Certain kids pick on the weak, the ones who can't retaliate. But when Max gets frustrated and explodes, *he* becomes the problem. The taunting becomes secondary."

"Are you worried about that happening?"

"It's inevitable. Not *if* it will happen, but *when.*"

"Which means you're always on edge, waiting for the phone call telling they have a *situation.*"

"Yeah, Mom," Molly replied. "Waiting for the volcano to erupt."

"Would it help to explain to the other kids how Max thinks?"

"What do you mean?"

"I mean we go in and talk to the class. Explain how Max's head works, how it is filled with noise at times, how he sees things differently. Like a Show-and-Tell. Create a connection, so picking on him is like picking on the kid in a wheelchair. Socially unacceptable."

"I have to think about that. Max might not want that, but Max is not the best judge of what could be helpful. And it could backfire. He wants to be accepted, but as normal."

"Well, think it over. I did it in Alaska with a family I was working with. Teamed up with the Mom and Dad. Their kid had Tourettes. The shit stopped, except for one nine-year-old sociopath, after we went into the classroom and had a *teachable moment.* But the better outcome was that they moved the little sociopath to a different class after the next incident."

They sat for a moment, sipping their wine, reflecting on how life-transforming removing a bully could be in a child's life.

"What about your classes?" Grace asked.

"Going fine. Feels like I'm in the right place. I'm finding more nontraditional students than in other majors."

"So psychology it is?" Grace asked.

"Well, as it happens, I met with the graduate advisor for the social work program two weeks ago." Molly almost laughed at how her mother's head jerked up from her bowl of chowder.

"You what?" That was Grace's degree, clinical social work followed by post-graduate training in family therapy. "I didn't know you were even considering it."

"Well, I'm considering a lot of things. But the M.S.W. has more flexibility than a master's level in psych. And insurance companies reimburse for the M.S.W. just like a psych Ph.D. So, if I want flexibility, that might be the best choice."

Grace kept her emotions in check. But it felt like a validation, after all they'd been through, that Molly would ever consider the same profession as her mother. Grace had an image—did private practices ever list like plumbers or painters? Grace envisioned a sign: *McDonald and Daughter: Finding the **Fun** in Dsyfunctional."*

Rein it in, she told herself.

"Well, let me know what you decide," was all she said.

Molly stood up, bringing the bottle of wine to the table, topping off their glasses. They were almost finished eating, but Max was content in the living room. Might as well enjoy whatever time was left.

"So, how are you doing?" Molly asked. "This has been a hell of a time for you."

"It has been. Dealing with my own guilt, the girl's parents, her roommate," explained Grace. "To top it off, I got an email from another client that the DA will not be indicting the guy who raped her. There is *insufficient evidence* to have any hope of a conviction at trial. I understand their position, but it's devastating for the girl."

"Did she go to the hospital when it happened? Call the Rape Crisis Center? Like right away so that. . ."

"She did it all," Grace interrupted. "But he isn't denying that they had sex. He says it was a *hookup*. And there apparently are kids willing to testify that she was flirting, mucho alcohol involved, she went willingly to his bedroom—and she said nothing to anyone at the party about being assaulted before walking out the door."

"Fuck," Molly said. "Cluster fuck."

"That's spot-on."

"So, what's your next step?"

"With her? To reinforce that she is believed, that her experience is valid even if there is no prosecution. But I need to understand, for future reference, this whole hookup culture, the mentality and protocols."

"Not my scene," Molly said. "There's been a significant shift since I was an 18 year old freshman."

Oh yeah, Grace flashed back, *when **your** college experience got messed with. But now is not the right time to bring that up,* she thought. *Stay focused.*

"So *how* is it different? What does 'hooking-up' mean exactly? I'm doing research here."

"Gee, who would have predicted? My mother researching hookups."

"How about start with the proper spelling. Does hookup have a hyphen? In my head it has a hyphen."

"I'm not sure."

"Okay, never mind that. Just explain."

"A hookup is a sexual encounter that does not imply anything about emotional involvement," Molly began. "People may have steady or regular hookups, like friends with benefits, but also one-time or intermittent hookups. Say you're at a party and you find someone attractive, you can end up having sex with them without either person placing any special meaning on it."

"So, it's like a one-night stand used to be, but people can choose to have repeats if they both want?"

"Yeah, and they're not exclusive. Some people have options for hookups, depending on what they feel like. Think different menu choices."

"That is so *gross,* " Grace interrupted.

"You're the one who asked."

"I know, I know. But *why* are kids doing this? Can you explain *that* to me?"

"No, because I don't really understand why. I can wrap my head around why some guys would, because they are penis-and-testosterone-driven and lack a moral compass. But I do not get why the girls are so willing," Molly answered. "I assume peer pressure or wanting to be seen as cool. Or some distorted idea of gender equality."

"All boys are **not** 'penis-and-testosterone-driven and lacking a moral compass,' " Grace replied. "There are plenty of decent young men who are not into hookups."

"Yeah, the ones who have taken some kind of Saving Myself for Marriage pledge, like Mormons and fundamentalists. The rest are only too ready to screw any girl who is willing. You won't see them saying 'Let's get to know each other first' or 'I want to take this slow' if the opportunity presents."

"I can't accept that, Molly. I've had too many young guy clients who are kind, thoughtful, and incapable of hurting or exploiting a girl."

"Well, those guys are not filling up the bars."

Grace tried a different tact.

"Are girls finding this sexually gratifying? I mean, not to sound like Health 101, but women are more sexually complex than men. So, unless female anatomy has made some changes, or the average young guy has become much more sexually skilled and sensitive, I do not see all these girls getting off on a hookup."

"Didn't we have this heart-to-heart when I was twelve? Never mind, I agree. That's what makes it hard to accept as a sign of equal rights—the *I can do anything a boy can do*. I see girls doing what the guys want but re-labeling it a sign of emancipation."

"So, if even the *good girls*, and I use that term loosely, are doing this, then what does it now take to be a slut?"

"Good question. Maybe more than one guy in a night? Advertising her promiscuity? Because that label—promiscuous—no longer applies. Not that it ever applied to men, only women."

"So nobody worries anymore about their *reputation*?" asked Grace.

"Not like they used to. But I think some girls are deceiving themselves if they think that hooking-up will not impact how they're perceived. There are no secrets in a world of social media. I'm not talking about the girl who has a long-term friend-with-benefits. That's a kind of relationship. But the girl who goes to frat parties, screws different guys every weekend, and thinks she's liberated? That she's in control?"

"So why do they?"

"Well, some girls have been giving blowjobs since they were fourteen. So, for them, not such a big transition," Molly said. "But a lot of girls arrive as freshman with beliefs that sex with virtual strangers is *not* okay. It does make them feel guilty. But if their peers are doing it, with no blatantly negative consequences, they try it. Over time it becomes acceptable."

"I don't get it. It's male-fantasy directed—a world where women will have sex with you without commitment, without even dating, and require *nothing* in return, not even their own sexual gratification."

"Yet the girls seem as invested in maintaining their *freedom*, or at least pretending they're not into commitment, as the boys," Molly added. "Only with a lot fewer orgasms."

"That's the word we've been circling around—orgasm," said Grace. "I want to interview a few hundred of the girls and find out just how many have orgasms with new partners the first time? Or ever? Are the boys invested in their partner's sexual pleasure?" Grace sighed. "We did not have a sexual revolution so that girls could put out without getting off. That is not equality."

"I cannot believe we're having this conversation," Molly said. "But I totally agree."

Chapter 25
(October 14th)

Grace hesitated before punching in the number.

"Hello, Lisa? This is Grace McDonald, Shelby's therapist. I don't want to intrude but I was hoping we could talk. I expect that this is painful for you and I don't want to make it worse, although really, nothing could make it worse. Anyway, I keep thinking that maybe if I knew a little more I could sleep. I hope this isn't too pushy. Would you call me back?"

Grace clicked off, hoping the message would not weird Lisa out. At least it was a Saturday morning and not late at night.

Grace had tried to *accept* that questions would persist about Shelby's death. She'd tried to *accept* that the facts—whether intentional suicide or accidental overdose or something in-between—might never be known. But she couldn't let it go.

Something had happened to Shelby, *something* had propelled her to take those pills, whether to die or simply to sleep, to escape, to not have to think or feel. And Grace wanted, needed, to know what that *something* was.

So, *accepting*—in this case—was *unacceptable*.

Five minutes later, Lisa returned the call.

"I'm sorry, I couldn't find the phone. It gets buried? Like under couch cushions or on the floor under newspapers? I heard your voice message, just not all the words?" Lisa's voice lifted at the end of each sentence.

"That's fine, Lisa. Look, I was calling to ask if you would be willing to meet with me, to talk. I keep thinking about Shelby. I have some questions and, maybe, between us, we could figure out more of what happened. I understand if you don't want to do it, that it might. . ."

Lisa cut her off. "No, I mean yes. Please. I need to talk, too. I wanted to call you, and I almost did one night, but felt like that was overstepping. When and where?"

Two hours later, Lisa and Grace sat across from each other at a booth at Wheatfields Bakery, each holding a tall mug of foamy latte. Once again, Lisa wore clothing that could have come from Goodwill but managed to make a fashion statement.

Grace plunged in.

"What can you tell me about this boy Shelby was seeing?"

"Not much," Lisa replied. "I don't know his name. I was hoping she told you. Shelby said they were in a class together last spring, were on the same group project team, and that she liked him. But I don't know which class other than business."

"So they met up again just as school was starting this fall? Did they have a class together again?"

"Not that I know."

"What did she say about what happened?"

"I probably know less than you do, I think. They had one date and it was nice. And they went out a second time, within a week or so, and she woke up naked in his bed. She couldn't remember anything. And this was *not* normal for Shelby."

"But she felt strongly that something had happened?" Grace asked.

"Yes. She asked the guy, like straight up, 'What happened last night?' and he got evasive. Then defensive. It was *weird vibes* was how she described it. And something about her clothes being folded. Guys just don't do that."

Weird vibes and folded clothing, Grace reflected. *Not a lot to go on.*

"She called him to ask again?"

"I think so. But no idea if he said anything," replied Lisa. "Felt to me that she never got any real explanation."

"Do you have any idea what might have put her over the edge?"

"No, I've gone over and over in my head, like what happened and what did I miss. I knew she felt depressed, but not *that* depressed. Not *I want to die* depressed."

"She may not have intended to overdose," Grace said. "She may have just wanted to not have to think and accidentally took too many pills."

"But she did die. And I didn't see it coming and did nothing to prevent it or help her," Lisa said, locking tear-filled eyes with Grace, almost as if she was expecting blame.

"That makes two of us," Grace replied, returning her gaze.

"So, what now?" Lisa asked.

"Can you find her class schedule from last spring?"

"Yeah, maybe," Lisa said. "We had copies on the refrigerator door so we'd have some idea of where we were on any given day. I'll look for whatever else I can find. Her parents took her clothes and her computer. I'm not sure what happened to her phone, but I haven't seen it around." Shelby paused. "But it's not like I've been looking. I haven't even gone into her room. I keep the door closed and pretend it's a one-bedroom apartment. And I just gave notice that I'm moving out at semester break, even if it means losing the whole deposit."

"I can understand that."

"It's so bizarre," Lisa said. "We were roommates, and we got along well, but we didn't have history, not like long-term BFFs. I don't even know if she had any of those because she never talked about them. We were on the same dorm floor and we each had sloppy roommates. Like gross-me-out sloppy. We bonded over that at first. And we were definitely becoming closer. I really trusted her. She was a good, decent person."

"Yes," Grace agreed, "she was a very good, very decent person."

They stared down at their empty mugs.

"I'll look for the class schedule," Lisa said.

"And anything else. Papers she wrote, loose notes, receipts, anything," Grace added.

"What exactly are you looking for?" Lisa asked.

"I have no idea," Grace replied.

Lisa found Shelby's spring schedule under some coupons in the kitchen junk drawer. She dropped it off at Grace's office Monday morning.

There were five classes total. Three were business: Integrated Marketing Communication, Introduction to Taxation and Human Resources Management, plus an English Lit and Italian 306. The names of the professors were listed.

Grace had no idea that Shelby had been studying Italian. Grace wondered if she just liked the way it sounded. Or maybe she'd had a dream of living in Italy.

Grace felt a pang. None of that mattered now.

She got on the university website in-between her appointments, jotted down the office numbers for the professors of each business class, then called and left a voice message.

"Hello. I'm tutoring a young man with Asperger's Syndrome. I'm reviewing different class requirements. Can you tell me if there are any group projects in your Intro to Taxation class?" She repeated the process for Human Resources Management.

It was a partial truth, a manipulated truth, so not totally alt-fact. She did "tutor" a young man with Asperger's Syndrome—or, more accurately, helped him with his homework. And she needed info on which business classes had group projects. But the connection was left to inference.

She hoped it would be a backdoor to information that she might not get if she said, *Hello. I'm trying to track down a guy who might have been in your class last spring and who maybe raped a fellow classmate who was on a group project team with him.*

When she got to Integrated Marketing Communication, the line was picked up.

"Dr. Hughes," a deep male voice announced.

Grace faltered a bit, then spouted out the same line as the voice messages.

"So, you want to know if I have group assignments or projects in the marketing communications class? That's it?"

"Yes," Grace replied. "I think that is it."

"And you tutor business students?" he asked.

Grace scrambled. "Well, more generic tutoring, staying task-focused, writing skills, and paper organization," she said. "I assist with executive functioning tasks," she added, hoping the word *executive* might add a modicum of credibility.

"Well, that's better. I'd hate to think a business tutor didn't know that group work is a core component of any marketing class. It prepares students to work on a professional team. Builds essential skills."

"I'm just doing some inquiries, learning for myself as well," Grace improvised. "So, you're saying that group projects are a key component of your marketing class?"

"Yes, all my marketing classes require some group projects."

"And what is the size, generally, of the Integrated Marketing class?'

"It varies, but anywhere from 40-50 students."

"That's all I need for now, sir," Grace concluded. "Thank you."

It took two days to track down the other two professors. Neither had responded to her initial message, so she called the main department office, got their office hours, and then called again during that time frame. There were no group activities in Accounting, but there were in Dr. Patel's Human Resources Management. And there were often 100 or more students total in the lecture component, broken down into small groups facilitated by teaching assistants.

If Grace assumed that there was a roughly even gender split in the classes, there could be 75 boys—plus or minus—that could be Shelby's *date*.

The next step was to find out from Dr. Hughes and Dr. Patel which of those young men had been on the same team as Shelby Stewart, now deceased.

But that would have to wait a few days. She was booked solid with appointments and sessions. She also needed a plan.

Chapter 26
(October 15th)

"You're coming to the house meeting, right?" the frat president asked, leaning through the doorway to Logan's room. It was Sunday night at 9 p.m.

"Yeah, sure, be down in a few minutes," Logan responded.

Logan had found a reason to miss the last few meetings. He knew he was avoiding his frat brothers, and he wasn't exactly sure why. While they were genuinely glad that he didn't have to deal with any legal shit, like, God forbid, being indicted for rape, which would have been, to quote several, a real _bummer,_ the tone of their commentary was that he had _gotten away with something._ That he'd caught a lucky break. Which is not how he felt at all.

Everyone concurred that the _skank_—the specific nouns and adjectives varied—had been all over him, flirting, drinking whatever he handed her, and had followed him up to his room, hand-in-hand, like a puppy. Then, whatever had happened, she regretted it and wanted to make him pay.

One brother had asked him, "Did she want to go out with you and you told her that was not happening, that she was just a hookup? That might have pissed her off."

But, no, there had been no discussion. It was a hookup.

House meetings were in the massive basement meeting room, _No Visitors Allowed,_ unless it was emptied out for a party. When Logan walked down the stairs, there were already about fifteen guys over by the big screen TV on the back wall. As he got closer, he could see the naked bodies gyrating on the screen. Sharing new porn with your brothers was a key feature of house meetings, something that a past president had formalized as a means of making the routine business meetings more palatable.

It was not as if Logan were some kind of prude. He watched porn. He'd started when he was thirteen, at the house of a friend with two older brothers. That kid had started watching when he was just ten. And then Logan had discovered the wide, wide world of internet porn. It was a click away, always available. He used the porn to get off whenever he felt horny. Five minutes later, he was good to go. Hell, he used porn to distract him whenever he felt bored. There were days when he used it to wake up. And he'd learned a lot from porn, like what turned girls on.

Two hours later, the house meeting was wrapped up: frat parties for the rest of the semester laid out, some pledge issues resolved, and sign-up sheets for the mandatory Christmas volunteer work passed around. The frat was big on volunteer work, and you couldn't weasel out unless you were authentically sick.

Logan carted his notebooks and laptop to a back table in the empty dining room. He needed to finish a paper for his Ethical Practices in Management class. He liked having a big table to spread all his notes and papers around instead of being stuck at the small desk in his room. And, once dinner was over, the room stayed empty until breakfast.

It was about 1:30 a.m. when Eric Johnson peered into the dining room, probably to see why a light was on, and then ambled over. Eric had longish blonde hair that looked sun-bleached even in winter, and muscles that he meticulously cultivated with two hours a day in the gym. He was getting a degree in Communications. Logan could not recall ever having seen him studying.

"How's it 'goin?" he asked in a street-slang-rapper tone.

"Okay," Logan replied. "Just got a paper to wrap up."

"Sounds like all that shit is over, right?"

"Yeah," Logan answered, taking his hands away from the keyboard and pulling his chair back. "As far as I can tell, the legal shit is over. Just waiting on the university."

"I didn't get it at all. I mean, you're one of the *nice* guys. You were even dating a girl for a while, no? That blonde business major? With the stupendous ass?"

"Yeah," Logan agreed, ignoring the ass comment. "But that's over. We weren't in the same place as far as commitment."

"Ain't that the truth. Start dating and they want a ring before you got your pants back on."

"It wasn't like that. . ." Logan started to explain, then stopped. He'd just gotten a whiff and realized that Eric was drunk. Eric wouldn't remember anything Logan said. Logan had been down this road with his father.

"Yeah, I felt bad that you're the one getting screwed over. If anybody was gonna' catch some girlie-flak, it should be me. Or Troy. Or Brent. Or. . ." Eric checked off fingers as he named other frat members.

"Hey, the night of the party, did you zero in on that one for any particular reason?" he asked.

Logan didn't know where Eric was going with this. But he knew that to ask for clarification would just prolong the conversation. Better to just answer.

"She was cute, Eric. That's all. Long hair and big eyes, dressed up like it was something special. But, no, I was not going *after* her. I just thought she was cute."

"Yeah, right, *cute*," Eric said, enunciating each word. "Me," he continued, "I look for the new ones. Just got away from Mommy and Daddy. I watch for the ones that keep looking at the other girls for how to act, how to dress. Maybe not virgins but close enough. They want to experience life. I figure I can help them with that."

"Where are you going with this, Eric?"

"No place in particular," Eric smiled.

"Look, I need to get back to this paper," Logan said, trying to keep his eyes on his computer screen to make it really clear that he needed to work.

"You keep track of how many you bag? You keep a little notebook, Logan?"

Logan looked genuinely shocked. "No, Eric, no. That's sick."

Eric laughed. "Yeah, maybe. I keep track, but do the police show up at the front door looking for me? You don't get nearly as much action, but *you* got slammed. How's that for justice?" Eric sighed. "It's not fair, man, not one bit. But it works for me."

"Glad that I could take some of the heat for you, Eric. But I don't think we're in the same league. I don't think like that."

"May not think like that," Eric concluded, pushing himself up off the chair and heading for the door. "But you got the moves."

Chapter 27
(October 17th)

Grace was taking a down day at home. She felt in dire need of time alone.

Grace had come to a different understanding of who she was, her core personality, over the past decade. She'd always assumed she was an extrovert who thrived on being with people, engaging and interacting. She could talk to anyone. Everybody said so. That was her image: Optimistic Grace! Happy Grace! Take-on-the-world Grace! But she'd come to recognize just how much of her behavior was a front.

She'd had plenty of time to think in Homer, Alaska. Time enough for memories to surface, willy-nilly, like fish coming to the surface of a pond in search of food, gaping fish mouths opening and closing, only to disappear back under the murky water.

But some memories took shape: a small girl in a sundress, playing by herself on the grass in a park. Her mother is standing over her, "Go play with the other children, Grace. You'll never have any friends if you keep on like this. Now go be nice."

And holidays at her cousins' home, a rambling house with what felt like a dozen bedrooms. There was always noise, talking. It hurt her head. She'd just wanted to read, to be alone. She'd go upstairs to find a bedroom with no one in it. She'd sit very still, reading her book, trying to be invisible. But then, always, her mother would come looking, take away the book, saying, "We drove all the way here so you could have time with your cousins. Now go downstairs and act happy."

In elementary school, she was a misfit. Her mother so wanted a popular daughter, perhaps to compensate for her own deprived childhood, or for some vicarious validation. But Grace was not, would never be, popular. She couldn't grasp all the unwritten, invisible social rules: how to talk, how to act, what to like, what to wear. She blundered through, never having friends who liked her as much as she liked them, always on the outside looking in.

High school was even worse. She was a dork, a goody-two-shoes. She respected the rules everyone else made fun of and was hopeless at sports. She fantasized about being a missionary doctor in Africa. That was before she realized that medical school required knowing math. She was abysmal at math.

College was better in some ways. She put herself through, so she was always working, mostly waitress and night-shift nursing home jobs. She joined no groups. There was an older boy who asked her out, intrigued, she later realized, with her innocence. She wasn't one of those *I've-done-everything-but-intercourse* virgins. She was the real deal. They spent seven months making out, slowly progressing though stages of intimacy. Five months of foreplay. She felt like his *project* but didn't care. He wanted to marry her. But he also wanted to screw other girls, which she did not discover until they were about to get engaged.

Grace didn't want to feel on the outside looking in for the rest of her life. She didn't see how she could transform herself with people who already knew her. It would be too—weird?

It took moving thousands of miles away, an exchange program with another university in California, to pull it off. She got on the plane as Grace, odd dorky Grace. She deplaned with an avatar. *Windy.* To everyone she met, she introduced herself as Windy. She was a free spirit. Windy could walk up to a group in the cafeteria and say, "Is this chair taken?" and sit down. The first time she did it, she thought she would faint. Faint or vomit. But no one realized, and a guy with a toothy smile said, "Sure" and pushed the chair in her direction.

Windy casually joined groups of students who gathered in the student union or cafes just off campus to talk about literature and drink cheap wine. She was not on the outside anymore, she was *in*. People listened to her. All those years of reading paid off when hanging out with a bunch of English majors.

Grace fell hard for a young professor with blonde hair and a Texas drawl. When he came on to her, she was authentically surprised. She did not feel exploited or sexually harassed—as she was later told she should have due to the power imbalance—but special. Chosen. For the first time in her life, she had a secret worth keeping. The sex was mediocre, but the validation of having a mentor, a professor, talk with her as an equal, tell her that she was smart, that she needed to go to grad school?

That was a gift.

In California, Grace reinvented herself. When she returned home, she dropped the avatar, the name, but kept the personality that went with it.

At the same time, she became intrigued with learning more about how people change, why people change, when it was possible, when it was not. After a few years, she shifted her graduate studies from English to social work.

Meeting Gil when she was in grad school had been a blessing, a salvation. He was also shy and had also struggled. But there was a completion she felt with Gil that felt right. She trusted him to understand her, to accept her. With Gil, she was the social one, the networker who set up dinners with other couples and kept connected with friends. They hosted potlucks and holidays. Grace did not feel inadequate with Gil.

But losing Gil, and then living alone, had brought back her former self. Her *original* self. She stopped pretending. She accepted that she did not like big parties or making small talk, and preferred one-on-one with a friend. She could happily spend a weekend totally alone. She accepted that she felt depleted rather than energized after a party. She could still do it, "rise to the occasion," as Gil used to say, but the next day she craved solitude.

Now, back in Kaw Valley, she was still learning just who she really was. Recalculating was the word that came to mind, a wayward GPS that had gotten lost on unmapped roads.

After ten hours hibernating, she felt the impulse to make one call.

"Mickey, it's Grace. I just want to say thanks, more than thanks, for the other night. I was in a bad way. So, can I take you out for dinner next weekend as a gesture of gratitude? Give me a call back as to the best night and time if you can. If not, you get a rain-check."

It had been two weeks since Shelby's suicide. Grace thought about her every day.

The morning after Mickey had come over, she'd awakened alone. He had silently slipped out at dawn, sparing Grace that awkward, *So, are you feeling any better?* She remembered that he'd put her to bed, undressing her, gently pulling off her socks and pants, the nightgown sliding over her head. But she had no memory of embarrassment. She'd been naked with Mickey Donahue, yes. Briefly. But the physical nakedness was nothing compared to the emotional nakedness. He had seen her as vulnerable as she'd been in many years. And he had not walked away, nor had he exploited it.

He had taken care of her, with tenderness.

That was something Grace knew she had to pay attention to. She'd avoided a serious relationship for twelve years. She'd been *involved* to some extent with a few different men, each of whom she knew in her heart that she would never really commit to. If there was no obvious reason to avoid commitment, Grace had poked around until she found one.

In Homer, Alaska, everyone had a few buried secrets.

Mickey Donahue did not fit anybody's picture of Mr. Right. He was average height, with a roundness to his belly and balding.

But Grace trusted him. And trust meant more than any of the other qualities that people might consider important in a partner.

So, Grace was examining why she was so avoidant. What she might even diagnose in one of her clients as relationship or commitment phobic? Besides, of course, the obvious trauma of how her marriage had ended.

She could not assume that Mickey wanted a relationship. There were too many complications. And before *anything* could happen, Grace knew she needed to figure herself out first.

Chapter 28
(October 18th)

"Dr. McDonald, this is Lisa. I found something."

Grace had given up trying to correct Lisa as far as the "Dr." part. She'd asked Lisa three times to just call her Grace. But Lisa had been raised to respect her elders. It would take a little time.

"Lisa, hello. What is it?" It wasn't that late, but Grace's friends did not call after 9 p.m. Grace had startled a bit with a ring at 10:05 p.m. For Lisa's crowd, she realized, this was no different than mid-afternoon.

"A thumb drive?" Lisa said. "It was in a little plastic box, like you'd put a bar of soap, you know? Like if you were traveling and needed to bring soap? It was in the bathroom, under the sink."

"Back up a minute, Lisa. A thumb drive in a soap container? Have you ever seen it before? What's on it?"

"No, I for sure never saw it and we for sure never stored flash drives under the bathroom sink. And it is really, really weird. Pictures. Naked pictures. And I'm pretty sure they are of Shelby. But the face is covered, so I can't be sure."

"What do you mean covered? With what?"

"Not like covered with something real, not like a blanket, but with a filter. You know? How you can change parts of pictures with filters?"

No, Grace thought, *I have no earthly idea what you are talking about.*

"You just need to see these," Lisa continued. "They're creepy. Can we meet somewhere? I'm downtown now so anywhere is fine."

Grace did not see herself getting into her car and driving to meet up with Lisa. It was already past her bedtime.

Oh well, she thought, *one more boundary bites the dust.*

"How about I give you my address and you just come over here?" she asked.

Lisa was at Grace's *casita* in fifteen minutes.

"Google maps just took me to the front house," Lisa said when

Grace opened the door. "You're, like, invisible back here. It was good you told me to walk down the driveway."

"Yeah, they don't know I'm here and I kind of like it that way," Grace replied. "Now, what do you have?"

Lisa took an iPad out of her shoulder bag and put it down on the dining room table. She touched a key and the screen came to life. Then she took a small red thumb drive out of her pocket and stuck in the side, and, in micro-seconds, pushed a sequence of keys to open the drive.

There appeared twenty or more pictures in small boxes on the screen of a naked young woman. Lisa clicked on one and it enlarged to fill the screen.

Grace gasped.

A woman's body was posed, legs spread, arms draped above the head. But in place of the face was what looked like the head of a pig. It was disorienting, disturbing.

"See what I mean? Like I really think this is Shelby's body but somebody put a filter on it so you can't see the face and be sure."

"This is a filter? How can someone do it?"

"It's just a program, like, you know, to alter the. . ."

"What makes you so sure it's Shelby?" Grace interrupted.

"Well, she is a red-head, right, and I've seen her naked. Not like we wander around like that, but going back and forth to the shower, or running into the bathroom to grab something. And that is just how her body looks, with the freckles, and really white skin. She's curvy and her pubic hair is red."

Lisa blushed a little at saying the word "pubic," then continued.

"She's kind of embarrassed about her freckles because she has a lot." Lisa did not seem aware that she was talking about Shelby in the present tense, and Grace was not about to correct her.

"But, honestly," Lisa continued, "who else would be on a thumb drive in a soap dish under our bathroom sink?"

The girl had a slam-dunk with that one.

Grace quietly and methodically looked at every picture. All were of the same young woman, and each was posed. Legs bent, legs straight, legs spread. Arms above the head, arms draped to one side, hand placed over pubic hair, hand placed over a breast. There was a long shot of a leg leading to her crotch. She was laying on a big bed with navy blue sheets.

"May I keep this?" Grace asked, gesturing to the flash drive.

"Yeah. I downloaded them already to my computer for back-up. Pretty creepy, huh?"

"Yes," Grace answered, "Very, very creepy."

"Creepy enough to make her do something?"

"Depends on if there was a message sent with them, or even an implied message. Or maybe not."

"Shelby was shy," Lisa said. "Bashful. Modest. Not like some girls who send shots of their breasts on Snapchat and don't care who sees them."

"Let me talk to a friend who's a police officer," Grace said. "I need some direction here. I don't think we can trace a thumb drive, but if he emailed Shelby and she put the pics on a drive? We could track the email to an IP address."

"Okay," Lisa replied. "Email me when you find out."

"Until then," Grace added, "I may need to see what those professors can tell me."

Chapter 29
(October 20th)

Grace was leaning against the wall outside Dr. Hughes' office in the School of Business building. After searching for a parking spot for forty minutes, she realized why apartments on the campus bus routes were so popular.

It was 10:45 before she saw a middle-aged man with a trimmed beard and a bulky briefcase ambling down the hall. He did not look in any hurry despite the fact that he was late for his own office hours.

Grace reflected, not for the first time, that she could have had a sweet life if she'd chosen to teach college.

"Dr. Hughes?" she inquired. "May I have a few minutes of your time?"

"Let me open the door," he replied. "But it looks like you're first in line."

He dumped his bag down and moved to sit behind a large metal desk piled with files, gesturing to one of the chairs on the other side of the desk. Grace sat down.

"What can I do for you?" he asked.

"I need to know which male students were on the same group project team in your Marketing 208 class last spring as Shelby Stewart. She was one of your female students in that class."

"How about we start with introductions," he said. "Like maybe a name."

Grace flushed. "I'm sorry. I'm Grace McDonald," she said, offering her hand to shake.

"And I'm Philip Hughes," he said, while shaking her hand.

"Now, what did you say you wanted?"

Grace repeated the statement.

"And why do you need this information?"

"Because the male student may have sexually assaulted the female student. And I'm trying to figure out which male student it may have been."

"It seems that the most obvious route would be to ask the female student," Hughes said. "No?"

"Yes, that would be the most obvious," Grace replied. "But it isn't possible."

"Why is that?"

"Because she's dead," Grace replied.

"What the hell?" Hughes' reaction was visceral. "When did that happen? How did that happen?"

"She died almost three weeks ago."

"But there wasn't anything in the paper. We should have heard something."

"The death was suicide or accidental overdose," Grace said. "Those deaths often do not appear in the paper. They are, for the most part, invisible."

"So where do you get a connection to a project in my marketing class from last spring?"

"Shelby told her roommate she had started dating a boy she met in a class last spring. They had worked together on the same group project. They met up again just before the semester started this fall. He asked her out. Something happened on their second date. She passed out despite not drinking very much and had no memory. She felt she was assaulted but could not prove anything. Four weeks later she swallowed pills."

"Wait a minute. Did you call me asking about whether I had group projects or team projects in my class last week?"

"Yes, I did."

"But you said. . ."

"I may have fudged a bit to get the info," she interjected.

"But what you really want is to know what male students were on the same marketing project team as this female student? So you can— what? Target them?"

"This female student was Shelby Stewart. The student who is dead."

Now it was Hughes turn to flush.

"I'm sorry. That was insensitive," he said. "But why did she think something happened? Sexual assault is a very serious allegation."

Grace hesitated. She was torn between respecting Shelby's privacy and tracking down whomever had done this to her. And she did not think this professor would understand without a visual.

Grace reached into her bag and removed a manila folder. She took out three of the pictures and placed them on Hughes' desk.

"Because of these. And more like them," Grace said.

Hughes flushed again. "Jesus Christ," he muttered. "How do you know it's her? I mean, there's no face."

"Her roommate identified her."

Hughes didn't answer. Then he blustered a bit, saying he needed a consult before he released any student names.

He called Grace a few hours later.

"I'm sorry, but I can't do it. Strictly against regulations. FERPA."

"FERPA?" Grace repeated. "What's FERPA?"

"You really aren't a tutor, are you?"

"Not for university level, no."

"FERPA is the Family Educational Rights and Privacy Act of 1974. It protects against a variety of disclosures. Like HIPPA but in education. We are absolutely not allowed to release any data on a student without the student's consent. "

"And if the student is dead?"

"But you are asking for the names of students who are alive, and they know nothing about you and have not given any permission to release their names."

"So, no one with the university can tell me who worked on the group project with Shelby in last spring's class?"

"That is correct."

"Is this the same law that wouldn't allow me to see my son's grades or be informed if he dropped a class when I was paying every penny of his tuition, room, board, books, and activity fees?"

"That would be this law, yes."

"So, the only people who might be able to tell me anything would be other students who were in the class? Because there is no law that says kids can't blab anything they want. Right?"

"Laws do not bind students from disclosing information, just faculty and staff."

"Then I have my work cut out for me. I was hoping for a short-cut. Any suggestions?"

"You managed to get into my office by lying. Maybe that will work elsewhere."

Grace went ahead and walked over to Dr. Patel's office. The sign on his door indicated that he would not be back in his office for an hour, so she went to the building cafeteria for coffee. It was filled with young people all animatedly talking—but into their phones. Grace counted eleven tables of students in which no one was talking to each other, and attention was fixated on screens of assorted sizes, from phones to tablets to laptops.

She felt a wave of sadness for these kids. She remembered the excitement of talking over ideas, debating some current political development, or the meaning of a paragraph in a 19th century novel. Life was so different then: no cell phones, no computers, no immediate or easy access to information. Research had required hours and hours in the library, taking copious notes, then writing up what was discovered on a typewriter. She remembered first getting an IBM Selectric typewriter, which could erase one letter at a time. It had been cutting edge.

Grace felt like a fucking dinosaur.

Dr. Patel was in his office when she returned. He echoed what Hughes had said: he could not release any names of any students of any of his classes past or present. He sounded like he was quoting the faculty handbook. But he also said that his projects involved more individual research, and the students just compiled their findings. Some never even met in person, but just did it all by email and Google Docs.

"I have no idea," he replied to the few questions that Grace did pose.

Chapter 30
(October 22nd)

Grace decided that the group projects in Dr. Hughes' class seemed the best place to start, closest to what Shelby had described. But it was Molly who came up with a plan to track down the names of boys who had been on the same team as Shelby.

"We set up a temporary dummy email account. That's the first step. Then we put out a request on Yik-Yak for anyone who was in Dr. Hughes' spring semester Integrated Marketing Communications class to respond to that email, with a $50 payoff to the first person who can come up with some desired info."

"And you think this will work?" Grace asked.

"Yeah, I do. People will see it and tell their friend who was in the class. Everyone wants to help someone get an easy $50. Or make it for themselves."

"What if they don't know the answer?"

"They may not. But unless they threw out *all* their papers from the class, I bet there was a handout, or something on-line, as to who was assigned to which project group. If nothing else, they'll be able to give us some names. And once we have names we can start tracking people down."

"Do it, Molly. It's worth $50 to me. So, what do we tell them as far as why we want to know who was in the group?" Grace asked.

"Humm—" Molly paused. "I'm not sure we have to explain. But if anybody pushes back, maybe we say we loaned Shelby books for research and she gave them to her team and now we can't find Shelby?"

"Sounds a little weird but it could work."

"You have a better option?"

"No, but I'll think on it."

Molly posted. They had four responses by the next morning. Three had been in the class. One provided the name and email of their friend who had been in the class, saying that if we got to her, and she had the information, that he wanted $25 as a finder fee.

Molly took down the posting, then responded to all four, asking if they had a class roster or, even better, a small group project assignment page. Or if they knew who'd been in the same project group with Shelby Stewart.

Grace and Molly considered that the guy Shelby dated might see it and respond or just get spooked. But there was no getting around that.

Within hours, BINGO! Two of the five emailed a scan of the handout where class members were assigned to semester-long projects. Grace was so surprised she said that each deserved the $50.

"Do you want me to write them a check?" she asked Molly. "Can you get their addresses?"

"No, mom. No checks. We'll use Paypal. Just go online and send $50 to each of their emails. Use a credit card."

When Grace looked confused, Molly laughed. "You really do live in your own little world, don't you? C'mon, I'll walk you through it."

It came down to four names. Four boys had been assigned to the same group project in Marketing 208 as Shelby.

Grace called Lisa, feeling very much the successful-detective. Molly had tracked them down, but Grace had the names.

"I think we start with Facebook," Lisa said. "See who we can rule out."

"You mean like try to friend them? What if they don't friend you?" Grace asked.

"Seriously? We're in the same university, so we must have some friends in common. I'll dress sexy and put on make-up and change my Facebook photo because now it's a bulldog. Better yet, I get my buddy Zach to friend them. He's a business major. Give me a few days and I'll get back with you.

It was only 48 hours. Lisa came over to Grace's house with her notes. She pulled out four large file cards, each filled with tiny scribbles.

"Zach friended them, then I checked them through his account."

"One is married," Lisa continued. "He posts pictures of his 10-month old. And he's carrying around some extra pounds post-partum. Plus, Shelby would never go near a married guy, let alone a married guy with a pregnant wife or new baby."

"Number 2 is gay. He waited for college to come out. His former teammates on the football team are not happy."

"Number 3 is a possibility. A junior. Accounting major. Like blues music. Didn't Shelby say that they went back to his place to listen to a CD?"

"Good work, Lisa," Grace said. "What about the last one?"

"Number 4 is low profile. But he posted about going to a photography exhibit in St. Louis. He must *really* like photography because that's a five-hour drive."

"We're down to two? Of course, that's assuming the info we have is correct. Do we have addresses on them?"

"Yeah. But they may be from last year. I'm amazed how often people forget to change their addresses when they move every year. But I can track that down."

Lisa reached into her backpack.

"Here are the addresses I have so far and a photo of each guy. I did facial blow-ups from pictures on their page. Is that okay?"

"More than okay. You have a future in investigations."

"It's okay, but maybe because I have a mission. Not sure it would be nearly as interesting just tracking down deadbeat dads and marital affairs. So, what are you going to do now?"

"I'll ask a cop friend of mine for advice. Until then, I may just park down the street from one of them and see what's up. Kind of old-fashioned, but I like the time to think."

"It's your call. Let me know what turns up and remember that the addresses might be wrong."

Grace met with Patsy the next afternoon to review the pictures on the thumb drive.

"There is no proof of a sexual assault," Patsy said. "You have pictures of a naked female body, no face, on a thumb drive."

"Look, a girl is dead. I'm pretty sure this is her body. And she came to see me about waking up naked in a guy's apartment with no memory," Grace retorted. "*Something* happened."

"But we do not know what or where or by whom," Patsy said. "And she is dead and buried. Well, I assume buried. Maybe cremated. But parents tend to not cremate their children, so. . ."

"Look, Patsy, if a guy sent her these pictures it was meant to be a threat. She was asking him what had happened, and he was really defensive. People don't just start doing shit like this out of the blue. He's done it before."

"Sure, Grace, but done *what* before? Taken pictures? Can you prove she didn't agree to have her picture taken? We'd have something if he sold the pictures. Without a release or contract, it would be an offense if he sold the pictures. Or if she even *is* your former client," Patsy continued, not waiting for a response, "what makes you so sure this is her body?"

Grace hesitated. This was getting messy. She'd contacted the roommate of the *former client* who'd helped by locating Shelby's spring class schedule and, then, accidentally—well, not exactly *accidentally* because Grace had asked to go over every inch of the apartment— discovered the flash drive under a bathroom sink.

It was Lisa who said it was Shelby's body, but that was just from passing each other in towels or the times they'd sunned together at the lake. Grace had no idea if the ID was accurate. Of course, finding the drive under the bathroom sink. . .

"Her roommate says so," Grace replied.

"So the roommate found the drive? And she contacted you? How did she. . ."

"No," Grace interrupted. "I'd already called her. We met and talked. We're both having a hard time coming to terms with this as a suicide. Plus feeling guilty for missing possible signs if it was suicide. I wanted to try and track down whomever the guy was that she'd been with. But that was all before finding the pictures."

Patsy ignored any minor ethical concerns that she might have voiced regarding Grace's contacting a former, albeit dead, client's roommate and collaborating with the girl to track down an alleged perpetrator.

"Track down some unknown guy and do exactly what?" Patsy asked.

"Well, that's the part I wasn't sure of. I think I just wanted to talk to him. Find out what happened."

"So, if this unknown man had assaulted this girl, you were hoping that maybe he'd just confess? Because you have such a *trust me-face*?" Patsy paused to inhale. "Are you out of your fucking mind?"

"Yeah, I guess I am. But something happened to Shelby Stewart that made her so distraught that she either intentionally or accidentally swallowed too many pills. And I want to know what put her over the edge and who did it."

"And there is no way that maybe she got drunk and did some stuff she later regretted or did not remember, in which case there is not some psycho involved as much as two intoxicated kids."

"Shit, Patsy, listen to yourself. Of course there is a *way* but it doesn't add up. She was not into hookups. And she reported having one drink, even told me the specific kind of drink, and then—nada. Zero memory. I found her very credible. So, unless she forgot about the other six drinks she chugged, *something was done to her*. This is not two kids experimenting with a camera for kicks."

"Okay, okay. Let's assume accurate self-reporting. But we're not sure the pictures are of her or if a crime has been committed."

Grace glared at Patsy, saying nothing.

"Okay, we don't know if we have a *crime* we can *prosecute*," Patsy amended. "So what is your plan now? Because you're sounding like Brenda Lee Johnson only without a police force to back you up."

"Who is Brenda Lee. . . ?"

"Never mind. I'll find it for you on Netflix."

Chapter 31
(October 26th)

Hunter was having the nightmare again.

He was in the living room of the house where he grew up. The room was filled with his mother's friends. He could never be sure what age he was, but it felt about thirteen. His father, who had taken off when Hunter was seven, wasn't there. Not that he'd ever really been there for Hunter. His mother, who drank too much, getting louder and more dramatic with each vodka gimlet, was sprawled on the sofa.

"I don't know if I'll ever have any grandkids," she was saying, gesturing toward him. "His pee-pee is too small. Hard to imagine it getting close enough to stick it in and keep it there long enough to do any damage."

This was not the first time she had made this announcement. She never remembered saying it the next day. And she never apologized. Hunter froze, his face getting deep, deep red, his eyes going flat.

"Shut up," he screamed in the dream. "Shut the fuck up. Just shut your stupid mouth."

But while his mouth moved, the words never came out. And when he woke up, he was always covered in sweat and his jaw felt locked and tight.

The dream was a re-enactment. The first time he had been only eight years old and had not understood what she was saying. When some of his mother's friends had tittered, Hunter did not realize that it was a nervous response to how wildly inappropriate his mother was being.

The pediatrician had told him and his mother that he had a condition in which his penis "at rest" was stubbier than most, just a few inches long, but would expand to "normal size" when erect. "It's nothing to worry about," he'd said in a reassuring tone. And Hunter might have managed to be okay with that had it not been for his mother's teasing. Because his penis did get a lot bigger when erect. But who wanted their mother to know that? What boy wanted his mother anywhere near his body, especially his penis?

Once, toward the end of a party, one of her so-called friends had cornered him in the kitchen. "Don't pay any attention to what she says, Hunter. It's not size that matters, it's how you use it. You get some moves, you'll do fine." And she had reached out her hand to touch his hair.

Hunter had kept his eyes on the floor, then pushed past her, going up the stairs to escape.

When he was sixteen, he'd fallen for a girl. She was cool, popular, with more street-smarts than him. They talked incessantly, about their families, childhoods, what they wanted or hoped for when they were older. And then they moved into messing around. After a few days of kissing and fondling and fumbling, she had offered to go down on him. But he had said no, he wanted to really make love. He'd used those words, too, because that was what he'd felt. *Make love.* As if the act of connecting physically would create something that would have a life of its own, that would exist between them. Their loyalty, their commitment, their love. He'd felt more for her than he'd ever felt for anyone.

Three days later they were in her bedroom, alone, door locked, her parents gone for the night. They spent almost an hour kissing, touching, slowly taking off each other's clothing until they were naked together. But just as he was ready to put on the condom, which he had practiced doing in his own bathroom weeks before, his erection had gone limp. And the girl, just a kid herself, didn't know enough to not take this *failure* personally, to not be hurt. In her world, that meant he didn't find her that attractive, that she wasn't hot. And Hunter did not have the words to try and explain. He didn't understand himself why his body had failed him.

After that, Hunter did not risk again. He found that he could perform just fine, rock solid, as long as no one was watching. He never thought that the same girls he targeted might have been supportive had he ever had the guts, the balls, to be honest.

Taking pictures was how he felt in control. He had beautiful women in his bed. He never hurt anyone. He repeated that to himself and he believed it.

Chapter 32
(October 27th)

Grace was sitting at the kitchen table at Molly's, watching her daughter chop onions, peppers, ripe tomatoes, and garlic for sauce. Grace had a glass of Syrah in front of her. It was pasta night. Katrina was coming over in an hour to join them. Grace inhaled with a sigh of pure pleasure. There could never be too much garlic.

While she did not want to spoil the perfection of the moment, she needed a *Molly consult*. And given how their schedules had been, if she did not get it tonight it could be another week.

"Ahhhhhh, Molly, I'm still working on that case and there are a few things I'd appreciate your help with. It won't take long." Grace's tone was pleading, and she gave her daughter a begging puppy look.

"You know, you've gotten awfully demanding lately," retorted Molly.

"I'm not demanding. I request. Like now I need to understand these social media sites. I know about Facebook, but I do not understand the differences between the rest of them. Let me check—I made a list."

Grace rummaged through her purse, pulling out a notebook.

"Okay, here we go—Clik-Clak? Is that one?" Grace asked.

"Not that I've ever heard of," Molly replied. "Are you maybe thinking of Yik-Yak?"

"I have no idea, but if Clik-Clak is nothing you recognize, then tell me about Yik-Yak."

"What else is on your list?"

Grace looked at her notebook.

"Instagram, Snapchat, Vine, Tumblr, Twitter, Tinder, Foursquare, and Whisper?" Grace read each one and checked it off as she spoke. "And what's a disappearing site?"

"That is quite the list," Molly said.

"Whatever happened to Facebook? Wasn't Facebook all the rage just a few months ago?"

"Okay, Mommy Dearest, using an expression like 'all the rage' really dates you. I mean r-e-a-l-l-y sets you back decades. And, no, Facebook was *all the rage* like a few years ago, which is a lifetime for some of these kids."

"So it isn't anymore? All the rage?" Grace asked. "Which is good, actually, because I never quite got the hang of it and now I don't have to."

"Mom, you never did Facebook. You said you would, but you didn't."

"I'm retro. I value *face time*. Screen-free. Being with a person and talking with them. Like we're doing right now. I got overwhelmed with Facebook. You can spend hours on it every day just trying to stay current with people's lives."

"That's the point: hours and hours and hours. That's what they *want* you to do." Molly stirred the saucepan, and the smell of peppers, garlic, and spices filled the room.

"So, okay, start with that first one—Yik Yak?"

"Yik Yak is like a university-wide bulletin board, where anyone can post stuff, and anyone can see it, so you don't have to know the people or be friends like Facebook, or following someone on Twitter," Molly started in. "What makes it feel different is that it's local—each university has one. Anyway, college students can look at other college's Yik Yak sites, which is called a *peek*, but can't post. And it's big on anonymous voting—think of an anonymous Facebook *like*—but with anonymous dissing as well. That gets people hooked. Lots of *thumbs-up* is validation. But *thumbs-down* can mess with a kid's head. Yik Yak is sometimes silly, short stuff like, 'Hey, I got so wasted last night at that blankity-blank concert down at the Jackpot.' More shout-outs, some Q&A, rather than serious discussion."

"That's good, Molly. I'm impressed. How did you learn all this?"

"Mom, you look at it three times, and you get it. It's not complicated."

"Not complicated for you, maybe. Now, are there rules about what can be posted? Like no naked pictures or. . . ?"

"It's a free app. I think that if you use certain language it will delete your post immediately. But not sure what the parameters are. They have rules, but not everyone follows the rules. When it started, it got real nasty, real quick with junior high and high school kids. Then the managers installed boundaries so that kids couldn't use Yik-Yak at school locations. I need to check on this, and I have *no* idea *how* they do it, that technology is like sci-fi, but I think it doesn't work in the location of a junior high or high school."

"Does everything disappear after a certain time?"

"Not sure. I think it just goes to the bottom of the pile and everyone is looking at most recent posts, but I'm not sure if stuff is deleted."

"So, someone could post something questionable and it could be seen before it gets deleted?"

"I'll check for you. There have been some bullying and harassment issues with the site because it is anonymous, no user name or password, so people were saying things they'd never say if they could be identified."

Grace was taking notes as fast as she could.

"Okay, got that one, more or less. Now, Snapchat?"

"Snapchat is a phone app, but it's not anonymous. But maybe you can use a fake handle? Anyway, it was the first site that was used a lot for sexting because you can send *snaps* to one person, but they disappear in like under ten seconds. Mostly people can take pictures, add a caption, a doodle, or overlay, and send out to all their followers or friends, or select just one or a few."

"So it's like Facebook for phones, but more focused on pictures, and the content, or whatever it's called, disappears?"

"Yeah, that's not bad for a beginner. But where Facebook is forever, Snapchat has this urgency to it. Like *gotta check, gotta check, gotta check*—or might miss something. Don't want to miss out because that is *death*."

"Who has time to do all this? And are they mostly selfies?"

"Adolescent and college kids are the big target audience. They make the time. This is what you see them doing all day, the constant checking."

"Don't they get bored? I mean, how many times can you see people doing stupid or even fun things—*Oh, gee, another of 100,000 pictures?*"

"Snapchat is way ahead of you, Mom," Molly said. "They added another feature to the app, to be able to create video stories, which is a sequence of pics and video, sound and all, which is now 'all the rage' as you put it. People make these mini-videos, a few seconds here and there, and can send out or assemble into stories, like narratives—*Here is what I did today.* Stories disappear after twenty-four hours. And people have scores based on number of views."

"Their *day*? Do they really think anyone cares about *their day*?"

"It's more about *how* you tell it, like really clever or funny. And the better you are, the more people will share and the more followers you get."

"And people want more followers because?"

"Because it is cool to have a lot of followers. But then the pressure is on to stay cool. But the flip side is that once you're really cool, then people may be out to bring you down."

"And this is supposed to be fun?"

"They act like it's fun, but it gets to be more survival in a particular social group. Don't do it and you're not *in* anymore. No one wants to be left out."

"This sounds like a lot of work, and for what? All that constant checking—having to be clever and recording your life—only to have it disappear?" Grace looked down at her notes. "Is there a censor protocol? Like Ick-Ick?"

"Very funny. Like Yik-Yak? I don't know. Listen, Mom, can we switch gears here for a minute because there's something I'd like to. . ."

Just then the back door opened and Katrina walked in, a bottle of wine in each hand.

"Oh my God, it smells fabulous in here," Kat said. "So, have you two been talking? What did I miss?"

"Nothing you want to know about," Molly said. "Don't get her started. Please, spare us all."

Later that night, after Grace and Katrina left, Max asleep in bed, Molly sat with the final half-glass of the second bottle of wine on her front steps. It was a full moon.

Twice that evening, before Kat had come, Molly had started to tell her mother something. Not so much a secret, nothing like *that*, but more just *private*. A private thing that it was now time to share. But each time she began, there had been a distraction. First had come a yell of frustration from Max when the TV remote wouldn't work. Then, just as she was trying to transition the conversation, Katrina had arrived.

No rush, she told herself. *I'll get to it.*

Chapter 33
(October 28th)

A letter arrived from the IOA. Hannah's hands shook as she opened it.

This letter is to inform you that the investigation regarding the allegation that Logan A. Whiteman violated the University's Sexual Harassment Policy has been completed. The IOA has submitted an Administrative Investigation Report to the. . .

Hannah's eyes scanned down to the next paragraph.

The complaint was handled in accordance with the University's Discrimination Complaint Resolution Process. The IOA used a preponderance of evidence standard, which means the facts at issue are probably more true than not. In order for the IOA to determine that a policy violation occurred. . .

At the start of paragraph three, Hannah's heart stopped.

Based on the preponderance of the evidence, there is insufficient evidence to demonstrate that Logan A. Whiteman violated Sexual Harassment Policy by engaging in non-consensual penile/vaginal intercourse with you on 9-1-2017.

Hannah's head felt like it was burning from the inside out—that if there had not been bone and skull to contain it, it would implode.

The IOA recognizes that this result may be disappointing to you. Should you choose to appeal the IOA's decision, you may submit a signed, written document articulating why. . .

Disappointing? Hannah thought. Getting a "B" instead of an "A" on a final was disappointing. This was. . .

But she had no words for *this*. She had never experienced *this*.

How can this be my life? How can this be happening to me?

Thank you for coming forward to make a report and for your patience and cooperation with this investigation, the letter continued. *Please know that the IOA continues to be available should you need support or services to keep you connected to campus and your academics. If you have any questions, please do not hesitate to contact..."*

Support? Services? Like what? What else could they possibly do?

Her instructors had been asked to provide her *interim measures*—allow extra time for tests, turn in papers late, receive *incompletes* in her classes without repercussions.

But Hannah did not want *interim measures*. She didn't want more *services*. She wanted her life back. She wanted to be what all the other girls were—*normal*.

Hannah wanted to stop seeing the panties in the nightmares that jerked her awake at 3 a.m. The panties she'd been wearing that night to feel pretty. They were red silk with a little edge of lace. They matched her bra. Hannah remembered how she'd looked at herself in the mirror before she got dressed for the party.

"Not half bad," she'd told herself, turning left and right in front of the mirror, making her long silky hair swing like in a TV commercial. "Lose ten pounds and you could be almost hot."

Now she remembered herself in front of that mirror, so excited about going to a real college party.

In the nightmare, she was in the hospital. She was handing the torn panties to a nurse. The nurse was wearing latex gloves as she carefully put the panties in a marked, brown paper bag.

Now her panties sat on a shelf somewhere in an evidence locker in the bowels of a police station.

When Officer Tsosie had called her to tell her that the DA was not going forward, she'd asked Hannah where she could return her clothes.

"I don't care what you do with them," Hannah had replied in a level tone. "I never want to see them again."

"Then I'd like to keep them in the evidence locker, just in case we ever need them," Tsosie had replied.

"Why would you need them?"

"If another report comes in on the same man, we could contact you and reopen the case."

"So, you can't prosecute him for raping me but, gee, after he rapes some other girl—or girls—then we might have a shot? Like a gang-prosecution? A jury would never believe *one* girl but maybe we have a chance if five testify?"

"I'm so sorry that you had to go through this," Tsosie had said after a long pause. "And you deserve justice. But, you're right. A jury almost never believes one girl with this set of circumstances. There's too much room for doubt."

It was after that call that another image first flashed across Hannah's brain. She didn't understand why, but it made her head stop spinning about what she could have done differently. She got to ask the questions she couldn't ask in real life.

In her fantasy, Logan was in an armchair, in a button-down short-sleeve shirt. His arms were duct-taped to the arms of the chair, his legs tied to the feet. There was duct tape over his mouth, so he had to breathe through his nose. He had a scared look, but also confused, probably close to the look Hannah had displayed when he'd first fondled her breasts and before he'd yanked down her panties.

"So why did you do it, Logan?" she asked. "I liked you, Logan. If I'm really honest here, I probably would have had sex with you, but not like that. We would have had coffee, gone on a few dates. You know about dates, don't you Logan? It's where a boy and a girl get to know each other. It's what happens before you have sex with them. Have you considered dating, Logan, as an alternative to sexually assaulting girls you've just met?"

So far, Logan did not answer. But Hannah was thinking that maybe she could, very slowly, peel off the duct tape and see what the boy had to say for himself.

Chapter 34
(October 30th)

Logan was having a hard time concentrating. The *incident*—as his parents now put it—had left him shaken. Having police show up at his frat house, answering all those questions, being accused of rape?

Rape? He was not a *rapist*. He wasn't a *violent* person.

Shit, he thought, *I've never even gotten into a fight since that weird kid in the fifth grade.* The other boy, an overweight, uncoordinated kid, a total loser, had come at him for no reason. Just lunged at him when they were waiting in line to go to the lunchroom. Yeah, he'd called him a retard and fat, just joking around, and had tossed his backpack in the dumpster a few times for laughs. But he'd never beat him up or anything. But that kid had gone wacko. Then he'd had to punch him a few times, which was all it took.

Logan wished he had someone he could really talk this out with, whose judgment he trusted.

Logan's father had been supportive, but in that critical, judgmental way that made Logan feel that he had somehow messed up. His dad had asked a lot of questions about the girl, like had he known her, did his friends know her, what had made him think she wanted to hookup. His father never called her *the girl* but always *that bitch* or *the little slut.* And then his father had settled on a reason, an explanation, for *why* the girl had accused him. She wanted money. She wanted to extort money. And that was what he told his friends, the guys he played golf with, anyone who would listen.

"My boy has been going through shit," he said. "The whole family dragged into it. This *girl* flirts like crazy, bats her mascara-coated eyelashes at him—and everybody who was at the party agrees on that— she drinks like a fish and holds his hand as they walk up the stairs to his bedroom. And then she has the fucking nerve to accuse him of rape? What kind of a trap is that? She goes to a bedroom in a frat house but then turns around the next day and says 'He violated my precious pussy.

I need compensation.' "

When he'd first gone home, he'd gotten a slap on the back from his dad's friend, along with, "Tough shit to go through, Logan, but we're here for you." A neighbor had crossed the lawn, put both his hands on Logan's shoulders and said in a very somber voice, "Your father explained the circumstances. It's a scary world to be a young man."

When the DA had declined to bring charges, the tone shifted. *Great news, Logan. . . Good to see that the legal system can still work. . . Knew they would see the light. . . Well, now you can go back to what matters, getting decent grades and having some fun.*

It had been the same with the frat house. The guys had been *very* relieved when they got the word that the District Attorney was not pressing charges. Having a brother indicted for rape was not good for a frat's reputation.

Before the DA decision, one of the board members had said that if Logan were to be indicted it might be best for everyone if he voluntarily moved out of the house until the matter was resolved. *So unfortunate, son, but it would only be a temporary measure.*

But the worst had not happened. And it was about to be over and done, finally—once and for all.

Today he'd gotten the letter from the university office with the weird name. The letter was convoluted, but the bottom line was that he was not going to be suspended or expelled. It had all been a misunderstanding, a miscommunication. At the same time, stay away from the girl.

No shit. Like he wanted to hang out with her?

So, Logan told himself it was time to move on. But he couldn't shake the feeling, the lingering anxiety, that it wasn't really over, that there was something else coming. He just didn't know what and he didn't know when.

And he could not answer for himself the question: *Why had the girl gone to the police?*

What he'd done, what *they* had done, was no different than what he'd seen a thousand times on his computer screen, not nearly as rough as a lot of the porn. No different from what guys described in their basement—*slams* a hundred times.

He had not been able to talk with anyone about how he'd *liked* the girl, liked talking with her. Yeah, he'd handed her drinks, the frat Everclear special—Jungle Juice. But she smiled at him and drank them. It wasn't like he forced her to drink. He'd wanted to hookup with her. What guy wouldn't? And it had looked to him, to everybody, that she wanted that too.

But maybe his father was right. If charges had been brought, she'd have been after them for cash to make the charges go away.

Waking up at 2 a.m., he sometimes tried to study. He was behind in his assignments, having trouble remembering and staying focused. And he had not had sex with any girl since that night. His usual drive to hookup, which had surfaced every weekend with predictable regularity, had disappeared.

November 2017

Chapter 35
(November 1st)

At 9 a.m. on Wednesday morning, Stacy marched into Hannah's room.

Hannah had not left her room, had not been out of her pajamas in four days. From the look of her, Stacy couldn't tell if she'd showered in that time either.

"Get in the shower, wash your hair because it looks like a damn bird's nest, and get dressed," Stacy ordered. "I need to get you out of here. I'm taking you shooting."

"What are you talking about?"

"Shoot guns at targets. I think it would be good for you."

"How can shooting a gun be good for me?" Hannah asked.

"Right now, anything that gets you out of these four walls would be good for you. And there is something about shooting a gun that releases anger. It requires total focus because you're, like, holding and aiming and shooting a potentially lethal weapon. Clears the mind."

"Oh, gee, Stacy, gun-therapy? Seriously? Is that what you're saying?"

"Just shut up and give it a try. If you hate it after ten minutes, then we stop. I'll treat you to the best BBQ this side of St. Louis at a place conveniently located mere blocks away. You're looking pale and pathetic. Nothing like a pile of ribs, brisket, and sweet potato fries to change that."

"You know the nearby restaurants? You've done this before? Where is this shooting place?"

"It's called a shooting *range*. This one is indoors, just five stalls, like bowling lanes. My cousins and I go there a couple of times a year to practice, stock up on ammo, before we go camping and hunting."

"You hunt? For real?"

"No, I actually do not shoot at live animals, just targets. But I like the camping part. I like being out in the woods."

"And you never mentioned this before because?"

"Because it never comes up in girly-girl conversations. So, are you willing to get out of those stinky pajamas and try something new?"

It took Hannah about 30 minutes to shower, wash her punky hair, and run her fingers through it with some gel. Then she stood in front of her closet, looking at the hangers.

"Whaddya wear to a shooting range?" she called out to Stacy. "Is there, like, a dress code?"

"The Gun Guys" was in a storefront right on Main Street in Ottawa, a town south of Kaw Valley. It did not have display windows, just a solid brick facade and a door.

Getting out of the car, Stacy popped the trunk of the borrowed Chevy and pulled out a bright yellow bag with a shoulder strap.

"My Glock," she said by way of explanation, slamming down the trunk and walking into the store.

Inside was spotlessly clean. Gray industrial carpet covered the floor, and shelving was neatly stacked with ammunition, silencers, holsters of assorted shapes and sizes for waists, legs, and shoulders. Hannah did recognize some product names: Smith and Wesson, Glock, Blackhawk. In a corner, T-shirts were hanging under a *Sale* sign. Some were pink and violet, with a picture of a gun on the front, ringed by flowers and read: *Some women read magazines. Some women load magazines.*

A long glass case displayed pistols. Behind it were racks of rifles.

"Hey, Danielle," Stacy said to the blonde woman behind the counter. "Range open?"

"Stacy," she replied with a big smile. "How are you, girl? Long time no see."

"Been busy with school. Not a lot of free time," Stacy said.

"Well, you're here now. And on Ladies' Day, to boot."

"Is it? That's helpful. This is kind of a last-minute *gotta-get-outta-the-room-or-die* visit."

"I've had plenty of those, "Danielle agreed, laughing and shaking her head up and down. "So, want two lanes? Might as well if they're free."

"What's Ladies' Day?" Hannah asked Stacy.

"Lanes are free for the ladies. Saves us $12 each. Now we just rent you a gun and some ammo and I'll show you the ropes."

"Like a Happy Hour," Danielle chimed in. "Better stress relief than alcohol."

"Show her some guns that would be a good fit, would you, Danielle? I'm going to get some ammo and I need a decent concealed carry holster."

Hannah stared at Stacy as if she were an alien. *Who was this girl?*

"So, let's start with the basics," said Danielle, turning toward Hannah. "What are you wanting the gun for?"

"I've never even held a gun in my life," Hannah answered. "So maybe just give me the *Guns for Dummies* intro."

"Hey, lots of the ladies that come in have never shot a gun, never owned one for sure. But something happens in their life that makes them want to have protection. Some realize that it is not a good fit for them, walk out, and never come back. Others end up in concealed carry classes and do target practice twice a month."

Danielle stepped back, eyed Hannah, then looked down at the display case.

"To start, let me introduce you to a Ruger SR22. We'll start small and move up. This is a Smith and Wesson, and over here. . ."

Hannah listened attentively as Danielle explained the features of a 22—how it was more compact, lighter, less recoil, trigger safety, adjustable sights.

"This is the magazine release, the slide release, the take-down pin when you want to clean it, the trigger safety." Danielle explained the function of each part as she spoke. Then she demonstrated how to hold it, index finger on the trigger, other fingers stretching out along the barrel.

It was smaller than Hannah had expected. Her hands closed around the small barrel, right index finger on the trigger, left hand also holding the gun, fingers touching as they wrapped around, arms extended as Danielle had done.

"It's good for close-up," Danielle said. "Small, but still can be deadly. Popular choice for home protection."

"It doesn't feel like I thought it would," Hannah said. "And it looks different from the ones on TV."

"On TV it can depend on what decade the show is set in. A lot of the TV guns look more round and silver. But almost all our guns are black."

"You can dry fire if you want," Danielle added. "Not good for a gun to do it a lot but won't hurt it for a few times."

"Dry fire?" Hannah asked, turning toward Danielle, gun in hand.

"Don't point at me," Danielle said abruptly, gesturing at Hannah to turn the gun away and back toward the wall. "Even unloaded, the most basic principle of gun safety is to *never* point at a person."

"Sorry," Hannah said, pointing the gun at the floor. "I wasn't thinking."

"You're thinking plenty, but this is a new experience with a lot of new rules. It takes a while for rules to become automatic and instinctive. Now," Danielle said, *"now* you can pull the trigger."

Hannah raised her arms, adjusted her hands so they cradled the gun. She pulled the trigger slowly, expecting a bang and kickback. But it was more a click than a bang. And the gun hardly moved.

"No real recoil with a dry fire," Danielle said. "Now let's try a Glock. The Glock 42 has .380 ACP."

Hannah was starting to lose track of all the acronyms.

"That means what?" she asked

"Automatic Colt Pistol," Danielle explained. "Developed by John Browning in 1908." When Hannah held it, it felt heavier than the 22, but smaller in size.

"Shoots bigger bullets. More recoil. No mechanical slide safety, just auto safety, so no extra step before firing. Least amount of parts. It's really streamlined."

"That's what I have," Stacy chimed in. "I like it. So, do you want to start with the 22? Or the Glock 42?"

"Whatever you say," Hannah answered.

Danielle looked at Stacy. Stacy shrugged her shoulders.

Danielle handed Stacy a gun along with a box of ammo.

"Let's go shoot," Stacy said.

They walked up a ramp to a steel door and pulled it open. It was a small vestibule.

"We don't open the door to the range until this door is fully closed," Stacy told Hannah when she reached to open the next door. "Protocol."

The *range* was a rectangle with five lanes, each twenty-five yards long. Diamond-plated steel dividers separated each lane. It was spotlessly clean, with a cement floor, wire shelving lining one wall for people's possessions. Each lane had a lever to control a paper target that could be set for a different number of feet away. There were cameras mounted so the staff could watch every lane, every person, from different angles.

Stacy opened her neon yellow bag and took out her Glock. She laid out the ammo and then carefully loaded each gun, demonstrating and explaining each step.

"I want you to watch me and then mirror how I hold the gun, my stance. You will not be pulling a trigger and the 22 has a safety that has to be released before you can. Just relax for now. Put on this eye and ear protection," Stacy added. "More protocol."

Stacy assumed the position, held out her Glock and fired. Hannah flinched at the loud noise, noting how Stacy seemed to absorb the recoil so that the gun did not jump. Stacy was aiming at a paper target she had set way down toward the end of the lane. She fired six more times. Each time, Hannah flinched, but never as much as the first time. Then Stacy pulled the lever and her target rolled back to her.

There were seven holes. Stacy had hit the target every time she fired, although not in the same core-marked center.

"Wow," Hannah said. "I guess you *can* shoot."

"Not great, but I'm adequate. I look like I'm better than I am when no one is here to show me up."

Stacy came behind Hannah in her lane and put her hands over Hannah's on the gun.

"Look down the barrel. Arms higher. Index finger on the trigger, the other fingers stretched along the barrel. Other hand also on the barrel, keeping it steady."

As Stacy watched Hannah hold the gun, she recalled the first time she'd ever held a gun. She'd been thirteen. She remembered the hard weight, cold and smooth to the touch. She remembered feeling grown-up. Being trusted to hold a gun, being taught to shoot, was a rite of passage.

Stacy had grown up with cousins who hunted and who had included her in some of their annual autumn camping and hunting trips. Her parents had required that she take gun safety classes before ever going out into the woods. She'd quickly realized that she didn't want to shoot deer, or quail, but she enjoyed waking up in a tent to the quiet of the forest, eating roasted corn around a fire at night while swapping family stories. And she'd liked shooting blanks at targets, usually empty bean cans.

Hannah and Stacy spent almost two hours at the range. By the time they left, Hannah was loading the pistol herself, had memorized some of the safety steps that Stacy kept reiterating, and was hitting a target most of the time. Of course, her target was not set at twenty-five yards at the end of the lane like Stacy's. It was much closer, five-to-ten yards, harder to miss. Pulling the lever, bringing the paper back to where she stood in the lane, counting the number of holes to see how many hits she'd made—it was a rush.

They drove the few blocks to *Smoked Creation* and snagged a window booth. Within five minutes they were sipping Blue Moons.

Stacy had a flashing thought that drinking beer with an underage freshman on her wing could get her fired. But if anyone was deserving of some slack it was Hannah. And it was not like she would rat her out.

"That was very *interesting*," Hannah told Stacy.

"*Interesting*? That's all you can come up with?"

"Yeah. You were right."

"I was?" Stacy asked. "Get specific. I love being right."

"It was the first time I didn't have room in my head to obsess about the rape. Or how I'm going to survive the university stuff. Or what my parents will say when they find out. I felt focused. And I did dump some anger in there."

"Ya think? Like when you aimed at a piece of paper dangling down the lane and yelled, 'Take this you mother-fucker-frat-boy-piece-of-shit?' before firing?"

"That would be one example," Hannah replied, sucking on the orange slice she pulled out of her Blue Moon.

The waitress arrived at their booth, laying down a platter of ribs, brisket, sweet potato fries, and slaw.

They stopped talking and focused on the food.

"Oh, damn, this is good. I'm starving," Hannah said, piling brisket on to a roll with her right hand while snagging a sweet potato fry with her left.

"For some reason, food tastes better after I shoot. But I don't know what the connection would be," Stacy said. "So, any epiphanies? What's your take-away from your first time?"

"I don't want to kill Logan Whiteman. But it was fun to pretend and shoot at the cut-outs," Hannah said, picking up a rib. She paused to gnaw, then spoke again, sauce dripping down her chin. "But I have to do *something*. I just don't know what."

Chapter 36
(November 3rd)

Grace and Katrina were in a window table at La Parrilla, making the most of Happy Hour. They'd started with ceviche and queso fundido, then split an order of tequila shrimp tacos. Their pitcher of margaritas was half empty.

Grace had a notebook open and, between bites, was intent on reading the contents to Kat, who knew enough not to protest. Plus, it was always easier to listen to Grace vent when consuming copious alcohol.

"Slut," Grace read out loud. "A woman who has many sexual partners. Adjectives are sluttish and slutty. Derivative unknown."

"And where are you getting this?" Kat asked, lazily picking at some shrimp that has escaped the taco.

"The Oxford American Dictionary and Thesaurus from 2009. Not up-to-date but close enough. These are words that have had a long shelf-life."

"Whore," Grace continued, looking down at the page. "A woman who has many sexual partners. Synonym is prostitute. Adjectives are whorish. Derived from Old English."

"Kind of redundant, don't ya think?" Kat commented.

"Nah. You can never have too many options for girl-slamming," Grace replied. "But boys get a different slant. Listen up."

Grace's voice adapted the melodious inflections of a radio announcer.

"Stud," she said. "A man who has many sexual partners or is considered sexually desirable." Grace bypassed the stallion part, although that too had a sexual connotation, albeit positive if not desirable, and ignored the "establishment where horses or other domesticated animals are kept for breeding."

"If you put it that way," Katrina observed, "the boys do get off easy."

"Cunt." Grace's voice grew louder. "1) a woman's genitals; 2) an unpleasant or stupid person."

The couple at the next table turned to stare.

"Twat," she continued, undaunted, "1) a woman's genitals; 2) a stupid or unpleasant person."

"More redundancy," Kat inserted.

"Prick." Grace bypassed the verb and went straight to the noun. "A man's penis, as well as 'A stupid or unpleasant man.' "

"Perhaps I'm incorrect, but 'prick' does not carry the same weight, the *gravitas* dare I say, as does 'cunt' or 'twat,' " said Katrina. "It lacks derogatory intensity."

"And prick has so many other meanings, which dilute the sexual connotation," Grace added in agreement. "Like, 'I pricked my finger.' Such an itty-bitty hurt. But twat and cunt are unambiguous. Also, prick is often used to describe a transient behavior rather than a permanent state of being. Like, 'Why is he acting like a prick?' which implies that there are many times when he is not acting like a prick. But, somehow, 'She's a slut' seems more intrinsic, an inescapable aspect of personality."

"Now," Grace continued, "there is a word that references men more often, has a pejorative connotation, but it lacks sexual specificity."

"And that would be?" Kat asked.

"Asshole," Grace replied, "as in 1) the anus, but also, 2) an irritating or contemptible person."

"Is it gender-neutral? Do girls call each other assholes? I don't remember doing that."

"You could be right but times change. Now here is one we never got to use *or* do," Grace said. "Hookup. It is both verb, as in 'to hook up,' and noun, referencing the person doing the verb, as in 'a hookup' or 'my hookup.' And do not be confusing this with a one-night stand, which implies a behavior different from a norm that would be other than one-night sexual engagements. They were practically a commitment compared to what the Oxford says: '2: a relationship initiated for a purpose, especially sex: *a date tomorrow night with my hookup from last week*.' "

"Oh my God," Katrina said. "Listen to that. We used to date *before* sex. Now even the Oxford has the hookup *preceding* the date?" Kat sighed. "This is so screwy."

"Screw," Grace said in a monotone. "Now that has a lot of

meanings, mostly having to do with small metal objects and assembling things. But scroll down to number 5 and you get to 'an act of having sex.' But then it is also 'to cheat or swindle someone, to extort or force, to make someone emotionally disturbed, to make something go wrong.' "

"That could cover it," Kat said. "How does screw differ from fuck?"

"Fuck is less complex, more just to 1) have sexual intercourse with someone, or, 2) damage or ruin something.' But 'Fuck-up' is also both verb and noun, as in to do something badly, to botch the job, or can describe someone who does all of the above, usually in a consistent manner. In the latter case, it often has nothing to do with sex, just incompetence."

Grace paused to stare at her notes and consider the myriad possibilities of their usage.

"There's a bunch more. Like skank. Do you think skank has any connection to skunk?"

"This is so not a girl-friendly vocabulary," Kat concluded.

Chapter 37
(November 6th)

Hannah and Stacy burrowed down in the front seat of a borrowed Toyota. They were parked down the street from the frat house. Stacy held a Nikon with a 30X zoom lens. Coffee, in tall, insulated mugs, rested between them in the console.

They were waiting for Logan Alexander Whiteman.

Every few minutes the door to the house opened and another boy would emerge, backpack slung over one shoulder, and start walking toward campus.

But, so far, no Whiteman.

*Well actually, all of them were **white men** but none were Logan,* thought Stacy, who had an affinity for those NPR games with word play.

They'd been positioned here for almost two hours and Hannah needed to pee. If Logan did not come out soon, they'd have to call it quits and return another day. It wasn't like they had an agenda or a deadline. They weren't even sure what they were going to do with the photos, but it would be *something*. There had to be some consequence for what he'd done.

But then Hannah saw him, walking across the front lawn, turning to yell something over his shoulder at another boy still standing on the front steps.

"That's him," Hannah said to Stacy.

Logan was walking down the street on the other side. In another minute he would pass the car and they would only have the back of his head.

Hannah's body flooded with anxiety. She had not seen Logan since the night of the rape. She did not want him to recognize her. She'd run stiff gel through her hair to make it spike and put on a pair of oversized sunglasses.

He looked thinner than she'd remembered. Hannah heard the click-click-click-click of Stacy's camera taking shots. Logan never even glanced in their direction.

"Got it," Stacy said. "A little zoom, a few cuts, and we'll have headshots. Good enough for Yik-Yak, that's for sure."

For Hannah, hearing from the police that the DA had declined to press charges had been difficult. She'd ended up talking with the woman cop again after her meeting with the District Attorney. Tsosie had patiently answered each of her questions.

It had been hard for Hannah to hear that the guy—she couldn't make herself say his name, Logan—had seemed genuinely surprised when the police told him the allegation. And even harder to hear about all the people who were willing to give statements and testify against her. On some level, she knew they were not *against* her, but their statements, their accounts, of how she'd talked to Logan for a long time, had been drinking, seemed to be flirting—which were all true—had nothing to do with what happened after, behind the closed door to his room.

It came down to *she said* versus *he said*.

Or, she realized, *she said* versus **they** said.

Hannah conceded that what the witnesses—the frat brothers and the girls there as well—reported seeing was accurate. They weren't lying. But what mattered was what they had *not* seen, what *no one* had seen.

The only two people who knew the truth of what had really happened behind that locked door were Logan and Hannah.

It had been just over eight weeks since the frat party. Hannah was behind in every class and her grades were going to be the worst she'd ever had if she couldn't pull herself together and focus. But, no matter how she tried, flashes of that night intruded. Not just the party, being raped, but every detail of what followed: the smell of the hospital, the doctor saying, *Now I am going to. . .* before every move, standing naked and exposed while a nurse took pictures of her body.

And she obsessed about how she'd answered the police when they questioned her, *Why didn't you tell people at the party what happened?...What stopped you from yelling for help as soon as he left the room and the door was unlocked?* She beat herself up for not having better answers. *I don't know. I just had to get out of there,* was true—but also insufficient.

I don't know, had been the answer to many of their questions.

Hannah woke up every night about 2 a.m., her teeth clenched, her arms held tight across her chest, her legs drawn up, and her head spinning out. How could she have been so stupid?

Stupid, stupid girl.

The first photo to be posted on Twitter was of Logan's back as he walked down the street. Stacy had captured how his left shoulder slouched under the weight of his backpack, how he walked. The brand of his backpack was visible. But no face.

Overlaying the photo were the words: *Do you know this guy? Pay attention girls.*

Two days later another photo, this time a side shot. If someone knew Logan well, they'd probably recognize him, but it wasn't a sure thing. The overlay text read: *Do you know this guy? Pay attention girlfriends.*

Two days after that, a profile, but more face*: Do you know this guy? Pay attention, girlfriends. He can be charming, but don't be deceived.*

By the third picture, there was buzz.

Why pay attention? What are you saying? some responded. *Just come out with it.* And, *Yeah, so what's up with him?* And, *Did he break your heart?* And, *Why are you directing the 'pay attention' to girls? Huh? Can't the boys take a look? He looks like he'd go bi.*

It was very hit-and-miss who saw it and who did not. It was there and then gone.

Chapter 38
(November 8th)

Grace sat at her kitchen counter staring at the computer. She'd just written and re-written the same sentence twenty times.

Write. Delete. Write. Delete.

She felt as if she would never, could never, find the right words.

Shelby's death had thrown Grace back into a maelstrom of emotions from over a decade earlier. She could not get Shelby's parents out of her head, even more so than Shelby. Their grief was so raw, their loss inescapable. So many hopes and dreams they would never experience, a future they would never share with their daughter.

Grace had not had any time, any goodbye, with Gil. Her husband had been there, fixing supper, listening to his favorite music, playing it loud, always so loud—and then he was gone. And her satisfying, safe, comfortable life had imploded.

But it was not Gil she was thinking of now. Or Molly. She and Molly had weathered some bad years, but now they depended on each other in ways many mothers and daughters never would. They had each other's back.

Grace was thinking of her other child, her oldest, her son. Alex was 33 now, a man. And the loss of that relationship, her inability to at least try to repair what was broken, was her deepest shame. It was a shame that went to her bones. And yet, shame had not propelled her into action. What resulted was more paralysis. She was an emotional quadriplegic. Nothing felt like it had a chance in hell of making a difference. And so, she did nothing. Or had done nothing.

Now she questioned how it was possible that she'd let him go. How had *years* past?

At the start, she'd been so terrifically hurt, so betrayed. She'd fixated on how it was *his* responsibility to come to her. To apologize to *her*. To beg *her* forgiveness.

But he had not. Not in the months after Gil died. Not in the years that followed. Grace had run away to Alaska, and Alex had run away as well, to the other end of the world. He'd finished college and taken jobs teaching English overseas. He went to Korea, Thailand, Chile, Panama. She did not know this from Alex but through Molly. Grace did not press for details.

She remembered the day—just two years ago—when Molly had explained to her what it had been like for Alex, and for Molly herself, after their father's death. How they had felt abandoned and how the choices that she'd made to save her own sanity had left them broken.

"Mom," Molly had said, "this is not just about you. Alex adored Dad, and he was in shock. You know how he can be rigid in his thinking, how if something isn't logical, then it can't be true. That was a part of his personality long before Dad was killed. Do you remember the paper he wrote in eighth grade, *Transubstantiation vs. Transignification* on why the host at Mass was not God and why we were all nuts to believe that it was? And that was for a religion class in a Catholic school. Not like he had the common sense to see that as a dumb move."

Grace had remembered—Alex's enduring insistence on proof. He didn't care if he made people upset. The boy required evidence. And, after his father's death, the *evidence* had not been with Grace.

"And remember how important traditions were to him? Like Christmas wasn't Christmas without checking off *every* item on his long list of essentials? When we put up the tree? What was on the menu? Did we ever have Thanksgiving without Alex's creamed onions? Hah, a travesty! The holidays were his bookmarks through the year. He lived from one to the other. And think about how he was with playing bocce. Was that just a game to him?"

Alex and bocce had been, at first, amusing. But his rigidity could get tedious if not bossy: the insistence on measuring every throw to the quarter inch, on mowing the grass so that every square foot was even.

"Alex lost Daddy, and then he lost you. Then we both lost everything: our home, our rooms, Thanksgiving and Christmas and Easter and even the stupid 4th of July. We lost having a place to bring our friends. We lost knowing that no matter what happened, we could always go home. *Everything* that made us feel secure. In less than a year, our father was dead, our mother disappeared, and our home was sold. Our shit was in some storage unit. When you went away, we had no *place* to go to. No *home*. Do you have any idea what that was like?"

Molly's words were like bullets, ripping into Grace. She had known, yet not known. She'd been so wounded herself back then that she had not been able to see how her actions wounded the people she loved.

Grace had apologized to Molly, over and over, sobbing. It was inexcusable. She did not try to justify abandoning her children. And, yet, for many years, she had justified it, at least to herself: they were in college, they had lots of friends, they seemed independent, she supported them financially, she paid for year-round apartments, they graduated without loans or debt, they could always go to Katrina's for a holiday, they could come visit her.

But a one-bedroom cabin in Homer, Alaska, was never their *home*.

After Molly had laid it all out, Grace had resolved to do something. She would find the right words. She just needed time.

But resolutions could not combat the fear that no matter what she did, this was unfixable. Then denial, ever familiar, kicked in. *Pretend like everything is okay and you can forget almost anything,* Grace thought. *Almost.*

But seeing Shelby's parents, so consumed with their grief, had brought it all back. Their child was dead. Her son was alive. Estranged, yes, but not dead. Although, she recognized, she might be dead to him. She felt as if she had been dead to him for these many years or he would have come to her, reached out to her.

She believed that, in Alex's heart of hearts, he wished she had died instead of his father.

And it was this cycle of thinking that left her doing nothing. Feeling the familiar hopelessness and then giving up. This was the point when she would put down her pen, or close the laptop, and go make a drink.

Later, she'd told herself a hundred times. *Tomorrow. I cannot do this today.*

But this particular *today* was, in some inexplicable way, different.

Alex is not dead, she thought. *I am not dead. Gil died, and he'd be pissed as hell at the mess we've made of our family. If there is some after-life, he is royally pissed, although maybe not totally, given what Molly and I are doing together.*

There are no right or perfect words, Grace thought.

"I am sorry. Very, very sorry," she wrote. "I can't make up for the years we have lost, or for the pain. I want to get to know you, who you have become. I will do this however works best for you."

Grace looked at what she'd written. She started to press *delete* but then pressed *save*. When the computer asked for a file name, she typed in *Hopeless*. Then she closed the laptop, stood up, and walked to the refrigerator. She kept gin in the freezer. If ever there was a time for a stiff martini it was now.

Alex McDonald was, at that very same moment, sitting on the stone patio in front of his home in Gorgona, Panama. He was sipping a can of Balboa, a locally brewed beer that was moderately acceptable if ice-cold but made him miss the heftier, flavorful beers of the microbreweries of Kansas.

Alex especially enjoyed this time of day, later afternoon but before the sun got so low in the sky that the almost-invisible chitras came out to bite. He would sit on the patio and watch children playing soccer in the street, or, as they called it, *futball*. Sometimes he'd read a newspaper or a book, but he usually preferred to just sit and feel the sun on his face, the soft breeze off the Pacific. He relished that he could sit on a plastic Adirondack chair in the shade of a coconut palm, just a few minutes' walk to the Pacific Ocean, and be home.

At about 4:45 he might catch the first glimpse of Graciela, his wife, as she turned the corner from the main street and walked up their lane. She would almost always have a small shopping bag in each hand, as she stopped each day at the market for some fresh food for their dinner and the bakery for some hojaldras for breakfast or crusty rolls to have with supper.

"Quieres pollo para la cena? O mariscos? Lo que quieras, mi amor," she would ask each morning before she left for work.

"Lo que tu piense que se ve sabroso es bueno," he would reply.

Alex felt that he had not been at peace, not complete, until he met Graciela. After graduating from the university in Austin, he'd been adrift, in transit, moving from country to country, signing on for one-year contracts to teach English to adults or children, sometimes re-upping for a second year, but never staying longer than that. With each move he would pack two giant nylon duffle bags with clothing and bedding, stuff his one sturdy suitcase with books and music, and leave the rest behind.

Alex felt he had learned the hard way not to get too attached to *things*.

It was during his sixth week in Panama that he'd met Graciela. He was standing in front of a wall of posters advertising concerts and lectures trying to decide what appealed. He just knew he could not stay in his small apartment alone for another Friday night.

"Prueba este," she'd said pointing to a poster. "Te hara querer bailar."

He'd gone to what she'd recommended, a local band with a reggae-Caribbean beat that did, actually, make him feel like standing up and moving his Anglo, midwestern, stiff white ass. The music loosened the tension in his neck, made him close his eyes and sway, shoulders lifting almost invisibly to the beat.

He did not know until much later that Graciela had been watching him. Graciela felt that she could judge a person's true character by how they responded to music when they thought they were alone. She accurately judged Alex as inhibited, a little intimidated by the novelty of his surroundings, but genuinely involved in the music. She watched as his body softened and small smiles flickered across his face, more so when his eyes were closed. She did not observe any macho-need to be noticed, did not see his eyes roaming, did not see him hit on women.

Graciela had positioned herself by the exit so Alex would have to walk right past her. She saw his face brighten when he saw her. He came right over and stood in front of her, making the rest of the exiting crowd go around him.

"Hola," he said. "Me alegra verte. Quieres tomar algo?"

"First you have to tell me your name," Graciela had replied in English. "And where you are from."

His face had reddened at her fluent use of English.

"I'm Alex and I'm from Kansas, in the middle of the United States."

"I know where Kansas is. I studied in Illinois. I am Graciela."

They talked that evening in a café for three hours, and then, a few days later, for almost six hours. By then Alex knew that he wanted to spend the rest of his life with her if she would let him.

It took a year for her family to understand that the lanky, tall American was serious about Graciela and that she was equally serious about him. Her parents and brothers were courteous but kept a distance. They did not see an American staying forever in Panama and they did not want to lose their beloved, only daughter to a gringo who could take her away. Falling in love was all well and good but it was not enough to build a life on.

Graciela and Alex did not discuss their relationship with her family, but Alex started showing up every weekend at their home. He would silently join in whatever they were doing, whether repairing a porch or digging in the garden. He always brought something—a bag of avocados, tomatoes, beer, a bouquet of flowers. He never gave these things to Graciela but handed them directly to her mother, Ines. The beer he gave to her father, Eduardo.

Her parents would, with a slightly formal Panamanian courtesy, ask him to stay for dinner, and he always accepted. When Christmas and then Easter came, Alex was waiting outside the church, dressed in a tie, when they arrived for midnight Mass.

In Panama, there were traditions for everything, certain foods for certain holidays: tamales, arroz con pollo, bollas, empanadas.

All of it was new to him.

Alex absorbed every facet of Panamanian culture, its holidays, traditions, and rituals. With each passing month, he felt more at home, and the memories and traditions of his own childhood faded.

At the same time, the emotional pain, the sense of abandonment that he'd felt for so long, abated. He adopted Graciela's family as his own.

When his father had died, Alex had been a junior at the University of Texas in Austin. He could still remember the moment, the phone call from Katrina, his mother's best friend, telling him that he needed to come home, that his father was dead. Woody Allen had been on the television screen when he'd turned down the sound to answer the phone. He remembered watching the screen, like a silent movie, as words that made no sense came at him through the telephone.

What followed was worse than the death. Not the funeral, which was a good funeral as far as funerals went. No, it was what came later, his mother's indictment and trial. The evidence he'd believed because it was so damning. There had been no logical explanation for the DNA that the prosecution used to make a case. Even his mother's attorney had no explanation.

Alex believed in logic. And DNA trumped love.

He had not returned home for her trial. He'd believed that she'd lied to him, that his parents had lied to him for years about their relationship. That everything had been a phony front.

And, with that, every grievance, the normal grievances of all children, had become significant. Every maternal flaw was magnified, while the good became insignificant.

And Alex had always felt a little out of step with his family. At the dinner table they would debate, his mother and sister waving their arms and interrupting each other over politics, movies, books, anything. But he was more reflective, holding back, waiting to be asked for his opinion. He wanted them to remember details of his life and inquire: "Hey, Alex, how did that paper on early immigration work out?" He waited for them to show that they listened to what he said. Not just, "How's it going?"

It had felt like his mother and father and sister had this triangle of connection and he was not included.

The spring of his junior year of high school, he and Gil had taken a road trip to check out colleges, visiting four colleges in four states in ten days. Something about driving made talking easier for Alex, maybe being side-by-side and not face-to-face. His mother had not come, so he'd been in the front seat, not cut off in the back seat while his parents talked to each other. On that trip, Alex and his father had connected in a different way, talking about music, books, politics, and ideas. Gil had shared memories of his own childhood, his own adolescent struggles, and disappointments in his own life.

After Alex went to college, ending up at U.T. in Austin, he and his father had begun taking long drives, lazy day-trips, every time he was home on break. They could go for hours without speaking, just listening to NPR or music. But when they did talk, Alex felt heard. He'd talked about what he wanted from his life, his anxieties that he would not measure up. His father had listened, without any agenda, without the incessant advice that his mother could not seem to stop herself from giving.

When his father died, Alex had become unmoored. He'd not had time to absorb the shock before his mother was indicted. He'd felt he owed it to his father to take a stand for truth.

And then everything became hopelessly twisted.

Alex believed in facts, in proof, in evidence. Words were just words. DNA was science.

It would have been different if his mother had stayed put and kept their home intact. But she didn't. She'd put their *home* on the market. She'd *sold* their family *home* to strangers, with no discussion. She'd *abandoned* him.

There was no warning, not even a farewell dinner. He remembered returning home to Kaw Valley, walking alone through the home he'd grown up in, a sale sign in the front yard covered by a big SOLD sticker, and making a pile by the front door of things he wanted.

Take anything you want, his mother had written. *I put some things in storage, but I don't want the rest. Whatever you don't want will get sold.*

What Alex heard was not just, *I don't want any of it,* but, *I don't want you,* or *I don't care enough to be there to help you do this.*

Alex had wanted all of it, every dish and end table, every holiday ornament, every damn lamp. But he had no place to put it. He had no five-bedroom house, nothing big enough. He took whatever he could fit in his car. Driving off, he'd felt a sense of loss so deep he thought he might faint.

For a while, he and Molly had not even known where Grace was. She left with no destination, no address. She would call, but often it was just voice messages—"I'm in Utah" "South Dakota" "Wyoming." When they finally did get an address—a P.O. box in Homer, Alaska—Alex had had to look at a map to locate it.

A dot on the end of a peninsula.

From Austin, Texas, it was the end of the world.

Then everything got mangled up in his head: 1) his mother was innocent of what Alex had believed she'd done; 2) the man who'd killed his father had done so to punish his mother; 3) his mother was thus complicit is his father's murder; 4) Grace had to have known that selling their family home and abruptly leaving would deeply hurt her son. *She had to.* And she did it anyway.

The shooter had killed his father, but his mother had killed their family.

His sister had told him that he needed to apologize, that his mother was devastated that he hadn't believed her.

They each carried in their guts a hard knot of betrayal.

After his mother was—whatever the word was—*vindicated?*

Released? Alex had not gone home but stayed in Austin for the summer. He got a job and took a few classes.

In his head, he needed time to process all that had happened. He had no idea how, but he'd figure it out. Then, maybe over Thanksgiving or Christmas, when they had the holidays to focus on, he and his mother would deal with it. Somehow.

But there was no Thanksgiving, no Christmas. There was never another family holiday. Alex was left with a bitterness that choked down whatever apology might have been forthcoming. He worked over Thanksgiving, went to a friend's home in Florida at Christmas. He sent cards to his mother and sister, with generic, impersonal notes that could have been to distant relatives. He finished his degree but ignored the graduation festivities. He looked for work that could take him far away, and stumbled on ESL, teaching English as a Second Language, overseas. His specific degree didn't matter as long as he completed an online training. It took him just three weeks and he left for a teaching assignment in Korea five weeks after that.

He'd seen his mother once. It was after Max had been born, and he'd returned to Kansas to meet his new nephew. Grace had also flown down, and they had overlapped by two nights and one day. Grace was staying in a hotel. The focus had been on Molly and the new baby, and Alex had kept himself busy by running errands for Jeff, Max's dad, who seemed befuddled by the responsibility of grocery shopping and other elementary tasks. Grace and Alex had been polite, but distant, and not spoken of anything that mattered.

"Tell me about Thailand," she'd asked.

"I like it. It has better beaches and food than Kansas," he'd replied. Then he stood, saying he needed to make a run to the hardware store. He never asked her about Alaska.

The divide had become an abyss, enabled by a shared genetic stubbornness.

But Graciela, and his life in Panama, had begun to thaw the coldness in Alex's heart. While he did not think of his mother very often, when he did, it was not with the same intensity.

Today he was not thinking of her at all.

Tonight, a Wednesday in November, would be like any other night. Graciela would drive home with a friend from the university in the city where she taught cello. She would greet him with a smile and a kiss.

He would bring her cold tea flavored with mango slices and mint. They would sit on the patio and talk about their days. Then they would go inside and, together, cook their supper. Alex would stand at the counter slicing tomatoes and avocados, then papaya or mango or watermelon, as Graciella browned chicken or fish or a small steak on the stove. They would re-heat some of the beans and rice they cooked every Sunday for use during the week.

After dinner, they would sit in their small living room, with music playing in the background, and grade papers or prepare their lessons for the next day—Graciela for her university students, Alex for the high school students to whom he taught English. Often, before going to bed, they would walk down to the beach, leave their sandals, and walk along the edge of the sea, froth bubbling up over their ankles, the white caps of the waves lit by the moon and stars.

Alex had never been so satisfied, so content. When he had formally come to Graciela's father and asked for his daughter's hand in marriage, Eduardo had said, "Si, eres un hijo para me." Alex had felt absolution.

Graciela's family had not understood why no one from his family had come to the small wedding, but they had not questioned his paltry excuses. Alex did not tell them that he had not invited anyone, not even his sister. He wrote Molly months later that he was married. He knew she'd been hurt, and he apologized. But he could not fully explain, even to his beloved Graciella, why he did not regret that decision.

Chapter 39
(November 9th)

Hannah and Grace were in the office. It was one of those sessions that seemed to go in circles, with no movement forward.

"I cannot fathom how frustrating it is for you to have the District Attorney come down with insufficient evidence," Grace said. "It's hard to imagine what more *evidence* they would need."

"They want lots of blood," Hannah said, her voice flat. "Bruises and black eyes and broken bones. Which I would have been happy to provide had I not been pinned down on the bed, unable to fight back enough to get them their proof. I wasn't thinking, *Gee, I better figure out how to make this look like rape for a prosecutor.* I was just trying to get enough air. I did resist, but then it felt hopeless and I just wanted it to be over."

"Hannah, you don't have to justify anything, not to anyone."

"Those are pretty words, but so not true. Yeah, I physically survived being raped, but what happened afterwards? It's been worse. It isn't a *good enough* rape. Not enough for the legal system, not enough for the university. I get that the courts need to have enough evidence to convince a jury, and what used to be hard evidence just doesn't matter anymore. But my *school*? The one I've cheered for and wanted to go to since I was a little kid? The university my dad and mom both graduated from? How could *they* not believe me?"

"It isn't a matter of believe or not believe, it's due process," Grace replied. "They can't just expel any student who is accused of something. They need—although not to the threshold of a criminal case—to have proof as well."

"***Proof*** that he pushed his fucking penis inside me? They got their proof. Look, I went to the hospital and police. I answered all their questions, which seemed to be mostly about *my* behavior. But it means *nothing*. The hospital collected semen, pubic hairs, DNA, but they don't matter. Because Logan Whiteman used the magic words: *consensual* and *hookup*. Who in their right mind would subject themselves to being treated like this if it were just a hookup? Maybe someone who is already messed up in their head, but that's not me."

"Hannah, it doesn't. . ." Grace started to speak, more empty words, but Hannah cut her off.

"I can't argue with what people saw. Yes, I was flirting with him. I thought he was cute, an upperclassman. I was flattered that he seemed interested in little freshman me. I trusted that this nice boy was offering what he told me—a room to rest for a while because I felt dizzy. Well, you can be sure I won't make that mistake again."

Hannah's voice escalated as she spoke.

"Here it is: *I wanted a date*. That's what makes this so crazy. I felt attracted to the guy and wanted to *date* him. Not to screw him in the middle of a party. I wanted him to like me and ask me out." Hannah paused to breathe. "How pathetic is that?" she asked. But it was not posed as a question. It was a judgment, flat and undeniable.

"No, Hannah. Not pathetic. There is nothing that you did that makes you culpable. Do you understand that?"

"Yeah, sure, great. But how can I believe it when so many people that I don't even know judge me. It's all over social media—Twitter and Yik-Yak and Facebook—how Logan has been *exonerated* from the terrible *false accusations*. He is *innocent*. And so, what does that make me? **Guilty**. Because you get to be the victim *or* the perpetrator. And according to everyone, he is the victim and I'm—well, I made the whole thing up out of some desperate, sick need for revenge or attention. That's what they're saying."

Grace felt her gut clench, a physiological response to what Hannah described. Yes, she did know. And it was awful beyond words. To be screaming inside, *I'm the victim here*, at the same time you're being publically judged and humiliated. Convicted without due process.

"It is very, very hard to believe your own truth when so many are tearing you down," Grace replied. "But you need to hold onto that truth. You *know* what happened."

"But knowing doesn't fix it. I'm not the same girl who went to that party. I can never, no matter how much I *know* what happened, be that girl again. Because it did happen."

Before Grace could form a response, Hannah stood up.

"I can't do this right now. I can't keep talking about it, like I'm supposed to talk myself into being okay with being raped and then being crucified by people I don't even know. *Why are we even talking? How does this help?"*

"Hannah, let's pull back and try to. . ."

But Hannah swept her hand through the air, as if brushing away any remaining words as she walked out the office door.

"It isn't your fault," she said over her shoulder. "I just can't do this now. I'll call you."

Chapter 40
(November 10th)

The pictures of Logan began appearing almost daily on assorted disappearing websites. The back shots and profiles were replaced by what was clearly Logan. Logan eating lunch in the cafeteria; Logan entering a classroom; Logan having a beer at the Nook; Logan with some frat brothers throwing a football.

And always the brief inscriptions—*Yeah, he looks so sweet. Like you can trust him. But should you?. . . What is it about certain white boys that they look so harmless?. . . Watch out, girlfriend, you may be 'asking for it' and not even know you did.*

Logan only saw them, or some of them, after his friends did. They sent him screen shots with questions, *Hey, what is this shit about?*

A girl he knew sent him three different shots. *You're getting quite the buzz. Do you want buzz?* she asked. *Is this about you being accused? I thought that was all dropped.*

No, Logan did *not* want buzz. He wanted to return to being anonymous. He wanted this to all go away. Why were they harassing him? The allegations had been investigated by the police and then the university. He'd been exonerated.

In a screen shot forwarded today, he was leaning up against a tree. He was wearing J. Crew khakis, a Ralph Lauren polo, Sperry Topsiders. A pair of Ray Bans perched on his head. There was a caption below: *A boy dressed for success, but success at what endeavor? Stay tuned. . .*

The shot looked posed, as if he'd been following a photographer's directions for how to tilt his head for the best light, for the camera to find the perfect angle, like a damn GQ magazine ad. But when could it have been taken? He went back through the week, his schedule, what he wore each day, to nail it down.

Wednesday. His classes had been over for the day. The sun had been shining. The leaves on all the trees on the boulevard had turned in a last hurrah of red and gold and bronze. He'd stopped to just feel the breeze. For a moment, he'd felt calm. Almost relaxed.

And someone had snapped this photo. He'd just stopped for a moment.

I'm being stalked, he thought.

And he felt a chill of fear course through him.

Chapter 41
(November 11th)

Max was sitting on the floor in a back corner of the Dusty Bookshelf. It was his favorite used bookstore, with a secluded area just for children's books. There were pillows on the carpeted floor for kids to curl up with a book. The walls were lined, floor to ceiling, with bookcases.

Max was so engrossed that he did not look up as the three boys quietly entered. He liked to face the wall, leaning on the pillow with his back to the open doorway. That way, he had his own private space.

"Hey, pansy, what 'ya doin'?" the voice whispered from behind his head. "Looking at pictures?"

Max flinched at the sound of the voice but did not move. He did not even turn around. He just froze. He knew this voice, knew who the boys would be. His mother had told him, *Ignore them and they will go away.* So, he was doing that. He would pretend that they were not there. That was ignoring them. She'd told him that then they would go away.

But they didn't.

"What's the matter, pansy, can't hear? We know you're dumb as shit, but now your ears don't work either?"

As the voice spoke into his left ear, a hand came around his head from the right and pulled the book out of his hand. The page he had been reading, which he had been holding, tore. The book was gone but he had the torn page in his hand.

This was bad. You weren't allowed to hurt the books. Even when you owned books, it was never okay, ever, to tear them or hurt them. Books were special.

Max turned abruptly to face them. He felt the sound starting in his belly. As it erupted, a howl, two of the boys looked startled. But the one boy, the one who had talked into his ear, smiled. Like he knew it was coming. Like—*but how could that be possible*—he'd planned it.

That boy, Roger, put out his arm and swept it along one of the bookshelves, causing all the books to fall to the floor. Then he did the same thing to another shelf. There must have been forty books falling, covering the floor, jumbled one on top of another. Max knew how many because he had counted how many books each shelf contained. He had done this years ago, when his mother had first brought him into the Dusty Bookshelf. The number varied based on how thick the books were, but it was always between thirty-five and fifty. And these were shelves where the numbers were usually about thirty-seven to forty-three.

Max was bellowing, "Go away, go away, go away," from where he still sat on the floor, now half-buried by books, when the fluffy-haired woman from the front counter came running in.

"What's going on?" she demanded.

"He just went off, ma'am," Roger replied. "I don't think he wanted to share the room with other kids. Then he grabbed those books off the shelves. And I think he ripped a page out of the book he was reading."

Roger pointed at Max's fist, which now clenched the torn page. Max had his eyes shut, the bellowing less loud, but repeating, "Go away, go away, go away."

When Max opened his eyes, Roger's face had changed. It didn't even look like Roger. His eyes were bigger and round. Like someone on TV trying to look surprised.

"You need to be quiet right now," the young woman said to Max. "*Q-u-i-e-t!*"

And Max, although he usually could not hear when having a meltdown, did seem to hear her. He did not stop but his voice lowered to a sort of chant, "Go a-*way*. Go a-*way*. Go a-*way*."

"Would you boys please step out to the main part of the store?" she asked.

"Yes, ma'am," Roger said. "Whatever you say, ma'am."

The young woman turned to Max. "You need to put every book back on the shelf, in alphabetical order. This is unacceptable behavior. You will be paying for the book you destroyed. And I need to talk to your parent because you cannot stay here alone again."

Max stared at her. Her words did not make sense. *He* had not taken the books down. *He* had not torn the book he had been enjoying reading. But, mostly, he did not understand. He was *always* welcome at the Dusty Bookshelf. It was one of his favorite places in the world. His mom would leave him there to read while she did some errands downtown. Then she came back and they'd sit together and he'd tell her about the books he'd read. And they always left with a new book. He had his own account.

He did not want this fluffy-haired woman. He wanted the manager-one, with kind eyes and a happy face, who smiled at him and asked which new book he'd discovered that day. She told him about the books she'd loved the most when she was his age. She saved special books that she thought he would like.

And Max wanted his mother.

Max started to moan and rock. Back-and-forth. Rock-and-moan.

When his mother strolled in about ten minutes later, not much had changed. The fluffy-haired woman told her what Max had done. His mother tried to ask questions: "Did something happen? Can you think of what might have set it off? Did you see anything yourself?"

"Three other children verified what he did," the woman insisted.

His mother asked to speak with them, but the three boys were long gone. They'd disappeared seconds after Roger had told his story.

"No, I did not get their names," she replied, impatient with the question. "They were just children."

"You can't leave him here alone again," she continued. "He cannot be trusted and is too disruptive."

Molly sat down on the floor and rocked with Max until he stopped moaning. Then they put all the books back on the shelves in alphabetical order. She gave the blonde woman $10 to cover the book that had been torn. She left a note asking the manager to please call her at home.

Molly did not ask Max questions she knew he would not be able to answer. Maybe later.

Chapter 42
(November 13th)

Grace had the four names and addresses. She wanted to visually check out all of them although Lisa had conditionally eliminated two. A morning with no clients scheduled was adequate for a little research. And, since she was awake at 5 a.m., she might as well do *something* productive.

She decided to drive past each of the residences listed on the cards. The first was a small box of a house with a chain-link fenced front yard and baby-sized play equipment strewn around. She swore they had the same Little Tykes plastic climber and mini-slide she'd had for her son, the one he'd gone up and down at least 20,000 times while she sat on a lawn chair and clapped. She looked over the detailed card Lisa had provided, matched the name to the mailbox, and moved it to the bottom of the short pile.

The next address was in an apartment complex near campus. She found the boy's name on a mailbox, #408. This was the recently out-of-the-high-school-closet-boy. The apartment was a fourth-floor walk-up. Shelby had not mentioned stairs, and certainly not four flights of stairs. It was a detail that Grace thought would have been included.

Possibility number three was about a ten-minute drive and turned out to be a run-down ranch on the east side. By this time, the sky was growing lighter, pink lines framing the horizon as the sun began to rise. Grace pulled up next to the large mailbox at the end of the driveway, close enough to see four names in block print on white paper in a sealed baggie taped to the mailbox. One was the name on her card. But, from what Grace remembered, it had sounded like the guy lived alone. So, unless he'd borrowed a friend's place for the night, a house with roommates was not consistent with Shelby's description.

The fourth address was for a triplex, just four blocks from downtown, each compact unit with a separate entrance, each entrance facing a different direction. Gauging how far it was from downtown,

Grace felt that this could be the place that Shelby had described.

She was just about to inch the car forward, to slide up close to the mailboxes to compare names, when a young man came around from a unit that faced away from the street. He was slim, smooth faced, wearing khaki slacks and a navy sweater. It was an LL Bean catalog look, casual but thoughtful.

He's good looking, Grace thought. Shelby would have found him attractive.

He got into a silver Kia that was parked at the curb. Smoke came out the exhaust as he warmed up the engine. Grace closed her eyes and slumped down a bit as the Kia drove past, music drifting out from inside the car. She did a quick memory game with the license plate, writing it down as soon as the car turned the corner.

After he was gone, Grace edged closer. She had to get out of the car to check which apartment matched which mailbox. The unit that the young man had come from was #2. The name on the #2 mailbox was Hunter Payne.

The fourth name on Lisa's list was Hunter Payne.

Now they were *maybe* getting somewhere. Grace felt suddenly voracious for a breakfast at The Roost. She visualized eggs over-easy, crisp bacon, dill potatoes, rye toast, and a latte topped with foam and whipped cream.

"Yes," she said out loud as she turned the car key. "Our number four could be it."

Chapter 43
(November 14th)

"*Something is going on,*" Molly said to Grace. "Max is pulling into himself, not sharing as much. He doesn't want to go to school. Not that he has ever been wildly enthusiastic, but he's never been so stubborn about it."

"What happened with the counselor and teacher and the kids who were picking on him?"

"It felt like they were more concerned about what he wrote, which was fantasy. . ."

"Or wishful thinking," interrupted Grace.

"Yeah, sure, or wishful thinking. But they were more worried about what Max wrote than what other kids might be doing to him to make him need to write it."

"Have you talked to him about whether the bullying is still going on?"

"I tried, but he starts to talk and then repeats the same phrases over and over, like, 'They sneak up on me' and, 'They hurt books' and, 'They do bad things.' "

"Which they probably do. What's the 'hurt books' one about?"

"I forgot to tell you. You know how he stays in the kid room at the Dusty Bookshelf when I'm running errands downtown? And he just sits there and reads?"

"You've done that for years. Never been a problem. The manager has always been sweet with Max."

"The manager *understands* Max, which is what matters. She lets him use the employee bathroom if he says, 'May I please use your bathroom?' They have conversations about their favorite books. She listens to him."

"So what happened?"

"So, the other day the manager wasn't there. Some new younger clerk was running the store. I didn't want to leave all these instructions, so I just made sure he peed before I left, and I was back in thirty minutes. But, when I returned, Max was rocking and moaning, and the clerk was saying he cannot be left alone at the store as he was too disruptive. She said he'd knocked two shelves of books from a bookcase to the floor and tore a page out of a book. . ."

"Whoa. No way. Max respects books. Not so much anything else, but definitely books."

"I would agree, except that he had a torn page clenched in his fist and two shelves of books were all over the rug. Not like I had a lot of room to argue."

"Why would he do such a thing?"

"The clerk said she didn't see it, just heard noise. But three other boys told her that Max did not want to share the space and pulled the books down and tore the book."

"Did you talk to them, ask them what had happened before that?"

"No, by the time I got there they'd left."

"How convenient," Grace sarcastically noted.

"Exactly. Meanwhile Max is moaning and rocking, gripping a torn page and surrounded by books strewn all over the floor and two empty shelves"

"There's got to be an explanation. Do you think it's the same boys?"

"It would be a big coincidence for two separate groups of kids to be harassing him. And he lumps them together when he tries to talk about them. I left a voice mail for the manager once we got home," Molly added. "I expect she heard a florid accounting of the incident. She's out of town until tomorrow."

"But she knows Max. She knows how he feels about books."

"Which is what we have going for us. For years, Max has sat there quietly—never damaged anything—like the invisible kid. Now he explodes? Empties shelves?"

"Molly, you know Max can lash out if he feels frustrated or attacked."

"Yeah, and not knowing what happened makes me worry more."

"This may not be the time to bring this up, or it may be the perfect time. Remember when I mentioned trying some sort of *intervention* with his class, trying to explain what it's like inside Max's head?"

"Sure I remember. But I'm still trying to decide if it would help

Max or make him more of an outsider. He's already the weirdest kid in the class."

"My vote is to risk it. Not like he's going to be more included the way things are going."

"You're probably right," Molly said with a deep sigh. "I just wish I *knew* what was the right thing to do instead of groping my way through a fog."

Three days later, having consulted with both teacher and counselor, Grace stood in front of a classroom of fourth graders. Max was not there. Molly and Grace had debated having him stay or not and decided it would be better all-around if the other kids could talk more freely. They'd also decided that Grace would present as she was not *the mom.*

It felt like walking a tightrope. They wanted the kids to better understand Max without making him out to be so different that they would not want to be his friend. So it was not okay to pick on him but okay to play with him.

Grace started with a model of the human brain she'd borrowed from Patsy, who used it to teach First Aid.

"Everybody has a brain with the same parts, but in some brains the parts do not talk to each other as well," she said. "It's like there's a noise or fog that blocks the different parts of the brain from discussing what's going on and what to do."

She asked the kids what it was like at home if the TV was blaring in one room and someone was asking a question from another room but you couldn't hear the question specifically but knew someone was talking, and you didn't want to get up and go to the other room and try and figure out who had been talking and what they wanted, so you just stayed put, and then someone was yelling at you because you weren't paying attention, and the TV was still really loud, and you just wanted to focus but you couldn't no matter how hard you tried. . ."

By the time Grace finished, the kids were all providing graphic examples of what it was like in their homes when all of that was going on, maybe a little more graphic than some parents would have wanted. And they did seem to *get it* when Grace played a CD of someone teaching a lesson, and then asked a kid in the back row to talk in a fast voice as she then kept trying to give directions. The kids got pretty frustrated and testy when everyone was talking over each other.

Then Grace turned off the CD. It took the kids a while to realize that and to settle down. And then Grace asked in a very quiet voice, almost a whisper, about the lesson that had been playing. And nobody knew. They couldn't remember much of anything.

"Well," Grace said, "that's kind of what it can be like inside Max's head. Not all the time but some of the time. All the parts trying to talk at once, and not being able to figure out which is important, or make the other ones be quiet. So it is extra hard to track what is being said and hear questions. It doesn't mean that Max is not as smart as any of you, just that his brain needs to work extra to sort things out. Mostly, what would help Max is having friends who will accept him as a good kid who talks a little differently, friends who won't let other kids be mean or bully him."

Grace had not intended to be quite so specific in the final few sentences. But when it came to it, she looked around the room and made a decision. There were a few kids in this room that were bullying Max and there were other kids who needed to see that for what it was and take a stand. And it was up to the adults to teach them how, and not pretend it wasn't happening with the *boys will be boys* bullshit.

When Grace asked the children what questions they had, she was surprised at how open and curious they were. Molly moved from the back of the room to the front and, together, they answered every one, until it was time to pass around the gluten-free cupcakes.

Chapter 44
(November 15th)

Between Molly worrying about Max and their classroom intervention, Grace had coffee with Lisa.

"Hunter, huh?" The *huh* got kind of swallowed as Lisa said it through a mouthful of cranberry scone. "Interesting choice of name."

"Now that you point it out, I have to agree. Had not made that connection," replied Grace. She, too, was talking through a mouthful, but of an almond-cream cheese pastry. They were in a booth at Wheatfields Bakery.

"So, what we have is a name," said Lisa. "And an address. But *nothing* that links Hunter to Shelby other than he was one of the guys on a group project in one of her classes last spring."

"When you put it like that it doesn't sound very solid."

"Well, that depends. If Shelby was telling the truth, then there are good odds that Hunter is the guy. If she was covering in some way, like telling me it was a student instead of saying it was her professor or a TA, for example, then we have nothing,"

Grace's head swiveled. "Her professor? Or a TA? You think that?"

"No, I don't think that. But I'm trying to consider all the possibilities. She never said a name, so other than her being a very private person, why would she hold that back?"

"Good question. No answer," Grace replied. "I say we focus on Hunter for now," Grace continued. "Follow the breadcrumbs. But if she *didn't* meet the guy on a group project in a business class, we are not just barking up the wrong tree, we are lost in the fucking forest."

Lisa considered commenting on Grace's very mixed metaphors. "So, do we have *anything* to give to the police? Can't they get a search warrant or anything?" she asked instead. "Get his computers? Find a date rape drug in his bathroom?"

"No," Grace said. "I'm no cop but there has to be *something* that adds up to probable cause. We have a hunch. Hunches do not fly."

"We need more," Lisa said. "We need a sting."

"A sting? And you learned this where?" asked Grace.

"I watch TV. Here's how it goes down: I position myself such that he cannot resist making contact. Then he asks me out. At which point I can get into his apartment."

Grace inhaled sharply. "No, Lisa, no. You're not making yourself a target when we don't know what the guy is capable of."

"We got zero. I'm going to find out who drugged my roommate, probably assaulted her when she was passed out, took kinky pictures, then sent them to intimidate her into backing off," Lisa argued. "I don't know if Shelby wanted to die or just take a break from a bad scene, but she wouldn't have been in that space if someone hadn't put her there."

"But putting yourself in danger won't. . ."

"Danger is an exaggeration. I'm fact-finding."

"Yeah, right. Look, Lisa, do not go rogue on me. We maybe can discuss a plan, but you're *never* to be alone with him unless I know exactly when and where."

"You can be two rows back in the movie theatre and three tables over at the restaurant. And I'll text you every fifteen minutes. Okay?"

"No, not okay. I need to talk to someone first."

"Whatever. You said it was a silver Kia, right? You got a make and model? How about a license plate number?"

Grace called Patsy and asked her to run a check on the Kia license plate. It came back clean. Grace put his name into the county and state data bases for past or pending charges. Nothing. But they didn't even know where Hunter was from or how long he'd been in Kansas. Grace made a note to ask Patsy for another favor.

A week passed with Grace booked solid with appointments and paperwork. She'd gotten behind in her custody mediations and could not afford to piss off attorneys who were counting on not having to go to trial over whether little Melody spent two or three nights each week with her daddy. They preferred to bicker over asset distribution and let Grace navigate the messier issues. And, for once, dealing with high-conflict custody issues felt easy. Grace knew what she was doing in *that* world.

Chapter 45
(November 20th)

"It's not enough," Hannah said to Stacy. They'd just posted a rather fetching picture of Logan with a caption that read, _It's the nice ones that can blindside you—but not if you remember your pepper spray._

They'd been posting shots of Logan for about two weeks, always on anonymous or disappearing sites, and always with a caption that was both ambiguous and yet leading.

"I want closure," Hannah said.

They were lying on the two twin beds in Hannah's room, theoretically studying for tests in their respective classes.

"What kind of closure?" Stacy asked.

"Closure-closure. Finality. An end to this shitty chapter in my life," Hannah said. "Because I thought, at least I did at the beginning, that there would be some kind of legal consequence, not necessarily a trial, but _something._"

"So, closure like revenge?"

"No, not revenge. More like retribution."

"Why not revenge? You're not entitled to revenge?"

"It's not a matter of what I'm entitled to or not. But there is a difference."

"Which is?"

"I think of revenge as personal payback. Vengeance. Getting even. Wanting to hurt someone with the sole intent that they suffer," Hannah said. "And while a part of me wants Logan Whiteman to suffer greatly for what he did to me, another part of me does not want him to suffer without _understanding_ what he did to me."

"So he has to _understand_ what he did, how he hurt you—and that is as important as him just suffering?"

"Yeah," Hannah was nodding now, working it through in her head. "I want justice. Something that makes it so he will never do it again. It's not like I'm the only girl he ever did this to. The punishment needs to be—" Hannah paused, searching for the right word, "*proportionate.* Which is different from payback."

"Proportionate is a very big word."

"Shut up. You know what I mean. Not a slap on the tooshie. A balanced retribution."

"And if he's incapable of understanding what he did? If a balanced and equitable retribution does not pan out? Then do you want a little bit of revenge?"

"I want him to feel *authentic* remorse," Hannah clarified. "And not just because he's scared."

"*Authentic* remorse is a very tall order. *Pretend* remorse, on the other hand, is readily accessible."

"I want Logan Whiteman to understand what he did and what I went through. I want him to experience something of what I experienced. I want him to feel afraid and helpless and trapped and violated," Hannah said flatly. "And that might need to include some penetration."

Stacy did not blink. "Then let's make ourselves some justice."

Once the door was open to thinking about justice, about retribution, being in control of the process instead of feeling helpless and dragged through the mud—it was fantasy payback.

"We could crash a frat party and go door-to-door of the bedrooms and interrupt all the sex that's happening. Kind of a 'Free Willy' scenario," Hannah started.

"We'd get arrested and the girls would all say they wanted to hookup."

"We could go to the frat in the middle of the night and make the guys stand in their underwear in the cold until they admitted they deliberately got girls drunk."

It took a day or so of silliness before they got down to business. They could not tackle guys in general. This was about Logan.

And to accomplish Hannah's goals, they needed to abduct him.

Stacy and Hannah were methodical. While they did not want to get in trouble, they recognized that the best of plans could easily get messed up.

"We need to do research," Hannah said. "But we need a computer with no connection to us. We can't have incriminating history on our laptops. Don't even want to use library computers that we have to log in on. I think they can trace someone by where they log in. But maybe not?"

Within three days, Stacy came through with an older laptop that belonged to her cousin, Bill. Stacy seemed to have an ample supply of cousins.

"I started to explain but he said he didn't want to know," Stacy told Hannah. "He just set up a new Google email account in his name, set a new password, handed me the laptop and said to erase whatever we could and drop it at his place when we're done. So, we're good to go."

They set a date, which was a bit scary as it made the fantasy more real. They picked the Thursday night before Stop Day—the Friday in early December when classes were over.

It was a *huge* party night.

"Now all we have to do is find a way to separate Logan from his fraternity, lure him to a car, subdue him, tie him up, bring him to a secret location, and figure out how to make him *understand*," reflected Hannah.

"What do we call this?" Stacy interjected. "We cannot refer to a pending *kidnapping* in an email."

"Heart-to-heart? Tutorial? Orientation?" Hannah listed options, checking each off on a finger as she went. "We want him to see the error of his ways. To understand how his behavior has hurt people."

"How about *intervention*?" Stacy said. "Like what families do with their alcoholics and addicts when they come together to show the fuck-up what needs to change."

The next step was figuring out where they would host their *intervention*.

"We can't do it in a hotel in case he makes noise or screams," Stacy said. "Even cabins won't work if they are close together. Maybe one of those state park cabins? They tend to be more spread out."

"Sure," Hannah said, "And when Ranger Rick comes by to see if we're okay, we stuff Logan in a closet?"

"Good point. No state park cabins."

"I'll check out the Airbnb website," Hannah said. "I read about some cabins for romantic weekends that sounded really isolated. But I want it to be within an hour max from town. I don't want to have him putting up a fuss for a long time in the car."

Hannah used her own laptop, as looking at romantic cabins did not seem incriminating. Stacy used Bill's to research other necessities.

Hannah found a cabin in the country about fifteen miles southwest of Kaw Valley: "2 BR, 1 BA, comfy LR, fully stocked kitchen, Wi-Fi, DVD player, cable. Watch the deer from rockers on porch overlooking 20 acres of Kansas grassland. Complete privacy and solitude." The owner was not on-site.

At $75 a night, they booked three nights using a pre-paid Visa debit card. Hannah said two, but Stacy pushed for another.

"Better safe than sorry," Stacy said. "We'll check in at 4 p.m., meet the owner, get the key. Say we have an engagement back in town that evening but will return later. Tell her how much we look forward to being *undisturbed.* Do you want to say we're studying hard for finals or play it as lustful lesbians?"

"Whatever," Hannah replied. "Oh, yeah, I checked the pictures and it has wood floors, not carpet, which is better in case there are some spills."

"I think we'll need a Taser," Hannah continued. "We're not strong enough to jump him or anything. It will take way too long to knock him out with drinks or a drug. We need him knocked out completely, just long enough to tie him up."

"Ahhhhh, Tasers," Stacy answered. "Did you know that the name is actually a reference to a novel for kids published in 1911? It was *Tom Swift's Electric Rifle* with a subtitle of *Daring Adventures in Elephant Land.* It was the sci-fi for the early 1900's, about this magical rifle that could bring down big game. It was also racist as far as any understanding of Africa and African people—the bigotry of the times. But it wasn't until about sixty years later that an actual prototype was developed by a Jack Cover. He marketed it under the name Taser, Inc., referring to the book. He added an "a" that was not in the title but I think because it made it easier to say 'T-a-s-e-r' than 'T-s-e-r.' There was a documentary that premiered in 2015 at Tribeca on the development of the Taser."

Hannah stared at Stacy, her mouth open.

"How do you know all this shit?" she asked.

"I liked to read *boy books* when I was a kid more than Nancy Drew," Stacy said with a grin. "More weapons, less tip-toeing around."

"So how do we get a Taser?" asked Hannah.

"On Amazon, of course. But we'll want a stun gun. Tasers and stun guns are not the same," Stacy explained. "A Taser is a stun gun that can be fired from a distance and totally disable someone without getting close enough to touch them. Actual Tasers are pretty expensive, like $400 to $1,500. All we need is a stun gun. We'll need to be close enough to touch him, but not until he's getting into the car. We can't lift that much dead weight, so we can't use it before then. Better if it's rechargeable, with a flashlight built in. It will be late at night, and hopefully, away from streetlights."

"Rechargeable? Are you planning on using it often?" Hannah asked.

"That really depends on Logan. But, no, I'm just thinking that we might as well get one that could prove useful in the future. While you were looking at cute Airbnb cabins, I found a 4+star rated one on Amazon: a VIPERTEK VTS-989 with 230,000,000—that would be volts or something like that—and over 600 positive reviews."

"How much?"

"Only $24.98."

"That seems really cheap. Is it strong enough to drop a grown man to his knees?"

"The reviews say it is. And reviews don't lie."

"Yeah, sure," Hannah said sarcastically. "Although there would be some pretty pissed off people if the stun gun failed to stun—pissiness on *both* ends of the gun."

"We'll use the pre-paid VISA, order on Bill's laptop, and have it delivered to Bill's address," Stacy said.

"Are you telling Bill what to expect?"

"He won't mind," Stacy said. "And the less he knows, the better. I'll just tell him to leave anything that comes for me on his back porch. That's what cousins are for."

Chapter 46
(November 21st)

Grace was binge-watching Crazy Ex-Girlfriend when the phone ring jolted her out of her chair. It was 10:15 p.m.

Lisa, she thought. *Nobody else calls me this late.*

"I've got a date," Lisa announced to Grace, without preamble. "Friday, December 1st, at 7 p.m. Movie at Liberty Hall. Then we grab a bite. But I will not go back to his place. This will be the first date, the one where he is a gentleman."

"Damn, Lisa, how did you pull this off so fast?"

"So I parked around the corner from his place and followed him to campus. Tailed him to his classes, which are in the Business School, then to the Student Union for lunch. I positioned myself at the next table, although I had to elbow two other kids out of the way who were about to sit down. I was rude but for a good cause."

"And how did you get from sitting at the next table to a date?"

"I asked him a question about a book he was reading. Said I was thinking of changing majors to business from English. Asked what he liked about the classes and what he wanted to do with the degree."

"And he didn't suspect?"

"It's not like I was coming on to him. Just a few friendly questions. Then I got all busy with my phone so he'd know I have a life."

"And so he just asked you out?"

"*No,* not *then.* That was last Friday. The asking out part was yesterday. I was going to call you right away but then I had to finish a paper. Anyway, I positioned myself where he'd been before. People are creatures of habit. They have preferred sections, preferred times, even preferred tables. Of course, he could have had another commitment, or a meeting, or class might have been canceled. Then I would have tried the cafeteria on another day or followed him after he left his class. But I got lucky. He showed up. So I smiled at him and he said 'Hey' to me and started a conversation."

"But from 'Hey' to a date?"

"I played it cool. Said I was busy for the first night he suggested, then said okay to December 1st, made eye contact, but then said I *really* needed to get to the library and left. It's not until after Thanksgiving. I didn't know if we'd need prep time. Do you still feel a need to be in the next row at the movies if I promise I will not get in his car or go to his apartment?"

"Let me think about it."

Chapter 47
(November 23rd)

Around 2 a.m. on the 23rd, Max woke up to his stomach making strange grinding noises. He felt something hot and bitter rising in his throat. He started to push back the covers, realizing he needed to get to the bathroom. But it was too late. He pulled himself onto his hands and knees, retching, as vomit exploded all over his sheets and comforter.

"Mommy," he cried, as another round rose from his stomach.

Molly startled awake, her body rolling out of bed and running into Max's room before her head stopped dreaming.

"Oh, shit," she muttered, smelling the puke even before putting the light on to see. "Shit, shit, shit."

"Mommy, make it stop. Mommy. . ." Max was wailing.

"It's okay, Max-boy. You're going to be okay. Mommy will take care of it." She picked Max up and went across the hall to the bathroom, throwing a few towels on the tile floor next to the toilet. "Just hang in there while I go get a bucket? Can you do that?"

An hour later, Max was all washed up, his teeth brushed to get rid of the bitter taste, in clean pajamas, asleep in Molly's bed. After three more *incidents* of projectile vomiting, she hoped the worst was over. It took her another 30 minutes to strip Max's bed, put the sheets and comforter in the washing machine on hot, and clean up the floors in the bedroom and bathroom.

Then she emailed Grace. *Hey, Mom—don't want to wake you with a call at 3:30 a.m. but Thanksgiving is not happening. Max is puking sick, sweats, and maybe fever. Let's talk in a few hours but don't call me until I call you in case he sleeps in.*

Grace saw the email about 8 a.m.

It would have been just the three of them anyway. Katrina had flown back to visit her family in New Orleans. The patched-together *family of friends* that had sustained her and Gil for so many years when the kids were young had long since dissipated. Molly had invited a few of her friends from school, but they'd gone home also.

Grace had bought a 12-pound turkey, down from the usual 24-pound one.

Might as well throw the bird in the oven anyway, she thought. *Bone it for later meals and make turkey noodle soup for Max for when his tummy settles down.*

Once the turkey was cooking, Grace crawled back into bed herself. In a way, she was relieved. Holidays were emotional minefields. Memories would often blindside her. And the day was cold and cloudy, with a wet chill in the air. She would have pretended to be cheerful, but it was a relief to not have to try.

She'd get up in a few hours and put together some Tupperware. She'd sauté onions and celery to doctor a box of stuffing, mash a couple of potatoes, use canned gravy. *I can throw that together in 40 minutes,* she thought, *and bring it to Molly's back door.*

It would be a good afternoon to zone out with the TV and she knew exactly with what. *The Marvelous Mrs. Maisel.* Now that girl could make her laugh.

Chapter 48
(November 25th)

Grace and Molly were hiking a trail along the lake outside of town. It twisted up and down ravines, close to the lakeshore, and then cut back into the woods. It was a four-mile loop, which, given the ups-and-downs, was all Grace wanted to tackle. The weather was perfect, one of those late fall days when the air was crisp but not too cold, when the sun seemed to have magical rays that made coats feel superfluous.

It wasn't often that Grace and Molly got time away from their houses together. They were either working or tag-teaming care of Max. But Max, who'd recovered from the stomach bug in under twenty-four hours, had been invited over to play at the home of one of the boys in his class. This was new territory for Max, as well as his mom and grandma. Everyone was a little anxious.

"What if Max has a meltdown and the mom freaks out?" Molly asked Grace.

"Didn't you tell me she has four kids? She's coped with meltdowns."

"The kid's name is Charlie. Max had mentioned him before, told me he's nice. And Max seemed pleased to get the invitation. Usually he just freezes up. But what if their other kids pester him and he starts moaning and rocking?"

"Max will do what Max will do, Molly. The mom has your cell if she needs to call. But I really think it will be okay."

"But what if. . ."

"Oh my!" Grace exclaimed. "Will you look at that? The lake is positively shimmering. Do you see the pattern the sunlight is making?"

Molly got the hint. Lose the worry and try to enjoy the day and the freedom.

They hiked for another twenty minutes and then stopped for a rest and water-break when they hit the midway point bench. It sat on the end of a small peninsula, with water on three sides.

Grace wanted to talk with Molly about Mickey. Not that there was anything yet to talk about, but she hadn't dated since returning to Kaw Valley. But, if she and Mickey did start something? Well, it'd be more than some hookup.

But each time she started to say something she hesitated, and then the moment was lost. *I'm just being silly,* she thought. *Just spit it out.*

"Molly," she began, "there's something I've been wanting to talk to you about. Do you remember back during the trial when Miguel took me to that polygraph expert in Kansas City? And then he testified at the trial?"

Molly gave her mother a long stare, then raised her eyebrows.

"Yes," she answered, "it was a very long time ago, in another life. But I do remember him testifying."

"Well, we sort of stayed in contact when I was gone, very intermittently, and we've had dinner a few times since I've been back. Then he helped me with that difficult custody case I had last year. He was a detective and works now as a P.I. as well as polygraph expert. He's a good person to talk to. A resource."

"Uh-huh," Molly said. "A *resource.* That you stayed in intermittent contact with for ten years when you were, as you so aptly put it, *gone.* Who you've had dinner with a few times. And would this *resource* drive a blue Camry like the one that was parked in front of the house from about 8 p.m. to 7 a.m. back in early October?"

Grace flushed. "Nothing happened," she said. "That was the night after the ER and my client's overdose. I needed him, and he showed up and was there for me."

"Jesus, Mom, you do not have to explain anything. I'm really glad that you have someone that cares about you."

"Well, it's not even like that. I mean, we've never had a date-date. Dinner, yes, but as friends. But I called him and asked him to. . ."

"*You* asked *him* out on a date? Way to go!"

"I asked him to dinner, period. But it's like this *possibility* has been on a back burner, ever since we talked about how we each have some emotional baggage, and maybe we needed to deal with that *before* we had a date. I mean, his wife died of cancer and he never even cleaned out her closet, just moved into the guest room for the last four years."

"Loyalty is a very valuable trait," Molly said. "And you both have dead spouses. That's something in common."

"You can be a real pain in the ass."

"Yeah, and it's something you admire in me. The big question is—can he cook?"

"Not that I know of, but he does know the best pizzerias."

Molly paused, looking out over the lake.

"Well, as long as you brought up needing to talk, I've got something I've been wanting to talk to you about."

Grace's eyes widened just a bit. "Really?" she asked.

"Really," Molly replied.

"Okay, then, spit it out."

"Remember Leah? Who moved to California? Who I was helping?"

"You did a lot more than *help,* but, sure, I remember Leah. How is she doing?"

"Great, or as great as anyone can be when totally cut off from the family she spent every waking moment with for her entire life. She's working, building a new life. She has hard days but never bad enough to want to return."

"And this is what you wanted to share?"

"No. But Leah gave my email and phone number to Mike, who was having adjustment issues with her nephew, David. He needed someone who knew something about his whole mess to talk with. So, we've been in contact."

Grace was truly—maybe not *stunned,* more—*What-are-you-talking-about-because-this-makes-no-sense.*

"What are you saying?" she finally asked.

"I'm saying that I've been talking with Mike Flores. We email. We talk a lot about our sons, who each present their own set of challenges. And then his Dad had a heart attack. Let's just say that life as a combat vet and single parent, with a kid whose family cut him out, has not been easy."

"Is his Dad recovered?"

"Yes, Abuelo is doing fine. That man has stamina."

Molly continued talking but Grace did not hear. The ease with which Molly had said *Abuelo,* and her familiarity with Abuelo's stamina? It meant she and Mike had been doing a lot of talking.

"And so I booked a flight last week to Florida for the week after

Christmas when Max is out of school," Molly was saying.

"Uh, you're going to have to back up, Molly. I did not hear a word after *Abuelo*. This is kind of a shock."

"It is a little complicated, because Mike was your client and all, but we never talk about you."

"That is the least of my concerns, Molly. It's a bit unorthodox to have the mediator's daughter take up with the client, but. . ."

"I am not *taking up* with anyone. We're friends. Leah is meeting us in Florida, and we're all going to hang out at the beach and let the kids build sandcastles and just stop having to be so damn responsible for a week, just let down and. . ."

"Which I totally, totally support," Grace interrupted.

Molly stopped talking.

"I guess I've been a little nervous about telling you. Like it would freak you out. It was a very tough case and you seemed weighted down after Mike and David left town."

"So Florida is where they ended up?" Grace asked. "I never knew where they went, although his mother told me it was by an ocean."

"Just a few blocks to the beach. A condo/town home development. Mike has a three-bedroom place and his parents are a block away. David goes to their home after school three days a week until supper. Mike is working and in school, part-time for both. Two classes a semester, which is all he can really handle between working and David and his, what do they call it? M-TBI. As if any traumatic brain injury can be *mild*."

"How is David doing? Has the adjustment been really hard?"

Grace felt a constriction in what could only be her heart. She'd gotten overly-invested in David. He'd had his life uprooted as surely as if a tornado had come through and destroyed everything. And yet there was a part of her that hoped, desperately, that he would have a better life because of it.

"He started out in public school, but Mike felt that he needed something with more structure. So—and this is weird considering how much his family despised Catholicism—Mike moved him to a Catholic school. It's just six blocks from home, small enrollment, and the faculty has been really supportive. Mike says David likes having religion be part of his daily life. He wants to be an altar boy."

"Does he still have his dog?" Grace asked, remembering how the puppy opened the door for David to connect with his father.

"Yeah, Moses sleeps with David every night. Loves the ocean and comes back from every walk on the beach coated in salt water and sand. They put in an outdoor shower just for the dog."

"Where are they in Florida?" Grace asked after a pause.

"By St. Petersburg. Not that far from Sanibel."

The rest of the walk they were single file and did not talk. Since a lot of it was uphill, they would have been panting anyway.

How the hell did this happen? Grace thought to herself. How did her daughter develop a relationship with Grace's former client, a man she has never even met?

But there was a natural, albeit convoluted, connection through Leah, Molly's friend. They shared overlapping history. And secrets.

The more she thought about it, the more Grace could see how Mike would value Molly's insight—just as she did—and Molly would value his dedication to his son. Mike was the total opposite of Jeff, Max's biological dad. Being single parents of kids with *issues* gave them plenty to talk about. And they were only a few years apart in age.

Molly's announcement made Grace's little disclosure, *Hey, I might ask this guy out,* pretty lame in comparison. Molly was going to fly to Florida to visit Mike Flores. And David. And his Abuelo and Abuela.

But Leah will also be there, Grace thought, *to chaperone.*

I'm certifiably nuts, she realized. *I'm the one who probably needs a chaperone.*

Chapter 49
(November 27th)

Grace had called Mickey the next evening, the Sunday after Thanksgiving.

"I've been wanting to take you out for dinner, but I may need more urgent help with something. It's related to the girl who overdosed. But I understand if you don't want to have any more to do with it."

"How about lunch tomorrow?" Mickey had replied. "I have to be back in Kansas City for a 4 p.m. meeting but the early afternoon is open."

Grace had looked at her planner, her *non-digital-write-down-the-appointments-for-each-day-with-a-pen*-planner.

"I can do 1:30. Is that too late?"

"No, pick a place and I'll be there."

They met at Little Saigon, a hole-in-the-wall Vietnamese place with the best pho in Kaw Valley.

"So, what's up? You sounded a little anxious on the phone."

"I am. There have been a few developments and it's getting a little twisted."

"Spill," Mickey said.

Grace spilled: Connecting up with Lisa; tracking down Shelby's classes from spring semester; Lisa finding the thumb drive with the pictures under the bathroom sink; finding out which classes had group projects; futile attempts to get rosters from the professors; dangling Molly's $50 carrot-incentive over social media to get info; Lisa doing Facebook searches; Grace driving around checking out where the *possibles* lived, assessing which place mirrored what Shelby had described; seeing who they now assumed was *the guy*; Lisa stalking him; securing a date for December 1st at 7 p.m.

Mickey had the decency to be impressed.

"You two plan on opening an agency? So you think this guy is the one?"

"Yeah, I do. But it's all based on what Shelby told Lisa and me. If that is off, then we're off, and if so, we have to start over. But my gut says he's the one."

"Oh, your *gut* says so? Is your *gut* also telling you what comes next? You got a hypothesis. But evidence? Not so much."

"Now we need to follow up, gather evidence."

"What sort of evidence do you have in mind?"

Grace reached into her bag, pulled out a manila file and handed it to Mickey.

"These are the photos that were on the drive," she said. "And I believe that this is not a one-time thing, that he has done this to other girls. He sets them up, dates them, drugs them, and assaults them."

Mickey opened the file and looked carefully, one at a time, at the pictures.

"How do you know this is Shelby?" he asked. "The face. . ."

"I know. It's a filter. Creepy for sure. But Lisa says it looks like her body: pale skin tone, freckles, red pubic hair. And who else would be on a thumb drive hidden in a plastic soap dish under their bathroom sink?"

"There is that. But it would not stand up in court. Not unless we have photos of Shelby to compare to. Which we could get from the autopsy if nothing else. So, say this is Shelby, then what?"

Grace realized that she did not have an answer, but it almost didn't matter. Mickey had said *we*. As in, *unless **we** have photos,* and *which **we** could get.* Not, *you.* Not, *what do you think you're doing playing detective?"*

"If he sent these pictures to silence or intimidate her, and I find them in his apartment, along with pictures of other girls. . ."

"Then you have pictures. If they show him engaged in sexual acts with unconscious women, you got something. But pictures of naked girls, however posed, not so much."

"If Rohypnol, GHB, or Ketamine are in his bathroom? Wouldn't that mean something?'

"Not for a good defense attorney. Anyone could have left it in his apartment. And you seem to be forgetting that this would be an illegal search, a breaking and entering, *criminal trespass*. So, you got nada."

"But at least I'll know he's the right guy," Grace protested.

"Which could make you totally crazy if you knew he was assaulting women but could not prove it."

"You mean like 90% of campus assaults?" Grace asked, her voice rising in exasperation. "Where evidence means nothing?"

"Yes. Sort of like that."

"So, you think this is nuts. That I need to just give up and go home and pretend like we don't know what we know?"

"I didn't say that," Mickey replied. "I just don't want you getting yourself in a hot mess. All you have here is conjecture—bits and pieces of what Shelby said linked together to make a narrative—and your gut. And even if your gut is spot-on. . ."

"Do you think this was a one-time thing?" Grace interrupted. "Or he did it before and will do it again?"

"It's ritualistic behavior. He's done it before."

"Should I just tell the police and let them handle it?"

"Their hands would also be tied," Mickey answered. "They can talk to him, maybe, but there's no basis for a search or warrant. And not like he'd confess."

They fell silent, staring at the now closed manila folder, thinking of the photos and what they might mean.

"So, when were you thinking of hypothetically breaking into this guy's apartment?" Mickey asked. "Because that's where this conversation is leading."

"On Friday at about 7 p.m. During Lisa's date."

Mickey was about to make a sarcastic remark, but the waitress was placing steaming bowls of pho down in front of each of them.

They stopped talking long enough to inhale, their faces leaning in over the bowls. Then they picked up the big spoons and started slurping.

"Are you sure," Mickey paused for a spoonful, "that this was an old-fashioned, traditional date? Not a hookup?"

"It was an uber-traditional date. So I have a window of time to check out Hunter's place. I can watch him leave, and Lisa will text me when they're settled in the movie theatre."

"*Nothing* you may find will be admissible in court. You do get that?"

"You made your point. So, can I borrow your lock picks?"

"It would take way too long to teach you. And I'd feel better knowing this was done right. Untraceable. Uncompromised."

"Do you think he could have an alarm system?" Grace asked, keeping her eyes focused down on her noodles as she felt a combination of relief and gratitude blanket her. "I woke up wondering about that possibility."

"Kids do not have alarm systems," Mickey replied. "Not unless they are very rich and have parents who think about those things."

"We could get in a lot of trouble if we're caught doing this, right? Like how much trouble?"

"It's a felony. But, without a record, you'd plea down. I'm going to assume that we don't get caught. The danger here could be nosy neighbors more than the guy himself."

"Nosy neighbors? I hadn't thought of that. Don't students avoid being nosy?"

"Which works if it's a student complex. But if someone's Aunt Bertha lives next door? Who takes it upon herself to know exactly who is coming and going?"

"So we pray there's no Aunt Bertha?"

"Exactly."

Chapter 50
(November 30th)

Hannah and Stacy were holed up in their dorm rooms. It was down-to-the-wire-with-no-room-to-procrastinate time. There was just one week left of classes for the fall semester and they each had major papers due. Hannah's grades had dropped dramatically from what she was used to getting in high school—mostly A's—to mostly C's. Hannah could not remember ever getting a C other than calculus and that was because the teacher had not known how to explain shit.

Hannah did not know how she was going to explain her grades to her parents. Stacy said to tell them she'd gotten sidetracked by her social life. Which was, in a convoluted way, true.

Stacy also said that stressing about her parents and grades was the last thing she needed to be doing.

They needed to be finalizing details for Logan's intervention.

The Airbnb cabin was confirmed. They'd already driven past to make sure it was as isolated as the description had made it seem.

Stacy would go down at 2 p.m. on Thursday to get the key and drop-off groceries, booze, and other supplies. They had a stun gun, an Amazon special order delivered to cousin Bill's address, plus Safariland Double Cuff Disposable Handcuffs, plastic restraints, a metal disposable handcuff cutter, two rolls of duct tape, and an assortment of First Aid supplies.

And they compiled a playlist.

"Music can have such an impact on mood," Stacy explained, her voice lifting in sarcasm. "We had an article about it my psych class. And, really, girls just want to have fun."

"Absolutely," Hannah agreed. "And we're brave and stronger, can run the world, and will survive."

There was only one disagreement.

"Not that one," Hannah told Stacy when Lady GaGa came up. "It's a downer. The rest are okay. And what about *Frozen*. You know which one I mean?"

They'd concluded that Stacy needed to be the one to go into the frat house. It was too risky for Hannah. She might be recognized. It was not likely as she now had spiky blue-green hair and large black-framed glasses, with zero resemblance to the long-haired, carefully made-up freshman Logan had hit on. But someone from the dorm who knew Hannah could be there and out her.

They also had a baggie of dynamite weed for Stacy to flash at Logan if she needed a bribe to entice him to come out for a hit. They talked about options for a *tease*, a story-line to get Logan to come out to the car just long enough to zap him and drive off.

The car was Stacy's Grandma's Twilight Blue Metallic '99 Buick Regal. It had a big back seat. "Take it for the weekend. I don't get my hair done until next Tuesday," Gran had told Stacy.

The Stacy makeover, so essential if she was to blend in enough to be invisible at the frat party, took work: a cut-and-color with blonde highlights, a borrowed set of hot rollers, mascara and eye-liner, and glistening lip gloss. She'd refused to wear high heels, convinced her unsteadiness would be a give-away, but had bought Seychelles block heel booties coupled with Free People slim jeans and a plunging black Zara sweater. She still had her curves, but they were now Spanxed. For a girl who shopped at Goodwill, it was a big investment.

"Holy crap," Stacy observed during the dress rehearsal. "I don't recognize myself. I've never, ever, been this hot. What have I been missing?"

December 2017

Chapter 51
(December 1st)

On Friday night at 6:40 p.m., Mickey and Grace were parked down the street from Hunter's apartment. The Kia, however, was not parked in its assigned *Unit #2* spot. They waited for him to leave but he never showed. Then, at 6:55 p.m., Grace's phone rang.

"We're at the theater," Lisa said in a stage whisper. "I'm in the bathroom."

"He wasn't here," Grace replied. "We didn't see him leave. I was getting worried."

"He must have already been out," Lisa said. "But he's getting popcorn now. Nobody's bought me popcorn in years. Even asked how much butter I like."

"How long is the movie?" Grace asked, although she'd already, obsessive as she was, checked the length.

"Two hours, but not sure if that includes previews."

"Text me when you get out, okay? And do not go anywhere other than a crowded restaurant with him. And watch your drink."

"Yes, Mommy, I promise," Lisa said in a whiny voice before hanging up.

Mickey and Grace left the car parked a block away and strolled down the street and to the doorway of Unit #2. The entrance was tucked around a corner, with a small front patio under an overhang. It could not be seen from the street. It was already dark outside, but a dim yellow bulb lit the doorway.

Mickey bent over the door, quickly but methodically doing something with the picklocks. Grace was holding a shopping bag. A black Baggallini purse draped across her chest.

It took Mickey two minutes before the lock clicked open, but for Grace it felt like twenty. She started to reach for the door knob, but he stopped her and handed her a pair of clear latex surgical gloves he'd pulled out of his jacket pocket.

They slipped through the door and closed it behind them.

"Don't move," Mickey said. Before he took a single step, he did a survey of the room, right-to-left, floor-to-ceiling, dividing it into quadrants in his head. He took four pictures with his phone. Then he moved toward the windows and tightened the blinds. They were already pretty much closed, but *pretty much* might still allow someone to see movement.

"Take off your coat. We'll leave them on the floor by the door," he said to Grace. "Take off your shoes as well. Nothing goes more than two feet inside the apartment."

Grace was feeling agitated. Her heart was pumping, her hands damp with sweat. Now that she was actually inside Hunter Payne's apartment, committing an illegal act, not sure what she was looking for or what she would do with whatever they might find. . .

"I would have made a lousy criminal," she said to Mickey. "You hear how thieves get an adrenaline rush? I'm more panic attack."

"Well, save the panic for later," Mickey said. "Let's get to work."

They started in the living room, Mickey directing Grace in how to methodically lift every cushion and feel underneath. Mickey turned the chairs and couch over and poked around the bottoms. He was meticulous when he put them back to make sure each leg exactly fit the pressed down space on the carpet where it had been. He opened every DVD holder to see if the DVD inside matched the cover. He opened each drawer of a cabinet and first looked carefully at the contents before ever reaching in. He lifted small plastic containers holding screws and paper clips and scotch tape to see if there were any envelopes hidden beneath.

In the kitchen, they went cabinet by cabinet, lifting each soup can, shifting the sugar and pancake mix in the Tupperware containers to see if anything was buried.

"Mickey. Look. Now."

Grace stood in front of an upper cabinet that was lined with glasses: six each of three sizes, a set that Grace recalled seeing at Target.

"What?" Mickey asked, standing next to her and peering into the cabinet.

Grace pointed at the shelf above the glasses.

"Copper mugs," she whispered. "Two round, hammered copper

mugs. That's what Shelby described that the drinks were in. She said he came out of the kitchen with two round copper mugs with Moscow Mules. She hadn't had one before and she thought they were cute."

"Good call, Grace. Every connection helps. But why are you whispering?"

"Because I'm very freaked out at what we're doing."

"You weren't so freaked out when you came up with the idea," Mickey replied. "You seemed pretty sure then that a break-in was a good move."

"That was last week. I was younger and more impulsive."

Grace moved to the refrigerator, starting with the freezer. She lifted each package to see if the actual weight fit the package description. There were no packages that were hand-labeled. They all had intact seals.

Grace stood, freezer door open, as a flashback hit her along with the cold air. It was Patsy Tsosie, describing how the gun, the most important gun in the world, had been discovered in a freezer wrapped up like a roast.

She looked up to see Mickey standing in the doorway, just watching her.

"Find anything in the freezer?" he asked.

"No," she replied. "Labels all intact. No Tupperware. No big roasts."

"Ready for the bedroom?"

Grace nodded yes. They walked to the bedroom. Grace felt as if she'd seen this room before, the color of the walls, the louvered doors of the closet.

"If there is anything in this apartment, it will be in here." Mickey said. "The bedroom is where he took the pictures. It's a more personal space. He stages intimacy."

They lifted the mattress and looked underneath, careful to not make the sheets any more taut than they found them, blankets precisely preserved with the same casual lumps.

Mickey tackled the drawers. They were not *military* but they were neat. The guy liked organization.

In the closet, Grace went through every hanger, probing every pocket. Mickey reached up and brought down the boxes from the shelves after taking a few pictures so he could make sure he put them back exactly as found.

And then, when they had begun to think that they would find nothing, with only a few boxes remaining in the far back of the closet shelf. . .

"Bingo," said Mickey.

It was a legal file box labeled with red magic marker: *Family Photos and Other Junk.*

Mickey opened the box very carefully, checking first to see if there were any hidden seals. He counted twelve manila envelopes. They were dated. The top one was September 2017.

In the envelope were the photos of Shelby, but before the filters were added to cover her face. Here she looked tranquil, deeply asleep— the way a child sleeps, draped across the bed, white skin against navy sheets.

"Pull out your phone, Grace," Mickey said. "I want shots of all of these."

Twelve envelopes—each with about fifteen to twenty-five 8-by-10's and 5-by-7's—of twelve very different young women. In most of the shots, they were posed naked. Some poses were repeated with each girl. With every sequence, except for Shelby Stewart, in the final shots the girls were at least partially dressed.

"He put their clothes back," Grace said. "Why would he do that?"

"So they won't know what happened," Mickey said. "No one but Shelby woke up naked. And if they can't remember anything, then they have to accept his version of what had happened."

"Which would be?"

"I don't know. But whatever the specific story line, Hunter is not the bad guy."

Grace was looking at one of the set of photos.

"She looks Indian or Pakistani," Grace said. "The jewelry is different also. Not from the U.S."

"Could be he was trying for diversity or targeting girls that he thought were more vulnerable," Mickey reflected. "Someone less adept at reading social cues or more wanting to fit in."

Grace did not reply. She was carefully lining up the photos, maintaining the original order from each envelope. By the time she finished, she'd taken over 230 pictures.

Grace was inserting the last set of photos back into the envelopes when her phone rang. She jumped.

"Yes?" she barked in a hoarse whisper into the phone. "What?"

"Hey, the movie is over. We're waiting for a table at Limestone," Lisa said. "I'm in the bathroom again. I can promise another hour but no longer. How is it going?"

"Going fine. We can do a show-and-tell tomorrow. We're almost done. Call me before you leave the restaurant."

Grace watched as Mickey put the box back on the top shelf. They looked together at the shots he'd taken of the shelves before he started to bring stuff down to make sure every box was exactly where it was supposed to be, precisely as far apart as they had been.

Grace felt exhausted. "Can we go now?" she asked Mickey.

"We still have the bathroom," Mickey said. "But it's more a one-person job so you can just watch, snap pics as I go, and make sure I get everything back exactly as we find it."

In the back of the linen closet, behind toilet paper and cleaning supplies, Mickey found a plastic bin labeled "Old Prescriptions, Cold Meds, Etc."

Jumbled in among a few dozen mostly empty scripts and medications was a bottle of pills. It was wrapped in masking tape and *Sleepy time* was written on the side.

"Take a picture," he told Grace. He positioned the bottle on the shelf, in front of the plastic bin with the label. Then he directed her to step back, to place it in the context of the entire bathroom.

"I'd like to take these now. Substitute aspirin or something," Mickey said. "Let him be surprised the next time he goes to use them and the girl doesn't pass out."

"Can we do that? Please?" Grace begged.

"Not if we want to get him down the road," Mickey said. "Now that we know what we know, we have to figure out how to share it legally. Meanwhile, I'll take one pill to have a lab see what it is. He may keep a count, but any count can be one off."

"I thought this would give me answers," Grace continued. "But I feel numb."

"We need a few days to think it through."

"What if he acts before then? What if we could prevent something and we. . ."

"He spaces them out," Mickey interjected. "And he has his sights set on Lisa now. I think she's the next target."

"Lisa," Grace groaned. "Who is probably saying good night to date-number-one right now."

They looked at each other with a sense of alarm.

"We need to get out of here *now*," Mickey said.

They stood in the doorway of each room, comparing their *intake* photo with the *exit* photo. Everything, down to the position of the throw pillow on the couch, needed to be exactly as Hunter had left it. Then they put on their shoes and coats, adjusted the blinds, turned off the lights except for the table lamp that had been on when they arrived, and stepped out into the cold night air. Then they peeled off the gloves and put them in the shopping bag.

"I could use a drink," Mickey said, opening the car door for Grace. "Would you care to join me?"

"What a splendid idea," Grace replied. "And food."

"Yes, perfect," Mickey said. "Drinks *and* food."

They drove downtown and found a space to park on a side street. Main Street in Kaw Valley on a Saturday night was hopping in the way that only university towns can. There was no separate *student district* of bars and clubs, coffee houses and restaurants in Kaw Valley. The downtown belonged to everyone. But there tended to be a time divide, like a shift change, with the 35-plus, or anyone with kids, the majority before 10-11 p.m. and the college kids taking the late shift, usually until 2 a.m. or later.

They settled in a table by the window at Zen Zero and ordered spicy curry and Boulevard Wheat. They did not discuss the evening. Mickey speculated on the back-stories of people passing on the sidewalk. Grace told him about *The Marvelous Mrs. Maisel*. When Mickey drove Grace home, she invited him in for a brandy.

They sat on the couch, a Bonnie Raitt CD in the background, as the hyper-vigilance of the evening waned and sheer exhaustion set in.

"That was so outside my comfort zone," Grace said. "And yet it was my idea. How does that work?"

"You want answers, Grace, and you're tenacious," Mickey

reflected. "You take risks, sometimes without appreciating the consequences. So, you get in over your head."

"So I'm not scaring you off?"

"Not happening," Mickey replied. "But seriously, I have some things to share if you're awake enough to listen."

"I can listen fine. It's talking that takes energy."

"I listened to what you said about *emotional baggage*. It took me a while, but I hired a young woman, very enthusiastic and energetic. We emptied every closet, got rid of so much stuff that I couldn't even tell you what half of it was. While I was gone on business, she had a crew paint every wall in the house with colors I'd never have thought of. Then some landscape guy tore out the dead bushes, planted some stuff to give it *curb appeal*. She's pushing me to move out so she can stage the house for the spring market."

"Damn, Mickey, that's huge."

"Well, what's weird is that once I started it's like I could hear Joanne's voice in my ear: 'Empty those kitchen shelves and give the young woman a big tip.' "

Grace started to laugh, a cackle that led to a deep, unquenchable laugh, with tears coming out the corners of her eyes.

"That's some voice, Mickey. Joanne is very specific."

"She taught elementary school, remember? You got to tell kids *exactly* what to do or they'll mess it up."

"Where did you find the helper?"

"That's kind of bizarre, actually. I posted an ad on Craigslist that an old widower needed help cleaning out his house. I got some responses from cleaning services and agencies, but one email that grabbed me. She told me that she had done this for her grandpa and it wasn't easy. She said she could get opinionated because she watched so much *HGTV*."

"How did you answer?"

"I asked her to come over and see what was involved before she took me on. And I asked what HGTV was. That's when she said I really needed help."

"How long did it take?"

"I'd say about twenty or so days over several months, plus the painting and landscaping that was done when I was gone."

"How do you feel about it now?"

"Well, anyone who sees it says it's an amazing improvement. And it's so much brighter, no clutter, closets mostly empty. It's like a totally different house, which, for me, will make it easier to sell."

"Where are you going to move? Do you want a condo or. . ."

"I'm not sure. Maybe a little ranch, with a small yard. Not sure I'm ready for apartment or even condo living. I really like what you've created here. It's manageable."

Grace looked around her home and saw it through his eyes. It was better than *manageable*.

When she looked back, Mickey was watching her.

"What I'm saying here is that I have been dealing with my *baggage*, and I've gotten clear that I want something more in my life."

Grace suddenly felt hot. Anxious. Unprepared. What was he saying? She felt her face flush. She couldn't look him in the eyes.

"Jesus, Gracie, don't go all weird on me, I'm not proposing or anything," Mickey said. "I'm just saying that I care about you, that I want us to be friends. To have each other's back. And more if and when the timing works for both of us, which is a complete crap shoot. Okay?"

Grace felt relief wash over her.

"Why the hell didn't you say that in the first place?"

"Because I thought you'd want to know I'd finally cleaned out my dead wife's closets before I said it. And how doing all of that was hard. And I appreciate you pushing me."

"I never *pushed* you."

"You pointed out to me that there were some things that might be problematic if I ever wanted to have another relationship."

"Yeah, I may have done that."

"For which I'm grateful. So, now, can I please finish, because this emotional *processing* shit is—how did you put it?—*Out of my comfort zone?*"

Grace nodded.

"We have some kind of hump to get over." Mickey continued in a rush. "You know, like in *Annie Hall*, that Woody Allen movie, which I liked before he went all creepy and it was no longer fun to watch Woody Allen movies? The scene with Diane Keaton where he says something like, 'Let's kiss now and get it over with so we don't have to worry during dinner.' "

Mickey abruptly stopped talking and leaned in toward Grace. Their faces were inches apart. She could feel his breath, warm and soft.

"I want to kiss you. I'm taking a risk here. Can you please help me out?"

Grace pulled back and looked into his eyes, then moved and gently let their lips touch. They stayed very still until Mickey said, "Ummmm," and moved his lips, ever so slowly, and inhaled deeply, as if to breathe Grace in.

They made out, tentatively, like adolescents who do not want to make a mistake. Mickey did not make a move for more.

When they came up for air, Grace felt shy. She had let him in, in some invisible way.

"Well, that's good, Grace. Quite, *quite* good. Now we can relax some."

He cleared his throat and started talking again.

"So, here is what I want, and I'm just going to spit it out. I want to stay over tonight. No sex. Just be in the same bed, in pajamas, and spoon. I want to rub your back. No big deal because we did this already when you were not in good shape and could hardly enjoy it. But I want to stay with you and wake up with you. That would mean a lot to me. But if you aren't ready, I can wait. You're worth waiting for."

"Are you saying that you brought pajamas? Are they in the car?" Grace asked.

"Yeah, smart ass, I brought pajamas. And a change of clothes, a toothbrush, and a gentleman's robe so I can read the morning paper in style."

"Go get your damn pajamas, Mickey. Let's do this."

Chapter 52
(December 2nd)

"We need the victims, the women," Mickey said. "No way to get anything on the perp without their personal accounts of what happened, or what they remember happening."

It was Saturday, mid-afternoon. Mickey, Grace, and Lisa were sitting at Grace's dining room table. Files of pictures, one for each of the unknown women, were stacked in the middle. There was also a file of all the pictures they'd taken of Hunter's apartment, and a file with a time-line and notes from when Lisa and Grace were in the initial stages of the *hunt* for Hunter. There were notes from professor contacts, other students, a background check, and more.

Mickey had printed out the pictures and Grace had assembled them. They were numbered to maintain the original order.

"Let's assume they all had a similar experience to Shelby," Mickey said. "They went on a date, had a good time, came back to his place, had a drink—and woke up groggy. No memory. The ever-helpful Hunter fills in their memories by telling them what happened. Since they're still at least partially dressed, and they have no memory of their own to argue with, they accept his version, and get the hell out of there. They know nothing about the pictures."

"Unless he tried to blackmail them. Could that be a part of this?" Lisa asked.

"Usually blackmail photos are much more sexually graphic," Mickey replied. "These are ritualized, a series of poses. *Artistic*. For personal gratification, not market value."

"So what do we need to get a search warrant?" asked Grace.

"*We* do not get a search warrant—the *police* get one from a *judge* by presenting an affidavit that an officer has a reason to believe that criminal activity has taken place. But what do we have? Say you tell a cop, 'Hey, I did a bad thing and broke into this guy's house and while I was in there I found all these pictures of sleeping young women posed naked—oh, and a bottle of something labeled *Sleepy time* in the back of his medicine chest. I have a feeling that something criminal is going on.'"

"What kind of charges would Hunter face if we did have *evidence* that could hold water?" Grace asked Mickey.

"Battery; aggravated battery if a DA could prove he drugged them without consent; invasion of privacy. A remote possibility of kidnapping if he took them from one room to another without consent or held them against their will. But that's a stretch."

"No sexual assault or attempted sexual. . ."

"Nothing to base that on. Zero, zilch, nada. At least as far as I know at this point."

"So, if I called 911 and said that my friend was at this address," asked Lisa, "and she'd just called me and said she felt she was in danger, that she thought he'd drugged her. . ."

"The police would go to the address and do a well-person check. That means they can enter, look into rooms, find the person and eRocnsure they are okay or safely escort them out. Whatever the person wants. But they cannot open a drawer or look under or behind things. Only what is visible on surfaces. *If* they do see something that, to them, indicates criminal activity, they can call the detective in charge and request a warrant. Meanwhile they can secure the location, like keep the resident from being able to flush drugs down the toilet, until they get a call that a warrant has been secured. Not like the movies where it always seems like they have to have a signed piece of paper in their hands. Now it gets scanned to a phone."

"This is a lot to process," said Lisa. "And none of it is helpful."

"I think that any kind of check would scare him off. There will be no evidence to find. He'll destroy it," Grace said. "From what you're saying, we have to track down some of the women in these pictures. Maybe like Molly did to find whoever was in Shelby's class—using social media?"

"Like how?" Mickey asked.

"I've been thinking. We have to get creative. This is out-of-the-box, but we could invent a *regional research group* that is collecting data on certain aspects of campus sexual assault. Develop a mini-questionnaire. Then we see if any responses match his MO. Can't be that many, and I'm assuming he focused on university women. Could go nowhere, zero responses, or we could luck out. What do you think?"

"And if Hunter sees it and freaks?" asked Lisa.

"We can keep it more generic at first, not as specific," replied Grace. "He may not even track these sites. But, yes, it could freak him. It's a gamble."

"We could try it, see if we get any responses," Mickey said, rubbing his chin. "Low risk, more back door, no lockpicks needed. Why not?"

An hour later, Mickey had set up a new email address, insufficientevidenceresearch@gmail.com, and Lisa and Grace had written an ad and posted it on two sites.

"Regional research group collecting data on invisible campus sexual assault wants to hear from university women who have had the experience of: 1) waking up with no memory of what happened the night prior; 2) in compromised circumstances outside their norm (i.e. in someone's bed, clothing removed, a *feeling* that something had happened or been done to them); 3) were then told a narrative that was inconsistent with their personal prior behavior or experiences.

Respond to this email and you will be sent a confidential questionnaire. If your experience fits our research focus, you may be invited to participate in a focus group (also confidential). Payment provided for focus group time."

Then they composed the follow-up questionnaire:

1) When did this experience happen? Month, day, year?

2) What year were you in college? How old were you?

3) Did this occur following a one-on-one date or a gathering (i.e. fraternity party, bar, club, etc.)

4) Did this involve one boy/man or multiple boys/men?

5) Did you know or have any prior relationship with the boy/man?

6) Do you know the boy/man's name? His first name? His address? (You do not have to provide it, but we'd like to know if you knew him.)

7) Did you report anything to law enforcement? Counselor? Crisis center? The IOA office of the university? If not, please briefly explain your reasons why not. If so, was the process or outcome satisfactory?

8) Can you describe what happened to you? Or what preceded it? Just describe your experience however you want.

Then it asked for a name and where they went to school.

Confidentiality will be respected was the final line in a large type size.

They sat back, somewhat satisfied with the last 24 hours: a date, breaking and entering, piles of illegally obtained evidence, setting up a dummy research foundation, posting about a fake project and focus group.

Just thinking about it would make anyone hungry. "What's on the stove, Grace?" Mickey asked. "I smell onions and garlic."

"Beef stew."

"Got some French bread to mop up the sauce?"

"Yes, as a matter of fact I do."

"Then let's get these files off the table and have ourselves some supper."

Lisa hastily excused herself. "I need to study. Exams are coming up. I'll let you know if we get any responses, but it may take a while because everybody is busy."

Grace and Mickey ate the stew, mopping up the sauce with a crusty, warm baguette, sipping their glasses of Pinot Noir.

"Damn, this is good. How do you make it?" Mickey asked.

"Use decent meat, fresh spices, red wine, broth. Sauté the meat first for a while before tossing in the carrots, potatoes, celery, and whatever other vegetables happen to be in the fridge."

"Which does not help at all. I need it written down, with measurements, precise quantities, like half a teaspoon of which spice and how much of each vegetable, and how much time is *a while* and what constitutes *decent meat*."

"I have no idea, Mickey. I've never cooked like that. You got lucky tonight. Sometimes it's a brown muddle. Want some coffee? Tea?" Grace asked, standing up and placing her hand on his shoulder.

"Coffee would be good. Then I need to take off. Busy day with work tomorrow."

Grace stood at the door watching Mickey toss his gym bag into his back seat. They'd hugged at her door, and he'd softly kissed her good-bye. She'd kissed him back, feeling a comfort and longing that had been long buried. This was scary, and she felt vulnerable in a way she had not for many years.

Chapter 53
(December 3rd)

Grace's phone rang about 11 a.m. Sunday morning. It was Lisa.

"Have you checked that email address?" she asked.

"No. I thought I'd give it a day or so."

"Well, I suggest you do it now because they're piling up."

"What? What's piling up?"

"Responses. There are 63 in the inbox and another one pops up every five minutes."

"From who?"

"Who do you think? From college girls who have woken up in someone else's bed with no memory of what the hell happened. This goes way beyond Hunter. I think girls who have friends that this has happened to must be forwarding it to them. And, really, *every* college girl has a friend who. . ."

"63? Did you say 63?" Grace asked.

"Make that 65. Two more just popped up."

"Take the posting down now. This changes. . ."

"I just did," Lisa interrupted, "but it hit a nerve. It's obviously being shared and re-posted to generate this much response. More will be coming in."

"Yeah, I get that. Can you come over here? We'll need to work through this together."

Within an hour, they were at work. Lisa methodically responded to each email with a cut-and-paste: *Thank you for responding. Here is a brief questionnaire. We appreciate that this is a very busy time for students, but we need your data in the next 48 hours to determine focus groups. So, if you possibly can, please take 10 minutes to complete the questionnaire and return it to the email listed.*

Surprisingly, or maybe not, over 80% returned the questionnaire quickly, many within an hour of receiving it. It was a marketing response rate that defied statistics.

Grace's printer got a workout as Lisa printed out each returned questionnaire. They were one-to-two pages each, depending on how much detail was in the answer to question number 8: *Can you describe what happened to you? Or what preceded it?* Lisa numbered each response for handy reference.

Grace reviewed each submission, sorting by: *Did this occur following a one-on-one date or a gathering (i.e. fraternity party, bar, club, etc.).* The one-on-one dates were then sorted again based on whether they contained any descriptive information that excluded Hunter.

Grace also selected a few that, while clearly not Hunter, were representative of the majority of the questionnaires. She put these on top of the pile for Mickey to review:

16 : *When I woke up, the guy was asleep next to me. I was still in the frat house. My panties and jeans were off, but my T-shirt was still on. I was totally freaked. But it was like nothing for him. I asked, "What did you do?" and he said, "What are you talking about? We had a hookup. You maybe drank too much. No big deal." I got my clothes on and got out of there as fast as I could. I never told anyone. I had two or three drinks but over four hours.*

42: *I'd known the guy for a year. We were friends. We're hanging out at a bar, a band was playing—the usual TGIF. I just nursed one beer because I was paying for my own drinks. After the band, we went over to his apartment. His two roommates were playing video games in the living room, so we went to his bedroom to watch some comedy skits on YouTube he'd told me about. He brought me a drink, said his roommate had a big bottle of Jim Beam that he'd mixed with Sprite. We put the comedy skits on. That's all. I woke up at like 11 a.m. the next morning in his bed, my capris and underwear were off. I shook him to wake up, and said, "What the fuck happened here?" He told me, "You know you've been asking for it for a long time." I left. He tried calling me, like we were supposed to be dating now or something, like we were still buddy-buddy. I told him to leave me the fuck alone. After a while, he did.*

And then there was one that made Grace's stomach turn over. She had to go into the bathroom and put cold water on her face. This one got a file all its own:

#56: *I woke up and I was naked in a room. This was 15 months ago. There were two twin beds but no one else was there. I found my clothes across the room on the floor. There was a blood stain on the sheets, and blood on my thighs. I knew something bad had happened because I hurt, just really ached and throbbed. And when I peed it stung. Later, when I had a bowel movement, there was also some blood. It's not like I was a virgin or anything, but I'd never hurt like that before, ever. After I got dressed, and went out the door, I realized I was on like the top floor of the frat. I'd never been up there, had only been in the downstairs and back deck. I walked down two flights of stairs, and it hurt to even do that. In the kitchen, about five guys were standing around drinking coffee. I asked where Joe was, because that's who I was talking to, the last guy I remembered. "Joe who?" one of the guys asked me. "I don't know. Joe with black hair, an engineering major, a junior, from Nebraska." "There's no Joe like that in this house," they said. "No idea who you've been fucking." I didn't go to the police, didn't tell anyone but two friends (and one sent me this email to respond to). I knew it would end up being my word against a dozen guys. I could not face being slut-shamed. I did go to a doctor and she said I had internal abrasions and cuts in my vagina and anus consistent with multiple forcible rapes. I got a morning-after pill and antibiotics. I was a freshman. I almost dropped out, and my grades sucked, but then I got it together. I'm okay now but I've never gone to another "party" and I have not had sex and I do not date. This is the first time I've said it all. No one has ever asked me what happened. Even my friends never asked for details. They think it was one guy and that I drank too much. But I didn't.*

"Mickey," Grace said into his voicemail, "I know it probably feels like you just left, but we need you back here."

When Mickey arrived, he found Lisa and Grace on the couch staring bleary-eyed at HGTV, the lovely fantasy of *Caribbean Life*.

"I want to live there," Grace said, pointing at a 1.3 million dollar *cottage* as he took off his coat. "Just walk out the door every morning and put my toes in the waves. That's what I want."

"And yet you moved to Homer, Alaska," Mickey commented. "That makes sense."

"I was in a bad place and felt that I deserved to suffer through subzero temperatures for 70% of the year," Grace retorted.

"You lived In Alaska?" Lisa asked. "I didn't know that. Why did you move to Alaska?"

"That is a very long story for another day." Grace said. "Now we have to get back to work. C'mon."

Piles of questionnaires were on the dining table, and the folders of photos and notes were in a legal file box on the floor. They had divided up the questionnaires by post-dates and one-on-one versus party.

"I say we start by reviewing every one of the possibilities—the one-on-one dates that could possibly be Hunter," Grace said.

"But if they go back a few years, and some do, are we sure he had his own place? Could he have lived with roommates for a while?" Lisa asked.

"Yeah, but this is ritualized, and he's probably a loner," Mickey interjected. "Needs to be in control. Not a party guy or someone who likes sharing space with messy roommates."

"Okay, that makes sense. Let's see what we have," Lisa agreed.

"We have twenty-nine one-on-one date responses. Eleven describe going to the guy's apartment, do not mention roommates, were not in a bedroom when they passed out, just sat in a living room," Grace explained. "That would be consistent with what Shelby said, but no guarantee that Hunter was that consistent. Eight are ambiguous—could be or not—like, *Went to his place. Had one drink. Don't remember anything else.* That adds up to nineteen. Then another ten of the one-on-one dates have something that points another direction, like there were roommates, they were naked when they woke up. . ."

"So, you got *nineteen* possible match options? Seriously?" Mickey sounded incredulous.

"We have zero matches without more data. We have to find a way to match the *photo shoots*, if we can call them that, with responses."

Mickey and Lisa read, and Grace re-read, the nineteen questionnaires, each taking notes.

"It could be any of these," Lisa said in a frustrated voice. "We should have asked for the name of the guy. That would simplify things. Why didn't we ask if they knew a name?"

"We had no idea there'd be this many responses. We didn't want to scare anyone off who might not want to share information they've kept secret and maybe want it to stay that way," Grace explained.

"Like we plan on using it?"

"Yes, precisely because we plan on using it. Now, when we narrow down the possibilities, we'll ask them the question and tell them what we know so they then can assess what they're getting into."

"But if they know he did it to other girls, wouldn't anybody want to do whatever they can to stop him?" Lisa persisted.

"They probably don't know they were photographed," Grace replied. "Not a single response of the one-on-one dates mentioned that as a possibility. Some girls reported being threatened with pictures, being told that there were compromising pictures that would be distributed on social media if they told, but they're all in the frat party or bar piles," Grace said.

"So, could we be creating trauma if they believed Hunter—that they fell asleep and nothing happened?" Mickey asked. "We have no idea what emotional closet they've put their Hunter date in—like, *Weird Date* or *Bummer* or *I'll never know so I put it behind me.*"

"Exactly," Grace replied. "Which is what Shelby probably would have done if she'd woken up with her clothes mostly on and not naked."

Lisa looked stricken.

"Oh, Lisa, I'm sorry. It isn't that simple. I shouldn't have said. . ."

"No, you're right. If she'd had her clothes on, she might have questioned him but not nearly as much."

"Both of you are ignoring that this Hunter maybe sent the other women photos," Mickey interjected. "Like he did with Shelby. To shut them up. And those women will probably not respond to any questionnaire. We could have zero matches."

"Let's look at whatever time frame they provided," Grace said, "and see if any patterns emerge. . ."

"Holy shit," Mickey interrupted. "We have the dates."

"Yeah, that was question #1 on. . ."

"No. I mean *we* have *Hunter's* dates. Each envelope had a date on it. Remember? Shelby's had *September, 2017.* Just the month, but that might be enough."

"Did we take photos of the envelopes?" Grace asked.

She remembered carefully laying out every picture and putting them back in the right order, but did they also take pictures of the manila envelopes the pictures were in? She could not remember. She'd been so totally anxious.

"I don't know," Mickey answered.

They both dove for the legal box on the floor with the photographs. Grace grabbed one folder and Mickey another.

"Yes!" Grace said, holding up a picture of an envelope. *November 2016* was neatly printed on the top right-hand corner. "I did take them. I just didn't remember."

It took three minutes to write down the Hunter dates, just the month and year, on blank paper. Mickey and Grace split the *possibles*.

"Okay, Lisa, you read out the dates and we'll see if we get matches," Grace directed.

Lisa started. "June 2016?"

There was no sound from either Grace or Mickey.

"November 2015?"

"March 2017?"

"Bingo!" Mickey said. "We have a match."

"Do you want to keep going," Lisa asked, "or stop and look more at..."

"Keep going," Mickey said.

Lisa read all nineteen dates. When she finished, they had seven matches for the months listed on the Hunter manila envelopes.

"Now what?" Lisa asked.

"We have a drink, move to the couch, and think this through," Grace replied. "Do you want whiskey or wine?"

"Whiskey," Mickey said. "Two fingers. Straight."

"Can I just have lemonade?" Lisa asked. "I still have to study tonight."

"Oh my God, Lisa," Grace answered, "Go home. Or the library. Wherever you go to study."

"Hey, Lisa," Mickey asked. "What's your major?"

"Aerospace engineering," she replied. "And I study at 24-hour coffee houses. I'll call you tomorrow."

Mickey and Grace retired to the couch, he with his Jameson and she with a Pinot Noir. He stretched out his legs, put one arm behind her shoulders, and began to softly knead her neck.

"Ohhhhhhh," she said, "that does feel good."

"That was my intention," Mickey said. "Your neck looked tight from clear across the table."

"So, to quote Lisa, 'Now what?' " Mickey asked.

"We email the women and ask if their date was with a man named Hunter. If so, we have some information for them. Or we just tell them about the pictures. We could do that also."

"Maybe ask them for a photo of themselves so we can match to the pics," Grace added. "Or get Lisa to do a Facebook search or whatever she does. Once we match names with the pictures, we have what we need to. . ."

"We have *nothing*," interrupted Mickey. "We aren't going to the police without the *consent* of the women."

"But we have. . ."

"We have photos. Period. Until the women identify as victims. Until they file a complaint."

"Then we need to move on this n-o-w," Grace retorted, standing up and walking over to her desk. Mickey did not try to stop her.

Her email was brief: *Thank you for your reply, and, by the way, was that date with a young man named Hunter?* If so, she had some information she wanted to share with them. She did not mention the photos.

Mickey, meanwhile, dozed off on the couch, the glass of whiskey empty on the coffee table.

She shook him, lightly, until his eyes opened, blinking at the lamp light.

"Would you like to stay over?" she asked.

"I didn't bring my pajamas," he said. "I didn't want to appear needy."

"That's okay. I ran into Walmart this morning and bought some masculine PJs in a dark gray. Size large. That red plaid you had on the other night didn't do it for me, although the robe was a nice accent. And I picked up a toothbrush, deodorant, razor and shaving cream."

Mickey grinned. "You did all that for me? Really?"

"Yeah," she said. "Didn't want to give you an excuse to sleep naked. We're not there yet."

Chapter 54
(December 4th)

There were seven responses in the phony research study in-box when Grace checked it at 10 a.m.

Three replied, "Yes," that his name was Hunter and just how did she/they know that and what was this all about?

Two said that, "No," they had never dated a Hunter.

Two said to take their name off of any list and not to contact them again. One of those added that they didn't know what kind of game this was, but she wanted nothing to do with it and if they contacted her again she would inform the authorities.

Grace emailed the three and: 1) Requested a photo, or link to a Facebook page, adding that she would be happy to explain why, when they could meet or talk; 2) To please send her their phone number or call her. She listed her cell number. She explained that she preferred to talk rather than email. Also, that she would prefer to meet for coffee and talk in person rather than on the phone.

She started to send the email to the two who had told her to take their names off any list, just to reassure them that this was not a part of some scam, but then reconsidered. Better to wait and talk to Mickey or Patsy.

Mickey had left at 7:30 a.m., showered and shaved, flashing her a big smile. He was in his day-old clothes, but, as he'd explained last night when they were spooning in bed, "I put them on at 5 p.m. before I came over, so they're not really day-old. Barely touched my body."

She'd rolled over, almost giggling, and they'd smooched. Then she'd rubbed his back, her left hand moving in slow concentric circles, like she had done when putting her kids down at night. "Inhale," she'd whispered. "Exhale. Now let it all go. No worry. Be happy." This time it was Mickey who had slipped first into sleep.

Grace wanted to just stay home and process what was happening. But she had appointments scheduled with a mid-afternoon break.

It was during the break, about 2:30 p.m., that she next checked the email. She found two responses. Neither girl was willing to send her a photo, nor a link, and were suspicious of what exactly was going on. In reading over the email sequences, Grace could understand why. It was all sounding creepy. She'd been so fixated on getting answers that she'd overlooked how it might be read or heard.

Enough, she thought. *Time to put **all** the cards on the table.*

She emailed all three young women separately from her business email, provided a link to her work website so they could see she was not a kook—although, given what was going on, that was debatable.

She tried to lay it out, explaining that they had each: 1) reported waking up with no memory of what had transpired; 2) had each dated a guy named Hunter; 3) that this was probably coming across as weird or creepy but that's because aspects of it were. She added that it would be easier to explain if they could meet in person, collectively rather than individually.

"I finish up with my appointments at 7 p.m. tomorrow evening. My office is downtown over the shoe store on Main St. I'll be at the bar in The Eldridge in a back booth at 8 p.m. Drinks (alcohol or not) are on me. I realize this may feel weird or creepy. If you can't make it then, I'll meet with you another time. If you want to bring a friend, like for back-up or support, that's fine."

No more games, Grace thought. *Enough already.*

Then Grace called Lisa, leaving a voice mail: "Can you meet tomorrow night at 7:45 at the Eldridge? I've invited the three *Hunter-responses* to come together. I think this will be a good thing."

The next day Grace had to work hard to stay focused during her last session. It was a couple with three children—a five-year-old daughter and two-year old twin boys—who weren't sure if they wanted to stay married. They reported almost no sexual desire, no energy, chronic bickering, feeling unappreciated and disconnected.

"If I have an hour, I just want to be alone," Melody said. "Not with Andrew. Just being with him feels like a drain."

"We used to share interests, liked to go places and do things," Andrew reported. "I know we have the kids, but she never wants to do *anything.*"

Grace asked questions, lots of questions, about their daily schedules, child-care, extended family support, finances, and more.

"I don't mean to be abrupt or dismissive," she said, "but divorce is a huge, serious, life-altering decision. It's also incredibly expensive—financially and emotionally. And, after listening to you both, my sense is that your current despair is situational."

They looked at her as if unsure this was bad news or good news.

"You said that your mothers get along well, correct?" Grace asked.

They nodded but appeared confused at the question.

"Good. Now here is what I want you to do. I need you to take this as a prescription. Not a mere suggestion, but a medical *necessity*. You each call your mothers and tell them that you're seeing a marriage counselor and that you're so depleted and disconnected that you've considered divorce. The counselor said you have *got* to go away for a week, no kids, to get sleep, start to feel human, talk, and, we can only hope, remember what it feels like to enjoy each other's company. You then say that while neither one of them would have an easy time taking care of the three kids alone, together they can manage just fine. Grammy bonding."

"I can't leave the kids," Melody said. "They've never been away from me overnight."

"You get divorced and they'll be away from you for three or more nights a week for the next sixteen-plus years," Grace said bluntly. "Want to ask them which they'd vote for? They know their grandparents and they'll be well cared for. It's a week, not a deployment."

"We've been saving for a family vacation for next summer, but I don't want to use that. . ." Joel started to say.

Grace interrupted. "Listen to what you just said—saving for a *family* vacation? If you folks don't get a break, time to breathe and re-connect, *there is no family*. There's exchanging the kids at a McDonald's parking lot on Sunday afternoons," Grace almost started shaking her finger at them like an elementary school teacher.

"A marriage started this family," she continued. "And that marriage needs CPR. Not a Band-Aid. No more waiting. You can't see it now, but this *is* in the best interests of your kids. They want married, *happily* married, parents."

Joel and Melody looked at Grace as if she were crazy.

"I'm not crazy," she replied. "But I'm not interested in taking your money every week for six months for therapy to work on communication skills when you're so exhausted and empty that you can't think straight. Go away, sleep for twenty-four hours, eat grown-up food without rushing, have a few arguments with enough time to make-up. Maybe even try some practice sex. Take your own alone time for five hours each day doing what *you* want to do. Then see if maybe, just perhaps, you look forward to being together."

Grace abruptly stopped, as if she'd run out of air.

"We could ask Uncle Ed if we could borrow his condo in Daytona Beach," Melody said softly. "He's offered, and we always say we can't."

"I'm off for the week after Christmas. I'd thought we could use that time to get the house squared away, but. . ."

"The house won't get squared away until they're all in school," Melody interrupted. "Maybe one room at a time." But her voice was not bitter or critical, just stating a fact.

"Are the grandparents local?" Grace asked.

"Just forty-five minutes," Joel answered. "South of Topeka. Close enough."

"I suggest you celebrate Christmas on the 23rd or 24th. Your kids won't know the difference. Flights are cheaper on the 25th, especially last minute. And there is something romantic about running away together on Christmas."

"I need a new bathing suit," Melody said.

"I bet they have them in Daytona," Joel answered.

After they left, tentatively holding hands while looking a little shell-shocked, Grace loaded the Hunter files into a briefcase, turned off the lights, locked the door and walked to the Eldridge.

Chapter 55
(December 5th)

"So two or three possible Hunter-dates may or may not walk in here in fifteen minutes?" Lisa asked. "For real?"

"Two responded that they would come, and a third has not," Grace replied.

Grace had nabbed a big booth, the ones that could hold eight people, in the far back corner. She'd told the waiter that they were having a meeting and to only come to the table when she waved at him.

"The whole picture thing could freak them out," Lisa said. "I say we warn them and let them decide if they even want to see them."

"That's what I was thinking. I brought blank paper to cover the body and leave the face if they just want to be absolutely sure it's them but do not want the visuals burned into their brain," Grace said. "And I reorganized the pictures in each file so the ones with clothing are on top and the most sexual, like the crotch shots, are at the bottom."

"It could also be that they don't match any of the photos. We won't know until we see them."

"Which means we got nothing," Grace said. "Nada."

"So, what do we say that we want from them? Because that's what this is about, right? Getting Hunter?"

"That comes later," Grace replied. "After they get sucker-punched."

"But we do explain that unless they're willing to come forward, collectively, and say what happened, that he will keep doing it to other girls?"

"We've had a lot of time to process all of this. They haven't. If we pressure them, they could disappear. We give them the info, say that this is kind of creepy and may take time to process. Then we ask if they are willing to meet and talk again."

"How long do we drag it out? I mean, winter break is in a few weeks. Something needs to happen before then."

"I don't think we can control that, Lisa."

When Grace glanced toward the front of the restaurant, she saw a young woman standing alone, her arms crossed across her chest, as if waiting or looking for someone. Instantly Grace realized that she was a match.

"There's one of them, Lisa. How about you go get her?"

By the time Lisa got to the front of the restaurant and introduced herself, Grace noticed that another girl had come in the front door. She gestured to Lisa. Match number two.

And then—surprise, surprise—the girl who had not responded to the email asking for a picture, but whom Grace had included in the invite to meet up tonight, also walked in. Match number three.

Lisa was shaking hands and doing introductions as all four walked to the back booth, stopping to hang up their winter coats and scarves at the coat rack.

Grace stood up as they approached. Lisa introduced Grace, and there was a flurry of, *Good to meet you,* and handshakes, followed by an awkward fumbling around as each girl tried to defer to the other as far as who slid in and who sat on the outside. "I'm so sorry, did you want to sit on the outside? I can slide in, no problem." "No, no, I'll slide in. You can sit on the outside. That's fine with me." "Are you sure? Because I'm happy to." "Yes, absolutely."

Lisa stood back until the three girls were settled, then slid in across from them. Grace followed. She was not about to debate Lisa on who got the outside position. There had to be some benefits to getting old. She gestured to the waiter who came over and took their drink orders.

Three faces looked expectantly across the table at Grace.

Carolyn. Amanda. Blair.

"Where do you want to start?" she asked. "How about you shoot me some questions?"

"How did you know to ask if the guy I had a date with was named Hunter? What's with that?" opened Blair.

"That's complicated," Grace replied. "I think I'll defer to Lisa to answer that for now."

Lisa gave her the evil eye.

"Here's a summary," Lisa began. "In the course of a private investigation, we found out that Hunter Payne had taken a young woman, Shelby Stewart, on a date. It was a traditional date, movie and a bite to eat after. He was engaging, listened well, courteous, not pushy. He asked her out again, and, when they finished eating, invited her back to his apartment to listen to a CD of a band she'd said she liked. He offered her a drink, a Moscow Mule in a copper mug. We believe that he drugged her with that drink. She woke up the next morning with no memory of anything. She was naked, in his bed. He denied sexual activity, told her that she'd come on to him, that she'd had too much to drink. But Shelby was not a drinker, and she never came on to guys."

While Lisa spoke, Grace had watched the girls' eyes, their non-verbal responses. By sentence three, two were nodding, as if this were somehow familiar. At sentence five, at the words *drugged her,* Carolyn started to breathe through her nose, Amanda gave a very small gasp, and Blair put her head in her hands, covering her eyes.

When Lisa finished, no one spoke. She continued.

"We believe that this was a pattern, and that Hunter repeated this scenario with other young women. So, while it was a long shot, we thought if we described the scene in general that maybe, just maybe, girls would respond, and we'd locate some of them. We believe that you are three, and that there are at least eight more out there."

"Why eight? Blair asked. "How did you come up with that number?"

"Because we've come into possession of 12 sets of photographs. Hunter took pictures of girls when they were passed out. We have no indication that he ever did anything with the photos, and believe that he took them for personal reasons, for himself."

"Shit," muttered Carolyn. "That sweet-talking, Mr. Nice Guy. 'You fell asleep, Carolyn, and I tried to wake you, but you were almost passed out. You had a few drinks. They must have hit you harder than usual.' "

"I knew something was off. I knew it," said Amanda. "I asked him what had happened, but he looked so, like, how could I possibly think he was not being truthful? He had this hurt face, like I was an attacking bitch and he was innocent. All I was doing was asking. But then I started to feel like I was over-reacting and I ended up apologizing."

"Me too," chimed in Carolyn. "I said I was sorry, like I'd really inconvenienced him. I said something like, 'Thank you for taking care of me.' "

"Did he ever contact you again?" Lisa asked. "Did you call or email him?"

"No," answered Amanda. "And I remember feeling relieved after a week, like I knew he wasn't going to, so I didn't have to figure out what to say."

"Same here. He was so nice at first, and I really liked him. He didn't want to hookup," said Carolyn. "He seemed to want to get to know me. But then it all got weird. A hookup would have been less weird."

"I knew he was lying, but he'd never admit it," said Blair.

"What bothered me the most was how it made me not trust my own judgment. How could I think he was so nice and then. . ." Amanda's voice trailed off.

"Where are the photos?" asked Blair. "Can I see what he took of me?"

"That's why I wanted to meet with you in person," Grace said. "This could mess with your head, although it sounds like all three of you felt that *something* was not right. But there is a big difference between a vague feeling that you can push away and concrete proof that someone violated your privacy and body."

"So, they're sexual," Blair said. "You wouldn't be talking like this about head shots."

"Yes. Some are posed, like erotic-artiste, and some are more blatantly sexual. And you're all clearly unconscious."

"Holy shit," said Carolyn. "I was not expecting this."

"There is no way anyone could have expected this," Grace said. "I just have the one set of photos, and I need to keep them for now, but I can make you copies."

"Why would I want copies? I don't even know if I want to see them at all," said Carolyn.

"*Then don't,*" Grace said. "I mean that. *Seriously.* Do not feel like there is any *I should look so I know* requirement. You can take what we've said and go home and think about whether there is any need for you to see them."

"So why did you tell us at all?" asked Amanda.

"Because it's your body and you have a right to make your own decision. But there was also a part of me that said, *They've probably moved on. Don't bring it up. They may have already forgotten.*"

"I hadn't forgotten," said Blair. "I just had no one to talk to about it, no way to describe it. I tried with some friends and they were, 'What are you making this a big deal? It wasn't like you got raped or anything.' One friend even said, 'Be glad you can't remember because then nothing really happened—even if it did.' "

"I said that to myself," added Carolyn. "Pull up your big-girl panties and move on. It was just one bad night."

"How did you decide it was us?" Blair asked.

"Each envelope had a date on it," Lisa replied. "When we collected the questionnaires, we first separated out any *experience* that was not after a one-on-one date, like those that were after club scenes or at frat parties, which were the majority. Then we narrowed down the one-on-one dates by excluding ones that did not match the Hunter scenario as far as what we did know—like if the guy had roommates, a fourth-floor walk-up, a studio instead of having a separate kitchen. We had asked for approximate dates and then matched the dates of the final possibilities to envelope dates. We then emailed the women who might be matches and asked it their date was named Hunter. You three responded, but we think there are a few more who just shut down at his name."

"How many responses did you get to the initial notice about the research project?" asked Caroline. "That sounds like a lot of sorting."

Lisa glanced at Grace, then replied. "142 before we could shut it down, but more dribbled in, mostly from women who had it forwarded to them by friends. As of yesterday, there were 197. Some were not at his university, but we assume friends forwarded the notice to them."

"Oh my God," said Caroline.

"Why?" asked Blair. "What made you do all of this work?" She looked directly at Grace and then at Lisa.

"Shelby Stewart was my roommate," Lisa answered. "So this is personal. Shelby wanted answers and kept after Hunter. I found a thumb drive of pictures of her, but with filters, so no face. We think he sent her that thumb drive or emailed her pictures to intimidate her, to make her shut up and leave him alone. We needed more proof that she was not his only target."

"Why isn't Shelby here?" Blair asked.

For a second, it was as if everyone at the table stopped breathing, as if knowing that this was a loaded question.

"Because she overdosed," Lisa replied. "Shelby is dead. Maybe it was accidental, maybe desperate. But I believe that Hunter pushed her over an edge."

There was silence as each girl absorbed what Lisa had said.

"I want to see the photos," Blair said. "I don't need to go home and think about it." The two other girls simply nodded.

Grace took out the files from her briefcase, selected three and placed them on the table. She looked at each girl, one by one, to see if they wanted their file. Each nodded.

It was a quiet five minutes as each girl reviewed her own file. Amanda gasped, again. Caroline kept blinking her eyes. Blair clenched and unclenched her hands with each photo.

Then Lisa picked up where she had left off.

"I'm asking you to consider talking to the police. With three of you, all reporting the same experience, with such similar photos, they should have a case."

"But a case for what?" Caroline asked. "What exactly would the charges be?"

"That's up to the district attorney," Lisa answered.

"Would there be a trial? Would we have to testify and have the pictures used as evidence?" Amanda's voice was plaintive. "I don't think I could stand for my family to see them."

"I think he would plea down," Grace interjected. "Avoid publicity and a trial."

"But you don't know that," Blair argued.

"There are no guarantees," Grace responded. "Look, I don't want to guilt you, but if you don't try, he will keep doing it. Over and over and over."

"Yeah," Blair said. "Like that's not guilting us."

"It's your decision," Grace concluded. "How about we proceed in stages? May I discuss your files with some police officers that I respect, but make it clear to them that you have not made a decision as far as participating? Could you email me by tomorrow if I can take that next step at least?"

That went well," Lisa said later that evening, somewhat sarcastically, to Grace. They were in Grace's kitchen.

"It's a lot to absorb," Grace said. "We've gotten used to it. But to see yourself so exposed, and to not know whether the pictures have been shared, if they were used for anything, if they are out there on the web somewhere—that's creepy and scary."

Not being alone, even if with strangers linked by the weirdness, had, Grace hoped, made it just a little less traumatic for them.

"Do you think they're posted? The pictures?" Lisa asked.

"Mickey doesn't think so, but this is a new world for us older folks. Things change so fast with social media. Our porn was a *Playboy* magazine hidden under the mattress. *Penthouse* or *Hustler* for the bad sleaze. They all seem so quaint now."

"It's not revenge porn," Lisa reflected. "That's like a whole separate genre. These are more like his little secret. Or power game."

"But it has to be illegal to post without permission, right?"

"If you think getting indictments are a challenge for physical rape, this is 1,000 percent harder. I did some research," Lisa replied. "Laws differ by jurisdiction, but the web does not respect state lines. A lot of the laws look at intent, like, was there *intent to harass* or specifically target a person by name. These would probably fall under a category of *nonconsensual porn*—pictures that go public but no slut-shaming *intent*. Like having your naked body plastered over a hundred websites should be less emotionally disturbing if the guy didn't do it to humiliate and harass you?"

"The more you describe it, the more awful it sounds."

"It is, especially if a name is attached, even without commentary. Because then, whenever someone's name is googled, the pictures and porn sites can pop up. That is not what you want when interviewing for a job."

Neither spoke as they considered the implications of one *bad* night with one jerk who thinks he's being cool showing off pics of the hot girl he fucked. Or naively believing that photos taken voluntarily—*We were just playing around. . . It's not like he would ever show anyone. . .We're in a relationship*—are ever really private.

"There is a national law being proposed, but I don't know specifics or if it would have any teeth," Lisa continued. "Platforms like Facebook and Google aren't liable for content they host, and there's kind of a face-off between victim advocates and the right to free speech. The positions reflect. . ."

"This is all I can take for tonight, Lisa," Grace interrupted. "I need some sleep and it might take a drink *and* a pill to get some."

Chapter 56
(December 6th)

By 9 a.m. the next morning, there were three emails in Grace's in-box. All three girls said it was okay for Grace to talk to the police—but also that they were not making any commitment.

Grace called Patsy. "There have been a few developments. It wouldn't be a bad idea to include Sam," she said.

"Whenever you use the word *developments,* Grace, I get nervous," Patsy replied. "Let me talk to Sam and get back with you."

"If you come to my place, I'll have lunch ready."

"Feed us and we'll be there."

So, at 12:15, Sam, Patsy, and Grace were seated at her table spooning up bowls of corn chowder.

"Have some more cheese bread," Grace offered.

"Why do I get a feeling this is a bribe of some sort?" Sam said. "Not that I am averse to food as bribe. It was my mother's first tool when it came to motivating me."

"Which may be why it still works," Patsy retorted.

"Enough you two," Grace interjected. "Finish up. I want to clear the table."

Grace had met Sam and Patsy under the kind of circumstances that rarely led to friendships, especially after more than a decade. But these two had colluded in a search of the truth. She doubted she would still be alive if it hadn't been for them—and especially Mandy, her former client. But that was a part of her life that she still kept locked away.

Table cleared, Grace brought out the files: Blair. Amanda. Carolyn.

She pushed them across the table. "Look at these and then I'll explain," she said.

They looked at each picture in each file the way that cops look: slowly, studying, absorbing—one picture at a time. Taking in the background, how they were posed, commonalities and differences.

It was several minutes before Sam spoke.

"What's the story here, Grace? Do you know these girls?"

"I do now. The story is that they each had two dates with the same young man. First dates were fine. He was respectful, courteous, engaging, not pushy. Kind of an anomaly what with the hookup scene. On the second date they each went to his apartment for a drink and to listen to music or watch a DVD. They each woke up the next morning in his bed, with no memory, but their clothes basically on. Each was told she'd had a few drinks and kind of passed out. The guy said he thought it best to let them sleep it off. They each felt something had happened, but they had nothing to refute his explanation. None of them ever saw him again."

"So, no memory of anything sexual as far as an assault?" Sam asked.

"No." Grace did not elaborate.

"How did they learn about the pictures?" Sam said, rubbing his chin.

"That's complicated," Grace replied.

"We understand complicated," Sam countered. "Spit it out."

"I came into possession of these photos, which is another story altogether. But how we identified the girls. . ." And then she explained about the fake research study, the number of responses, the matching of months, the reaching out.

"There are more?" Sam asked. "More women?"

"Yes, and then there is what got me started," Grace said, handing him the file with Shelby's pictures.

He startled at the filter but studied them closely. "Why the filter?" he asked.

"Shelby Stewart also had a date with the same guy. But she woke up naked. We believe that she kept pressuring him to tell her what had happened. She didn't just back down like the others. We believe he sent these to Shelby as a threat, to intimidate her to shut up and go away. The other girls did not know until last night that any photos had even been taken."

"Where is Shelby?" Sam asked.

"Dead. Either accidental overdose or suicide."

Sam did not flinch, but his eyes dropped to the table, to the photos. He looked up and back at Grace.

"Where do you fit in?" he asked.

"I was, very briefly, her therapist."

Sam considered this for a moment.

"And you never saw it coming?"

"No," Grace said. "She never told me about the pictures. I never saw it coming."

"So, you did what, Grace?" Sam asked. "How did you get these pictures?"

Grace said nothing, staring at Sam. He stared back. Patsy looked out the window.

"I did some legwork. I believed that this guy, Hunter Payne, was the man who took the pictures and then sent them to Shelby. But it was all conjecture. I wanted proof. I picked the lock to his apartment and did a search. I found these pictures and what I think is a date-rape drug in his bathroom."

"You took the pictures?" Sam, asked.

"No, that would have tipped him off. I took snapshots of the pictures and had them printed."

"You had help on this excursion?" Sam continued.

"No, just me," she replied, looking Sam straight in the eye.

"You picked his lock?"

"There are video instructions on YouTube," Grace answered. "It's not that complicated."

"Right." Sam said, looking at Grace and shaking his head. "Not complicated at all."

"I'll need these photos for now," Sam said as they stood up from the table. "But I'll make copies."

Sam said they would confer with their chief as far as how to proceed. He expected having the photos and Grace's report would be sufficient for a search warrant. The girls would need to come forward for any charges to be made. But he was unsure of what the charges would be.

"You will have to say how you came into possession of the pictures," Sam told Grace as they were leaving. "If you cannot do that, we need to know now."

Chapter 57
(December 7th)

Grace's cell buzzed about 4 p.m. Thursday afternoon.

"We executed a search warrant late last night," Patsy reported. "The judge took a look at the pics, our summary of your report, and she signed off. We found a box with photos in his closet and a bottle with what we expect will be a drug in the date-rape family in his bathroom. It's been sent for analysis. Found another bottle of another drug in a pair of rolled up socks in his neatly organized sock drawer."

"How did Hunter take it?" Grace asked.

"It was about midnight and he'd been sound asleep. But he didn't say anything incriminating if that's what you were hoping. Kept his mouth shut. Just asked for legal counsel. He used those words, 'I want legal counsel.' "

"Where is he now?" Grace asked.

"Spent the night in county jail. But I heard he has an attorney to bail him out."

"What are the charges?"

"That's why I'm calling. Can you meet with the DA tomorrow?"

At 2 p.m. on Friday afternoon, Grace was sitting across the desk from an assistant district attorney. It was the first time she'd ever been in the DA's office suite at the courthouse. It felt awkward, bizarre even, to be on the same side as a DA when her personal history had created an abyss of suspicion.

Patsy sat in a chair beside her.

Mark Sorenson was in his mid-thirties; trim, wavy hair, wire-rimmed professor glasses perched on his nose. He cleared his throat and his chin dropped so he could look at Grace over the glasses.

"Thank you for coming in, Ms. McDonald. From what Officers Hillard and Tsosie have told me, you were instrumental in providing evidence in this case."

"Am I in trouble for that?" Grace asked.

"Not at this time," he replied. "And I'm hoping it will not be an issue. Unless we go to trial, in which case defense counsel would bring up how the police obtained cause for a warrant."

"But you can use what they found with the warrant? No matter what led to it?"

"Yes, we can. We can use evidence uncovered in the course of an illegal act, or as a result of an illegal act, as long as that act was not a part of a government action. You are a private citizen, so we can make use of it and you."

"What charges can be filed?" Grace asked.

"That's what I want to explain," Mark answered. "And I also wanted to meet you. Your case was used as an example of overzealous prosecution when I was in law school."

Grace flushed. It had been over thirteen years since her indictment and trial. But one mention and she could be flooded with panic and fear. Grace had developed coping strategies for her PTSD, but had accepted that she would have times, until she died, when the PTSD took over.

Inhale, she told herself. *Exhale. Look out the window at the trees, their branches with no leaves.* She angled her head slightly to look back at Mark.

"Well, here I am," she said. "The cold-blooded murderess returns."

Mark was the one to flush. "I didn't mean. . ." he began. "I was trying to say. . ."

"Of course not," interrupted Patsy. "So, what charges could be on the table?"

Mark looked back and forth between Grace and Patsy. Then he cleared his throat and replied.

"Battery," he replied. "That's what we're starting with. For aggravated battery we need to prove *great bodily harm. Great* can also be a *potential for harm*, as in giving someone drugs without their knowledge that could kill them or cause a fatal or near-fatal reaction. Sometimes it has been used for causing someone to lose consciousness for several hours if that puts them in circumstances with the potential for greater harm. Then there's a Level 8 felony, *eavesdropping,* which includes using cameras or video to record without the subject's knowledge."

"Like with cameras, in store-dressing room cases?" Grace asked.

"Yes, where there is a breach of privacy."

"What about sex offender stuff?"

"There is sexual battery, which is touching someone with the intent to arouse oneself. It's a misdemeanor, but conviction means registering as a sex offender for fifteen years. Most people prefer to plea to a straight felony with no sex offender strings attached. And, in this case, we cannot prove touch."

"What would sentencing for battery look like?"

"Realistically, with no criminal history, it could be probation for eighteen-to-twenty-four months."

"That's it?" Grace's voice was incredulous. "For drugging and taking naked photos of twelve young women?"

"We do not have twelve, we have three. And we do not even know if they will follow through. I have not yet interviewed them. I don't even have their names."

Grace avoided the obvious: that she knew the names, the DA did not, and whether or not they would cooperate fully was still a crapshoot.

"What about Shelby. The dead girl. Doesn't she count?" Grace asked.

"Of course she counts," Mark countered. "But with no proof that the defendant sent her the photos and she is not present to testify to her circumstances, we are left with. . ."

"I get it," Grace said, cutting him off mid-sentence. "It just makes me crazy."

"It makes me crazy too," Mark replied. "Case after case comes across my desk, and I know that a serious crime has been committed, but what used to be evidence is now erased with a single word—*consensual*."

"Say Hunter Payne decides he wants a trial. He's willing to take the risk. Then what?"

"Then we'll need the three women to testify. Then we'll go for every charge we can throw at him. But it will fall apart unless there is a chorus of women describing the same experience."

"Do you think a trial is likely?"

"No. I anticipate that he'll want no publicity, no trial, no confrontation. He'll hire a good attorney who will poke holes in the evidence and then will plea down."

After the meeting, Grace emailed Amanda, Blair, and Carolyn.

The police got a search warrant. They found the pictures and drugs in his apartment, she wrote. *I met with the DA. He wants to meet with you. He can then explain the process, his expectations of how it would progress (which is that Hunter will plea down and not want a trial) and what would be expected from you. You can withdraw at any time. I have not given your names yet. May I provide your names and emails so he can contact you directly?"*

Within five hours, they each replied.

I'm in, wrote Blair. *The more I think about it, the madder I'm getting.*

It's a little scary but I'm willing to meet with the DA, wrote Amanda.

I'm willing to meet, emailed Carolyn, *but if this goes to a public trial, then I want the option to reconsider.*

Grace emailed Mark Sorenson with the names of the three young women and their contact information. She copied Patsy, Sam, and Lisa. Mark emailed the girls that he would contact them after January 8th to schedule a meeting.

It was now out of her hands. From what Patsy had described, the process could drag on for months, with attorneys scheduling hearings and then asking for continuances and then more scheduling and more continuances. Or it could be resolved very quickly and quietly if Hunter, now officially *the defendant,* wanted to plea down with no publicity.

It also appeared that she was off the hook unless there was a trial. In which case it could get awkward. An old line from one of Grace's favorite TV shows, *I Love Lucy,* popped in her head: *You got some 'splaining to do.*

Hell, Grace thought, *it wouldn't be the first time.*

Chapter 58
(December 7th)

By 10 p.m. on Thursday evening, Hannah and Stacy were as ready as they ever would be.

"Hannah," Stacy said as they threw extra clothes in gym bags, "This might not work out. Logan could blow me off. We have to get him to voluntarily leave his frat party and walk to a car and then get into the car. A lot could go wrong."

"I understand," Hannah answered. "And if it doesn't work, then okay. But at least I'm doing *something.*"

At 11:33 p.m., the frat house was lit up like the 4th of July. Despite being December in Kansas, the big double-front doors were open and people spilled out onto the front porch and yard. Hannah and Stacy circled the block looking for a parking spot. There were none. Some spaces for one car were crammed with two small cars at angles, bumpers touching.

"Well, this is unfortunate," Stacy said. "I guess we could have predicted it but we're not party animals."

"I'm staying in the car so we could double park," Hannah said. "Or block a driveway on a temporary basis. But it will be hard to position ourselves so no one can see us."

"I should have parked the car here earlier. We could have Ubered over."

"No more second-guessing. We did a lot of planning."

"And it might all get blown to hell due to one oversight," Stacy interrupted.

"Hey, we're not in any rush here. We have, literally, all night. Let's circle a few times and see exactly what could be workable."

They drove, at five miles an hour, around the block. It was a big block, two sides lined with the old mansions that had been renovated and expanded into fraternity and sorority houses mixed in with lots where the old places had been torn down to make room to build new frat houses designed to look like southern plantations (brick and columns and porticos) or New England (white with green shutters, dormers, three-sided covered porches). On the other two sides were a hodgepodge of blocky student apartment buildings and smaller houses broken down into multiple one-room studios with mini-kitchens and shared hall bathrooms.

"See that space under the tree," Hannah asked. "I don't see anyone around who'd make a fuss even if it is alongside the driveway."

Stacy stood behind a tree across the street from the frat house. She was a university senior, but this sort of social situation made her feel like she was in junior high.

It had hit her in the last day or so that if this went really, really bad, she could lose everything she'd worked so hard to achieve. Years of work to create a different life could go down the drain.

Stacy was the first in her immediate family, first among all of her many cousins, to go to college. Some had done one-year or even two-year technical programs through a community college, but always while living at home or working full-time and going to school part-time. But she'd left home for a university and lived in a dorm. Having to support herself was the reason she'd remained in the dorm long after her friends had moved out and into apartments. Being an RA paid her room and board plus a small stipend.

When Stacy had arrived on campus as a freshman, her parents' car stuffed with checklists from articles on "What Every Freshman Needs," she'd known nothing about Greek life. While other freshman girls were consumed with Pledge Week and having hysterics about whether they would get their top sorority picks, or how it wasn't fair that they had to compete against legacies, Stacy had observed from the sidelines. To pledge cost money, sororities cost money, and every cent she'd saved over four years of high school was going straight toward tuition and textbooks. And Stacy saw that there were other costs as well, the *costs* of a sorority lifestyle—the clothing and haircuts and getting your nails done—everything associated with being in Alpha Chi Omega or Kappa Alpha Theta or Delta Gamma.

Stacy had adapted by being a nerd, not anti-Greek but, *It's not my thing.*

So, walking into *this* frat party was going to be the first time she'd ever gone to *any* frat party. It was hitting her that she maybe should have tried a few practice runs.

Too late now. Plus, she was shivering. She'd left her coat in the car. If she left the party abruptly, and she assumed she would, no way she could go looking for a coat. From the look of the girls on the wide porch, looking hot was totally more important than freezing.

Stacy walked across the street and up the front steps of the fraternity house. She plastered on a big smile, repeating, *Excuse me,* in a sing-song voice as she made her way through the packed entry. Within ten minutes, she realized that she had grossly miscalculated how easy it would be to: 1) Locate Logan Alexander Whiteman, and 2) Extricate him from the party. She could spend the next three hours in this body-to-body mash and never see Logan.

She headed for the broad staircase to the second floor. Looking down would have to be an improvement. Pushing through, she got up seven steps before turning around.

Better, she thought. But there were still so many people and they all blended together. She tried to search more methodically, first going around the outskirts of the room, then focusing on the next *layer*.

"You'll never find who you're looking for in this mess," a voice shouted into her ear. "Let's get a drink instead."

Stacy startled, turning to see a compact young man with black hair and an amused look.

"Why do you think I'm looking for someone?" she shouted back.

"Because you're standing on the staircase and searching the crowd. And you're not chugging a drink. You're not here to party."

"I could be here to party once I find my friend," she said. "But I'm late and for all I know she moved on to a better party."

"There are no better parties," he said, with a very stern face, then grinned. "Who is your missing friend?"

"Ahhhh—" Stacy said, stalling. "No one you would know. She's just up for the weekend."

"So, want a drink while you look?"

"Yeah, sure. Where's the bar?"

"Bars. Plural. You must not be from around here either if you don't know that. One on every floor."

"I'm just not a party girl," Stacy retorted. "I'm doing this to entertain the friend who has gone missing. She wanted to check out the local party scene."

"Well, you found it. Party fucking central. C'mon," he said, gesturing down the stairs. "Time to get pushy."

"Hey, maybe you can help," Stacy suddenly realized, reaching out to tug at his shoulder. "She's a Facebook friend with a guy in this frat. Logan? I forget his last name. She was going to look him up. I think he's a senior."

"Logan Whiteman?" the guy asked.

"Yeah, that sounds familiar. Maybe she found him. But I have no idea what he looks like."

"Then let's find Logan. Better than standing on the stairs." He turned, then twisted his head to look back. "I'm Gabe."

"Michelle," she replied.

They elbowed through the crowd, calling, *'scuse me, 'scuse me, coming through, 'scuse me.* Gabe did the hard work and Stacy followed in his wake.

They angled up to a long table with two huge punch bowls. Plastic cups were piled at one end. Gabe scooped out two glasses and handed her one.

"Jungle Juice," he said over the din. "Party favorite."

"Thanks," Stacy said, bringing the cup to her lips and taking a tiny sip. Then she remembered where she was, and what she was supposed to be.

"Just what I need," she added, putting a wide, cute-girl-at-frat-party-smile back on her face. "So, let's find this Logan guy. Okay?"

"There's dancing in the basement," Gabe said. "We can start there and move up."

"You're the boss," Stacy replied, lifting her cup in mock salute. "Lead the way."

The basement was, if that were even possible, louder. Stacy felt sweat forming and dripping down her back. In the middle of the massive cement-walled room were people dancing.

No, not dancing, Stacy thought. For dancing, couples generally faced each other. This was grinding. Gyrating. The girls' hips swayed and jerked. Some were alone, as if on display. Others had young men plastered to their asses.

"There he is," Gabe yelled, pointing to a tall guy glued to the butt of a blonde in a micro-mini who seemed oblivious, her eyes closed, as they pumped in synchrony.

Stacy recognized him immediately. But she stalled.

"Which one?" she asked Gabe. "I'm not sure who you mean."

"Tall, brown hair, pounding the blonde." He pointed again and she pretended to follow his arm.

"Is that your friend?" he asked, gesturing, Stacy assumed, at the micro-mini.

"No. But I'll look around."

"I'll go get Logan," Gabe said, and started into the mob before Stacy could object. "Stay put until we get back."

Stacy watched, her mind spinning, as Gabe maneuvered across the dance floor toward Logan. When he reached him, Gabe pointed back to her and Logan looked in her direction.

Stay in character, Stacy reminded herself.

Stacy smiled at Logan and gave a little wave. *Trust me*, she thought. *You have to trust me.*

Logan said something to the blonde and he and Gabe started back.

"Did Emily find you?" she asked, or more like yelled, when Logan was within possible hearing range.

"What?" Logan asked. "Who?"

"Emily Smith. She's a Facebook friend. She's in town visiting and wanted to look you up."

"Emily who?"

Stacy tried to look both adorable and exasperated. It was tough to pull off.

"Emily Smith," Stacy repeated. "You know? You guys are, like, Facebook friends? She's here from Colorado visiting and wanted to meet you? I think she's hot for you?"

"I don't remember an Emily but then I have a shitload of Facebook friends."

"Yeah, I think she said that," Stacy agreed.

"And who are you?" Logan asked. "I haven't met you before, right? You go to school here?"

"Oh, me? I'm Michelle. Yeah, but I'm in nursing so not like we'd have the same classes."

Stacy looked away, back at the bodies, taking a sip from her cup of punch. *What now. . . what now. . . what now. . . shit. . . shit. . . what now?*

"So where is this Emily?" Logan asked.

"I was hoping she was with you," Stacy replied. "She's gotta be around here somewhere. And I've got to get some sleep because I have to work tomorrow. But I don't want to leave without knowing if she wants to stay."

"So you're taking off soon?" Gabe asked.

"As soon as I find Emily."

Stacy noted that his interest in her took a nosedive. *Oh, you fickle, fickle boy,* she thought.

Stacy pointed to the micro-mini blonde who was still gyrating. "I bet she's available," she said to Gabe.

"C'mon Logan," she added. "Let's go find your secret admirer. And then I can leave because I know she'll be in good hands."

Stacy and Logan started pushing their way up the steps to the main floor. This time she was in front.

"Michelle," a voice said. "Hey, Michelle?" A hand touched her shoulder.

Oh yeah, Stacy thought with a jolt. *I'm Michelle.*

She turned her head to face Logan. "Sorry, the noise makes me nuts. What did you say?"

"What does Emily look like? What is she wearing?"

"Well—she's like 5'3" and has long brown hair, runs 5K races like all the time, it's ridiculous how fit she is. Wearing a blue sweater with some bling. Jeans. Tan suede boots."

"Gotcha," Logan said.

"Let's try the front porch," Stacy added. "We said we'd meet up at the car in two hours if she didn't find you and it's almost that long."

They maneuvered through the crowd to the front porch.

There were people all over the porch and steps, many of them smoking. It was cold but most did not have jackets.

"I don't see her," Stacy said. "Hey, the car is just a few doors down. I bet you anything she went to the car because it's so cold. We were set to meet in, like, eight minutes. Come on! We can move fast. I know she really wants to meet you. Let's surprise her!"

Logan looked, for just a moment, as if he were evaluating the cost/benefit ratio of walking a half block in the cold weighed against meeting an unknown and possibly hot girl who had come looking specifically for him. The benefits won out.

"Where are you parked?" he asked.

"In the next driveway. Just about there," Stacy replied, her voice growing louder with each word. "There it is, see, that classic Buick. Don't make them like that anymore. Ever drive one of those, Logan? Huh?" *Just keep talking,* she told herself. *Just keep talking.* "Oh, hey, I was right. There she is, just like she knew to expect us. C'mon, let's slide in the back and I'll do the introductions."

They approached the car from the passenger side and Stacy jerked open the back door. "Quick, I'm freezing, slide in," she told Logan, lurching against him so that he nearly fell from her weight. He was half in and half out, body on the seat, legs dangling outside. Stacy was standing, one hand on the door and the other on the roof of the car.

Logan could see that there was a girl in the front seat, the passenger seat, but she didn't turn around. He felt a micro-second of confusion because he could see the back of her head and the hair was short, very short, and spiky. But Michelle had described her hair as. . .

And then she did turn and looked him right in the eyes. "Hello, Logan," she said. "I've been waiting for you."

Then something was pushing against his side and he felt an intense, blinding pain. He made a moaning noise from some place very deep and far removed.

"Get out, Hannah, quick. Grab under his arms and pull. I can't get him all the way in just by pushing," Stacy said in a rush. Hannah jumped out and opened the other back door, pawing at Logan's shirt, trying to get a grip under his armpits.

"You guys need some help?" a male voice said.

Stacy popped her head up and saw a guy with his arm around a girl, peering from the shadows of the sidewalk.

"Nah. He just passed out. Well get him home and to bed," she said. "Not like this is our first rodeo." This last she almost yelled, with a laugh.

"Okay, just asking," the guy answered as he and the girl moved away.

"That was close," Hannah said.

Logan groaned again and started to move.

"Put these ties on," Hannah said, pushing two plastic restraints toward Stacy.

In ten seconds they were done. Logan was lying in a semi-fetal position on the Buick's back seat. His ankles were looped tightly together, and his wrists as well, with an extra-long tie linking the ankles and wrists so they would stay below his waist.

"Hog-tied. Nice job," Stacy muttered. "Let's get the hell out of here."

Stacy ran around and hopped into the driver's seat. From now on this was Hannah's play to direct.

Hannah watched Logan from the front passenger seat. He was already twitching. Then one eye opened. It took him a minute to realize his situation. Hannah watched as he tried to move his arms, then his legs.

"It will be better for you if you don't fight it," Hannah said. "Just relax."

"What the fuck do you think you're doing?" Logan's voice was a hoarse growl. "Let me out of here."

"No, those are Safariland Double Cuff Disposable Handcuffs. So, sorry, but not happening for a while," Hannah answered.

Logan's response was to start to buck and twist, trying to break out of the restraints.

"You need to be a good boy and lie still, Logan. Do you understand?" Hannah said, holding the stun gun where he could see it.

Logan kept trying to kick his way out.

"Okay, Logan, this is going to hurt you more that it hurts me." Hannah said as she pushed the stun gun against his side.

And it did.

When Logan came to for the second time, he lay still, panting.

He looked—well—stunned.

"How about some music?" Hannah said. "And turn the heater up. Poor Logan didn't bring a coat."

They looked at each other, a Thelma and Louise, *We did it*-moment of exhilaration and relief, coupled with, *Now what the fuck do we do?*

Stacy cranked the CD player and "Fight Song" blasted through the car. Without looking at each other, they sang along as loud as they could.

Chapter 59
(December 8th)

It took just fifteen minutes to get to the highway exit, and another twenty-five to reach the cabin. There were no cars on the rural roads. As they left the highway, Hannah reached back and tossed a towel over Logan's head.

He made a grunting noise but did not attempt to shake it off.

There was a long, winding gravel drive to get to the cabin. It was impossible to avoid the potholes in the darkness. Logan was bounced around, and Hannah heard a cracking noise along with a grunt, as the top of his head smacked against the door.

They parked on the far side of the cabin, which could not be seen from the distant road. Their supplies, food and all, had already been dropped off. All they had were duffle bags of clothing.

Logan did not move.

Stacy and Hannah got out of the car and stood to one side.

"He's too heavy to lift and carry, so we have to cut the tie between his hands and feet," Stacy whispered.

"But what if he tries to run or yell?"

"His feet are tied together. We can make him hop."

"And the yell part?"

"Mention the stun gun is inches from his body if he tries *anything*."

They opened the back door on the driver's side. Logan's head almost bounced out.

"We're going to cut the tie holding your handcuffs and foot ties so you can stand up," Hannah said in a tone that sounded like a pre-school teacher describing bathroom line protocol. "You'll have a pillow case over your head. You'll have to hop from the car to the house. We'll stay on either side so you don't fall down. If you try anything at all, from yelling to trying to make a break for it, I will use the stun gun again. It's in my right hand, about nine inches from your body. So, any questions?"

"Who are you and what is going on?" Logan asked.

"That part comes later," Hannah replied. "Any questions about what

I just described?"

Logan grunted but said nothing.

"I'll take that as a *no*," Hannah said, as Stacy leaned in and cut the tie with the metal handcuff cutter they had purchased from Amazon. Logan groaned as he stretched out his shoulders and legs. With one smooth movement, Stacy pulled off the towel and slid a pillowcase over Logan's head.

"Now sit up and slide out, real slow, put your feet on the ground and then stand up," Hannah continued. "Otherwise we can haul you out. Your choice."

Logan swung his feet to the floor of the car and inched his butt over toward the open door. Then he lifted his feet out and gingerly, stood up.

"Good boy," Hannah said, in her preschool teacher voice.

Getting to the house was easier than they'd anticipated. Logan was a surprisingly good hopper. It took thirteen hops to get to the steps to the porch, then five hops up, then another eight hops into the living room. They had him hop right up to a chair.

"You can sit down now," Hannah said. "There is a chair right behind you."

Logan hesitated. Hannah had the urge, almost irresistible, to pull the chair out from under him and watch him fall on his ass.

"It's an armchair, a little low, but solid," Stacy said, as if reading Hannah's mind. "We're not going to pull it out from under you, as appealing as that idea is."

Logan lowered himself into the chair twisting a bit with his handcuffed hands to feel for a chair arm to hold.

Stacy and Hannah took stock of the situation.

They now had a 6'4" man in handcuffs, his feet tied, a pillowcase tied over his head, sitting in a chair in a living room in a one-bedroom cabin on twenty-plus acres of Kansas prairie. For three days.

"I could use a drink," Stacy said. "How about you?"

"That sounds good to me," Hannah replied. "Make it a double."

"Water," said a mumbled voice from under the pillowcase.

"Did you say something, Logan?"

"I need water," the voice said again.

"Could you say *please*?" Hannah countered. "As in, *Please, may I have some water?*"

There was silence.

"You are going to be one thirsty boy if you can't follow directions," Stacy said. "In the meantime, I'm having a Horsefeather. This is a night that requires whiskey."

When Hannah awakened, light was coming in between the blinds in the bedroom. She could smell coffee brewing in the next room. She was still dressed, but her shoes and sweater were gone, a comforter loosely draped over her body.

Her mouth felt very dry and icky. She lay trying to decide what she needed more—to brush her teeth or drink some coffee. The teeth won out.

When she went into the living room, Logan was curled up, fetal position, in a corner on the floor. His head rested on a chair cushion and a plaid blanket was over his body.

Stacy was on the couch, sitting up, legs extending to the coffee table, a cup of coffee in her hand.

"The view from this couch is lovely," she said, keeping her voice almost at a whisper. "I watched the sunrise through the big picture window as a deer family did a dance in the meadow. There's a word, *gamboling,* that I don't think I've ever used before. But I can say it now. The damn deer were *gamboling.* "

"I don't think that's a word," said Hannah.

"Yeah, it is."

"Okay, but I reserve the right to debate this later on," Hannah said, then looked over at Logan. "Uhhhh, is he restrained?"

"His feet are still in the slip ties that we can only get off with the handy-dandy metal cuff cutters. Even if his hands got loose, he can't get the ties off. He can hop, and whip out his dick to pee. Not so sure about wiping himself when the need arises."

"Yeah, I don't want him wiggling out and racing to the road screaming that he's been kidnapped.'"

"He hopped a bit and then kind of half-fell to the floor. I put the pillow there and found the blanket in the hall closet. This is a nicely equipped Airbnb."

"Let's be sure and write a good review."

"Coffee is hot," Stacy added. She patted the couch next to her,

"Come sit down and I'll get you a cup."

Hannah did not protest. She sat on the couch, but within seconds moved her head to the armrest.

"What happened last night?" Hannah asked.

"I think all the anxiety caught up to you," Stacy answered. "I made you a Horsefeather, a double, and you only got half-way through it before going in to see what the bedroom was like. Guess you tried to see what the bed was like because you were down-and-out when I went looking for you."

"I'm sorry," Hannah said, "I didn't mean to desert you or leave you with guard duty."

"No worry. I crushed up two Trazadone and put them in few jiggers of whiskey and fed it to Mr. Whiteman. He was quite thirsty, chugged it down fast."

"You are such a Girl Scout, Stacy. Always prepared. Where did you get the Trazadone?"

"My very own supply. The health center nurse wrote me a script last year when I was having issues sleeping. But I didn't like waking up groggy."

"Yeah, those side effects can ruin a good pill."

They sat quietly, sipping their coffee. Snores emanated from the body in the corner.

"Now what?" Stacy asked, her voice still low.

"I was just wondering about that," Hannah replied. "I think I've been so focused on actually getting him here that the specifics of what I want to accomplish—and how—have gotten fuzzy."

"You said you wanted some form of *justice*, and *retribution*. How he has to *understand* what he's done, really *understand* the hurt he caused, and *feel* some of the same emotions that you experienced in his room," summed up Stacy. She ticked off each word on a finger as she said it. "The word *penetration* was mentioned but I'm not sure what your plans are for that."

"Shit, did you take notes?" asked Hannah.

"Of course. Oh, one more—*remorse*," she said ticking off another finger. "And not fake remorse just to get out, but *authentic* remorse. *Truly, truly sorry. Contrite.*"

Hannah said nothing, as if considering just how all of that could be accomplished. Because there was another word, the one she had originally said she did not want—*revenge*.

Hannah had never deliberately, intentionally, hurt someone in her life. She swatted flies and mosquitoes, but when mice invaded the kitchen she'd put out humane traps so the mice could be released into the woods.

Inflicting physical pain would be crossing a line. But at this precise moment, she was not sure which direction she would go. She had used the stun gun, which decidedly hurt, but had been necessary. Somehow that felt different.

"How do you want to start?" Stacy asked.

"Naked," Hannah said. "He'll need to be naked."

"Want me to wake him up?"

"No, no rush. We have all weekend. Let's just enjoy our coffee."

"Oh look, Stacy, the deer are back. They look like they're jumping around for the fun of it."

"Yeah," Stacy said. "That's gamboling."

Logan snored on for another two hours. The pills, whiskey, trauma, and very late hour had elicited a deep sleep despite the hard floor. Hannah and Stacy had time to take showers, wash their hair, and put on clean clothes.

They convened in the kitchen. Hannah sat at the kitchen table with a notebook, looking through the French doors at the fields, as Stacy sorted through a plastic bin of foodstuffs. She lifted up a Tupperware container filled with what looked like flour.

"What's that?" asked Hannah.

"Scone mix," Stacy said. "My grandma's recipe. With walnuts and dates."

"Yummy," said Hannah. "You're a marvel. Sleeping pills *and* scones."

It was about noon when Logan started to wake up. There was a smell in the background, somehow familiar, and he thought for a moment he was dreaming he was in a bakery. But he was cold, lying on something very hard, and he couldn't see. He couldn't move his hands apart. And his feet. . .

He started to thrash around before it all came back. The party. . . going to a car. . . the sudden pain. . . coming to and being hog-tied. Hopping.

He went very still, taking stock. His ankles were bound together but he could stretch his legs out to their full length. His wrists were also bound, one wrist on top of the other, facing down, but he could move his hands and stretch out his arms. Something covered his head and neck. It was light material, not transparent, but he could breathe okay. He tried to tug at it, but his hands could not get up much past his waist. His shoulders and body were stiff and sore, and he felt a throbbing pain in his side, like a deep bruise, when he tried to move.

Stacy and Hannah silently watched Logan's initial movements from the couch, also staying very, very still.

Logan cocked his head under the pillowcase, as if trying to determine if he were alone. He shifted his body to one side and put his hands down in front to brace himself as he tried to sit up. Once sitting, his legs stretched out in front of him, he felt around his body, unable to reach back. He felt an urgent need to urinate. He started to scoot his butt along the floor, trying to retain balance with his hands. He bent his knees, and tried to lift himself up, rocking a bit and using his hands for ballast. Once on his knees, he leaned far forward and then threw his body back, lifting from his toes.

He was standing, lightly panting from the exertion, but also trying to make no noise.

"Going for a stroll, Logan?" Hannah asked.

Logan's head jerked toward her voice and he stopped moving.

"Who are you? What is going on?" he said, almost in a growl.

"Excellent questions," Hannah responded, "and you'll have some answers soon enough."

"Where's the bathroom?" he said.

"Oh, we can take care of that," said Stacy in a sing-song voice. "At least if you just need to piss. I have a handy little bucket."

"What the hell is this? Where's the fucking bathroom?" Logan started hopping, as if movement alone would get him there.

Stacy stood up, reached down behind the couch, and brought out a small lime-green plastic bucket with pictures of frogs and a pond on its side. "Discard from my nephew's sandbox," she said to Hannah by way of explanation.

"I have a bucket here, Logan. You can feel it, but probably not hold it and your penis at the same time to piss. So, if you want to try to lower your zipper and grab your penis, I'll hold the bucket."

"Get the fuck away from me," Logan said. "What kind of sick shit is this?"

"Okay, your choice," said Stacy. "But you know you really need to piss. And if you think you'll just whip it out and piss on the furniture or rug, I want you to know there will be a consequence. Remember that stun gun from last night? That's what happens if you make a bad choice."

Hannah watched Stacy with detached incredulity. She sounded so calm, so reasonable.

"You're really good at this," Hannah whispered to her.

"I have brothers," Stacy said.

It took fifteen minutes for Logan to concede to the demands of his bladder. He had hopped in one direction, and then another, arms extended, until he hit a wall. He stood there, panting, for a good five minutes until he said, "Get the pail."

"Get the pail, *please*," responded Stacy.

Another minute passed.

"Get the pail, *please*," Logan finally muttered.

When Logan was finished, Stacy took the pail into the bathroom. They could hear the toilet flush.

Coming back, Stacy gestured to Hannah to go into the kitchen.

"How do you want to start?" Stacy asked softly.

"I think we get down to basics. He's gotta be naked."

"He will resist," Stacy said.

'Yeah, but that's why we have a stun gun and duct tape and those handy cuffs. I say we just get the scissors and start cutting his clothes off."

At that moment, they heard the ring of a cell phone. They walked quickly back into the living room. It was coming from Logan's back pocket and he was frantically trying to twist his cuffed hands around to be able to get it out.

"Let me help with that, Logan," Stacy said. But as she got close to him and started to reach for his back pocket, he lunged at her, a full body slam, and they went down with a crash. Hannah was across the room in a mini-second, kicking hard at Logan and pulling Stacy away. Hannah must have connected with something sensitive because Logan curled up on the floor, the fight gone.

"Logan," Stacy said, breathing heavily, holding onto a chair as she climbed to her feet. "Let me explain the ground rules. You are not leaving here until we say so—when we're done—at which point we will return you to your frat house or whatever location you prefer. We do not want to hurt you, but we will—with no hesitation—if you attempt this kind of shit again." Stacy walked over to the table and picked up the stun gun from where its battery had been re-charging, "Now, Logan, I am going to reach down and remove the phone from you rear pocket. If you so much as flinch, I will poke you with the stun gun. Understood?"

There was no response from the floor.

"Another ground rule is that you will respond. So, if I ask, you need to answer. *Understand?*"

"Yes," Logan muttered from under the pillowcase.

"Yes, what?"

"I understand."

Stacy reached into his pocket and pulled the phone and started to check it out. "You have two messages and six texts," she reported. "From different numbers." She pressed play and put it on speaker: *Hey, man, where are you? Thought we were gonna throw some hoops this morning to warm up before studying? What's up?*

Next was: *Where'd you go? You were supposed to supervise the pledges with clean-up. They're fucking useless alone. Call me back pronto.*

She pulled up the texts: *R u AWOL? Who was chick you left with? She was hot. Text me now.*

Another: *Dude. Where r u? We need study. Exams in 3 days!!!*

The rest of the texts were about the same.

"Let's see," ruminated Stacy. "How shall you reply that would make sense to your bros? Maybe piss them off but something they would understand?"

Stacy started punching in letters: *Shit, sorry, but count me out of everything. Am hooking up major league. I'll make it up, swear, but going off-grid for a day or so. No worry, be happy.* She stopped to silently re-read it, then read it out loud to Hannah and Logan.

"That works," said Hannah. "Who will you send it to?"

"The six numbers of the texts and voice messages. And I'll use it for any others that may come in," Stacy replied. "Half the frat is still asleep, so we may get a few more later. Anything you want to add, Logan?"

Logan grunted, then spoke. "Who the fuck are you? What kind of fucking prank is this, because you have gone way, way over the top."

"Excellent question, Logan, and one I will answer shortly," Hannah said.

Stacy placed Logan's phone on top of the refrigerator, behind a box of cereal, and plugged it into a charger. *Don't want to miss if his buddies send out search parties,* she thought.

"Well, that's a start," Stacy said. "How about we get the dude here in the chair?"

Stacy and Hannah went over, each grabbing hold of an arm, and hauled Logan upward as his feet scrabbled out from under him, trying to get balanced.

"Three hops forward," Stacy said.

Logan hopped.

Hannah put the chair down behind him. It was not a chair from the cabin but one that Stacy had brought—an aluminum lawn chair with plastic strips for the seat and back. The kind of chair that you could hose off, that allowed access to any body part simply by spreading the strips apart a few inches.

"Wait a minute," Stacy said. "Stand still. I forgot something."

She went into the kitchen and rummaged around in a box, coming back with a five by five foot square of heavy blue plastic.

"For under the chair in case of accidents or spills," she said. They spread the plastic and put down the chair.

"Two more little hops, Logan."

Logan complied.

"We're going to take off the cuffs in a few minutes, Logan, but first we're going to cut your clothes a little and use some duct tape. You're going to follow our exact instructions. The stun gun is turned on and ready, but we prefer to not have to use it."

In sixty seconds, Stacy had cut off his pants to above the knee, removed his socks, and efficiently duct-taped one of Logan's legs to a leg of the chair. His leg secure, she cut the ankle cuffs. Then she duct-taped the other leg. She sliced up the front of the shirt in one smooth move and repeated the same in the back, flipping the two halves so they were gathered around his lower arms and hands. Rather than cut the ties, she sliced once again along the arms of the shirt and pulled at the pieces so they fell to the floor. Logan was sitting there shirtless, with the pillowcase still over his head.

"What the hell are you doing?" Logan said, the pitch of his voice escalating.

"Not quite done, Logan. Do not move a muscle or you *will* be hurt."

Stacy pulled his pants out from his body and sliced down in one jab, cutting pants and underpants both.

Logan flinched and cursed under his breath.

"Oh, did I nick you? I'm sorry. You'll need to stay really still so I don't accidentally nick a more sensitive part. And I may switch here from scissors to box-cutters. The scissors are not cutting it. A double-entendre, as they say."

In sixty more seconds, Logan was stark naked, seated in the chair, his feet taped to the legs and his hands taped to the arms. Only his head and face remained covered.

Stacy and Hannah looked at Logan, then at each other. They turned and went into the bedroom and closed the door.

"So how exactly do you want to proceed?" asked Stacy.

"I'm not quite sure," replied Hannah.

"There's no rush if you want to take some time."

"I think I'm ready to take off the pillowcase," said Hannah. "Make some introductions."

"In that case, let me brush my teeth and hair, maybe spruce up a bit," Stacy said. "First impressions are so important."

Thirty minutes later, having changed into low-cut sweaters, dangling earrings, a touch of make-up and squirts of perfume, they returned to the living room.

Logan was hunched down in the chair as if trying to get his body to disappear into the plastic weaves. With his ankles taped to the legs of the chairs, his knees pulled somewhat apart, the penis had no place to hide.

His pillow-cased head hung down on his chest.

"Okay, Logan, sit up straight," said Stacy. "We're ready to answer some of your questions."

Logan complied.

Stacy went over, cut the tie that had been holding the pillow case in place, then pulled it up and off Logan's head, sweeping her arm as if in a magic act. Voila!

Logan blinked in the light, eyes darting around the room.

"Where am I?"

"Don't rush ahead, Logan, first things first. You've asked, 'Who are you?' a few times. We'll start there. But we begin with a question for you. Who do you think we are?"

"You're the girl that was at the frat party," Logan said, gesturing with his chin at Stacy. "You told me that your friend, Emily, was a Facebook friend of mine and wanted to meet me. And we walked to the car because that's where you guys had agreed to meet."

"Excellent, Logan. Good memory. But I have some sad news. It was all made-up. There is no Emily."

"So why? What was. . ."

"We wanted to get you to voluntarily leave the party and come to the car so we could stun you, load you up, and bring you here," Stacy continued.

"So you're not. . ."

"Michelle?" Stacy laughed. "No, I just pulled that name out of thin air."

"The bigger question, Logan, is **who am I**?" Hannah asked from across the room, more behind him, where she'd been standing. She took a few steps toward the center.

Logan looked. It was the first time he'd ever seen this girl.

She was only about 5'3", with spiky, short hair that stood straight up, with a blue tint. Big, dangling earrings. And big, black, square glasses.

Not his type at all.

"Okay," he answered. "No clue. Who are you?"

Hannah's jaw moved, but no words came out.

She was authentically stunned.

In the scenario that had played in her head, he would look at her, perhaps puzzled for a moment, but then see beyond the superficial changes in hair and glasses. He would recognize *her*.

But he didn't. It had been three months. While his face, his smell, his hands, his eyes, had hourly intruded into her brain—her dreams—every time she tried to go to sleep, whenever she was trying to focus—he could not *see* her.

"I'm Hannah, Logan. Remember Hannah? From the frat party on September first?"

Logan went white, the blood draining from his face.

"What is this? You can't do this. It's kidnapping. You need to stop right now and let me go!" Logan's voice rose until he was yelling.

"Logan, Logan, Logan," Hannah said, her voice brittle. "You're getting awfully worked up for someone who did nothing. What's that phrase: *doth protest too much?*"

"What do you want from me?" Now his voice had an almost plaintive tone.

"We want you to learn from your mistakes, Logan. To become a better man. And to stop hurting girls."

"I don't hurt girls. You're a nutcase. It was a hookup and you know it." He practically spit it out.

Hannah felt the room begin to spin. She grabbed hold of the back of the chair in front of her. Logan didn't sound like he was covering up. He sounded as if he believed what he was saying.

"Are you okay?" Stacy's voice intruded.

"Yes. No. I need some air." Hannah stumbled across the living room and out the front door.

Stacy looked at Logan. "Oh fuck," she said. She went into the bedroom and grabbed her coat and Hannah's coat and headed back out.

"Don't you move," she said to Logan as she closed the front door.

Hannah was sitting on the top step to the porch, arms tight across her chest, her body rocking back and forth.

"How could he say that? Like he really believes it? He was there. He knows what he did. He has to. . ."

"Put on your coat, Hannah," Stacy interrupted. "It's cold out here."

"He didn't recognize me. How could he not recognize me? How could. . ."

"Because it's been three months. Because he saw you for a few hours and he was probably half-drunk at the time. Because you had long brown hair and contacts and now you have punky blue hair and monster librarian glasses. Your own mother might not recognize you. Meanwhile, we've stalked him and taken his picture like a thousand times. And he's changed nothing about his appearance. He is exactly the same."

"For a second, I almost believed him. He sounds so convincing."

"Yeah, he does."

"Could he really be so twisted that he thinks what he did was a hookup? Could he believe. . ."

"I don't know what he believes. And I'm not sure that what he believes changes anything. Maybe he didn't *intend* to rape you, but he did. I saw you that night. You were raped. That was no hookup."

"But if he doesn't believe he did anything wrong? How can I make him. . ."

"Stop right there. Checklist time. This is about *justice*, which does not measure intent. Drunk drivers do not get a pass because they did not *intend* to run over the kid. He needs to *understand* what he did, which is even *more* important if he is as clueless as he just sounded. Then *remorse*, which, again. . ."

"Okay. I get it. He just really threw me off."

"So, we take it slow, maybe tweak how to proceed?"

"Yeah, tweak and proceed."

"Good, because if we stay out here I need to get a hat. My ears are freezing."

Stacy went to hang up their coats and Hannah went into the kitchen to make some fresh coffee. Logan was shivering from the blasts of air that had come in when they opened the door. Being naked didn't help.

Stacy picked up the comforter from the floor and draped it over his shoulders and around his chest.

"Thank you," he said.

Gee, Stacy thought, *not totally hopeless. The boy has manners.*

Hannah came back in the living room and dragged the easy chair, the comfy one, over in front of Logan. She put it really close, then reconsidered and pulled it back a few feet.

She sat down, placed her coffee on a side table and cleared her throat.

"Your name is Logan Alexander Whiteman. That name will forever bring back the worst night of my life thus far. But I now wonder, since you didn't even recognize me, if you know my name. What is my name, Logan?"

"Hannah," he said, looking at the floor.

"And the rest of my name, Logan?"

He shifted in the chair. "I don't remember," he finally answered.

"Hannah. Marie. Larson," Hannah said, enunciating each syllable. "I am Hannah Marie Larson."

"We never said last names."

"No, I guess we didn't. It was on those IOA papers, but maybe it didn't register. Of course, I'd assumed we'd get to last names later in the evening, like when you asked for my number. Do you regularly fuck girls without knowing their names? Is this a habit?"

"What do you want? Why are you doing this?"

"I'm asking the questions today. I will assume the answer is *yes,* and that you have fucked girls without knowing their names."

Logan thought for a moment. *Yeah sure, but they didn't care. You don't do a background check for a hookup.* He started to say so but then stopped. He was duct-taped and naked in some cabin being grilled by a psycho-bitch. *Play along,* he thought. *Do whatever she says, give her whatever what she wants to hear.*

"Rule #1. From now on, you will know a girl's complete name before engaging in sex. Got it?"

Logan nodded.

"Okay then, next question. What made you think you were somehow entitled to fuck me?"

Logan did not know the right answer. *Because. . .*

"Logan, answer the question."

"What answer do you want, huh? Because that's the one I'll say." As soon as he blurted it out, he regretted it.

Hannah considered his question. It was not unreasonable in light of his circumstances.

"I want to understand why you did what you did to me. I *need* to understand what you were thinking. *And I need for you to understand what I was feeling.* And we will sit here until that happens."

"So you kidnap me and. . ."

"I did not expect you'd be a willing participant."

"You're right about that," Logan said.

"So, why did you feel entitled to fuck me?"

"You came on to me, okay? You were all cute and flirty and we stood and talked and you touched my arm and smiled a lot and you weren't looking around the room to check out other guys. You were into me, or I thought you were."

Yeah, Hannah thought, *I was.*

"I get all that," Hannah said. "You read me right. I was a newbie freshman and you were a senior. A *senior.* A senior was giving me his full attention. *You* talked just to me. *You* didn't look around checking out other girls. *You* kept filling my drink. *You* touched my hair and my shoulder, too. We laughed. I flirted with you. It was fun."

Hannah paused to inhale.

"But what about that made you feel entitled to fuck me?"

"Everything," he said. "All of it. And you wanted it, too."

"When did I *say* I wanted to have sex with you?"

"You didn't have to say it," Logan replied. "You showed it."

"I was showing that I *liked* you. And I thought you liked me."

"I did like you. I wouldn't have stayed talking with you for an hour and a half if I didn't."

"But you lied to me. How could you do that? Like me and lie to me?"

"What do you mean?"

"You gave me drink after drink, which you knew were stronger than they seemed. When I got dizzy, you offered that I could go lie down in your room for a little while and see if I felt better. You told me if I didn't that you would take me back to my dorm."

Logan struggled to remember exactly what he had said. Yeah, he'd handed her drinks, so what? That was just being nice. And everybody knew that frat punch was strong. That was the point of it.

"Everybody knows frat punch is strong. Any frat. You had to. . ."

"No. I'm a freshman. You're a senior. It was my *first* frat party. I told you that. But you kept bringing me drinks."

"And you kept drinking them."

"And I got woozy from them. And you lied to me."

"I didn't lie. I offered my bed and room to lie down. You accepted.

What was I supposed to think?"

"That I was woozy and needed to stop drinking and lie down?"

"That's not how it works."

Hannah felt a vibration run through her, like an electric current.

"*That's not how it works?* What does that mean?"

"You took my hand and went to my room. That means something."

"Because you offered. Because I thought you were being a nice guy and taking care of me. Like a friend would."

"I was."

"But then you came back into the room and raped me."

"I did not rape you, dammit. It was a hookup. You were into me and now you talk like you never flirted. *You were into me*." Logan leaned forward in his chair. His voice increased in self-righteous volume with each sentence.

"Yes, we've covered that. I wanted to date you. But I never, ever, in any way, said I wanted to have sex with you right away. I do not have sex with boys I just met. Ever."

"How was I supposed to know that?"

And, with that, a tight knot of pain imploded inside her gut.

"Because I *told* you, asshole. I said *No, no, no*. I said, *Stop, stop, stop*. I said, *Please, please stop*."

Hannah was now ten inches from his face, her voice hoarse. "I didn't kiss you. I didn't try to touch you. I did *nothing* that would show you that I wanted sex or reciprocated in any way what you were doing to me. That's how you were *supposed to know*."

"I didn't hear you saying those things. Not for real. I thought you were just saying it like girls say things sometimes."

"*Like girls say things sometimes*? What the fuck does that mean? So you did hear me and didn't stop? Didn't stop long enough to check it out? I thought there was a remote, wildly remote, chance that you maybe really had not heard, because you were *smothering* me, had my face pushed against a pillow, and the music was loud. Now you say you did? You heard me and ignored me?"

"I was not *smothering* you. You're making that up."

Hannah stopped cold and appeared to reflect. "Let me show you what I mean," she said.

She went behind his back, yanked the comforter up over his mouth and nose and pulled it tight. She jerked his head back, hard, not releasing her grip on the comforter. He struggled, trying to get his face loose. She braced her hand and arm against her chest, put her other hand alongside the first, elbow digging into his back, and hung on. Logan's body started heaving, and the chair almost came off the floor as he swung from side to side, his lungs desperate for air. Hannah hunkered down as if riding a bull, as if holding on was her lifeline.

"Let go, Hannah. Let go now!" Stacy was yelling at her and pulling at her arms. "*LET. GO. NOW.*"

Hannah dropped her grip and took three steps back.

Logan was gasping, leaning over, his chest visibly moving in and out, hungry for air. His legs and arms were shaking uncontrollably.

Hannah looked at him, then at her hands. She started to tremble, just barely, then walked across the living room and into the bedroom, closing the door behind her.

"What the fuck. . . does she think. . . she's doing?" Logan's voice came out in tight gasps.

"You'll figure it out," Stacy said. "You're a smart boy."

"Cut me loose. CUT ME LOOSE NOW. That bitch is going to kill me."

Stacy leaned in so close that Logan could feel her breath on his face. "You better change your attitude about women if you plan on walking out of here. And, for the record, I'm on her side."

Then Stacy flashed him a wide, fake, toothy grin. "Now, how about a little water? Wouldn't that taste good? Or lemonade? Because it smells like maybe you puked a bit into that comforter. Happens to a lot of people when they need air."

It was two hours before Hannah came out of the bedroom. Stacy had given Logan both lemonade and a cup of hot coffee, holding the glass and mug to his mouth so he could drink. Then she'd placed the bucket on the floor underneath his slatted chair. The comforter was in the washing machine. He was hunched over in the chair.

Stacy was at the stove. Hannah inhaled as her stomach rumbled,

"That smells awesome. What is it?" Hannah asked.

"Chicken and mushrooms in a cream sauce. To be served over herbed rice. A Julia Child recipe that I simplified."

"Was all this in the one bag of groceries you brought? You planned this?"

"Yeah," Stacy said. "We need to keep our strength up. I pre-mixed all the spices and put them in mini-baggies. That saves a lot of space."

"That Girl Scout planning again. Unbelievable."

They closed the door from the kitchen to the living room. No open concept in this cabin. That was handy because they did not want Logan in their line of sight while they ate.

Might spoil their appetite.

After their supper, Stacy put some chicken and rice in a small bowl and cut it up into baby-sized pieces best eaten with a spoon. As Hannah did the dishes, Stacy fed Logan. His earlier refusal to eat, several hours back, had been reconsidered.

After the dishes were done, they sat at the kitchen table over a cup of tea.

"That was scary, Hannah," Stacy began.

"It was scary for me, too."

"I'm a little nervous about you losing it with a knife in your hand. I'm not that quick."

"I get that," Hannah said. "Something cracked. But I think I can do what needs to be done without losing control again. I've been thinking."

"Are you sure you want to continue?"

"Yeah. I considered bailing, but I want to see it through."

Ten minutes later, Hannah was again seated in front of Logan. In a weird way, she'd almost gotten used to him naked and duct-taped to a chair. She felt safe with him like this.

Logan, however, almost started to tremble when Hannah sat down.

"I got a little out of control, Logan. I expect that you felt really scared when you couldn't breathe. I remember how terrified I was. I hope you'll remember how you felt when you're on top of a girl. Like make sure, if she is face down, that she can breathe okay? And stop fucking her if she is trying to talk until you understand what she is saying? Can you do that for me?"

"Yes," Logan said.

"Now we're going to discuss appropriate touch. Good touch and bad touch. You will listen carefully and ask whatever questions you want. Do you understand?"

"Yes."

"When you came back into your bedroom that night, you lay down beside me, like spooning. I remember you ever so gently rubbed my back and shoulders. I liked that. It was like you understood how shitty I was feeling and wanted to make me feel just a little bit better. Do you remember doing that?"

Logan did not really remember doing that, but he replied "Yes" anyway.

"And then you reached up under my blouse and undid my bra. Did you ask if I wanted you to undo my bra?"

"No, but I thought you'd like it. I think you made some noise when I rubbed your back, like *ummm*."

"So, making a sound when you rubbed my back was an obvious message that it was okay to un-do my bra and then put your hands all over my breasts and twist my nipples?"

"I already said that I thought you wanted it."

Hannah casually leaned forward and grabbed one of Logan's nipples, pinching it hard, then rolling it back and forth between her fingers.

"Stop, dammit," Logan said, trying to pull back.

Hannah stopped, hands dropping to her sides. She was looking directly into his eyes.

Logan was panting, quick shallow breaths, the fear and rage of a trapped animal. She could do anything to him and he could not defend himself.

"How did that feel, Logan? Was that good for you?"

"No," he growled.

"Gee, since you did it to me, I just assumed you would like it. The difference is that I stopped when you said to."

"I never did that. Not like that."

"Well, actually, you did. Then you pulled up my skirt and pulled at my panties until they ripped and then rubbed your fingers and hand against me. You were rough and it hurt. Do you understand what that felt like? To have someone you don't really know putting their hands all over your private parts? And you can't move and can't make them stop?"

Hannah had maintained eye contact with Logan. Now, in one fluid motion, she grabbed his penis, holding it tight, as her other hand slipped under his balls and squeezed. Not harsh, just a light squeeze to show she could.

"Stop it," he yelped. "Your sick, fucking game has gone far enough. Cut me loose."

"But I thought all the boys like a girl who makes a grab for their cock. And I can play with it, too," Hannah said. "Would you like that, Logan? And, really, we haven't even got to the *fucking* part of this—how did you just put it? *This sick, **fucking** game?* This is just the warm-up. The fucking part comes after."

"What do you want from me?" Logan's voice was hoarse.

"I want for you to *understand*. But what is frustrating me is that you continue to insist that you didn't do what you did, that you're not accountable."

"Look, I'm sorry. Okay? I didn't understand. I couldn't have heard you or I would have stopped."

"Now that is one piss-poor apology. Mr. Nice Guy would have stopped if he'd just heard? So, it's *my* fault? I didn't communicate clearly or loudly enough? Ever heard the term *Narcissistic Personality Disorder*? It describes people who lack empathy, who project their own feelings and needs onto others. Narcissists are always the victims. Nothing is ever their fault. Does any of that fit for you?"

"This is bullshit. Bullshit. I didn't hear you. I didn't understand."

But even as Logan said it, the word *bullshit* ricocheted in his brain as a memory intruded.

He was about ten years old. He'd been driving somewhere with his father. It was a long trip—all day. They stopped at a restaurant. His father had said, "I'm starving. You must be starving, kiddo." Logan had said that he wasn't hungry, that he didn't feel so good, that he didn't want to eat. But his father hadn't listened, or hadn't heard him, and ordered them deluxe cheeseburger platters. It was a huge amount of food. His father dove in, making smacking noises with his lips. When he noticed that Logan had just eaten a few bites, he said, "Finish it up. I paid a lot for that meal." Logan said, "I'm not hungry," and his father got angry. "Why didn't you tell me you weren't hungry? I wouldn't have wasted the money on you?" Logan said, "I did tell you," and that made his father more mad. "Bullshit," he'd said. "Bullshit. Don't lie to me now." Then he made him eat more and more, counting every bite. "You were hungry," his father had said. "I knew it. No bullshit."

Logan had ended up puking in the back seat an hour later. He remembered it as one of the worst days of his life, a combination of emotional fear, physical pain, and the sense of being trapped with someone who could not hear him, who never seemed to hear him, who was supposed to love him but. . .

When he looked up, Hannah was staring at him. She had let go of his penis and balls. He didn't remember her letting go.

"I'm not that," he said. "I'm not like that."

"Seems like a good stopping point for tonight," Stacy said from the sidelines. "Let's sleep on that."

Chapter 60
(December 9th)

In the morning, when Hannah emerged from the bedroom, Logan was still asleep on the floor wrapped in a comforter. And Stacy was in the kitchen, the coffee freshly brewed.

"I'm sorry I abandoned you last night, Stacy. Again. How did you get the tape off and. . ."

"No problem. It's one leg at a time. Cut the tape, move that leg over, cuff it to the other one, then cut the rest of the tape holding him to the chair. We even got to the bathroom. He sat on the toilet for twenty minutes, with the door open, of course. And I never saw a boy so happy to be given a toothbrush. He had both wrists banging against his face as he went at it, but he brushed those pearly whites. Then I gave him another special cocktail to drink."

Stacy gestured at the sleeping, snoring form. "He'll be out another few hours I think."

"Coffee?" she asked.

Hannah didn't answer the question. She looked out the window at the fields. There were no deer. Then she turned to face Stacy.

"I don't think I can keep doing this. I'm so sorry. I know I started it and dragged you into it. I thought it would make me feel better, like I was doing *something*. And all that shit about needing to make him *understand*. That it wasn't revenge, but *retribution*. . ."

Her voice trailed off.

"I wanted to hurt him, Stacy. Humiliate him. And I did. And then I lost control. But after that, it was like there was a shift in my psyche. I got so cold and deliberate. And when I said last night that this was just the *warm-up,* I surprised myself. Like who is this woman and what is she doing? Am I really going to rape him? Like that will make me feel any better? That will make him understand?"

"Okay," Stacy said. "First off, stop with the apology. I have no regrets. You didn't *drag* me into this. I'm with you. And you can choose to end it whenever and however you want."

"Yeah, I've been thinking about how to wrap it up. Might be stronger with both of us involved."

"So shoot, girl."

"Well, to start, both of us are talking. And we go through what has happened but do it from the perspective of. . . "

When Logan opened his eyes, groggily blinking against the light, he saw Stacy and Hannah sitting on the couch staring at him. It all rushed in: where he was, what was happening, terror at what they might do, what they'd told him they were planning to do.

"Good morning, Logan," Stacy said in her sing-song voice. "How did you sleep? Ready to face another day? How about some coffee? And a warm, buttery biscuit? I made some biscuits. C'mon, time to sit up."

His eyes darted around the room, searching for something, anything, that could help him escape. His stomach was a tight, hard knot. He felt as if he might vomit.

"Oh, dear, you do look a bit worn," Stacy said. "Not looking forward to today, are you?"

Stacy turned toward Hannah. They smiled at each other and did a fist-bump.

"There's been a change of plans, Logan. We've decided to just bring you back to the frat house," Hannah said. "We don't think that this process will accomplish our initial goal of you having an epiphany as to what a total asshole you've been."

"Yeah, the goal was that you truly *understand* what you did and feel deep *remorse*," added Stacy. "And then you'd resolve to treat women with respect and stop playing mind-fuck and other fuck games."

"But that isn't going to happen so we're done. Is that okay with you?" asked Hannah. "Do you want to go home?"

Logan knew this was another piece of their sick, sadistic game. They would promise to cut him loose and then pull it away. He said nothing.

"Okay, so you aren't feeling chatty this morning," continued Hannah. "No problem. We can do the talking. But you have to listen really, really closely, and there will be a quiz at the end. Boys who don't know the answers could be in big trouble. Are you ready?"

"Wait, wait, wait," Stacy interrupted. "The boy needs some coffee first. And maybe a potty run. And to sit in a comfy chair and not on that hard floor. "

Fifteen minutes later, Logan was seated in the comfy chair, still naked but wrapped in the comforter, with a cup of coffee in his hands. Stacy had cut off the handcuffs from the night before and put on new ones, but with 12 inches between them. It was enough to hold a cup to his mouth and feed himself.

"So, Logan, let's talk about what you're going to do as soon as you get home," Stacy began. "Let's say we drop you off. I bet you'd like to take a hot shower and grab some clean clothes." She smiled at him as if waiting for him to agree, then continued.

"You'll need to have a few story-lines ready for when your frat brothers ask where the hell you've been. It's important to get your story straight from the start. So be thinking about that, okay?"

"So, after you clean up and grab a bite to eat, what next?" Hannah chimed in. "I think the first step is to file a report with the police. Tell them how you were kidnapped."

"Yeah, these two psycho-girls abducted you from your frat house in the middle of a party," Stacy continued. "Okay, so like a hundred people saw you leave with a girl—that would be me, and I was pretty damn hot that night. So, anyway, they saw you leave, and walk down the street, but really, it was what happened after that when no one was watching that matters."

Stacy looked at Hannah.

"So, you willingly walked to this car," Hannah said, picking up the narrative, "where you'd been told you'd meet a chick named Emily who was a Facebook friend who you'd never met, but the hot girl, Michelle, had told you that Emily had the hots for you. . ."

"Only, it will turn out when the cops do their investigation into your report, that you don't have a Facebook friend from out-of-state named Emily," interrupted Stacy. "Gee, that's odd. Why would you make that up?"

"Anyway, you get to the car, but then these girls—one hot and one not-so-much-anymore—grab you and stun you and handcuff you and then drive off to somewhere."

"Yeah. Somewhere. A cabin, like, somewhere—in the middle of

nowhere."

"Then, after they drugged you for a night, they *tortured* you. Like Guantanamo. Cut off all your clothes, duct-taped you naked to a chair, started asking you hard questions."

"You need to tell the cops how the girls were really *mean* to you. And how you were so embarrassed to be naked when you weren't the one in control—tell them how that is so *not* fun."

"Oh-oh, and how one of them almost smothered you. And she pinched your pretty pink nipple really hard. She said she thought it would be a turn on, but it wasn't. And then she grabbed your cock and balls when you didn't tell her first that she could."

"That sounds about right, doesn't it Hannah?" Stacy concluded, turning to Hannah.

"Uh-huh," Hannah replied, shaking her head up and down in agreement. "Let's review, shall we?"

"So, two girls abducted you from a frat party in front of hundreds of people, stunned you, tied you up, took you to a cabin somewhere, made you hop, duct-taped you naked to a chair, asked you so many questions, and were really, really mean. Of course, they did feed you and ply you with alcohol and drugs. Then they drove you home and dropped you off by your frat house."

"Oh my, Hannah," said Stacy, opening her eyes wide as her voice shifted into a fake drawl. "What will we do? If the po-lice come and take us down to the station for questioning because Logan has filed a report? Oh, golly, gee, girlfriend, what could we say?"

"We just 'fess up and tell them our side."

"And what would that be?"

"Well, Logan did leave the party with you, Stacy, no question. And you were definitely hot that night. He got into our car and we all drove to the cabin. But there must be a *misunderstanding*—a *miscommunication*— because we'd explained that we wanted a hookup, a three-some actually, and we'd heard he was into S & M," Hannah gushed. "So we did. But it was all role play. He lost a little hair from the duct-tape but that's to be expected. And the handcuffs were, you know, part of the game. We'd bought two dozen cuffs, just in case, but we didn't need that many."

"Yeah, he was into it big time. I remember he texted his friends and frat bros that he was into a major hookup and wouldn't be home for a while. How many friends did you text, Logan? Was it six? Eight?"

"We never actually got to the *real* sex, which was a major disappointment, because he just petered out. Could not get it up. That Limp Dick Syndrome can sure ruin a good time."

"Is there anything else we can help you with, officer, sir?" Hannah asked, her voice innocence personified.

Later, Logan would have no idea who had said what. It became a blur. But he remembered the feeling of sinking down, then deeper down, of knowing that whatever had happened to him would need to remain a secret, forever, and that any attempt to go after the girls would drag him through mud so dark and sticky he would never get it off.

Their dog-and-pony show completed, Hannah and Stacy finished loading up the car. They'd considered coming back to the cabin and actually studying, because they had paid in advance for three nights, but nixed that idea. The cabin did not have good vibes. Not now.

Stacy went out to the trunk and returned with a plastic grocery bag. There were clothes inside. "These will work until you get to your room. Anyway, it's this or nothing. Got them at the Salvation Army. You ever shop there, Logan? Quite the bargains."

She cut the footcuffs so he could pull the pants on, then re-cuffed him. She repeated the protocol with the handcuffs. She stood just two feet away, pointing the stun gun directly at his cock and balls. Once Logan was dressed, in jeans and a flannel shirt, she slipped new cuffs on his hands and ankles.

Before they left the cabin, they did one last check, left a tip for the girl who would come to clean, and slipped a pillowcase over Logan's head. Then they hopped him to the car and he slid into the back seat.

"Do we really need the pillowcase?" asked Hannah. "Do you think it matters?"

"Probably not, but when will I ever get to use it again? This is my Thelma and Louise moment," Stacy replied. "We will need to pull it off once we hit the turnpike or we'll freak someone out."

"Yeah, our kidnapping days are over," Hannah sighed. "Back to the real world."

The ride back to Kaw Valley was uneventful. They played music loud. Coming off the backcounty roads, as they turned onto the highway, Hannah pulled off the pillowcase.

"Sit up now, Logan." she said. "Look out the window."

"Don't you think the Flint Hills are beautiful no matter what the season, Logan?" she asked, turning her head around to face him in the back seat. "I love spring when all the wildflowers come out but also when the fields are all *amber waves of grain.* Do you have a favorite season?"

Logan started to say, "No, not really," but stopped himself. It was like nothing had ever happened. Like they were out for a weekend drive in the country, music playing, watching the scenery go by.

He felt like some character in a sci-fi movie, with alt-facts. It was disorienting, disturbing. And he still could not believe that it was really over, that they were not going to shoot him in some deserted field where they'd already dug a hole. That was where his fucking mind had gone last night. Into the fucking hole.

Twenty-four minutes later, they pulled up a block from his frat house.

"We'll just drop you here if that's okay, Logan," Stacy said. "And if you try to memorize the license plate—not that you'd do that, not that it would matter—just an FYI that we traded with a car that's been parked in the dorm lot for two months and we'll be switching them back tonight."

"So, before we leave, any questions?" asked Hannah

Logan felt bile rise in his throat. Yeah, he had a few questions. Like, what the fuck happened? Why did they do this? What made them think they had a right to. . .

But he swallowed the bile, swallowed the questions.

"No," he replied.

"If we bump into you on campus, Logan, you are instructed to ignore us, walk away, say nothing. We are dead to you. Got that?"

"Yes," he said.

"So, you can go now."

"The ties?" he said.

"What?" Hannah asked.

"The cuffs are still on."

"Yes, as a matter of fact they are. But you can manage. You hop pretty damn well."

"Jesus, please, just cut them."

"Logan, Logan, Logan," Stacy interrupted, getting out of the car and opening the door to the back seat, the cuff cutters in her hand. "Can you not take a joke?"

They drove off, Stacy behind the wheel, leaving Logan at the curb rubbing his wrists. They did not look back.

"Reach into the glove box, will you?" Stacy asked Hannah.

Hannah reached in and pulled out five CDs.

"Put in *Frozen*," Stacy instructed. "And turn the volume way up."

Within seconds "Let It Go" filled the car. By the second stanza they were singing along at the top of their lungs. By the third round their fists pounded the dashboard.

Back at their dorm, Stacy brought out a rolling cart so they could bring up everything in one load. They went about emptying the car, wiping it down, and shaking out the floor mats. They would switch back the plates after dark. They worked as a team, without speaking.

Back in their rooms, they continued to put things away. The handcuffs, stun gun, duct-tape, and more, went into a green plastic bin headed for a cousin's garage.

"How do you feel?" Stacy finally asked Hannah.

"I feel—purged. Whatever happened out there, it was closure."

"What about retribution? Or justice? Any of that happen?"

"Forget justice," Hannah replied. "But there was some retribution. And a few moments of pure revenge."

Hannah paused for a moment. "Do you think Logan was hurting out there? Was he really scared?"

"Yeah, Hannah, Logan was hurting. And he was really scared. He felt trapped. He maybe felt more horrible than he ever had in his life."

"But did he *understand*? Did he feel *remorse*?"

"That I don't know. Maybe not now, but later? Over time? Maybe he'll connect the dots. That's up to him."

"I'm glad he was scared and hurt. I'm glad that I, me, personally, directly, made him feel that. That would be the revenge part, right? What does that make me, Stacy? That I wanted him to suffer?"

"Human, Hannah. That would make you human."

Chapter 61
(December 10th)

Molly, Max, Grace, and Katrina were at Vespers, the annual end-of-fall semester concert that combined all of the university choirs, orchestra, and some special groups. It was a family tradition that had marked the start of the holiday season when Grace and Gil were raising Alex and Molly. Grace remembered her young children peering over the balcony railing at the people below.

Now it was her grandson looking down. But Max, Grace realized, was counting the rows, organizing what felt to him to be chaos into something his mind could process.

Grace closed her eyes, allowing her mind to free-float through Christmases past. She and Gil had been faithful to this particular tradition for almost two decades, missing only one or two years when the kids had been sick. Until she'd abruptly left Kaw Valley, abandoning her children and all of their family traditions as well.

But she was back now, and so was Vespers.

Every year was somewhat different, except for the concluding audience sing-along to traditional carols. This year would open with Tchaikvosky—parts of *The Nutcracker Suite,* segue into a more contemporary "Gloria" from *Misa Criolla,* then a cello solo, a spirited sing-along medley, the requisite "Ose Shalom," more Tchaikovsky, and wrapping up with "Go Tell It On The Mountain" and "Coming Home."

Grace had not invited Mickey. She was still trying to figure out where and how he would fit into her life. A part of her wanted to keep him private. But privacy was not a realistic possibility when she lived in a reconverted garage behind her daughter.

After the concert, they would go back to Molly's for sour cream chicken enchiladas that were warming in the oven. Max had chosen the menu. Part of the tradition was that the kids got to pick their favorite meal. Then they would, together, decorate the tree that they'd already set up with lights.

Grace felt that the anxiety, even desperation, that had driven her behavior, her choices, for so many years, had diminished. She had an image of a future she'd thought impossible, where she once again might have both family and a partner.

Except for the dark empty place in the corner of her heart. Except for missing Alex.

Chapter 62
(December 12th)

Grace sat, notebook in hand, in the third row on the right side of the small courtroom. She was here to observe a trial for rape.

Patsy had called a week ago and suggested she might want to sit in for a few days to get a better feel for the court process. Grace had rescheduled appointments to make it work.

Trials are like weddings, she thought, watching people come in and quickly find their place. *People sit on the side they are connected to or identify with.* She visualized an usher showing people to their seats with classical music playing in the background.

"Are you with the victim or the perpetrator?" the usher would inquire softly. "Defense or prosecution?"

Only one woman, other than herself, sat on the prosecution side. Grace assumed she was a relative of the victim. Across the aisle, however, sat fifteen or so people, family and friends of the young men on trial.

She'd missed voir dire, the process of jury selection, the day before. But today was opening arguments. Then the prosecution would present their case. The defense would cross-examine each prosecution witness. The defense presented last.

This was a case of a freshman at another college who'd been raped by two young men. They'd all known each other from their hometown. The boys—roommates—lived in the same co-ed dorm but were older. They'd all been hanging out with other friends in the guys' dorm room, but then it had dwindled down to just the three of them.

And then they turned on her—these friends she'd trusted—and raped her.

"All rise," the bailiff intoned. And the trial began.

The opening arguments were basically position statements: *this is what we will show you, prove to you, and this is why you will be compelled to reach a conclusion of guilty—or not guilty.*

The attorney for the defense was a woman, in a dress that was both tight and low-cut. *There must be a reason,* Grace thought. *Perhaps to keep sex and seduction in the jury's visual field at all times?* Whatever, this attorney had the D-cup to do it.

An assistant DA was for the prosecution. He was methodical, fact-focused, organized, and believable. One of the good guys.

Much of what followed was tedious. Police were called by the prosecution to explain what they saw and did, their specific protocols, which were then attacked by the defense. For hours and hours.

It took just one morning in real court for Grace to appreciate how *real time* was so **not** like TV. *Law and Order* did in an hour what took the real legal process months, if not years to do. No three-month continuances in TV land. And other shows, like *CSI* and *NCIS,* had created totally unrealistic expectations for investigations and evidence.

"So, the clothing was placed in paper bags and then in the trunk of the police car?" the defense attorney queried. "Was an officer present at all times to secure the evidence?"

"The trunk was locked," the officer replied.

"So, no one was protecting the evidence from being tampered with?" This time her voice communicated incredulity if not suspicion of some sort of cover-up.

"The trunk of the police car was locked from the time we placed the bags with the evidence in the trunk until we delivered it to the evidence locker at the station. That is our protocol."

"But an officer was not assigned to stay with the vehicle at all times to prevent tampering?"

"No. We have limited staff and all of our officers were on tasks required for that stage of an investigation." Now his tone, which had been completely flat-line, had an edge of frustration.

"So, the number of officers was not adequate to both conduct the investigation and secure the evidence?"

"I did not say that. The evidence was secured in a locked trunk of a police vehicle at all times. Officers were doing their assigned tasks."

"But no officers actually watched the vehicle."

"Correct, but. . ."

"Thank you, officer. That's all for now."

The dorm director explained what the dorm rules were, procedures for enforcing the rules, and what he had or had not observed on the night of the alleged crime.

The ER nurse was called to explain and review the rape kit protocols and findings. The nurse described abrasions and vaginal tears, visible trauma to genitalia, vaginal bleeding, bruising. She explained coagulation and clotting factors, and how they affected vaginal bleeding. She listed medications given a rape victim, such as antibiotics for possible STDs or medication to prevent conception.

All of which the defense ignored. Their focus was on the poor quality of the photographs taken of the victim in the ER. The pictures were fuzzy. And, if the camera had messed up, could other aspects of the rape exam be relied upon? They questioned the nurse's credentials and why she did not belong to a particular organization of forensic nurses. They exploited any sliver of inconsistency in testimony, even if just word choice. The defense insinuated some degree of collusion between the hospital and police.

Grace felt, despite the intensity of the cross-examinations, that this was a slam-dunk case. They had a rape, a report, medical findings, and DNA from both men. Both men admitted having had sex with the victim. The defense kept trying to poke holes in the credibility of the evidence, how it was attained or secured, what protocols were or were not followed by the cops or the ER personnel or the dorm resident supervisor who had checked the halls and heard nothing. But, to Grace, it was solid. The conclusion was obvious.

Until the girl took the stand. Then it became clear that *she* was also on trial. When the words *Rape or Regret?* were plastered on a big screen in the courtroom as backdrop, Grace felt her stomach turn over.

The girl was grilled for hours. The prosecution was respectful, leading her through a timeline of the night. But, when the cross-examination started, every word was scrutinized and picked apart. She was forced to describe, in second-by-second detail, which boy had held her down, where exactly his hands had been on her body, how she had resisted, exactly how her arms sand legs were positioned when the other boy had penetrated her.

"So, you say he had his hands on your shoulders and was holding you down. Did you use your arms to push him off?" the attorney asked.

The defense put pictures of the dorm room on a screen. The implied expectation was that she should have total and consistent recall of a trauma that had happened over a year before. Every, *I'm not sure,* was framed—through the sighs, eye rolls or dismissive tone of the defense attorney—as intentional obfuscation. The goal was to discredit her, to impugn motives for a false report, right down to holding up the girl's thong underwear and asking if this was the underwear she had been wearing.

This is crazy, Grace thought, watching the attorney dangling panties in front of a jury. Like any girl who wears a thong must be secretly asking for it? Because you sure couldn't tell from the clothes the girl had been wearing—sweat pants and a T-shirt. Hardly the clothing of a seduction. And most teenaged girls had some version of the same undies in their dresser drawers.

Parading in front of the jury, the defense attorney signaled more sexual interest and availability than the girl ever had, Grace realized as she walked out of the courtroom.

"This was one time that selfies were useful," Grace told Molly that evening. "The prosecution had pictures of six or seven kids all goofing off, sprawled on a bed and the floor, laughing and smiling. And all wearing *hanging around the dorm* attire."

"What exactly is that?" Molly asked.

"Comfortable and totally a-sexual. Gender aside, they all had on sweats and T-shirts. Maybe even pajama bottoms, the ones with crazy prints with no matching tops."

"Yeah, Mom, because *matching* went out in the 90's. Now finish your soup. I've got to get Max going on homework."

The next day, after the prosecution rested, the defense hit back even harder. They had their own expert witnesses. Medical professionals testified that bruising and vaginal tearing could happen from any form of *rougher* sex. Or it could even have resulted from a previous sexual encounter. A retired detective from another state critiqued the Kaw Valley police department's protocols and findings.

After two hours, Grace couldn't take it anymore. She slipped out of the courtroom, almost breaking into a run to get outside, to breathe in the crisp autumn air and feel the sunlight.

Tomorrow, she told herself, *I'll come back tomorrow.*

But the next day was worse.

Grace tried to focus but she was impatient for the defense to put the defendants on the stand. She wanted to hear how they would explain, justify—how they would be under scrutiny and pressure. So, when the defense attorney stood up and said, "The defense rests, your Honor," Grace was stunned.

Closing arguments started after a lunch break. The prosecution reviewed the evidence. Not that the two boys had had sex with the girl—they had admitted that—but how all of the evidence pointed to rape. Piece by piece, they re-built their case.

Then the defense found fault with the evidence, arguing that if one part was flawed, how could the jury trust that the rest was reliable? They pointed to every verbal *I don't remember* from the victim, every minute inconsistency. They questioned her motives, her history, her character.

The judge gave the jury their instructions: what testimony was to be weighed and considered and what was not; how to request clarification; a brief reiteration of the threshold for reasonable doubt.

The verdict came back after one day of deliberation. Grace read about it in the morning paper.

The jury was hung. Deadlocked. It was a mistrial.

"What did you expect?" Patsy asked her later that night over vodka gimlets and medium-rare steaks. They were at a window table at *715*, a Main Street continental bistro with both exquisite food and drinks. "That it would be a balanced process? Defendants have a right to face, even interrogate, their accusers. That's the law."

"Yeah, but when the accuser, dare I say *victim*, is also on trial? She was *interrogated* for hours. But the guys never took the stand. The jury didn't get to see them fumble for words or admit that they couldn't remember or get flustered and confused."

"Defendants do not have to take the stand," said Patsy, "and juries are instructed to not take that as meaning anything as far as their guilt or innocence. That right to not self-incriminate. Although most defendants deflect that back to their attorneys: *I really wanted to testify but my attorney wouldn't let me.*"

"But it *does* mean *something* or at least it feels like it means something."

"You're preaching to the choir on that one, Grace."

"I was *sure* it would be a guilty verdict. The same evidence ten or fifteen years ago would have been plenty."

"We have higher conviction rates for almost any other crime. I believe that the criminal justice system needs to look, pragmatically, at setting gradations for rape like we do for homicide. With homicide we have 1st degree, 2nd degree, manslaughter, involuntary manslaughter—all related to the degree of intention and planning versus reactivity and impulse. Sentences are very different for each gradation." Patsy stopped to sip her wine. "I think juries would convict at a higher rate for rape if the consequences were not so rigid and extreme."

"So, it's not that they don't believe that a rape happened, but they don't accept a one-size-fits-all?" Grace asked.

"Sort of. They see a difference, and I can too, between a stranger with a gun and a frat boy with alcohol. A gun is a weapon no matter who wields it or what the circumstances are. Alcohol is not. A gun, or knife, clarifies intent and planning. Alcohol is ambiguous. And, usually, everyone is drinking. So, the threshold to reach the *beyond a reasonable doubt* standard is fluid with rape in a way it is not with other assaults."

"I can see that. I used to hold to *rape is rape*. Period. And if *dead is dead* is not a bottom line for charges, and intent is even weighed in sentencing, then maybe we do need to re-define. But isn't that another way to victim-blame? Like, *We can only charge third degree rape because the victim was drinking and flirting?*"

"Maybe. But that's how it is now. And girls have always been seen as culpable. Like if they do *anything* that can be perceived as seductive: what they wear, how they act, if they drink. This is a crime where victims are seen as contributing to their own victimization. It's warped but pervasive."

"So there would be more convictions absent the alcohol factor?"

"With campus-related assaults? Absolutely. Alcohol complicates prosecution. Drinking is perceived as a mitigating factor for the guys. Like they would never have done anything like *that* if they'd been sober, so they're not *really* rapists. It's how people who drive drunk make excuses: *It was just this one-time mistake; the cops were unfair or targeted them; their friend must have made the drinks doubles and not told them."*

"But it's different for girls."

"Totally," agreed Patsy. "If a girl drinks, she is perceived as *more* responsible for what happens to her—sometimes more responsible than the man who is sexually assaulting her. If she's too drunk to consent, her inebriation is taken as a free pass, like, *I thought she wanted to because she didn't say she didn't.*"

"I'm feeling guilty because I've thought that," Grace said slowly. "But it is so unfair. Unless the girl abstains, she's complicit."

"Juries get confused in rape trials. The whole *miscommunication* piece is quicksand. People know drunk driving is criminal, and being drunk isn't an *excuse* for the accident, it's the *reason* the person got arrested." Patsy paused for a bite of steak. "Circumstances that could be ruled as an *accident* if the driver was sober are taken as intentional and causative if the driver had been drinking. The assumption is that it would not have happened without inebriation. Drink and drive and you break the law. But drink and fuck? The lines blur."

"But do they have to? Beating someone up is criminal. We don't tell people, *Yeah, he knocked you down and hit you but it was a* **miscommunication.** Or ask, *How did you communicate that you didn't want to be hit and kicked?* Assault, with fists or a weapon, is criminal. The perpetrator can't say, *Yeah, I did it but I didn't mean to.* But sexual assault. . ."

Grace stopped mid-sentence. She picked up her glass, downed the remainder of the gimlet.

"I know you've been dealing with this a lot longer than I have," Grace continued. "But I feel so helpless, so angry. How can you not be yelling in the street?"

"I'm yelling on the inside," Patsy said. "I was raised on a reservation. Alcohol abuse was rampant. The lack of employment and educational options made it worse. But domestic abuse and sexual assault were almost normalized because of the alcohol. Like it's an ugly part of life but you just have to live with it."

"Were you raped?" Grace asked Patsy.

"We all were assaulted in some way. Many of my friends. Our mothers and aunties and grandmothers. We excused it, buried it, made up stories so we could live with it. Like, *That's not how Daddy really is—*

it's the booze making him be that way."

"I had this suburban, protected childhood," Grace said. "Whatever happened, we were in the dark. Like we naively assumed that if we played by the rules, which don't even seem to exist anymore, we'd be safe. But, in the grown-up world, denial is not a useful life skill."

"I think I became a cop so I could carry a gun, not be a victim, and help keep people safe by locking up the creeps," Patsy shared. "The first two are working out okay but the third one gets harder every day. Enough!" Patsy announced abruptly. "No more depressing shit about what we can't control. Our glasses are empty and your steak could use a warm-up. I, on the other hand, somehow managed to eat an entire Kansas City Strip and still talk."

As Patsy spoke, she gestured to the waiter, pointing to their glasses and then holding up two fingers.

"We need another round," she said.

Two hours later, during a 30-minute hot-hot-hot soak in her tub, Grace puzzled over a lingering question.

What impact did it have for a jury to face the defendant's family and friends, all seated on *his* side of the courtroom, day after day of a trial? When a guilty verdict would put their son, grandson, brother, and friend in jail for years? Would it make a difference if *her* side was also filled rather than empty? If juries had to face the victim's parents, grandparents, siblings, and friends with every verdict of not guilty? *Was justice ever really blind?*

With homicide trials, she reflected, families come together. They show up no matter how long it's been. But with rape? People want to erase rape. Many families don't want to hear the details. They want to move on, get over it. A trial a year after the rape brings it all back.

We don't blame someone for being murdered or robbed like we can with being raped.

This is a variable that needs to be examined, Grace thought. Women can volunteer a morning or afternoon to simply bear witness. But who makes a commitment to research? It would need to be a movement: *We Believe You.* Get women to show up for rape trials, even if they just sit in the courtrooms and knit, even in shifts. Then see, after a year, if conviction stats are impacted.

Right, she thought, reaching for a towel. *Another one of my crazy ideas.*

Like I have the time to tackle that project.

Chapter 63
(December 18th)

Lisa had called Shelby's parents. She'd told them that she'd connected with Grace McDonald, Shelby's therapist. That they had some information on what might have been going on with Shelby. She'd offered to email them a summary or to meet with them in person.

"So you and the therapist know why Shelby took the pills?" Bill had asked.

"No, we don't know anything for sure, but we do know more than we did in October."

"I want to do this face-to-face," Bill had said. "We'll drive to Kaw Valley. When can you meet? Both of you?"

They'd scheduled for today at Grace's office, at 10 a.m. Grace had told Lisa that *whatever* they wanted, she'd make herself available.

So, at 9:45 a.m., Lisa and Grace were discussing strategy in the office as they waited.

"You take the lead, Lisa. They're pretty angry with me. They might be able to hear it better from you."

"I don't think it will matter, not really," Lisa replied. "Do we show them any pictures?"

"I have them in my desk. But I'd hate to have those images seared into my brain if it were my daughter. I'm not going to offer unless they insist."

They heard the door to the waiting room open. The Stewarts had arrived.

After a few moments of hanging up coats and Grace's offer of tea, they sat, Bill and Diane on the couch and Lisa and Grace in chairs across the coffee table.

"Just tell us what you found out," Bill started in. "Don't sugarcoat it."

Lisa looked at Grace and then began to speak.

"It started with Ms. McDonald calling me and asking to meet with me. She wanted to know if Shelby had said anything that might be a clue as to why. . .”

At their daughter's name, Diane and Bill both seemed to flinch, and then Diane began to blink away tears.

Lisa hesitated for a second and then continued.

"Anyway, we believed that she'd had two dates with a young man whom she said she met in a business class last spring. Shelby told us they were on some small group project. She'd said that she woke up in his bed after the second date and could not remember anything. That's when she'd called Ms. McDonald, for an appointment. But that was it."

"That much we know—what Ms. McDonald told us," Bill replied. "So what else?"

"I looked for Shelby's class schedule from last spring. Ms. McDonald then called each business instructor and asked whether they had group projects in their respective classes. She then went to each professor who did and asked who had been on Shelby's team. But none would say due to national privacy regulations called FERPA."

"Yeah, like those regulations that Ms. McDonald quoted as to why she didn't contact us when our daughter was hurting?" Bill's tone was hostile.

"No, that's HIPPA. This is FERPA," Grace answered. "Educational rather than medical privacy."

"So what did you do then?" Diane asked, gently placing her hand on her husband's arm.

"We realized that we had to find a backdoor to get the information. And, while professors have FERPA, students can tell anyone anything," Lisa replied.

Grace listened as Lisa neatly summarized the process: how they used social media, offered money for information, received replies, came up with some names, researched the names, selected one as the most likely, and then how Lisa trailed him, finagled a date, and went out on the date.

"You can take it from here," Lisa said, turning to Grace.

"While Lisa was on the date with the young man, I enlisted the help of a retired detective and we broke into his apartment to search it," Grace said, her affect as flat as if she were describing the weather. "We found envelopes with pictures of girls, 12 in total, in a box in his closet. One of the girls was Shelby."

Bill punched the arm of the couch. "That prick," he muttered. "That fucking prick. What did he do to my daughter?"

Diane simply sat very, very still, staring at Grace.

"This will be hard to hear, but you have a right to know. He took pictures of girls after he drugged them," Grace continued. "But we have no evidence at all of sexual assault. We subsequently identified three of the young women in the pictures, which is another story, and have met with them. Their experiences mirrored each other, but they had no idea about the photos. We notified the police, who secured a warrant to search the guy's apartment. They found the pictures and two drugs that might have been used."

"You know who did this to Shelby?" Diane asked. "You know his name?"

"Yes," Grace said. "He was arrested and some charges brought. The specific charges may be amended after further investigation. The DA has the names of the three young women we identified and will meet with them in early January. After that, we may have a better idea of what the process will look like."

"Who is he?" Diane asked. "What is his name?"

"Hunter Payne," Grace replied.

"Where is he now?" Diane asked.

"He's out on bail."

"So, there will be a trial? He will be prosecuted?"

"That is one possibility. But more likely, at least according to the DA, he will plea to lesser charges in order to avoid a trial."

"I want him locked up. For a long time," Diane continued.

"I don't think that's likely," Grace answered. "What can be proven is that he took pictures, which will probably play out as battery. There is no evidence so far of sexual assault. But the DA will make those determinations."

"You said that the other girls didn't know about the pictures. Did Shelby know?"

"Yes, at least we think so. We believe that she was standing up to him, demanding answers, and that he sent her a thumb drive with the pictures, probably as a means to intimidate her, to make her back off. We don't know if there was a message with them, such as a threat to make them public."

As soon as Grace said those words, Diane started to cry, moaning sobs of despair.

"It's high school all over again, Bill," Diane choked out the words. "No wonder she cracked. She didn't want to die. She just cracked."

Bill was leaning forward, his face contorted, looking stunned.

"What are you talking about?" Grace asked at the same moment that Lisa asked, "What about high school? What happened in high school?"

It took a full three minutes for Diane to stop sobbing. Bill kept patting his wife on the back, mumbling, "We didn't know. We couldn't know."

Grace brought Diane a glass of water and more Kleenex. Bill moved closer. He kept his hand on her shoulder as she started to speak.

"In high school, Shelby was a junior when she started dating a senior boy," Diane said. "He seemed nice enough. But he talked Shelby into taking some pictures of herself and sending them to him," Diane finally said.

"Oh my God," Lisa said. "No wonder she was so private."

"Shelby was pretty outgoing back then. She liked to have fun with her friends but hadn't really dated. He was Shelby's first love. She was really smitten with Brad. That was his name. Brad."

Grace reflected on the word. So quaint, so sweet. *Smitten*. Shelby had been *smitten*.

"But Brad started getting controlling, wanted her to account for every minute of her time. And he was jealous. He started accusing her of keeping secrets, of wanting to have sex with other boys. That's when she knew she was in over her head. She came to us and told us what was going on. So, the next time he was over, we asked him to come sit down in the living room. Shelby told him that she did not want a relationship with him—and Bill told him to stay away from her or he'd call the police."

"But he didn't stay away?" Lisa asked.

"Oh, he never went near her, not physically, but the pictures she sent him began showing up all over social media. And he'd taken some of her also, even more sexual. His friends started calling her names. *Slut-shaming* was what the counselor told us. He said that it was not that uncommon."

"She must have thought it would all happen again," Bill said in a whisper. "Poor baby, my poor baby."

"What happened after that?" Lisa asked.

"She was an outcast," Diane said. "Her friends, her supposed friends, most of them at least, dropped her. One day she woke up and simply refused to return to school."

"And so what did you. . ."

"She home-schooled for the rest of junior year and senior year. We wanted her to go to the high school in the next town over, but she wouldn't consider it. She said they probably already knew or would find out as soon as anyone saw her there. And the kids would believe it because gossip trumps truth."

"Did she keep up with any friends?" Lisa asked, beginning to understand Shelby's reticence to self-disclose.

"There were two girls who came to the house, but that went from once a week to once a month or less over time," Diane explained. "Shelby said that they had nothing to talk about other than what was happening at school, dating and break-ups, gossip and drama. And Shelby couldn't do that. It made her nauseous."

"So she had no social life?" Lisa asked.

"She got into some on-line chat rooms for homeschooled kids. But a lot of them were from religious families. If they knew, she said, they'd judge her and cut off."

"But she ended up here for college?"

"That was a shift too," Bill answered. "She'd been leaning toward small schools, but then she said she just wanted to go someplace big and out-of-state, where she could be anonymous."

Bill reached for Diane's hand and clutched it tightly.

"Let me get this straight," he said, looking at Grace. "Did you say you broke into this man's apartment? Looking for what? What did you expect to find?"

"My detective friend thought that the pictures on the thumb drive reflected ritualized behavior. He felt it was probable that he'd done it before. We wanted proof of *something*. And searching his apartment seemed the only way to find the *something* that could, maybe, be enough for the police to use for a warrant."

"Had you done anything like this before?"

"Never."

"This took a lot of time and effort and risk here. Why?"

"Because Shelby deserved it. And you do as well."

They spent another thirty minutes answering more questions from Diane and Bill, reviewing how they'd located the other young women. Bill shook his head when Lisa described setting up the pretend research foundation and the surveys.

"If you hadn't done this, and some of it does sound pretty screwball, we wouldn't know why Shelby. . ."

But he could not finish the sentence.

"What he means to say is *thank you*," Diane said. "We've been in hell blaming ourselves. But now I believe that our daughter didn't want to leave us, didn't want to die. She just cracked."

Grace gave them the DA's name and number.

"He said he can meet with you, to answer any questions, but it would be best to wait until after he meets with the other young women. And be prepared that any consequences will *never* equate to justice. It will probably end up in a plea bargain for a minor charge."

And then Bill and Diane stood up, shook hands with Lisa and Grace, collected their coats and left.

Lisa and Grace sat back down.

"That was exhausting," Lisa said. "And tomorrow I'm supposed to be out of the apartment. I'm moving stuff into a storage unit until after the break."

"Do you have a new apartment lined up?"

"I've got possibilities. I'm looking at studios. I cannot handle new roommates. There are always apartments in early January when people dropout or switch around. Landlords will even discount rent so they don't sit empty for the semester."

"Any plans for the break?"

"Sleep, eat, read for fun."

"That sounds like my dream vacation."

"So, what now?" Lisa asked.

"You did amazing work here, Lisa. You're a caring and loyal friend. And I apologize again for my bias when we first met."

"Blondes with high voices have a hard time being taken seriously.

Some cultural stereotypes are embedded," Lisa replied. "And not like I was bias-free when it came to you."

"So we were both surprised?" Grace asked, laughing, and Lisa nodded.

Grace locked up the office after Lisa left.

Only a few more days, she thought, *and I'm off for two weeks.*

Chapter 64
(December 20th)

The voicemail was so unexpected that Grace had to replay it.

"Hello. This is Hannah. Hannah Larson. I know it's been a while but I kind of left therapy in a weird way and I wondered if you have any time today or tomorrow to fit me in. I'm done with exams and I'm leaving tomorrow evening. I know you reached out to me after our last session, like a few times, and it was rude of me not to reply. So, anyway, would you please call or text me if you can? I know this is last minute so I understand if you can't."

Of course I can, Grace thought.

She left a message that she had clients booked from 11 to 4, but would be happy to see her at 4 p.m. If that didn't work, then anytime tomorrow morning.

Hannah texted back that 4 p.m. would work and she'd see her then.

When Grace opened the door to her waiting room, ushering out her 3 p.m. appointment—a woman struggling to juggle care for her elderly mother with dementia while setting boundaries with young adult kids who had returned to the nest—Hannah was waiting.

Grace was a little startled by Hannah's change in appearance. The first time Grace had met with her, her brown hair looked like a freshly shorn lamb and her eyes had darted about as if mapping escape routes. In subsequent sessions, Hannah had been alternately anxious, depressed, edgy, hyper-vigilant, hyper-reactive—standard PTSD responses. But they hadn't had time to engage in what Grace considered *treatment:* then the social media slams, then when the DA declined to prosecute, then the IOA ruling—those had sucked up their session time.

Now Hannah looked, well, *different.* It was not just her physical appearance—hair punky-short with a blue-green tint, jeans, baggy sweater, big black glasses. The changes were more something in her eyes, her face.

"Hannah," Grace said. "Please, come on in. Thank you for calling.

I've been thinking about you."

Hannah stood up and smiled at Grace. "I wanted to see you again," she said, walking into the office and sitting down on the couch.

"I want to explain," Hannah started. "I feel bad about how I walked out. You were helpful to me, but. . ."

"No apologies. You were absolutely right. It is crazy-making to be told that what happened to you is *insufficient* for any consequences. Meanwhile, you're being publicly maligned. And some therapist wants you to process it, as if talk-talk-talk will somehow make it better."

"But I did need to process it, and it did help, a lot, to have someone validate what happened, to believe me and not make me feel that I was somehow accountable, that I must have *done something* that allowed a man to feel *entitled* to rape me."

"Do you still feel that? It's pretty normal to struggle with those kinds of feelings."

"No. I did for a while. I felt so stupid, so naive. But I think I'm past that. My struggle now is what direction to take with my life because the *college experience* I'd imagined is not possible. I look at girls primping in their rooms to go to a frat party, or any party, and I want to block the door. Tell them it isn't worth it. That bad things can happen to good girls."

"What are you considering?"

"I know that I want an education, to complete college and even grad school. But I don't know in what area. Anyway, the learning and education part of college feels disconnected from the social part now. The sports stuff, football and basketball games, tailgating, frat parties, developing close friendships. . ." Hannah paused to smile, ruefully. "I remember arriving in August, moving into the dorm, looking around and thinking, *Some of these girls will be my friends for the rest of my life because we will share the happiest and most fun time of our lives.* I really believed that."

"And none of that is possible? Are you sure?"

"I've tried but I feel separate from the other girls. I can't participate. I cannot imagine going to a party without having a panic attack. I break into a cold sweat just thinking about it. Or listen to some girl describe her hookup? I'd go ballistic and come across as some maniac pussy police."

"Have you been able to talk, really share, to *any* friends?"

"Just one, Stacy, the dorm resident assistant, the one who helped me after I was raped. She's been a lifesaver."

After I was raped. . . Hannah realized she had just stated the rape as a fact, a valid part of her personal history. Was this the first time that she'd owned it? She wasn't exactly sure what that meant, but it felt different.

Grace heard it also, heard that *I was raped* would forever be a part of Hannah. It would not define her, but it would influence her choices on so many levels. Her life was now divided by *before* the rape and *after* the rape. When she had felt safe and trusting and when that changed. It might make her stronger as a woman, but at what cost?

"So just Stacy?" Grace asked. "It sounds like she did a lot more than the usual RA."

"For sure," Hannah replied, smiling. "Stacy has done way more than any job description could ever cover."

And that was all Hannah was going to say about Stacy. She had decided there was no reason to share with anyone, not even this kind, lady therapist, what they had done. She was not ashamed. She had no regrets. But she had no need to disclose.

Grace sensed a door closing, so she moved on.

"So, tell me more about the possible directions you're considering. Are you thinking about a transfer to another school? A leave of absence for a semester?"

"I've thought about a transfer, but that would be the same issues with different furniture—you know? Colleges mirror each other in so many ways. They share a culture. And I don't fit in. A semester break won't change that."

"So, will you work for a while?"

"That's one way of putting it," Hannah replied, a half-smile playing across her face.

"I enlisted last week," she continued. "In the Navy. I went to a recruiter, took some tests, and scored really high for medic. I start Basic Training in seven weeks. That gives me time to go home and deal with my parents who will think I'm totally out of my mind."

Grace sat with her mouth hanging open.

Hannah laughed. "Aren't you going to say something? Have I thrown the therapist a curve ball?"

"Yes, I think you have. I did not see that one coming. Why Navy? Is that something in your family?"

"My grandfather served in the Navy, but, no, not like it's a family tradition. I do prefer water and ocean to sand and desert. And I like the idea of being a medic, learning specific skills and helping people one-on-one. Being part of something much bigger than me. It sounds cliché but it's also true. And it will be a totally different experience."

"Those are the reasons a lot of young people decide to enlist."

"Well, it's not all altruistic. I want to learn how to kill someone if I need to, or at least to make them really regret coming after me."

"That's probably not a goal you ever expected to have."

"I'm not the girl I was four months ago. One night changed everything I'd imagined for my life."

"Will you explain to your parents why? They might understand more if you. . ."

"I don't know," Hannah interrupted. "I've never made a big decision on my own. My parents have always had the final say, especially if they were paying for it."

Hannah grinned, then giggled.

"It was so weird talking to the recruiter. I kept waiting for the guy to demand a permission slip. But, apparently, I'm legally an adult. Who knew? And I withdrew from the university, cancelled my dorm contract for spring semester. So now my plan is to have a *normal* Christmas and wait until after the holidays to drop the bomb."

"Which bomb? Enlisting or. . ."

"Enlisting. Sooner or later I expect I'll tell them about the rape because a secret like this is pretty big to keep forever. But I want to feel strong enough that if they start to grill me about why did I drink, or what was I wearing, or why did I go to his room—I need to be in a strong place inside so I can explain without getting defensive or angry."

"You think they'll react that way?"

"It's not that they're mean, but they carry around some serious bias-baggage. Maybe that's their way of coping, like, *It will never happen to our family as long as we cover every contingency.*

"You're in a very different emotional place than you were, Hannah. I really respect how hard you must have worked."

"Thank you. It's taken a lot of work, and going through some very weird shit, to get here."

There was a shift in Hannah's affect as she shifted her body on the couch, and Grace sensed another door closing. They talked, lightly, about how her classes had resolved, coping with "C" grades, and how she was storing her stuff at a friend's garage until after she'd told her parents about enlisting.

Then Hannah glanced at the time on her phone. "I'm meeting someone for an early supper," she explained as she stood up. "Need to get going. But, honestly, thank you for your support."

After Hannah left, Grace sat in her chair and thought. Something had happened to Hannah. Something she had *not* shared. Hannah had moved from victim to a new version of herself. It had not come from talking. That much was clear. *Something* had *happened*.

And she, Grace McDonald, had little to nothing whatsoever to do with the transformation. Grace knew she would probably never see Hannah again. That was one of the downsides of being a therapist. People entered the office, shared intensely painful, difficult or intimate parts of their lives, seeking resolution or guidance or a reality check. Then they left, days or weeks or months later, hopefully with a plan, but often with much still unresolved. Because life is never *resolved*.

Still, she thought, *it sure would be nice to get a postcard someday*.

Later that evening, Grace walked out to the mailbox to collect the mail. She stood under the streetlight, separating out her mail from Molly's, bills mostly, coupons and sale notices from assorted stores, and holiday cards. There was one red holiday envelope addressed to Molly that caught her attention. It was from overseas. There was no name, just an address. Grace slipped it into her jacket pocket and walked back to her casita, stopping to slip Molly's pile inside her back door.

Chapter 65
(December 22nd)

"So this is window-shopping?" Mickey asked Grace. "Just strolling along and seeing if anything *grabs my fancy?"*

"So, you're calling it your *fancy* now?" Grace retorted.

"You seem to be finding sexual innuendo in perfectly benign comments these days, Ms. McDonald," Mickey said. "I was just asking about shopping protocol."

Grace laughed and took his hand. *I'm strolling down Main Street holding hands with a man,* she realized. It was the first time she'd done anything so public in years. And it felt, in this moment, more intimate than the sex with other men, men she did not care for as much as she was growing to care for Mickey.

And Mickey was right. She was hearing sexual innuendo in perfectly benign comments. It was as if her brain was awakening, her bones and muscles loosening, the tension that had gripped her for over a decade slowly melting.

I want sex, she thought. *Not just because it's expected. Not because a man wants it. I want to make love.*

I want to make love with Mickey Donahue.

She abruptly stopped walking.

"What's the matter?" Mickey asked. "See something that grabs your fancy?"

"Yes," Grace answered. "As a matter of fact, I do." Looking him in the eyes, grinning like a fourteen-year-old girl, she leaned forward to kiss him, ever so lightly, on his lips.

They stopped, at Mickey's suggestion, for lunch at a Korean café. He ordered jjajangmyeon, bibimbap, bulgogi, and, of course, kimchi. He did so without hesitation, in Korean, barely glancing at the menu.

"You speak Korean?" she asked, incredulous. "And you learned that where?"

"Ah, that would be Korea," Mickey said. "I did two years there in the Marines. I was just a kid but the culture fascinated me. I'd hop on a bus every chance I could, then get off in whatever village looked interesting. Mostly I speak restaurant Korean—just enough to get fed."

"How do I not know that you were in the Marines?" Grace asked.

"I may not have mentioned it," Mickey replied. "It was decades ago. I think we both have enough history that there will always be surprises popping up."

After lunch, they walked all of Main Street, down one side and then back the other, with forays into some side streets as well. They stopped at whatever store—or window—caught their fancy.

Five hours later they were curled up on Grace's couch, John Coltrane in the background. Grace was reading a mystery she'd found at the Dusty Bookshelf. Mickey reached his hand over to massage Grace's neck.

"How are you doing?" he asked.

"Good," Grace replied. "I am, at this moment, quite good."

"So, if I ask you to put the book down and kiss me, would that ruin the good or enhance the good?"

She slowly smiled, laying the book down on the coffee table.

"Just what I'd hoped," Mickey said.

They had not yet had *sex*. They kissed, they nuzzled, they massaged each other's shoulders and backs. But they had circumspectly avoided erogenous zones.

Mickey kissed Grace ever so gently on the lips. He stroked her hair.

"You have very shiny hair," he whispered. "It's quite lovely."

"Thank you," Grace whispered back. "I considered shaving my head but decided against it."

"Good call. Hair looks better on a girl. Bald is for boys."

"Like you?" she asked, stroking his head.

"I'm not bald," he said. "I'm balding. It's a process. Takes years to perfect."

"Well, you're moving in the right direction."

Now or never, Grace thought. *Just do it.*

Without giving herself time to think, she turned toward Mickey, lifting her right leg up and over his legs so that she straddled his lap.

For a second, Mickey looked genuinely startled. Then he laughed.

"That was one smooth move, missy."

Grace did not answer. Instead she reached up under the back of her sweater and unhooked her bra, slid one shoulder strap down over her right arm, then the other over her left arm, then reached up her front and pulled it out like a magician pulling a bunny from a hat.

"Viola!" she announced, tossing it over her shoulder.

"I'd really like it if you touched my breasts," she whispered. "Maybe through the sweater to start so they don't get scared off."

"Oh, dear Gracie, I thought you'd never ask."

Mickey touched one breast and then the other, cupping his hands under them, circling, slowly and gently. When his fingers grazed her nipple, she let out a sharp gasp.

His fingers retreated. Mickey spoke in a very low, quiet voice.

"Do you want more of this?" he asked, the palm of his hand moving against the whole of her breast. "Or this?" his fingers circling her nipple. "Will it be A?" he asked, again with his palm. "Or B?"

"A," Grace said. "For now, I really want A."

"Then A it is."

Grace felt as if her body had become electric. Each touch sent ripples down—deep, deep down.

"Would you try B again?" Her voice was almost raspy, and when Mickey did try B, Grace inhaled sharply.

Mickey very gently, still through her sweater, put the forefinger and thumb of each hand around a nipple. Not really squeezing, he touched, an almost invisible twirl. Back and forth. Grace had leaned forward, so that his face was just inches from his hands, from her breasts.

"Oh, oh, oh."

"Was that a whimper?" Mickey asked. "Is that a good sign?"

"Yes, it's good. It's very, very good."

"Then I'll do it some more," he whispered, placing his face between her breasts and closing his eyes.

After a minute, Mickey slowly moved his right hand down and then up under her sweater.

"Do you like this?" he asked, his fingers circling her naked breast, ever so barely brushing her nipple. Then his hand stopped. "Or this?" as his left hand still moved outside the sweater. "Do you want A or B?"

"A," she said. "Let's go with A."

"Excellent," he said, moving both hands upwards.

Grace had been bracing herself against the back of the couch by her arms. But now she leaned back and, in one fluid move, peeled off her sweater.

"It's getting really hot in here," she said, her lips feigning a pout. "Do you feel hot?"

"Oh, definitely. I definitely feel hot."

Grace leaned even farther back and then started to unbutton his shirt. With each button she leaned into him and kissed the skin that became visible.

Now Mickey was groaning, a soft, deep rumbling of anticipation in the back of his throat.

Grace slid off his lap and onto the rug, now kneeling between his legs. When she finished opening the final button, she reached for his belt.

"So, if *A* means we stay in the living room, and *B* means we move into the bedroom," she whispered. "Do you want. . ."

"B," Mickey said. "B-B-B-B."

They stood up and walked, not touching, into the bedroom. Grace did not turn on a light but left the door to the living room open enough to cast shadows.

Grace returned to the belt, unzipping his pants and sliding them down his legs until he stepped out. She reached for his socks and pulled as he lifted his legs, one at a time. She stood up and unzipped her own jeans, dropping them to the floor and kicking them to a corner of the room.

Mickey took her face in his two hands and cupped it, one hand on each cheek. "Do you want this?" he asked. "No regrets? No second guessing?"

Grace looked into his eyes, so level from her own.

"Yes. No regrets. No second guessing."

Mickey grinned. "Good decision," he said.

They lay down on the bed, and began exploring each other's bodies, stroking thighs and backs, nuzzling earlobes and necks. Mickey rolled Grace over and gently palmed her ass, running his hand down her thighs, then up between her thighs. He did it again, then again, until she moaned.

"Was that a good moan or a. . ." he whispered into her ear.

"Please," she whispered back to him, "please touch me. I can't wait any more."

Grace turned onto her back, looking at him, as he lay on his side next to her.

His hand cupped each breast, feathered each nipple, and then moved, slowly, over her belly and down to her groin. Then he simply rested his hand, barely touching, over the soft mound of pubic hair.

When he started to move his hand in concentric circles, Grace gasped, an inhalation as much as gasp.

"Softer?" Mickey whispered, "Or harder? Or about right?"

"Sweet Jesus," Grace moaned.

"I'll take that as *about right*," Mickey whispered.

"Faster?" he asked. "Or slower?"

"Slower," Grace said.

Mickey could feel the wet, and he moved his hand, slowly, softly, as Grace's breath quickened. Two fingers slipped between her labia and touched her clitoris. He pulled back a bit, teasing, not too direct, listening to her breathing, feeling the tension mounting in her.

"Would you please get on top?" he asked. "I really want to look at you."

Grace silently rolled over and straddled Mickey, wrapping her hands around his penis, then lifting herself up, guiding him as he entered her.

She did not move at first, just sat, almost trembling. Then she started to rock, up and down, feeling him inside her. He took one hand and placed it against her, his thumb now against her clitoris, moving in time with his cock.

Grace came first, in three quick spasms of release. Mickey followed. She lay, her head on his chest, her breath unsteady.

"Well, that wasn't bad for a first try," Mickey said. "I think we have potential if we practice regularly."

Grace chortled. "Define regularly."

"Once or twice a week?"

"Not every day?"

Mickey made a noise that was half-laugh and half-snort.

"You want quantity or quality?"

"Quality," Grace replied quickly. "Definitely quality."

"Me too," Mickey said.

"I really do not understand these guys that say they can't figure out if girl wants sex or not. They just need to ask the right questions."

"And make the right moves," she said, curling up against him. "Don't forget about the moves."

Chapter 66
(December 24th)

By 4 p.m. on Christmas Eve, Grace was ready. Her presents were wrapped to bring over to Molly's house. She'd swept and mopped, dusted and sprayed, washed towels and sheets. White mini-lights twinkled around her front door and railing.

Her casita was holiday fresh.

The artificial wreath that her children had made decades ago, decorated with red bows and mini-teddy-bears, the wreath she'd carted to Alaska and back, hung on her front door.

In a few hours they—Grace, Molly, and Max—would go to Mass together. Grace rarely went to church anymore on Sundays although she did sometimes slip into a back pew for the 7 a.m. weekday Mass at St. John's. She had a hard time explaining *why*, and she felt almost sneaky, secretive, when she went.

There were times when Grace yearned for the simplicity of a trusting faith in a loving God, the faith she'd had as a child in parochial school. She'd tried to set aside her doubts, the part of her brain that nit-picked at dogma. But she could not make herself believe that Catholicism, or Christianity, was more right, a greater truth, than other religions. And she reacted viscerally to those who were self-righteous in asserting that their beliefs were the only path.

But the rituals of Catholicism were in her bones. The Mass, with its continuity over centuries, could be a solace.

Grace accepted that she would probably die still questioning. In the meantime, she maintained some rituals. She held hands with her grandson and said a blessing before they shared a meal. She talked with Max about being a good person and what that meant. She tried to act ethically and with compassion. She sang *Gregorian Chant* in the shower.

They would go to the 7 p.m. Mass, the family Mass, which would be crammed to the rafters with over-stimulated children and exhausted parents who prayed only that their kids would fall asleep quickly so they could finally assemble whatever was the much-desired toy of the season.

Then they would come home and have a late supper of chowder. Grace would read *The Night Before the Christmas* to Max until he fell asleep. She would keep Molly company as she wrapped whatever remaining presents had been hidden around the house.

Tomorrow morning, she would walk the few steps to Molly's back door in her slippers and pajamas. Molly would hand her a mug of hot coffee, and the house would be filled with the smell of cinnamon rolls in the oven. She and Molly would sit on the couch, with Max on the floor by the tree. Then, with coffee and cinnamon rolls, holiday music playing, they would open presents. They would take turns. Max would reach under the tree and hand a package to each of them after he opened his first present. Grace and Molly would finish after a few boxes, and then the focus would be on Max.

They were a family and this is what they did.

Chapter 67
(December 25th)

It was 1 p.m. on Christmas Day. Grace was still in her pajamas. She was back in her kitchen after the morning with Molly and Max. A hefty roast beef was cooking in the oven. She was washing up the first round of dishes and pans. Then she'd peel potatoes.

Dinner wasn't until 4 p.m. at Molly's so she had plenty of time. Katrina was bringing shrimp remoulade and a Yule Log cake. Her New Orleans dishes were an essential part of their holiday rituals, which now included lining the front walk with luminaries and playing zydeco as background music. Both of Kat's sons were gone for this holiday, one visiting his in-laws and the other on a trip abroad with friends.

Mickey was coming as well. He had no children, no siblings (well, none still living), no geographically accessible relatives. When Grace had asked what he usually did, he'd said that he volunteered with prep for the free holiday dinner at a church and then delivered Meals on Wheels.

"I'm usually done by 1 p.m.," he'd added. "Then I take a nap."

"In that case, would you like to come over for a late afternoon dinner at Molly's?" Grace had asked him.

"You want me to come? Won't it be weird for Molly and Max to have some strange man intrude on their holiday?"

"I can check with her, but I can't imagine she'd say no. It's Christmas. Not a time to turn poor, lonely orphans away from your door."

"So, that's how you're presenting me? A poor, lonely orphan?"

"I'm breaking them in slowly," Grace had replied. "Don't push your luck. You're getting a free meal."

Standing at the kitchen sink, Grace found herself thinking, seriously thinking. For many years, holidays were something she endured. They were times when the reality of all she'd lost made her heart constrict. But she'd put up a good front, always gracious and smiling as she counted the hours until it would be over.

Attitude of gratitude. She'd been telling herself that for years with limited success. Be grateful for what's in front of you, not yearn for what you think should have been.

Three sharp knocks at her front door made her jump.

Mickey stood on the steps, both arms gripping a big, big box. On the steps next to him was a shopping bag.

"This is damn heavy, so could you please let me in?" he said. "And, baby, it's cold outside."

"I just heard that song on NPR," Grace retorted. "Some holiday medley. What in the world is in that box?"

"A token of my appreciation for your daughter. A little wine."

"Little? This is more than a little."

"Cheaper by the case. Much better deal."

"You brought a *case*? We'll never drink all that."

"Sure we will. Well, not all tonight, of course, but eventually. And the girls can each take home a few favorites."

The box now planted on the counter, he went to get the shopping bag on the steps.

"Mickey, you didn't need to. . ."

"Please, Grace, stop. Of course I didn't *need* to. And I'm not trying to buy the good will of your daughter and grandson and friend. Well, maybe, a little bit, if it works, but that isn't the primary motivation. It's just been so long since I've celebrated *anything*. Yesterday afternoon I walked through a mall. Not only did I shop, but I *enjoyed* shopping. But, if you think it's too much, I'll leave the presents here and. . ."

"Yeah, right," Grace interrupted. "Like that's an option. You bring presents they're going to get opened. So, what'd you get?"

"You'll see when everyone else does," he replied, moving past her to stand by the oven. He inhaled, deeply, closing his eyes. "Damn, this place smells wonderful."

"Take off your coat. I'm putting you to work," Grace said.

Forty minutes later, the peeled and diced potatoes were boiling, sliced carrots glazed, and a red wine-garlic-mushroom sauce was just barely simmering.

"I chopped more garlic for the mashed potatoes," Mickey said, gesturing to a small dish. "You were planning on roasted garlic mashed and not just bland, boring mashed, correct?"

"When you put it that way, sure."

"What now?" Mickey asked.

"Now I take a shower and you relax on the sofa with the newspaper."

Grace went into her bedroom, turned on the shower to warm up, and stripped out of her pajamas. Her shower was a four-foot square of tile and glass, with handy cubbies built into the tile wall for shampoo and such. She stepped in, closing her eyes, letting the water massage her shoulders.

When she opened her eyes, Mickey was standing in front of her, on the other side of the glass, his face pressed to the glass.

He, too, had stripped.

"I got all sweaty delivering those Meals on Wheels," he said. "And carrying in that wine. We could save water if you invited me. . ."

Grace pulled the glass door toward her and Mickey walked into the shower. She felt a wave of shyness come over her. This was different. This was being naked with each other in the light of day, not in the dark or shadows of her bedroom. There were no sheets to coyly drape. She felt exposed.

"Turn around," Mickey ordered. "You're looking at me like you don't think this is such a good idea."

Grace turned.

"That's better," he said, reaching past her for the body wash.

Grace faced the shower now, and the hot water coursed down her face and over her breasts. She braced herself against the tile wall, both arms extended. She felt his hands, slippery with the body wash, first knead her shoulders, then move down her back in long strokes. Up and down. When they got below her waist, he stopped, then started in slow circles over her ass, one hand on each, circling, his fingers massaging ever so gently.

"You have a spectacular ass," he whispered.

"It's big," Grace whispered back. "And droopy."

"Oh, God, no. It's a womanly ass. Not like those skinny college girls with little bumps on their rears. This is *goooooood* ass." He'd added a little accent, an emphasis, to the words.

"Now," he said, his lips brushing her ear. "I want you to keep your arms up, just where they are, and stay very, very still so I can wash you all over. You got that?"

Grace nodded.

"You'll be so clean when I'm finished," he added. "It will be the best shower ever."

With that, Mickey moved in closer, not pressing against her, but their bodies touching. His hands moved up her sides, then forward. Each hand cupped a breast, as he ever so softly began to massage.

"You also have splendid breasts," he whispered, nipping an earlobe as he rubbed the palm of his hands over her nipples. They hardened, quickly, and Mickey responded, one finger now gently rubbing a nipple, the rest of the hand holding a breast, barely moving, with just a slightest squeeze.

Grace felt small electric jolts zapping through her body, and heat building in her groin. She started to turn, but Mickey took her arm, quickly but gently, and placed her hand back on the tile wall.

"You said you'd stay still," he said in a low voice. "We're not done yet. Unless, of course, you want to be done. Do you want that?"

Even as he spoke, his right hand slid down from her breast over her belly and down. His fingers were slippery with bath gel. They slid back and forth, touching her, and then pulling back.

"Oooohhhhh…" Grace whimpered. Her legs felt rubbery.

"I'm going to fall," she whispered.

"No you're not," Mickey whispered. "I got you." He pressed himself tight against her back. "But you are going to *come*—no rush—we have all the time in the world." His left hand still held her breast, his fingers brushing her nipple, and his right hand was sliding and slipping and. . .

Grace came with a moan, sweet waves of pleasure. Her body shuddered. Her arms dropped from the tile wall as she twisted to face Mickey.

"Oh. My. God," Grace said, looking into his eyes.

"So, was that the best shower ever?" he asked her, placing soft, small kisses on her face which was now inches from his. "Do you feel all clean?"

"Yes, Mickey, I am so, so clean. And now it's your turn, no?"

"If you're asking if I got off, that happened about a minute after I started rubbing up against your magnificent ass."

"I didn't even realize. . ."

"You were a little distracted. And I was having so much fun it even took me by surprise."

Twenty minutes later, they were dried, dressed, and seated at the kitchen counter with mugs of coffee. Looking at the clock, Grace walked over to the stove and began the task of mashing potatoes with melted butter, cream—and garlic.

Mickey watched from a counter stool, a mug of coffee in his hand.

"How are you feeling about me being a part of the holiday?" Mickey asked. "Any second-guessing? Any guidelines you'd like to share but are too polite to say?"

Grace did not look up from the stove for a few seconds.

"I did realize about ten minutes ago that I've never included a man in *anything* with my daughter, let alone grandson. Never even introduced anyone. So there may be some adjustments."

"For your daughter?"

"Molly will be okay. Katrina may do a little cross-examination, but just humor her."

"How will I be introduced?"

"As an old friend who has no place to go for Christmas. A friend bringing wine and gifts. That's enough to get you in the door."

And it was.

The wine was a big hit. Molly, Kat, and Grace sat on the living room floor around the case, lifting out bottles, while Mickey watched from the couch.

"Pinot Noir for me. And Pinot Grigio," said Grace, "and Sauvignon Blanc."

"Oh, a Tempranillo. That goes in my pile," chimed in Kat.

"I'll take the Malbec and Syrah," Molly said.

In ten minutes the case was empty.

The next two hours passed in a blur of eating, toasts, and storytelling about awkward Christmases past. The latter was to please Max, who loved hearing embarrassing anecdotes from people about themselves. Each detail elicited a giggle.

"Did you really hide all your brother's presents? And tell him that Santa said he'd been too naughty for any presents?" Max asked Katrina. "That was really, really mean." Then he giggled some more.

After dinner, they moved to the living room, settling down on the couch and chairs, groaning from having eaten too much food.

"More presents!" Max announced. "It's *more presents* time! Can I pass them out? Please?"

Molly, Max, and Grace had already had their Christmas morning, so this exchange was more limited.

Grace had a small box for Katrina. Kat had one for Grace. Max took them from under the tree and solemnly handed them out. They opened their boxes at the same time, then burst out laughing. Each contained a winter scarf.

"Just what I wanted!" Grace said.

"How did you ever guess?" chimed in Kat.

"Is this from Weavers?" Grace asked. "Because I think I saw it there and liked it."

"Yeah," answered Kat, already draping her gift around her neck. "On a display about two aisles over from this one."

"This happens a lot," Molly explained to Mickey. "One year it was gardening related, then mystery books, IKEA stuff when the store first opened. . ."

"Great minds think alike," Grace interjected.

Within ten minutes, they were done. Kat gave Molly and Max books; Molly gave Katrina a tin of homemade cookies; Max presented Kat with a brightly hand-painted mug with her name on it.

"For your pens, on your desk," Max explained. "Not to drink with."

Mickey watched from an armchair.

"All done," Max announced. "All done until next year."

"Well, Max, not quite. See that big shopping bag in the corner? Go bring it over," Mickey requested.

Max had to look for a minute before he found the shopping bag as it was mostly hidden behind a chair.

"Where did this come from?" he asked. "It wasn't here when we cleaned up this morning."

"From Mickey," Grace answered.

This elicited simultaneous—*Oh, you shouldn't have* and, *But we didn't get you anything*—from Kat and Molly.

"Enough," Mickey retorted. "Stop whining, ladies."

He turned to Max. "Would you help me with these?"

There were no names on the wrapped gifts, but Mickey seemed to know what was inside each one as he carefully lifted a present and then looked, thoughtfully, around the room.

"Let's try this matching one with Molly," he said to Max. "Although, really, they're all for everybody. You'll see."

And they were. Because each present contained a game or a toy. And not one required batteries.

There was an Etch-a-Sketch, Checkers, Scrabble, a bag of multi-colored marbles, sidewalk chalk, a Lambchops puppet, Pick-Up-Sticks, Monopoly, and Clue.

"I got these when I was seven," exclaimed Kat upon opening the marbles. "We'd make up games to play on the driveway."

"I remember buying Molly an Etch-A-Sketch when she was in first grade," said Grace.

And then, for another two hours, they played with the toys and games with the mindless abandon of children.

"Where did you find all of those?" Grace asked later that night as they snuggled under her down comforter. "It was brilliant."

"I was walking down the street and every kid I saw was staring at a cell phone. I thought, *How did we manage? What did we do?* When I saw that really great toy store on Main Street, I walked in and asked if they had an old toys section.

"That's what they called it—the *old toys* section?"

"*Classic* was how they described them. *Classic* toys. Like antiques. Non-electronic. No keyboards or screens."

"Well, I cannot imagine a better idea. I didn't think anything would top the wine, but the toys—*brilliant.*"

"So you think I might get invited back?"

"Yeah, Mickey, I'm thinking that might just happen."

An hour later, Grace long since fallen asleep, Mickey lay awake reflecting on the day. This holiday had been the best gift ever. All of it felt to him like an unanticipated gift, a lottery win.

He and his first wife had married young but postponed having kids. And maybe that was the right decision because she was killed in a car crash when a distracted kid plowed into her. The kid was not a bad kid, not drunk, just distracted. Just being a kid.

An accident.

After that, for a long time, Mickey was angry. Everything pissed him off. He worked fifty-sixty hours a week and drank too much. Not every day but it was how he coped with days off.

Then he met Joanne. She was a fourth-grade teacher. He'd been doing a Safe Kid program for the police department in her school. She was Italian, with an infectious laugh. Joanne told Mickey he was a *vecchio irritabile* and *basta con la faccia triste*. She brought him back to life, one Saturday night date at a time. They married within a year. They talked a little about having kids but were already in their forties. Joanne worked every day with children and appreciated having a respite at home. They were good together—kind and thoughtful, shared the same politics and values, talked about whatever books they were reading, enjoyed a movie and a drink. And they were each deeply grateful to not be alone.

Then the doctors discovered her cancer. Colon. Stage 4.

When Joanne died, Mickey felt ashamed at the waves of sheer relief. But he'd been grieving over the two years that the cancer chewed through her organs and into her bones. He'd felt her pain, felt the impotence of not being able to stop it. Toward the end, when she'd asked him to help her die, he had not been able to do even that.

The night after her funeral, he'd closed the door to their bedroom and slept in the guest room. And he never went back. His clothes migrated, shirt-by-shirt, drawer-by-drawer, as if of their own accord, to the guest room as well. Mickey went to work, ate take-out on a tray in front of the TV, and read formulaic mysteries he could easily forget.

On some level, he knew if he tried he could find someone else to share at least parts of his life. But he also knew he could not survive another loss. And he did not want to endure, or inflict on someone else, the indescribable exhaustion, as much emotional as physical, that came with caring for someone who was slowly dying. And, at his age, not old-old, but the high end of middle-aged, everyone was going to die. Of course, anyone could die at any time, and losing Bethany had proven that. But when people are in their late 50s and 60s, the obituaries feel more real. Death is no longer an anomaly.

This conflicted mess of emotion was triggered every time he felt stirrings of need or desire. Because to need, to want, would eventually lead to loss. To love again could only end in pain, loss, and death.

So now, lying in bed next to Grace McDonald, after his first *family holiday* in many years, sharing a dinner, listening to their jokes and how they teased each other, being able to give gifts and make people laugh— it had been not just *normal* but extraordinary.

It forced Mickey to face what he longed for. Mickey wanted a family. He wanted to *belong*, not just visit.

And what was growing between him and Grace was more than he'd ever let himself desire. She was smart, funny, curious, stubborn, generous—with a rogue streak that matched his own.

On top of all of that, which was plenty, he found her beautiful. He loved caressing her body. Giving her pleasure made him feel powerful. With every touch, he felt his own body awakening as if from a deep sleep. What he'd done earlier in the day, stripping off his clothes, standing on the other side of the shower glass and making some inane joke to get close to her, was something he'd never done before.

He might have thought it, but he'd never followed through.

With Grace, he felt that he was bypassing boundaries he'd always imposed on himself. He was acting on his impulses, not censoring them.

And all of this, the complexity and potential, made him dizzy.

This was the Full Monty.

Mickey clutched a pillow to his chest. It was all he could do to stay, to not slip out of bed, gather up his clothes, and ever so quietly, disappear into the darkness before it all came crashing down.

Chapter 68
(December 26th to 30th)

Around 11 a.m. on the 26th, Molly and Max took a shuttle to the airport to fly to Florida for a week on a beach with Mike, David, and Leah. Grace had not pressed Molly for her expectations of this vacation, but she was really looking forward to hearing all the nitty-gritty details when Molly returned.

Grace had become emotionally invested in David and his dad, Mike. She'd been stunned by how the custody case had resolved. It had involved a fundamentalist, gay-bashing, funeral-picketing family and church. She'd found their beliefs, based on what she regarded as a twisted and selective interpretation of the Bible, abhorrent. It had been a professional challenge to maintain neutrality.

Grace waved goodbye to Molly and Max from the driveway as the shuttle van pulled away.

And then, for the next three days, Grace played sick.

She stayed home, in her pajamas, slept an inordinate amount of time, took hot, hot baths, colored her hair, shaved her legs, painted her toenails, binge-watched a TV series she'd been hearing about all year, and read a novel she'd been wanting to read. She put an *I am unavailable* message on her phone and email.

Grace had, for many years, often fallen ill soon after the holidays, a probable result of exhaustion and germ exposure. She'd ended up sniffling and coughing, feeling miserable but also woefully unprepared: no soaking salts, no trendy nail polish, no pile of books. Nada.

At the same time, she'd preached to her clients how important it was to take *mental health days* once in a while to recharge. She'd emphasized how *planning* a sick day was more healing than actually being sick.

But Grace had always been more nurturing and supportive with her clients than she was with herself. They deserved breaks. But she needed to be stoic, strong, tenacious—*Pull up your big girl panties and stop whining*—was her self-talk.

But just a few years ago, she'd had a belated epiphany, as if a voice from the heavens spoke directly to her: *Stop being such a damn martyr,* the voice said. *And take better care of yourself.*

The voice had sounded an awful lot like Gil, her dead husband.

That was when she'd decided to start a new tradition: *post-holiday sick-days for stressed out, over-worked women—PHSD.*

Grace hadn't gotten around to actually explaining PHSD to Molly, Katrina, or Mickey. It was, at this point, a *secret* tradition. But once she'd decided to do it, she hadn't felt the usual cold coming on. No fever and no nausea.

Mickey called late afternoon on the 29th.

"How are you feeling?" he asked.

"Better," she answered.

"Better enough to have company for dinner if I bring the food?"

"I think so. What kind of food?"

"Vietnamese. Maybe Thai. Pho or bun."

"Perfect. What time?"

"How about seven? I've got to finish up with work and drive over."

"I'll put on less-smelly pajamas," Grace said.

"Not on my account," Mickey replied.

By the time Mickey arrived, Grace had showered and changed her pajamas. They put bowls of pho and a small platter of spring rolls on the coffee table and sprawled on the couch.

"Those are very bright toenails you have there," Mickey said. "What do you call that shade of blue?"

" 'Aqua Ecstasy.' That's what the bottle said."

"Very perky. And here I thought red was hot."

"Too many *Playboy* magazines when you were young. You got imprinted with red as the sexy color. I did too. But I'm breaking the bonds of middle-aged conformity. Starting with my toes."

"Which are conveniently covered up in winter," Mickey said.

Their banter continued. It was lazy banter, easing them back into what was now—surprise, surprise—a relationship.

After supper, Mickey cleared off the coffee table, returning with two small glasses and handing one to Grace.

"Courvoisier," he said. "Good for whatever ails you."

Mickey sat down on the couch, turning to Grace as he started to speak.

"Is there something going on, Grace? You just seem a little distracted. Are you having second thoughts?"

"About you? Or us?" Grace responded in surprise. "No, Mickey, no second thoughts."

"Then what is it? Because you're. . ."

"You know I met with Shelby's parents on the 19th. Lisa and I filled them in what we found out, about Hunter, all of it."

"But I thought that went okay," Mickey said.

"It did. But it also brought back all my unresolved shit with Alex. I look at how many years have passed and ask myself, how did it ever come to this?"

"Your son is an adult. This is not just on you."

"But he was not an adult when his life collapsed. And I'm his mother. I made some really poor choices as a mother even if leaving Kaw Valley felt like the only way to save my sanity at that time."

"Okay, you had twenty years as a great mom and then your life, and his, went to hell. But he survived. He. . ."

"There's something else, Mickey," she interrupted.

"What?"

"About a week or so ago I went out to get the mail. There was an envelope for Molly with a return address in Panama. No name, just an address. I thought that it might be from Alex. I took it and opened it."

"Was it from Alex?"

"Yes."

"Did you tell Molly?"

"No. I've just kept it in my drawer."

"Maybe not the best decision," Mickey said. "What did it say?"

"It was a Christmas card, with a one-page typed letter enclosed. The letter just talked about his life, what grades he's teaching, how he might start a bocce league, and, oh yeah, that his wife is now playing in the national orchestra. But in the last few lines he was apologizing, *again*, for not telling her some time ago that he was getting married."

"Alex has a *wife?*"

"Yes. *My son is married.* And I knew *nothing* about it. He describes his wife, Graciela, and she sounds lovely. She teaches music at the university. He teaches English at the local high school. They live in a beach town outside Panama City. He sounds happy."

"Can I read it?" he asked.

Grace did not reply. She got up, went into her bedroom, returned with a red envelope and handed it to Mickey.

He read the letter. Twice. Then put it back in the envelope and lay it on the coffee table.

"He sounds okay. Not traumatized or anything. Isn't that what you want?" he asked her.

"I want to be in his life. I want him in my life. I don't want this very high and thick wall between us."

"So, climb over the wall."

"It's not that simple, Mickey. He lives in another country. We've been estranged for years."

"So go to him. Just go to him and tell him what you want and that you're sorry."

"Right. And when he tells me he wants nothing to do with me?"

"Tell him again that you're sorry. Tell him again that you love him, that you will do this at whatever pace he wants, but that you want to build a relationship with him."

"And if that doesn't work?"

"Then you're no worse off than you are right now. At least then you'll know what you're up against. The not knowing will make you crazy."

"I'm already crazy. You've just been too polite to point that out."

"I've been holding back."

"So, I write him and ask if we can talk?"

Mickey was silent, considering his words.

"No, Grace, I don't think so. I think you just *go*. You have an address. That's more than you've had for years. You go and stand on his doorstep, face-to-face, and ask to talk."

Grace stared at Mickey as if he'd gone bonkers.

"Just hearing you say that makes me shake. What if he closes the door in my face?"

"That's what's kept you stuck—fear. And I seriously doubt he will turn you away from his door. He'll be too shocked to do anything but ask you in and offer you coffee."

"But if he feels manipulated? If he gets more entrenched in his position?"

"First off, you don't know what his *position* is because you and he have never talked this out. He has never heard your apology. If he does not accept it, then you know where you stand. But I don't want you wondering ten years from now if you should have tried *something, anything*."

"I'll think about it. Really. I'll think about it."

Even as she said the words, his other words repeated in her head, *I don't want you wondering ten years from now*, spoken with the unconscious but implicit assumption that they would, in some way, be together then.

"Are you listening? Huh? Look, you've been thinking for a very long time and nothing has changed. Enough with the thinking."

"And did you not hear me when I said it's not that simple?"

"Maybe it is that simple, Gracie. Maybe *something* is better than nothing."

Mickey paused, then spoke again. "We're going in circles here. And we can't resolve this tonight. C'mon, let's do the dishes and go to bed."

They washed and dried the few dishes in silence.

"Just to be clear, so we don't have any *miscommunication*, we're not engaging in any sexual activity tonight," Mickey said as they walked to the bedroom. "Tonight we spoon and rub backs and hold hands. Maybe I rub your ass, but that is as far as it goes."

Chapter 69
(December 30th)

When Grace woke up at 8:30 the next morning, Mickey was gone.

On the dining room table, he'd left a note.

"Your flight is at 2 p.m. I'll be back at noon to drive you to the airport. Start packing. And you need to call the airline with your passport number. Here is the flight info."

Grace punched in Mickey's cell number. He picked up on the third ring.

"What the hell is this all about? I cannot just get on a plane this afternoon." Her voice was indignant. "What do you think you're doing?"

"Sure you can, Grace. You're off work for the next week. You get on a plane to Panama City. You take a taxi to the town. I'm working on booking an Airbnb for you now. It's cute—a tiny cottage by the beach. You crash there, get some sleep. Then tomorrow morning you get up, have coffee, take a shower, walk four blocks to Alex's house and knock on his door."

"How do you know it's four blocks?" Grace asked.

"Google maps. You can find anything."

"This is crazy."

"Seriously? You don't talk to your kid for over a decade and you think a plane ride is crazy?"

"It feels so risky."

"It's a risk. Sure. But doing nothing is also a risk. Last night you were asking, *How did it ever come to this?* Well, as I see it, it came to this from doing nothing."

"Yes, I get that. But isn't there a middle ground here?"

"Probably. But with this you see your son tomorrow morning. If you want to think, then think about that. *Tomorrow.*"

"What if he's not there? What if they went away for a holiday?"

"They live by a beach, Grace. Their lives are a holiday. But, if they're not home, you would be forced to swim and sun for a day or so until he gets back in time for school. It starts back January 3rd."

"How do you know when school starts?"

"Again, Grace, it's Google."

Grace felt a seismic shift, a cracking in her core.

"The ticket must cost a fortune, Mickey. I could get it a lot cheaper if I plan ahead."

"Merry Christmas, Grace. Not your worry."

"I cannot let you pay for a ticket to Panama."

"You are not postponing this because of money. You'll start to obsess about every possible downside. Meanwhile, another year will pass. Besides, my house is ready to stage for the spring market. My agent says I'm going to make a bundle."

"I don't care. I'm not letting you pay. . ."

"We'll work it all out later," Mickey interrupted. "I've always wanted to go to New York City. You can take me."

"You haven't been to New York?" Grace asked. "Seriously? To Korea but not New York?"

"Is my limited travel history what you want to be discussing right now?"

"Well then, so now what?" she asked.

"Pack a carry-on bag. Remember your bathing suit. And flip-flops. It's going to be in the 80's most days and 70's at night. And maybe some afternoon rain, so bring a mini-umbrella or poncho."

When Mickey arrived at 11:45, Grace's small suitcase was by the door. She wore jeans, sneakers, a black T-shirt, and a loose, silky coral over-shirt.

"You can do this," Mickey said.

"It feels surreal."

"It's a first step. One step at a time."

"Until I step off the cliff?"

"No cliffs. It's sea level, remember?"

"You know what I mean—oh, never mind."

"Want to do a check of the essentials? If only so I don't worry?"

"Sure, Mickey. Bring on the check-list."

Mickey reached into his jacket pocket.

"Passport?" he asked.

"Yes," Grace said. "In a zip lock baggie in the side pouch of my Baggalini."

"Money and credit cards?"

"$400 cash, three credit cards, and an ATM card, stashed in different places."

"Bathing suit and flip flops?"

"In suitcase."

"Book to read?"

"My Kindle is charged with ample choices. One question: Do I need a voltage converter? Are the plugs different?"

"No, Panama has the same system as the U.S.—no worries there."

Mickey placed the suitcase in the back seat of his car. Grace walked to the passenger side but then just stood there, not opening the door.

"Grace? Is something wrong?" Mickey asked.

"No. Yes. Maybe?" she answered. "I feel like I'm going to a doctor for a diagnosis. Like, *will I live or die?*"

"You'll live, Grace, no matter what happens. The treatment may be difficult but worth it." Mickey paused. "Now get in the car."

Mickey put on NPR and they listened. There was nothing more to say.

Halfway to the airport, Grace began to search her purse for her cell phone.

"I have to tell Molly," she blurted. "I can't just go to Panama and not tell her."

"I was thinking about that," Mickey replied. "This is your issue with your son. You tell her and then she's in the middle again—should she tell Alex that you're coming? Should she try to talk you out of this wild, crazy, impulsive move? If it doesn't work out, she'll feel like she's responsible for the bad outcome, like she didn't do the right thing. So maybe just let Molly enjoy Florida with Max. Leave her out of it."

Grace pondered what Mickey was saying.

"Okay," she said. "But Molly is not a fan of surprises. Me neither. Alex especially." Grace looked out the window at the bleak and empty fields, a small huddle of cattle on the horizon.

"You've all been traumatized by surprises. Maybe in the long run showing up will be a good surprise. It shows both your kids you're determined."

When they got to the airport, Mickey dropped Grace by the ticketing counter and went to park. When he returned, she was waiting outside the security area, still bundled up in her winter coat and scarf.

"Give me your coat," he said. "I'll bring it when I pick you up. You don't need to be lugging it around Panama."

Grace looked at her coat as if it belonged to someone else. She took it off and handed it over.

"I never thought of that," she said. "I feel like there's a lot that I haven't thought of."

Mickey took an envelope of papers out of his inside coat pocket.

"When you arrive, there should be a driver standing past Customs with a sign with your name. He'll drive you to Gorgona, to the Airbnb. He has the address and has been paid, tip included. The hosts are expecting you to be late. The driver can fetch the key. They'll have the refrigerator stocked with some basics, coffee and tea. You'll have food for a snack and breakfast at least."

Mickey handed Grace the envelope.

"This has the contact information for the driver, the agency he works for, the Airbnb owners who live next door, and the names and phone numbers of a few hotels close to the airport in case something doesn't work out."

The surprises just keep on coming with this guy, Grace thought.

"Were you a travel agent in a past life?" she asked. "Because this is damn impressive."

"Heck, lady, I'm an ex-cop. We gotta' pay attention to the details. Otherwise we get fired."

"Speaking of details," Grace continued, "what about my return ticket info?"

"In the envelope as well."

"And when would that be?"

"January 4th."

"And what *exactly* am I supposed to do for four or five days if Alex closes his door in my face?"

"You like to travel. Go see the Canal. Walk on the beach. Drink fruity cocktails. Read. People-watch. You'll figure it out. And keep showing up at his door each morning to make it clear that you're not leaving until he talks."

Grace did not reply. Emotions were flashing across her face like clouds before a storm, volatile and swirling. She looked away. She had an urge to run.

Mickey put his hands on her shoulder and gently turned her to face him.

"If you don't get on that plane today, you will regret it," he intoned. "Maybe not today, maybe not tomorrow, but soon and for the rest of your life." Then he grinned. 'Damn, I've waited decades to say that."

Grace offered a tentative smile,

"Would you just hold me for a minute?" she asked.

And he did.

After the hug, Grace kissed him, lightly, on the lips, and turned to go through security. Mickey watched through the glass walls as she walked toward the gate.

I sure as hell hope this doesn't blow up in my face, he thought.

Chapter 70
(December 31st)

When Grace awoke, she could not remember, for just a moment, where she was. It was a bedroom, with blue walls and white lace curtains, a yellow chair in the corner, a suitcase on a low table.

My suitcase, she thought. *That I packed. To fly to Panama. To reconcile with my son.*

She pulled the sheets up over her head.

After ten minutes, the need to pee compelled her to stop hiding under the sheet, get out of bed, and walk across a tile floor through a small living room and into the bathroom.

I'm up, she thought, *so might as well make some coffee.*

The kitchen was original, with orange, green, and blue tiles. There was a small brightly painted table with two chairs. The stove and refrigerator looked to be from the 60s. But the coffee maker was a generic version of a Keurig, and she found multiple choices for coffee, tea, or cocoa in a plastic container on a shelf above. There was juice, milk, fruit, and yogurt in the refrigerator and instant oatmeal and cereal on a shelf. When she needed a spoon, the tableware was exactly where she expected.

It had been so dark when she'd arrived the night before that she had not been able to see anything of the outdoors and was too tired to pay attention to anything but crawling into the bed. She didn't remember a town at all, just the driver stopping the car and saying, "Estamos aqui, senora." He'd gone to the house next door and collected a key, then carried her bag inside.

Now, looking out the kitchen window, she saw a back garden. A hammock was hanging between trees. There was a gravel patio off the back door with a round table and four chairs.

In the living room, she looked over the café curtains and through a large front window. Sunshine filtered down through some trees. There was another small patio with two plastic chairs. She opened the front door, coffee mug in her hand, to check the weather.

It was like stepping into a different universe. She was enveloped by warm air, the smell of salt water, the distant sound of waves. A rooster was crowing. One tree had what looked like huge clumps of red bananas. Another tree of—was it papayas? Mangoes? Grace couldn't remember which shape was which. Then she saw avocados. And oranges.

It was a market in the front yard.

Grace sat down in a plastic chair, closing her eyes and turning her face to the sun. She was in pajamas, but she didn't care. For a minute she just sat, inhaling the ocean air, feeling the warmth of the sun on her body.

And then she remembered—why she was here and what she needed to do. The fear that had flooded her when leaving her home—as if dreading a diagnosis—gripped her again.

If I delay, she thought, *I could chicken out.*

She knew she could easily end up spending a day, two days, scripting just the right words to say, as if word choice could determine outcome. She knew because she'd already done it a hundred times.

An hour later, Grace was dressed in beige capris, sandals, a sleeveless aqua tank, and a white, cotton-with-lacy-edges open blouse. She looked down at her glossy blue toenails.

"I never expected to see you outside the house," she muttered to her toes. "But here I am in sandals in December."

Mickey had put a map of downtown Gorgona in the envelope as well. There was an *X* by the cottage she was staying in and another *X* in the middle of a street four blocks over.

Grace put the map, some cash, lipstick, and a brush in a small cloth purse and walked out the door. Then she went back inside to find the key to lock the front door.

She walked very slowly, absorbing the town. Some signs she understood, or whatever was featured in the front window made obvious—Panaderia, Frutas, Muelbles, Ferreteria. Under a *Café* sign was a patio where a few couples and old men sat reading a newspaper and drinking coffee.

This is where Alex lives, she thought. *This is his home.*

Within ten minutes, she was standing in front of a small house, similar to every other house on the block. It was painted white, with a red front door and a stone patio in front. Two plastic Adirondack chairs were on the patio with a table between them.

Grace walked up to the door and knocked.

A young woman opened the door. She was slender, with glossy dark hair and deep brown eyes. She was wearing jean shorts and a T-shirt.

"Si? Puedo ayudarlo?" she asked.

Grace could not, for just a second, find her voice.

"Me llama Grace McDonald," she said. "Soy la madre de Alex. Eres Graciella?"

Graceiella's smile disappeared as her eyes widened. Emotions flooded her face. She looked stunned.

Grace felt a stab in her gut. This was not a good idea. Sweet Jesus, what had she been thinking? After thirteen years? You don't just show up at someone's door and. . .

But Graciella's face had changed again.

"Eres la madre de Alex?" Graciella asked. "Eres mi suegra? De verdad?"

Grace had used a translate function on her laptop during the layover in Houston to jot down some phrases. Whatever Spanish she had once known had long ago disappeared into the black hole that was her memory. She had no idea what *suegra* meant, but she shook her head anyway. She did know she was Alex's mother.

"Si," Grace answered, nodding.

"Dios mio! Estas realmente aqui." Graciella said, smiling, and reached out with both of her hands to hold both of Grace's hands.

"Esperaba este momento, Gracias, muchas gracias por venir, Entra por favor. Dejame hacer un café. Alex fue a la pananderia para hacer pasteles."

Grace caught the words for *coffee* and maybe for *pastries*. And then she walked through the door and into Alex's home.

"Oh my God," Graciella said, turning to face her again. "I am so happy that I forgot to speak English."

"You speak English?" Grace asked, which was a very dumb question she would later realize given that Graciella was already speaking English.

"Oh, yes. I studied at the Music Conservatory in Chicago," Graciella said. "For two years. Now, come to the kitchen. Sit while I make the coffee."

Grace sat down at the table. Graciella was filling a pan with water from the sink when she suddenly turned.

"Is Molly okay? And Max? Because you are here and. . ."

"They're fine," Grace said. "All healthy."

Grace realized she needed to explain why she'd come, with no warning, to her son's home.

"I am here to apologize," she said softly to Graciella. "I hurt my son, badly, and I'm here to try to repair that. I miss him so much." As she spoke the words, tears came to her eyes.

In an instant, Graciella was in front of Grace. She slipped to her knees.

"So many times I have tried to tell him that he needs to go to you to apologize. That he cannot have this wall with family. But he gets very quiet and will not discuss it. He can be very stubborn, your son."

"He may get that from his mother."

When Alex McDonald returned fifteen minutes later from the bakery, he called out to his wife from the front door.

"Sorry I'm late. I ran into Antonio and we had a quick talk about the fireworks tonight. . ."

In the doorway to the kitchen, he stopped, frozen.

His wife was sitting at their kitchen table.

His mother was sitting across from his wife.

They were sipping coffee.

"Oh, good, the pastries are here," Graciella said. "Just in time."

Grace stood up, looking at her son. *He's so tall*, she thought. *When did he get so tall?* He was tan. His hair was shaggy. He looked almost exactly like his father had at that age. It was like seeing Gil all over again.

"I've come to apologize," she said. "I'm so sorry for what I did. I didn't understand how much I hurt you and Molly. I can't make up for that but I'm asking. . ." And then her voice cracked, and she sat back down, tears running down her face.

Alex had not blinked. He'd spent so many years grieving, being angry. He had a new home, a new family. And now his mother was *here*? Saying *what*? Like any apology could erase. . .

Then Graciella was at his side, taking his empty hand in her own, making him look at her.

"Think first about your words, my love," she said, very softly. "You can never take them back from this moment. Whatever will happen now will take time, so do not be hasty with your words."

Alex looked at his wife, at the black center of her soft brown eyes as her words jumbled together in his head.

This, now, after so many years? No, it was too late. He couldn't start over. . .

Grace's hands clutched the mug of coffee, her body suspended in time, as she waited for her son to speak.

Book Group Discussion Questions:

Questions have been put in three areas of focus: Overall, Legal, and Literary. They are not discrete, but different book groups may have different interests. For broad-ranging discussions, groups may opt to consider questions from each of the three categories.

Overall Focus:

1) Before Chapter 1 there was a disclaimer, advising readers who may have experienced sexual assault that the first chapter could be triggering, so to perhaps start reading from Chapter 2. Was this necessary? Was it challenging as a reader to dive directly into such an intimate and painful scene?

2) The characters in *Insufficient Evidence* discuss and argue about different issues. Did you find yourself agreeing more with certain characters? About which issues?

3) Do you see differences between a *one-night stand* in the 1970s or 1980s and a *hookup* today?

4) What benefits do you see young men getting from the social acceptance and normalizing of hookup culture? What benefits do you see young women getting from hookup culture?

5) Kraus quoted statistics from the documentary *The Hunting Ground*. Did you find them surprising? Did they impact your own ideas about levels of sexual assault, reporting, charges brought, trials, and convictions?

6) Some readers have described the intimate scene with Grace and Mickey as *anti-porn*—a depiction of sexual intimacy that is mutual, consensual, respectful, and satisfying for both partners. What was your response to the Grace and Mickey sex scene? Were you put off by it? Can mature sexuality scenes fit in mainstream fiction?

7) Did you learn anything about social media in this novel? Do you know of incidents in your own life, or lives of your family or friends, where social media has caused damage?

8) How has your own upbringing, community, religion, race, and ethnicity informed your sense of security? How about your trust in, or distrust of, law enforcement and the legal system?

9) What are some different ways that friendship is expressed in *Insufficient Evidence*?

10) There were a few chapters in which Grace becomes irate about how language is far more pejorative and condemning of women than men when it comes to sexual behavior. Were you surprised or offended by any of the specifics?

11) Hannah wanted retribution, and some semblance of justice. She wanted Logan to *understand* how his actions had hurt her. What would you call what happened in the cabin?

12) Take the expression, *The ends justifies the means*, and apply it to different characters and choices in *Insufficient Evidence*. Are people entitled to break rules under certain circumstances? Are ethics sometimes situational? Have you had times or experiences in your own life when the ends justified the means?

Legal Focus:

1) The title of the book is *Insufficient Evidence*. What has constituted *evidence* in the past as far as sexual assault? Why is that no longer *sufficient*? What level of evidence is now required for a jury to convict someone for rape or sexual assault?

2) What are the requirements, as you understand them, between *beyond a reasonable doubt* and *preponderance of evidence*? Do you see differences in what is required for legal prosecution and/or for consequences imposed by a university?

3) The offices of Institutional Opportunity and Access have dual roles: a) to provide support and help for students regardless if they choose to make a complaint, whether or not they choose to do *anything* legal; b) to hear complaints, investigate, compile facts, reach findings. Is it reasonable to expect that a university office can adjudicate sexual assault cases when the legal system and juries cannot?

4) In the rape trial that Grace observes, the young woman is unnamed. Does anything change with your emotional response if you give her a name? The name of your daughter? Your sister? Your friend? Do you think it makes a difference to the world at large that many rape victims are not named publicly to *protect their privacy*?

5) Kraus first dealt with the fragility of *reputation* in her novel *Fall From Grace*. That novel was set over a decade earlier than *Insufficient Evidence*. How has social media impacted our public understanding of *reputation* and *character*? Is it easier now to destroy someone's *reputation*?

6) Do you agree with Patsy that juries would be more likely to convict if there were gradations of sexual assault, as with 1st degree homicide, 2nd degree homicide, manslaughter, for example? Or if sentences varied considerably as well? What do you see as relevant factors? Is alcohol a mitigating factor? (It isn't with DUI, but should it be with sexual assault?) How could intent be measured?

7) There have also been discussions about applying standards of contribution as is done with some civil cases. For example, if a young woman drinks too much, and is thus realistically unable to consent, is she culpable in some way? Are there any other areas of criminal prosecution where victims are held accountable in part for what happens to them?

8) Imagine yourself on a jury in a sexual assault case. What would you need to know for sure in order to convict someone? What is your *beyond a reasonable doubt*? How do you measure *reasonable*?

9) Do you think that television shows foster unrealistic expectations as far as standards for evidence? Have these expectations been exploited by defense attorneys in your communities? Is it feasible to hold every county to standards depicted in NCIS or CSI?

10) Trials are public and open to anyone to observe. Have you ever gone to your local courthouse when you know a trial is in progress for a rape or sexual assault case and simply observed the legal process? Is that something that you and a friend might do as a means of developing a personal awareness of the issues?

Literary:

1) Writers are often advised to *write what you know*. The author is a therapist and mediator. Did you find the tangent chapters about Grace's other cases distracting or informative? Do they add or subtract from the overall substance of the novel?

2) The timeline of *Insufficient Evidence* is just four months—September 1st to December 31st. This is very different from the expansive timelines of *Fall From Grace* and *All God's Children*. Does your experience as a reader change with such different timelines?

3) Are there minor characters in *Insufficient Evidence* that you find memorable? Are there any for whom you feel a stronger connection? What does the author do, or fail to do, to make the minor characters more real?

4) Does *Insufficient Evidence* fall into a specific genre? Does it extend across genres? Do you experience it as more about relationships, or mystery, or psychological drama?

5) There are multiple endings in *Insufficient Evidence*: for Hannah, for Shelby's parents and Lisa, for Grace. Two bring some closure, while one leaves the reader hanging. With the latter, did you re-write the ending in your head? What does Alex say or do in your ending?

6) In each of Kraus's novels, readers know critical facts before the characters do. Can readers still feel literary tension when they know *who done it*?

7) In many novels, the bad guys are *all* bad. But, in each of her novels, a consistent feature is how Kraus creates *bad guys* with complexity. Do you feel any empathy for Logan? For Hunter? What specifically allowed for that empathy? Did feeling empathy impact how you thought about the issues?

8) Grace is not a typical protagonist. In *Fall From Grace,* she was a victim. How does Grace change in the course of this novel? How do you respond to a flawed, vulnerable protagonist?

9) What adjectives would you use to describe Hannah at the beginning and then at the end of the novel? What about Logan? What other characters change in the course of the book?

10) There is a genre evolving called *Socially Responsible Fiction* or *Socially Conscious Fiction*. It is literature that prioritizes factual accuracy, addresses bias, and tackles polarizing or misunderstood social and political issues. Do you see *Insufficient Evidence* as falling in that category? Did it cause you to reflect differently on any issue?

Suggested Reading and Resources:

Against Our Will: Men, Women and Rape; Susan Brownmiller, Simon and Schuster, 1975

Against Rape; Andra Medea and Kathleen Thompson; Farrar, Straus and Giroux, NY, NY, 1974

Asking For It: The Alarming Rise of Rape Culture—and What We Can Do About IT; Kate Harding; DeCapo Press, 2015

American Girls: Social Media and the Secret Lives of Teenagers; Nancy Jo Sales; Vintage Books, Penguin Random House LLC, 2016

American Hookup: The New Culture of Sex on Campus; Lisa Wade; W.W. Norton & Company; 2017

Girls & Sex: Navigating the Complicated New Landscape; Peggy Orenstein, HarperCollins Publishers, 2016

Missoula: Rape and the Justice System in a College Town; Jon Krakauer; Anchor Books, Penguin Random House LLC, 2015

Sex, College & Social Media: A Commonsense Guide to Navigating the Hookup Culture; Cindy Pierce; Bibliomotion, Inc; 2016

Rape is Rape: How Denial, Distortion, and Victim Blaming Are Fueling a Hidden Acquaintance Rape Crisis; Jody Raphael, JD; Lawrence Hill Books, Chicago, 2013

The ABC's of Sexual Assault: Anatomy, "Bunk" and the Courtroom; Michelle Ditton RN; Laurie A. Gray, JD; Socratic Parenting LLC; 2015

The Morning After: Sex, Fear and Feminism on Campus; Katie Roiphe; Little Brown & Company, 1993

__Insufficient Evidence__ can be triggering for those who have experienced sexual trauma. Here are some resources if you want to talk:

National Sexual Assault Telephone Hotline (RAINN) 800-656-4673

Women Organized Against Rape (WOAR) 215-985-3333 (out of Philadelphia but 24 Hour Hotline)

Google "Rape Crisis Hotline in __________" or "Sexual Assault Support in __________" and put in your city or state.

Acknowledgments

Against Our Will, the groundbreaking book on rape and rape culture by Susan Brownmiller, was released in 1975. Shortly after, I trained as a volunteer for the Austin Rape Crisis Center (the first crisis center in Texas, now SAFE: Stop Abuse for Everyone). Any acknowledgment begins with Susan Brownmiller and the staff and volunteers of *every* Sexual Assault / Rape Crisis Center in the United States.

I began work on *Insufficient Evidence* some years ago, a response to working with university women who had experienced sexual assault in the context of hookup culture. It was mostly written prior to the "Me Too" movement, when so many voices were still unheard.

My deep appreciation to:

Thea Rademacher, JD, of Flint Hills Publishing, for her insight, enthusiasm, patience, and pragmatism.

Rachel Asbury, who from the day she showed up on my front door, as a college sophomore, has been a consultant, friend, cheerleader, and my go-to woman in times of need.

Kelsey Kimberlin, book cover photographer; Ashley Honey, cover graphic artist; Jen Sharp, web design; Jeffrey Ann Goudie, eagle-eye edits; Pam Grout, pointed interviews.

Nathan Pettengill, my cherished editor at Sunflower Publishing.

Sara Shepherd, reporter for the Lawrence Journal World, who really knows what goes down.

The legal folks: Mark Simpson, Assistant DA for Douglas County, Kansas; DA Charles Branson; David Brown, JD, for always being available for a consult; Rick Frydman, JD, for the defense perspective.

Jennifer Brockman, director of the Sexual Assault Prevention and Education Center, University of Kansas and Shane McCreery, JD, past Director/Title IX Coordinator, Office of Institutional Opportunity & Access at The University of Kansas. Their commitment to serving the needs of students, in providing protective measures and resources, is palpable.

The director, staff, and volunteers of the Sexual Trauma and Abuse Care Center, Lawrence, Kansas, for their front-line reality checks.

The students and clients who shared their experiences with hookups, frat parties, relationships, social media, the bar scene, sexual assault, blowjobs, and orgasm inequity.

Antonio and Pamela Dominguez, for their gracious invitation to come to Panama to write. There would be no book without that month in

Panama.

Dairy Hollow Writers' Colony in Eureka Springs, Arkansas, and director Linda Caldwell, for the award of a residency that provided time and support to get to the home stretch.

I am blessed to have a village to turn to, friends who have never turned away: Emily Kofron; Jeffrey Ann Goudie and Tom Averill; Harriet and Steve Lerner; Margaret and Will Severson; Alice Lieberman and Tom McDonald; Michelle and Mel Berg; Marcia Cebulska and Tom Prasch; and Peggy Hiltman. My extended family: Kate, Mark, Tess, Zoe, Ross Brilakis; Marjorie Kraus and daughter Amy; Nancy and Danny Fox and the nieces—Alyson, Megan, and Lindsey; John Barthell; Antonio, Pamela and Joel Dominguez.

My mother, Anne Kraus, who managed, despite 92-year-old memory loss, to consistently inquire, "How's the book coming?"

My children, Sarah and Ben, who keep me honest and humble.

Most of all, my husband, Frank Barthell, trusted reader and critic, for bolstering me when I despaired, pushing me to get away to write, taking over chores, taking care of Mom and massaging my neck after too many hours at the computer. It is a blessing to have him as my partner in life.

About the Author:

Susan Kraus is a therapist, mediator, and writer. Taking to heart the adage, "Write what you know," Kraus uses her decades of professional experience to take readers behind the closed doors of therapy, mediation, and intimate family relationships. Her novels tackle polarizing social and political issues, always raising more questions as she makes the political personal. But, mostly, Susan just likes to write stories about ordinary people trying to manage the challenges of ordinary life. Not strictly genre, her books may or may not have a murder, because, as she puts it, "Sometimes dying is the easy way out. It's living that takes guts."

Susan has written non-fiction for over 25 years and is an award-winning travel writer. *Insufficient Evidence* is her third book in the Grace McDonald series. The other books include: *Fall from Grace (The Grace McDonald Series Book 1),* and *All God's Children (The Grace McDonald Series Book 2).*

www.susankraus.com